THE CHILD'S PAST LIFE

THE CHILD'S PAST LIFE

CAI JUN

TRANSLATED BY YUZHI YANG

amazon crossing

Text copyright © 2013 Cai Jun
Translation copyright © 2014 Yuzhi Yang

Previously published as 生死河 in China in 2013 by Beijing Publishing House. Translated from Chinese by Yuzhi Yang. First published in English in 2014 by AmazonCrossing.

Published by AmazonCrossing, Seattle
www.apub.com

Amazon, the Amazon logo, and AmazonCrossing are trademarks of Amazon.com, Inc., or its affiliates.

ISBN-13: 9781477825921
ISBN-10: 1477825924

Cover design by Edward Bettison Ltd.

Library of Congress Control Number: 2014910636

Printed in the United States of America.

PART 1:

ROAD TO ACHERON

CHAPTER 1

I died on June 19, 1995.

The dictionary says that *death* is a biological state relative to a living entity: the permanent end to all biological functions that keep an organism alive. Things that cause death include aging, malnutrition, diseases, suicide, homicide, accidents, injuries. No known organisms can avoid death.

After death, the material remains of a human are usually called a corpse.

Scientists say that at the moment of death anyone might experience an array of sensations, such as entering a tunnel of white light, or feeling one's soul fly up and looking down on one's body, or seeing dead relatives or a flashback on one's life.

Or seeing Jesus, Buddha, saints, Doraemon.

What is one's world like after death?

Bracing cold like a freezer? Burning hot like a microwave? Barren like a planet ravaged by intergalactic wars? Or maybe a lush paradise like *Avatar*'s Pandora?

When I still lived in the basement, I asked the old man to give me a simplified version of *Strange Tales from a Chinese Studio*. I really believed in those stories—reincarnation, evil people being tortured in eighteen levels of Hell, wronged souls stuck inside souls like Nie Xiaoqian. It wasn't until junior high, after I learned about Karl Marx's dialectic materialism in political science class, that I realized so-called reincarnation was rubbish.

Once we die, there is nothing. Right?

When I was sixteen and playing around too roughly at school, a piece of glass fell out of nowhere and crashed into bits right in front of me. A few jagged shards stuck into my leg. If I had been a second faster, or if the glass had fallen a few centimeters off, I would have suffered a big hole in my head and died on the spot, or I'd have become a vegetable. While the wound wasn't serious, I threw up, had diarrhea, and was hospitalized. All kinds of nightmares woke me up every night. I was either being slashed in the throat, getting run over by a truck, or falling off a building.

The way I feared death, so do you.

June 19, 1995—Monday, 10:01 p.m.
I died. I was murdered.

CHAPTER 2

I believe death makes itself known before it arrives.

Two weeks before I was killed, death kept dropping in front of me like ripe apples in front of Newton.

June 5, 1995—Monday, 6:00 a.m.

Screams outside my window woke me.

I thought the noise was from my nightmare, which hadn't come in years. I tried to get up but couldn't. I felt powerless, as though someone was crushing me. Many people have experienced the same thing—it's called "Ghost on bed."

In the predawn darkness, I saw a blurry face attached to a strong male body. I wanted to scream the way I had as a kid, but no sound would come out. My throat felt pinched.

I heard more screaming from outside the window—another scream, and another. Shrill female screams gave way to husky male screams.

Those screams saved my life.

The face in the nightmare disappeared in the dawn. The poster in front of my bed remained. In it, Diego Maradona was holding the World Cup. He was the only idol from my youth.

I was working at Nanming High School. I looked out from my fourth-floor window. A woman in white was lying on the library roof. Although I was at least 100 meters away, I recognized her. It was Liu Man. Her body was contorted and still. Her black hair fell like a waterfall on the red roof tiles. It made me think of *The Red and the Black*, a book I'd read countless times.

She was dead.

Liu Man was a senior in class Section 2. I was her teacher for both homeroom and Chinese.

My name is Shen Ming. Shen as in *Shen Ming*, and Ming as in *Shen Ming*.

I graduated three years ago with a bachelor's degree in Chinese and was assigned to Nanming High as a teacher.

I ran out of my room wearing only pants and a shirt. The building was filled with the male students' commotion; most had never seen a dead body before. I tripped and fell by the stairs, then scrambled to get up again. I didn't feel my forehead bleeding.

The school's sports facility was quite wide. A standard soccer field was in the middle and its outer rings were used for track events. A forest of oleander stood behind the field. There was plenty of space in this rural setting.

On this very field is where I'd become the men's 100-meter champion ten years ago.

I ran as fast as I could. Time froze as if a deep river separated me and the library. The female student dorm was behind me, filled with screams and cries. Girls leaned against the windows to watch; their attention moved from the body on the roof to me running.

It took me one minute and twenty seconds to run from the dorm to the library.

The buildings of Nanming High were relatively new, with the exception of the two-story library, which had been there for god knows how long. It even had a traditional thatched roof. There was a little attic inside where no one ever went. The mysterious attic had a window through which a faint light could be seen at night. This was the setting for some of the students' favorite ghost stories.

I scrambled to the second floor. Filled with paper and the smell of ink, the whole building was empty except for the dead body on the roof, and me.

The attic door was locked from the outside with a simple slide bolt, so it was easy to undo that and walk in. A dark room stood before me. The narrow window let in a glaring stream of light. The room was filled with old books and choking dust, along with a strange smell.

The window was open.

The wind tangled my hair as I crawled out the window and onto the roof. I felt tiles and grass under my feet. The girl in white lay in front of me.

I stumbled toward her. I almost slipped. I heard distant screams from the girls' dorm. A tile fell and crashed.

There was no mistaking Liu Man's face. She was the prettiest and most gossiped-about girl at Nanming High. The worst of the rumors involved me.

Her frozen expression told me she'd died in pain. Her eyes stared at the sky. Had she been looking at the moon or the stars in her last moment?

Or maybe the killer's face?

Why did I think this was murder?

The way she died was elegant.

Like a plucked rose, she faded in her own unique way.

I was afraid of death but not of dead people. I leaned down carefully and touched her neck. Screams from the girls' dorms grew even more piercing. I wondered whether I seemed brave or strange in their eyes.

I touched her. Only the dead felt this cold and had that certain stiffness.

Even though I was mentally prepared, I fell onto the tiles and scooted backward a bit. My fingertips felt electrocuted, ready to decay.

I crawled closer to Liu Man and lay with her on the roof like I, too, was a corpse. I couldn't see the moon or the stars, only a cloudy morning sky where the souls of the dead floated. Across the bleak air over the sports field, hiding among a group of girls gathered at a dorm window, a soul watched me in silence.

CHAPTER 3

"This is a murder."

The man was in his thirties. He wore a dark uniform, his face tanned and stern. He wore no expression, and his voice was toneless.

"Are there any leads on the k-killer?"

Damn! Why was I stuttering? I rubbed the bottom of my shirt. Just the two of us were inside the teachers' office on the second floor. Students passed by from time to time, trying to look in. The teaching director shooed them away.

Six hours ago on the library roof, in the presence of a doctor, I'd confirmed the death of Liu Man, senior in class Section 2.

"I am Huang Hai. I'm in charge of this case."

"I can't believe something like this would happen in my class. It's only a month before the college entrance exams. The principal and I just met with Liu Man's dad. I kept apologizing, but he still slapped me. I don't blame him."

I rubbed my still-burning cheeks; I wanted to look at the floor. Huang Hai's gazing eyes were like powerful magnets. It was hard to hide from their invisible power.

"Mr. Shen, someone said that you two talked privately in the classroom last night after evening study. Is that true?"

His voice was slow but forceful. It crushed me like a steam-roller.

"Yes."

"Why didn't you say so earlier?"

"I . . ."

Obviously I'd become a suspect.

"Don't be nervous, just tell me what happened."

"Last night, I passed that classroom. Liu Man stopped me to talk. She asked me about some hard questions in the mock tests for Chinese, like Cao Cao's 'Haiku,' and the source for 'Green is the gown, my heart yearns for your talent.'"

Was this a police interrogation? I felt the sudden urge to pee, but all I could do was press my legs together.

"Is that all?"

Police officer Huang Hai waited for me to say more. His terrify-ing patience reminded me of the way Liu Man had looked in death.

"Also, she asked about Bai Juyi's 'Pipa Song,' and how to explain the 'hair comb' in 'Hair comb trimmed in gold was crushed, the red skirt stained with wine.' That's it. I left as soon as I answered her questions."

My mind was filled by the image of a "red skirt stained with wine."

"Mr. Shen, what was your impression of Liu Man?"

"She was a bit odd. She loved to ask about all sorts of things, and there was no school secret she didn't know. Some kids disliked her. But a girl that pretty was always popular with boys. She had not dated yet. She was braver than a lot of boys. She was probably the only one who dared to go to the library attic in the middle of the night."

"How do you know she went by herself?"

"Oh, her killer was there, too, of course!" I hadn't killed any-one, but everything I said seemed suspicious to the cop. "Was there a third person besides the killer and the victim?"

Huang Hai shook his head calmly. "Sorry, I am not here to discuss the case with you."

"Liu Man seemed outgoing, but she was actually quite a loner, probably because she came from a single-parent home. She grew up with her dad and lacked a mom in her life. Her grades were bad, and she was easily distracted. She knew a lot of random people from outside the school. Nanming High is a really prestigious boarding school and sends a lot of kids to elite universities. But I'm not sure Liu Man could have even gotten into college. As her homeroom teacher, I was worried about her, so I tutored her at night."

"I'm sorry, what I need to know is—"

"I know what you want to ask," I said, slamming my fist on the glass table. "This is ridiculous! There was this shameless rumor at school the last two weeks, saying Liu Man and I had some sort of relationship. This is the ultimate insult to my character and profession as a teacher. This is slander!"

"Mr. Shen, I talked to the principal and a couple of teachers about it. The rumor is unfounded, just talk among students. I believe in your innocence." Huang Hai lit up a cigarette and puffed on it hard. "I heard you also graduated from here?"

"Yes, I spent my high school years here. I remember everything, every plant and every flower. I couldn't believe I was assigned to work at my alma mater after graduating Peking University, but I was fortunate to be named a People's teacher."

Cliché sayings like this came out of my mouth effortlessly, mindlessly.

"You remember *everything*?" Huang Hai said, frowning.

"What's wrong?"

"Mr. Shen, you're only twenty-five and yet already so enlightened. It's quite impressive." His face was covered by blue smoke, making it hard to see his eyes. "I heard you're leaving Nanming High soon?"

"I am really reluctant to go, as I have been here only three years. This is my first and also my last senior class. I'll transfer to the city's Education Bureau Youth League Committee after the exams in July."

"Congratulations."

"I'll miss teaching. It will be hard to adjust to a government-agency life."

He nodded without an expression and stubbed out his half-smoked cigarette. "I'd better get going. You won't leave town any-time soon, I trust?"

"No. I live in the school dorms. Exams are next month, and I can't leave my students now."

"Keep in touch."

Huang Hai swooped out of the room like the wind. I looked at the teaching director in the corridor. He shied away from my gaze and left with the cop.

I'd lied to the police.

Liu Man may have liked dreamy poems, but she knew little of classical Chinese poems. She would never have asked about "hair comb trimmed in gold."

Last night in the self-study classroom, she told me, "Mr. Shen, I know her secret now."

Did this have to do with the school's Dead Poets Society?

My heart beat rapidly. I wanted to leave so no one would see us and make trouble. This girl had already given me enough trouble. I hoped she would disappear that night.

Five minutes later, she said things only dead people knew. Using "witch" to describe her was apt.

"What does all this have to do with you?" I asked.

Though there wasn't even a whisper of wind in the classroom, the fluorescent light overhead kept shaking, casting our shadows on the floor.

She leaned against the blackboard and said, "At this school, I know everyone's secrets."

This is what we really talked about last night.

But I didn't kill anyone.

June 5, 1995. Noon.

Everyone went to the cafeteria. I sat alone in the office. How could I have an appetite after touching a dead body?

In the afternoon, I taught one Chinese class and corrected the tests from a few days ago. There was an empty seat in the classroom.

Someone put an oleander flower on the desk. The students stared at me from time to time and whispered. I spoke faintly, not daring to mention Liu Man. It was as though the dead girl had never been in our class.

After school, I hurried out of the classroom. People ogled me in the corridor, as if "killer" had been scrawled across my face.

Outside the multipurpose building, a few male students huddled in conversation. They scattered as soon as they saw me. Only Ma Li stayed behind. He was the best student in class, and also my favorite.

"Were you talking about Liu Man?"

"Mr. Shen, didn't you hear?"

Ma was lean. He looked like Nicky Wu but had hair like Aaron Kwok. He always seemed melancholy.

"Know what?"

"Liu Man was poisoned!"

"I'd guessed as much. I didn't see any wounds on her this morning."

"The whole school knows. When the cops looked over the crime scene and found some liquid on the floor, they figured that after she was poisoned, she climbed onto the library roof through the attic window. She couldn't get out through the attic door because it was locked from the outside. Our chemistry teacher went in to do some testing after the cops left. You know how he talks."

"What did he find?"

"There was a lot of oleander glucoside in the liquid."

"Oleander glucoside?"

I suddenly understood, but I tried to look confused for Ma.

"The chemistry teacher said you can extract it from the oleander. Half a milligram of pure oleander glucoside is enough to kill someone. He told us to stay away from oleander."

There were a lot of oleander bushes next to the sports field. They bloomed bright red every year at exam time. Red oleander was the most poisonous.

"Don't spread rumors like this. Nobody will really know how Liu Man died until the police autopsy report is out." I patted Ma Li's shoulder and whispered into his ear, "Rumor kills! You know what I mean."

"Mr. Shen, I don't think Liu Man would go to the haunted library attic without a reason. Someone must have asked her to. Who do you think it was?"

His eyes were so clear that they made my heart clench. I backed away two steps. "You don't trust me, either?"

"I'm sorry, but everyone is saying—"

"Shut up!"

I ran away from Ma Li. The robust oleander bushes displayed countless red flowers among the greenery; they made me nauseous.

I now understood why Huang Hai had taken note of my remembering "everything."

CHAPTER 4

June 5, 1995. Late night.

My room was number 19, the very last room on the fourth floor of the men's dorm. Next door was a cluttered storage room. My fiancée, Gu Qiusha, had only been there twice. She said my place was worse than a doghouse. She insisted that we were to live in a spacious and comfortable home.

We were going to be married in a month.

The wedding was set for after exams, which is when I was leaving Nanming High before starting a new job at the Education Bureau. We were supposed to pick up our marriage licenses on June 19, two weeks after the exams.

I called her that day. I was afraid to tell her what happened— just that I might be in trouble but it wouldn't last long.

My Swiss-made designer watch showed ten o'clock. It had been a gift from Gu Qiusha's dad, my future father-in-law; he'd bought it in Hong Kong. That watch had caused quite a stir in the teachers' office. I was afraid to use it for fear of wearing off its shine, but Qiusha insisted that I wear it every day.

I sat at my desk. I stared at the watch's face, which reflected *my* weary face. Ever since returning to teach at my alma mater three years ago, I'd lived alone. The paint on the walls was peeling, the ceiling was moldy and cracked, and I had little else besides a rickety single bed and a fuzzy color TV from the flea market. I liked this room, though—I'd spent my high school years in it, too.

Back then, it had three bunk beds, and six of us slept in here. In 1988, on the night before the college entrance exams, one roommate hung himself. We woke up in the morning and saw him hanging from the ceiling fan. Unfortunately, I slept on a top bunk. The boy's stiff body swayed before me. Its exposed belly button was at my eye level, and it looked like a single eye staring at me.

The school's investigation went nowhere. The conclusion was that he was afraid of not doing well and decided to take his life. All of us in the room had a hard time accepting those findings. We had nightmares for weeks. After we graduated, no one else wanted to live in our room. Nearby rooms were haunted, too, so the school just gave up on the whole block of quarters.

Four years later, I returned as a newly minted teacher, as well as the only Peking University graduate. I had no housing, however, and the school had no place for me to stay, so the haunted room became my staff dorm room.

I would be moving next month and saying good-bye to this room, where I'd spent six years of my life.

My new place would be official housing from the Education Bureau; it was an exception. I had only taught for three years, yet many teachers who taught their whole careers were still cramped inside a leaky old house with their kids and grand-kids. Two months earlier, I had gotten my keys. The place was a two-bedroom apartment—the best the Education Bureau could offer. Top education administrators lived upstairs. My fiancée's family was renovating the place for us and had moved in imported furniture and appliances just the day before. They'd already spent more money than I made in a whole year.

I knew that a lot of people felt envious, and some of them even hated me.

I didn't feel like sleeping, but I turned off the light early and lay in bed. When I heard a knock, I opened the door, feeling scared. Huang Hai, the same policeman who'd interrogated me earlier, was standing there. His gaze swept past me and looked things over.

"Good evening, Mr. Shen. May I inspect your room?"

He presented a search warrant. The teaching director, Yan Li, stood behind him. He was a sincere middle-aged man, but tonight his eyes were full of pity.

"Are you . . . am I a suspect?"

"Mr. Shen," Yan Li said, "you're known for your verbal skills, but tonight you seem rather—"

I blocked them from coming in. "Mr. Yan, are you—"

"Sorry, are you not letting me in?" Huang Hai's voice was almost toneless.

"It's fine—please come in and check! I didn't do anything wrong. Why would I be afraid of a search?" I showed the cop my room and pointed to a necklace hanging off the writing desk. "Be careful not to break it," I said.

Huang Hai didn't tell me to leave, but I left anyway. I was embarrassed. Where could I go with a cop trailing me everywhere?

I walked into the cool moonlight. The male students were coming out of the dorm. They'd probably decided that I was the killer and the police were arresting me. The time I spent waiting for the search to finish felt endless. I turned to look at the girls' dorm and saw their young faces in the windows. But she wasn't there.

Huang Hai came downstairs carrying a clear bag with a plastic bottle in it. The night's darkness hid his face. He didn't talk to me again. Two policemen escorted me to the front of the school and out to their waiting car, parked with its flashing lights on.

"Sir, please lock my room—I have important things inside." This was the only thing I said when they arrested me.

As I was being shoved into the police car, I saw a man standing on Nanming Road. His face was so pale under the streetlight that it was scary.

His name was Zhang Mingsong.

CHAPTER 5

My first night at the police station was sleepless. I begged to call my fiancée but was refused. Huang Hai promised me they'd let her know. They knew Qiusha's father. But by dawn there was no further word. The detention room had no mirror, so I couldn't inspect my face. I probably had dark circles under my eyes. My breakfast tray sat on the floor. I couldn't eat with my stomach in knots.

June 6, 1995. The first interrogation.

Before Huang Hai could say anything, I asked, "What did you find in my room?"

"We found that plastic bottle on your dresser," he said. "It was empty, but it had traces of oleander extract. The lab tells us it had been procured in the last few days."

"You're saying I made poison out of oleander and killed Liu Man the night before last?"

"Right now, you're our primary suspect. But that doesn't mean you're the killer."

There was no point in explaining. Everyone saw me as the killer. They'd decided I had some sort of immoral relationship with Liu Man. Since I was getting married soon people assumed that she was an obstacle to me. She could have harassed me after graduation. I lived on campus and had the perfect opportunity. The school had oleander everywhere. No one else dared to go up to the library attic after dark. Only I could have lured Liu Man up there.

"I didn't kill anyone!"

"I checked your college records. You took a toxicology class. Isn't that rather strange for a Chinese major?"

"Did you also check how my mother died?"

Huang Hai answered quickly: "Your father killed her when you were seven."

"She was—she was poisoned." I became calm again, like I was recounting something I'd heard on the news. "My dad added the poison to her medication daily. I didn't cry at all when my mother died. I ran out of my house and I bit a cop on the thigh. Then they sent my mom for an autopsy and found out how she died."

"Your father was executed. I read the file last night. So that's why you took the toxicology class—because your mom was poisoned?"

"Why else would I take it? Or do you think I'm psychic? That years ago, before I ever met Liu Man, I knew I wanted to kill her—so I took a class to learn how?"

"Shen Ming, what about the rumors about you two?"

"That's nonsense. She only liked to ask me questions. Sometimes she said strange things. As a teacher, I know to keep a distance from students, especially pretty girls like her. I was extra careful."

"You must have been popular with the girls when you were in high school?"

I lowered my head and stayed silent for a moment. I'd never felt like a heartthrob. At most, I looked clean-cut, like someone from an awards ceremony. Occasionally someone would say I looked powerful, that my face showed a hero's fate. Would girls today even like that kind of look?

"I don't know. I'm easygoing. I don't talk much. I like to write classical poems. You know how moody eighteen-year-old girls are. Maybe they admire me for that. But that will change in a few years."

What was I rambling on about? Had I just admitted that Liu Man had a crush on me?

The stenographer quickly wrote down what I'd said. Huang Hai nodded.

"Let's change the topic, Shen Ming. Tell me about your past."

"My past?"

"Start with high school. We talked too briefly yesterday. I heard you had guaranteed admission to Peking University?"

"My dream college was Peking University, but I wasn't sure I would get in. A month before the exams, about seven years ago today, something big happened across from Nanming High. There was nothing but the woods and a factory on Nanming Road—as well as some illegal housing units, shacks built by migrants. A big fire broke out. A bunch of kids climbed up the wall to watch. I was the only one who ran across the road to save people. I was lucky to survive. Because I'd been a Party member since my senior year, the city gave me an award. Local TV stations and newspapers interviewed me, and I almost got on the national news broadcast."

"So that's how you got the coveted guaranteed admission?"

"Mr. Huang, do you believe in fate?"

"No."

"Neither did I. I studied really hard in school, I did nothing else and had excellent grades. But at graduation time, people who did worse than me, some of whom had terrible grades, were assigned to government jobs, while I was sent back to my hometown to be a high school Chinese teacher."

"You've got the best opportunity now, though." Huang Hai lit a cigarette and blew smoke over my head. "I heard you're getting married soon. Can you talk about your fiancée?"

"Two years ago, when I took the bus back to school, I noticed a thief pickpocketing her. No one on the bus cared. The ticket seller actually opened the bus door. Just as the thief was about to get away, I ran up, knocked him to the ground, and dragged him to the police station. That's how I met Gu Qiusha. She was so grateful. She asked me to dinner a few times. She worked at the Education Publishing House and was in charge of high school textbooks. We had a lot to talk about, and she became my girlfriend soon after."

"Have you ever had a relationship before?"

"No, she is my first girlfriend." I scooted back to avoid Huang Hai's smoke rings. "I didn't know that her father was an administrator at the Education Bureau until we'd been together for six months. As you know, he's a university president now. Qiusha lost her mom when she was young, and her dad spoiled her. Guys like me who have nothing aren't popular with most people, but her dad likes me. He also graduated from Peking University. When his secretary quit to have a baby, I was transferred from Nanming High to the university and worked as the president's secretary for three months. I worked really hard and stayed by his side day and night. I made sure he had everything he needed. All of his bosses and professors loved me, too."

I stopped talking all of a sudden. Why *did* my future father-in-law like me so much? It seemed odd that someone with nothing was getting a chance to have it all. But President Gu only has one daughter. He needed someone to continue his legacy so his retirement wasn't too cruel. Perhaps it was better to cultivate a hardworking kid's loyalty than to marry off his daughter to someone with connections.

Huang Hai broke the silence. "I heard your engagement ceremony was in March."

I couldn't have dreamed of a more elaborate ceremony. Everyone came—university officials, Education Bureau administrators, the Writers' Association president, even celebrities like TV hosts. They all flattered me. My future father-in-law meant well. He wanted to give me access to his social circle. Everything would be easier with his connections, including getting me out of a police station.

I didn't share these useless thoughts with the police. Instead, I focused on the key: "A month ago, the school heard from upper management that I was leaving for the Youth League Committee after exams. I am also Nanming High's Youth League Committee secretary. Qiusha told me that her father has ensured that in two years I'll be the internal candidate for the city's Youth League Committee secretary. Everyone heard about it."

Huang Hai stubbed out his cigarette and tapped the table with his knuckle. "So a lot of people must have been jealous," he said. "This is what you wanted to tell me?"

"Mr. Huang, have you read *The Count of Monte Cristo*?"

"I have no time for novels. I know what you're saying, though. So tell me, who is out to get you? I'm talking about revenge, not just jealousy. Even I feel a little jealous after hearing your story. I worked my butt off for years. I've apprehended so many killers and have the wounds to prove it. But I still don't have a single apartment for my efforts. You're about to have it all. Who wouldn't be jealous?"

"I understand. This is persecution via murder, not just jealousy. Can I have something to write with?"

Huang Hai stared at me before pushing over some paper and a pen.

I wrote down a name: Yan Li.

CHAPTER 6

Yan Li was the teaching director for Nanming High.

Why would he want to frame me? I wasn't 100 percent certain. But I knew he was a bad guy. Others may have gossiped about me, but Yan Li was one of those people who appeared docile—until he stabbed you in the back.

All high school teaching directors are very conservative and stubborn. Yan Li seemed that way at first, too, just like his name, which means "stern," would imply. He was in his early forties and divorced. His wife had custody of their kid.

One night I was up very late, correcting homework in my office. I opened the window to look at the stars and noticed someone leaning on top of the multipurpose building. Worried that it was a student, I ran to the roof to check. I was surprised to find that it was actually the teaching director training a telephoto lens on the girls' dorm. I was too embarrassed to say anything—he was my boss after all. I snuck away when he wasn't looking. After that I started keeping an eye on him. The school showers have very tall windows, but with the thick forest outside, no one could easily look in. The teaching director had all the keys, however, so he could peek from the roof. One night as I watched Yan Li I saw Liu Man and two other girls going into the showers. That was the final straw. I went up to the roof and gave Yan Li a beating. He didn't even fight back. He knelt in front of me and begged for more. He swore he'd never do it again. He asked me to not say anything and promised to do whatever I asked. He agreed to replace the girls' shower windows with frosted glass. The next day, the windows were changed, so I kept my mouth shut. What a Wolf of Zhongshan.

Now that I was about to leave for the Education Bureau, I wanted to secretly investigate Yan Li and drive him out of the school. He must have known his days would be numbered once I left Nanming High.

One night, just three days before Liu Man was killed, she told me that she saw Yan Li wandering through the girls' dorm hallway. Dorm rules prohibited all males, even teachers, from going into the girls' dorm at night. She called out to him and demanded to know why he was there. He was really nervous and threatened her, telling her he was there on official business and if she told anyone she would be in trouble. Most girls would be too scared, but not Liu Man. Yan Li must have known this.

As the teaching director, Yan Li could have done things in the library; so he poisoned Liu Man to shut her up. The next day, he could have snuck into my room to plant the bottle with the left-over oleander juice—killing two birds with one stone.

Huang Hai detained me, despite hearing my theory.

So I was a high school Chinese teacher locked up in a tiny, dark cell, right next to killers and rapists. Other prisoners started beating me almost as soon as I arrived. I tried to fight back but was only beaten even worse. When Huang Hai interrogated me, he saw my bruises and asked the warden to give me a new cell. Now I was bunking with common thieves and embezzlers, so I had a fighting chance.

My fiancée didn't visit me once while I was locked up; my all-powerful future father-in-law was absent, too.

Huang Hai said he'd talked to Gu Qiusha, but he didn't tell me what was said. I couldn't guess from his silence. Even though the crowded cell was hot, I had a scary premonition that chilled me to the bone.

Was this punishment for what I'd done that summer?

Friday, June 16.

Huang Hai finally released me. He said he'd been unable to find a connection between Liu Man's murder and me. No traces of my fingerprints or hair were at the scene. Liu Man's autopsy didn't implicate me, either. The police leaned toward the theory that I'd been framed. I almost collapsed into Huang Hai's arms with relief. The man who'd sent me to prison was proving to be my savior.

After collecting my belongings from police custody, I put on the watch Qiusha's dad had given me, and I put away my wallet and keys. I finally looked into a mirror: I had a clean-shaven head, dark bags under my eyes, cuts and bruises, and the first white hairs at my temple. I looked like a corpse ready for a coffin, not a twenty-five-year-old man.

Those ten days in jail were definitely the longest ten days of my life.

I spent all my cash after getting out. I had just enough to buy a new shirt. I went to a bathhouse to scrub away all the grime. I rubbed my skin raw with soap. Finally, I was ready to go see my fiancée. Luckily, my bus pass had not been lost.

I rushed to the publishing house where Qiusha worked. The receptionist at the front desk said that Qiusha was in an important meeting and she'd left word that I was to wait for her at home.

Go home?

Half an hour later, I arrived at my newly remodeled apartment. It was on the twelfth floor of a building in the quiet part of downtown. I'd been regularly inspecting the renovation's progress, but now my keys didn't work. Nobody answered the door, either. A neighbor lady that heard me knocking came out and said that someone had changed the locks yesterday.

I kicked the door, and then regretted the deep dent I'd caused. This was my home. What was wrong with me? My toes burned as I hobbled to the elevator.

It was summer, and the temperature was over 30 degrees Celsius. All sorts of swampy odors festered on the bus, but that didn't stop me from almost falling asleep. The dense clusters of buildings outside the window gave way to spotty construction, until finally, a steel factory with smokestacks appeared. The bus stopped on Nanming Road. The school entrance stood between two expansive walls. A brass plaque that read "Nanming High School" hung above the door.

Friday was when the boarding students went home. People were surprised to see me, and no one—teachers and students alike—dared talk to me. I saw Ma Li and his roommates. Even they avoided me. Students faded away from me like a receding tide leaving behind a dry island.

"Mr. Shen, please come to the principal's office."

The creepy voice had snuck up behind me. I turned and saw Yan Li. Why was he still here? Shouldn't he be in jail?

I followed him in silence. As we turned at the staircase landing, he said in a low voice, "That cop, Huang Hai, came looking for me a few days ago. You actually told him what I did?"

I didn't want to speak to Yan Li. I could guess what his next words might be: *Do you have evidence? Any photos? I already talked with the principal about this. Who would believe a murder suspect?*

I arrived at the principal's office still having not said a word. The principal's face was pale. He kept wiping sweat from his brow. Seven years ago, he'd personally given me the award for fighting the fire. He'd also decided to sponsor me for guaranteed admission to Peking University. Three years ago, he'd stood at the school entrance to welcome me back and give me a place to live. Just last month, he said he'd pay a visit to my future father-in-law.

"Mr. Shen, I am very glad to see you. I announced an important decision today: Based on your immoral conduct and your violations of the ethical code for People's teachers—and to protect our school's reputation—we have decided to terminate your position. Effective immediately."

For a long time I stood like a statue before truly understanding what he'd said. I spit out two words: "Thank you."

The principal was surprised by my reaction. He exchanged looks with the teaching director before shaking his head. "I'm sorry," he said, "but there's another announcement you need to hear. Top-level administrators have decided to terminate your Party membership as well."

"Fine. I just want to tell you that I am innocent. I didn't kill anyone, and the police believe me. Why are you doing this?"

"Mr. Shen—" The principal realized that I was no longer a teacher. "You're just twenty-five. You have a long road ahead of you. Don't be discouraged. Everyone has setbacks. You went to an elite university, and you will always be able to find a good job. You might even do better elsewhere."

"Who decided to terminate my job and Party membership?"

"It wasn't me. The city's Education Bureau made the call about your job, and no one at the school disagreed. The Party committee voted unanimously, too."

"But the Bureau chief just spoke to me last month about grooming me for the future."

The principal turned his back and sighed. "Things change."

He was trying to make me leave. I didn't want to have to beg like a dog.

The teaching director walked me downstairs. He whispered, "Mr. Shen, there's something else. Your room will only be available to you until Monday night. By Tuesday morning, it will be a Ping-Pong room. Please start packing now. Let me know if you need help with anything."

I shook for half a minute, my shoulders spasming like the wings of a wounded bird. Finally, I turned to Yan Li with a clenched fist, but he was long gone.

The night wind blew the scent of oleander toward me. I stood for a long time like a dead man. The cafeteria was already closed. Not that I was hungry, anyway.

I returned to my room to find that it had been turned upside down. My books were scattered all over the floor, and students' homework had disappeared. I was no longer their Chinese teacher. Frantically, I searched for the only possession that mattered to me. I fell to the floor and looked everywhere. I finally found the dim strand of beads in a pile of trash in the corner. Holding it tightly, I carefully cleaned and kissed it.

Next, I restored the room to the way it was before my arrest. Imagining what might happen if I called my fiancée, I thought it best to let Qiusha and her dad have a good night's sleep.

Lights off. In bed.

In another three days, *this* bed would no longer be mine.

Who would sleep on that big Simmons mattress in my new apartment?

CHAPTER 7

The next day—June 17, 1995. Early morning.

I changed and took the bus downtown. I wanted to catch them before they left the house.

It was ridiculous to think of it now, but I remembered being so excited and clumsy during my first visit to my girlfriend's place. I'd carried all sorts of outdated gifts, and Qiusha made fun of me. Her dad was easygoing, however. He talked about the education system's problems from his perspective as a university president. Luckily, I was prepared. I showed off my unique point of view, which really impressed him.

At 9:00 a.m., I arrived at the Gus' home. I tidied my clothes and hair and, with a shaky hand, rang the doorbell.

There was no response, so I ran to Qiusha's office and learned both father and daughter had left home in one of the company cars. They were supposedly taking a vacation in Yunnan.

I looked up and let the sun sting my eyes as I imagined my fiancée's face melting out of focus. I'd never in my life wanted to see anyone as much as I wanted to see her in that moment. Had she abandoned me just like everyone else?

I arrived at the six-story apartment building before noon. I pressed the fourth-floor doorbell.

"Who is it?"

A woman in her forties opened the door. She held a spatula and was confused by my unexpected arrival.

"Is Prosecutor Shen Yuanchao home?"

I knew who she was, but she didn't seem to recognize me.

Before she could reply, a middle-aged man appeared next to her. He frowned and said, "I know why you're looking for me."

He pulled me into the apartment and told his wife to keep cooking. Then he sat me down on the sofa and closed the living room door.

"She does know who I am, right?"

"Yes, but she hasn't seen you for seven years." Shen Yuanchao poured me a cup of tea. "You don't look too good."

"You heard?"

"Shen Ming, does anyone else know what we know?"

His formality made me grimace. *Of course* that was his biggest worry.

"I've never said anything. But for some reason, there was a rumor going around at school last month."

"It's obvious that someone is out to get you."

"They want to kill me!"

Shen Yuanchao paced the living room. "Who else knows?"

"Other than my grandmother and the three people here, no one else knows."

"Don't suspect my wife—she would never say anything."

"That's not why I came here." I didn't know the proper way to ask; I had no choice but to just spit it out: "Can you help me?"

"To vindicate you?"

"The police already let me go. They know I was framed. Others don't know yet."

"I'm worried about what I'll have to do if you *were* framed and the police send your file to the Supreme People's Procuratorate to make a case."

Shen Yuanchao had a face like a hero popular in those 1980s Chinese martyr movies. It disgusted me whenever he said things like this.

"What would you do if I died?"

This made him pause and frown. "What happened?"

I told him about losing my job and Party membership, as well as how my fiancée's family was avoiding me. I stopped talking when I couldn't describe what lay ahead for me. I finished my tea and then nervously chewed up and swallowed the tea leaves.

He listened to me calmly before asking, "What have you been doing recently?"

"Not too much. Preparing to get married, renovating our apartment, and helping students with exam prep."

"Have you been unfaithful to your fiancée in any way?" He patted my shoulder. "You're twenty-five years old, and you know what I am asking."

I couldn't answer while looking him in the eye.

"You're not telling me everything," he said.

"I'm sorry. I don't think I can tell you yet. That's not what I'm dealing with right now."

"Everything is connected. Trust me. As a prosecutor, I've dealt with so many criminals. I know everyone's motive and what they're thinking."

"Give me a break—I am not a killer. I am the victim here!"

"You're too young to handle this on your own. If you tell me everything, I might be able to save you. This is the only way I can help you."

I unbuttoned my collar and looked out the window. The sun was beaming down on his Kaffir lily. I shook my head and said, "No, I can't."

"That's unfortunate." He walked behind me and whispered into my ear. "You remind me of myself when I was your age." He continued pacing the room. "Are you hungry? You can eat with us."

Before I answered, he went to the kitchen to let his wife know. It was noon and I had nowhere else to go. The hosts brought out the food. This was the first time I'd ever taken a meal in their home.

Two rumors had circulated about me at Nanming High a few weeks earlier.

The first one involved Liu Man, the prettiest girl in the senior class. She was supposedly having an affair with me. The romantic version had us reenacting a classic romance novel, *Outside the Window*. The more sordid version claimed that while Liu Man was out sick, she was actually having an abortion.

The second rumor said that I came from a lowly background. That unlike the information recorded in my residency registration, my father who was executed when I was seven wasn't my biological father. My biological mother was a frivolous woman, and I was an out-of-wedlock child born into shame.

The story about my being born out of wedlock was true. The man who gave me life now sat right in front of me: Prosecutor Shen Yuanchao.

I'd never admitted who he was, however, and he'd never acknowledged me as his son.

His wife had known about this for a long time. She should have remembered who I was. She showed no animosity and instead kept adding food to my bowl. It was the first proper meal I'd eaten since being in jail for those long ten days.

After lunch, Shen Yuanchao walked me downstairs and outside. I didn't know what else to say. As I prepared to leave, he stopped me with a light hug. The last time he'd hugged me was over ten years ago.

The one o'clock sun was fierce. We stood in the shade of the oleander trees for a moment before he said, "Be careful." Then as his lips shook, he added, "My son."

He'd finally called me his son. But I never called him Dad. I nodded awkwardly and left.

This was the last time he ever saw me.

I got back to Nanming High School two hours later. The old man from reception called out, "Mr. Shen, the hospital called—you need to get over there right now!"

CHAPTER 8

My grandmother was fading fast.

It was almost 11:00 p.m., and I was at the Zhabei District's Central Hospital. The scents of alcohol and disinfectant filled the ER. Under the sickly light, the pale walls revealed human-shaped glob stains. A lonely old man was abandoned on a stretcher, his only company the IV dripping into his veins. When he died, the nurses would ask the on-call doctor to do some perfunctory resuscitation, then he would be sent to the mortuary with disgust. A woman had just been sent in; she was young and pretty and looked like she was in college. Her shiny dark hair draped over the bed, and the scent of her shampoo was still strong. A middle-aged couple trailing the stretcher cried and said she'd taken a whole bottle of sleeping pills. The on-call doctor pumped her stomach. The woman's mom said, "She's pregnant" and then proceeded to curse some man. The young woman was unable to throw up the pills. The doctor put out his hands in resignation. Just when the family was about to kneel in front of the doctor, a bunch of people rushed in holding a bloody young man with a knife sticking out of his chest. He looked clean-cut, not at all like a thug. A woman fell upon him and cried, "He's just a baby, just a baby." The doctor tried for a few minutes and shook his head, saying, "Prepare for a funeral."

"He's just a baby."

It wasn't yet dawn. I waited by my grandmother's side, stroking her white hair until her EKG showed a flat line. The doctor signed the death certificate and left in silence.

This was Sunday, June 18, 1995, at 4:44 a.m. My grandmother was sixty-six years old.

I was calm and didn't shed one tear. I arranged for everything. By daybreak I was in the hearse. I wasn't at all afraid to be with my grandmother at the funeral home. I had no other family, and no one else was going to pay attention to an old housekeeper. The family she worked for sent 200 yuan. My fiancée and her family never met my grandmother. There was no need for a memorial. All she needed was for me to say good-bye to her. I was the person she loved the most in this world.

I signed my name so many times that day. Once the final piece of paperwork was filed away, I watched her slight body being sent into the cremation chamber. I thought of the expression "Every hope dashed."

I picked up her still-hot remains and placed them in the urn, which I kissed. I had no money for a cemetery plot. My hands were covered in my grandmother's ashes, but I didn't want to wash them. On my arm I pinned a black sash with a small red patch that showed my grandson status. I boarded the bus to Nanming High.

It was late when I got back, and I was exhausted. As I walked into my room, I noticed that someone else was there, too. I picked up a wooden rod and was about to hit him on the back of the head when he turned and shouted, "Hey, it's me."

Yan Li backed away in a panic. Could he be any slower? How could this be self-defense?

He raised a big chain of keys.

"Don't worry! I'm on call tonight. I was just checking your room."

As I lowered the rod, he noticed my sash. "Mr. Shen, I apologize—I didn't know your family had a funeral today."

I stood at the door and stared at him. If looks could kill.

Yan Li wanted to linger. "Mr. Shen, you still haven't packed? The workers are coming to set up the Ping-Pong table the day after tomorrow. Can you move out by tomorrow night?"

Nonchalantly, he walked to the desk and fingered my strand of beads.

"Don't touch that," I shouted in a rage, charging at him and grabbing his arm. I didn't expect him to struggle. He may have been in his forties, but he was taller than me, and strong. As we both tumbled to the floor, I heard the strand of beads breaking and scattering.

The saying "Pearls, large and small, on a jade plate fall" seemed wrong here.

I searched the floor for the beads as though I had lost my mind. It took me half an hour to find them all, until my head was dizzy and my legs felt numb. Yan Li had run out long ago. I tried restringing the necklace, but the hand-drilled holes in the beads were so irregular that it was difficult to do once it had all come undone. I kept trying until early morning, but it was no use. I slammed the floor, not caring if the students downstairs heard me.

My fist was bruised and it hurt like hell. I found a fabric pouch to hold the beads and lay on the bed like a zombie, still tightly grasping the broken strand.

Tomorrow night. I was waiting for tomorrow night.

CHAPTER 9

Why do we kill?

First: to protect oneself. Second: to usurp someone else's possessions. Third: to eliminate competition for the opposite sex. Fourth: revenge. Fifth: to follow a superior's orders. Sixth: to make money. Seventh: for no reason.

Which was my reason?

The Dead Poets Society had once discussed this topic. I wanted to etch these words on my tombstone.

June 19, 1995. Monday morning. I was still alive.

The sun illuminated the top of my bed. I opened my eyes in a daze. This must have been the third period. This was the first time I'd ever slept in at school, but of course I no longer had the right to teach.

I stood on a stool to retrieve an army knife I'd hidden in a ceiling crevice. I was lucky the police hadn't found it. "Factory 305" was etched into the blade, which had a blood reservoir on the tip. Lu Zhongyue had given this to me two years ago. He was my best friend, my high school classmate—and he'd been my roommate in this very room. His dad worked for the district government and often got his hands on weird things like imported liquors and cigarettes, army boots, and smuggled watches.

The blade's frosty glow reflected my face like a distorted mirror, an image so ugly I hardly recognized myself.

I tied the knife inside my pant leg.

Breakfast had already ended at the cafeteria. I walked around campus. As I passed senior class Section 2, the lecturing math teacher saw me and nodded. Some students noticed and turned to look. No one could concentrate on what they were studying. They just whispered and acted like they'd seen a zombie.

Two teachers from elite universities worked at Nanming High. I'd come from Peking University, and Zhang Mingsong had come from Tsinghua University. He was seven years older than me. While I was still in high school, he taught me math. His math was impeccable. He'd qualified as an elite teacher before he turned thirty. His students all did really well. Since math was so important to the overall score in the college entrance exams, countless parents fought to have him tutor their kids.

I stood outside his classroom, keeping my back straight as a board. I regarded the students with a cool gaze. I'd been their homeroom teacher just two weeks earlier, as well as the advisor for the Nanming Literary Society. The window reflected my weary and moody face, like something out of a nightmare. I stared at my favorite student, Ma Li, but he avoided eye contact, the sadness on his face hard to hide. Even though we would all scatter next month after the exams, saying good-bye like this made everyone misty-eyed.

I started crying in front of all of my students. Zhang Mingsong came into the hall wearing a pained look. "Sorry, Mr. Shen, but you're interfering with our class."

"I'm sorry. Good-bye."

My body felt heavy as I walked downstairs. My pocket held that strand of necklace, and my pant leg hid an army knife with a blood reservoir.

June 19, 1995. It was the last Monday in my life. My last night, too.

I took off my watch from Qiusha's dad and ate my last dinner in the cafeteria. The chefs looked at me like I was a killer. No one sat near me; they all stayed at least ten meters away. I ate heartily. I used up all the meal tickets I'd been saving.

9:30 p.m.

Thunder rolled through the night sky.

Yan Li was still at school, just chatting with someone. He seemed well; occasionally he laughed in his own wretched way. After the conversation ended, he smoked by himself. He didn't recheck my room—he was probably afraid of getting beat up again. He patted his clothes and walked outside the school gates. I followed him to Nanming Road, hiding in the darkness of the trees. He was heading to the bus stop, but I couldn't let him get that far. If he made it to a crowded place, it would be hard to act.

There were no streetlights on Nanming Road and no pedestrians, either. Flickering starlight lit the way, shining on the half-closed steel factory. I took out the knife, held my breath, and caught up to Yan Li. Just as he was about to turn at hearing my footsteps, I stabbed him in the back.

The night before, I'd practiced so many times—I'd visualized hitting him right in the middle of his back. But in the darkness, I couldn't tell where the knife went in, though it did meet great resistance. I stabbed deeper. I heard Yan Li's muffled yelling. With a violent force, he turned to grab me, flailing like a dog about to be put to sleep. His blood splattered across my face.

Movies always made killing a human seem easier than killing a chicken. It wasn't until I tried it that I realized just how difficult it really was. After a heart-pounding sixty seconds, Yan Li collapsed on the ground and stared up at me. I groaned and leaned over him. I'm sure my face looked as horrific as his.

A few raindrops fell on my head, and a moment later it was raining cats and dogs. The cold rain cooled my boiling blood. My adrenaline seemed to stop pumping, too. In that moment I felt a little sorry for Yan Li.

Why do we kill?

I suddenly felt more afraid than if I was about to be executed.

It was too dark to see one's own hands, but Yan Li knew who I was. He coughed hard, his mouth dripping with blood.

"Shen . . . Shen Ming!" he gasped. I . . . I swear . . . I . . . I didn't . . . hurt . . . hurt you."

The rain fell into Yan Li's open mouth. He couldn't say another word or take another breath.

He didn't hurt me?

Blood muddied his face. I felt for a pulse, but he was a corpse.

Last month, I saw a French movie called *Léon: The Professional*. In it, Léon said, "Everything changes after you kill someone."

My fate could no longer be different.

41

CHAPTER 10

June 19, 1995. Before the exams. A rainy night on the rural Nanming Road.

A few minutes ago, I'd just killed someone. He was my school's teaching director.

Before I turned myself in to Huang Hai, I needed to go somewhere. I dumped the body next to the road and stumbled forward. I was very familiar with this landscape. The walls around the steel factory had almost all crumbled; the structures sat mutely in the rain, like graves with no souls to honor. I walked around to a small rear door on the largest building.

Students called this area Demon Girl Zone.

I took out the strand of necklace and clutched it in my hand. I didn't care whether I stained it with blood. I lit a still-dry match in the putrid air. All I could see was rusty machinery. I looked outside anxiously. Thunder and lightning tore through the sky, and the second the light seared my eyes, blackness took over the sky again, leaving only the sound of persistent rain.

Why wasn't she here yet?

From the tunnel that reached down into an even blacker darkness, I heard soft cries that faded in and out after circling endlessly in the damp, decaying air.

It took great effort to walk. My hands were bloody. Shakily, I clutched the walls and faced the tunnel. The opening looked like a hole leading to the center of Earth in a Jules Verne book.

Thunder rolled.

My left foot stepped down.

June 19, 1995—9:55 p.m.

The cries turned into soft and resilient strands: They looped around my neck, dragging me down into the tunnel.

The hatch was open.

Demon Girl Zone.

There was a round handle on the outside of the hatch. One twist and it would lock the tunnel.

Why was the door open?

Flames danced. My shadow swayed across the spotty walls, and with my mourning sash it looked like a cave painting from ten thousand years ago. Every time I came to the Demon Girl Zone, the air was so damp—like a blanket in the rainy season. My skin felt like it could leak water.

A nauseating smell smacked me in the face. The match only remained lit for a few meters before the wind from the tunnel snuffed it out.

The last thing I did in this lifetime was turn around.

My heart was filled with regret—the same type of sadness those who jump to their death feel during their fall.

It hurt so much. A piercing pain flared across my back. Metal had entered my body.

The world spun.

I widened my eyes in the darkness. I could feel myself lying on the cold ground in dirty water. Blood spurted out of my back. My fingers shook a few times before I stopped moving altogether. I tasted the metallic tang of my own blood, flowing endlessly into my mouth.

Frantic footsteps sounded next to my ears. My eyes were open, but I saw nothing.

Time disappeared. It felt like a few seconds, or maybe decades. The world became quiet. I had no sense of smell; my lips were not my own. My body floated, and the pain disappeared. I didn't know where I was.

A life for a life. My punishment had been delivered quickly.

June 19, 1995—10:01 p.m.

I died.

In the last second of my life, I did not believe in reincarnation.

CHAPTER 11

June 19, 1995. Year of Yihai, month of Renwu, day of Xinsi, May 22 on the lunar calendar, and 10:01 p.m. According to the Twelfth Earthly Branch on the traditional Chinese calendar, it was "a bad time to do anything."

That's exactly when I died.

On every Grave-Sweeping Day and Winter's First Day, I visited my mother's grave. With each visit, I understood death even more. If someone remembered you after you died, then you hadn't really died. You still lived with them. You may be in a grave, but you lived in your children's DNA. Even if you had no descendants, your name and photo remained on ID cards, residency registrations, library cards, swimming membership cards, homework sheets, and exams.

But still, I was afraid of being forgotten.

My name was Shen Ming. I used to be the homeroom teacher for Nanming High's senior class, Section 2.

I killed someone, and then I was killed by someone.

Someone stabbed me in the back in the Demon Girl Zone under the abandoned factory.

I believe my eyes stayed open. I still wore the mourning sash. I did not rest in peace. But I also didn't see my killer's face.

Did I stop breathing? Did I still have a pulse? Were my arteries still pumping? Was my blood still flowing? Did oxygen still reach my brain? Was I brain-dead?

I couldn't feel myself at all.

Is it death when you can't feel yourself exist?

People said dying was painful, whether it was by stabbing, hanging, choking, suffocating, poisoning, drowning, falling, or illness. That endless loneliness followed.

I vividly remembered a reference book in college describing the process of death: paleness and a stiffening starts setting in after death; livor mortis—the settling of blood in the lower body; algor mortis—a drop in body temperature, which gradually lowers until it matches that of the immediate environment; rigor mortis—the limbs become stiff and hard to move; decay—the body decomposes, producing a strong odor.

My memory was pretty good, right?

Suddenly a stream of light lit up the ground. I saw a fantastic tunnel lined in white marble. It looked like the tunnel to Demon Girl Zone, or an ancient underground palace. A young boy was crying under the light. His thin clothes were covered in patches. Runny-nosed, he was sobbing on top of his dead mother. A cold man stood nearby, smoking. A shot rang out and then the smoking man was dead, too. Blood oozed from the bullet hole and pooled on the ground, covering the boy's feet. A middle-aged woman took the boy to a quiet street. The address seemed to be Road of Serenity. The house was old. The boy lived behind the window in the basement. Every cloudy day, he looked out at the rain-slicked road, watching people's shiny or dirty shoes pass by. The boy never smiled. His face was as pale as a ghost's but for the two spots of red on his cheeks that looked frightening when he was angry. One late night as he stood by his window, a scream rang out from inside a big house across the street. A girl ran outside and sat down on the stairs to cry.

I wanted to cry, too.

But I was only a corpse. I could no longer cry, just leak pus.

Soon, I would turn into ashes. I would lie in a mahogany or stainless-steel box, six feet under. Or I'd stay on the ground in the Demon Girl Zone and decompose into a dirty mass, turning into something not even the rats and bugs would eat. Eventually, microorganisms would eat away at me, leaving behind a young skeleton.

If the soul existed, I could have left my body and observed myself as a corpse, seeing my killer. I could have sought revenge as a fierce ghost. I'd have spread the bitterness brought to life by my death from the Demon Girl Zone and all through Nanming High.

But the world after death knew not of time. My bitterness would probably last forever.

Yet people don't live forever. Death is always present.

Didn't people always wait for death after birth? My wait had been too short.

Maybe one of you would be smart enough to discover the truth behind my murder—and catch my killer.

Who killed me?

What if reincarnation was real? What if you could relive everything? What if you could avoid all of your mistakes and missteps? If I saw Yan Li in another world, I'd say, "I'm sorry."

I felt like I'd slept for a long time, and I could feel my body again. It felt very light, like I could fly away with the wind. I also felt joy. Was this reincarnation?

I stood up without meaning to and left the Demon Girl Zone. The road ahead seemed unfamiliar. The dilapidated factory was gone. The surroundings looked more like an embroidered painting. I walked aimlessly for a while, then I followed a dim passage through the sparse trees. Bones stuck out of the soil; ghostly light flickered; owls screeched overhead. Birds with human faces flew over me. The birds' bodies looked female. Were they the mythical Ubume birds?

A river stopped me. The water ran blood red and a hot wind carried a fishy smell from across the shore. The current seemed to hide human bodies, as if several boats had sunk right there. I walked along the bank, unafraid. I found an old bridge. An old white-haired woman sat at the entrance to the black bridge. Her hunched figure made it hard to tell her age. I thought of my grandmother who'd just passed away. This woman held a chipped porcelain bowl filled with hot soup. She looked up at me. Surprise peeked out from behind her cloudy gaze. The soup's greasy surface filled me with disgust.

"What is this place?"

"Drink this soup, then you can cross the bridge and go home."

I hesitated but took the bowl, forcing myself to drink the soup. It didn't taste horrible; it reminded me of the tofu soup my grandmother used to make.

The old woman moved out of my way. "Hurry up and cross the bridge," she urged. "There is not much time."

"Is there time for reincarnation?" In high school, this had been my favorite saying.

"Yes, child."

As we talked, I crossed the old bridge over the water. It was tangled with weeds as long as women's hair. When I got to the other side, nausea overcame me. I knelt on the cold riverbank and vomited. All the soup was on the ground in front of my, as though I'd never eaten it.

Before I knew what was happening, the river crested behind me and swallowed me up. In the dark water, surrounded by skeletons, a strange and beautiful light shone toward me and lit up a face.

It was a dead person's face: It was the twenty-five-year-old Shen Ming.

I was about to become someone else.

I never believed what old books said—how the dead always crossed the gate of Hell and took the road of Acheron to the underworld. There was also the River of Forgetfulness. After you crossed the River of Forgetfulness on the Bridge Over Troubled Water, you would be reincarnated. An old woman named Meng Po sat by the Bridge. If you didn't drink her soup, you would not be allowed to pass the River or cross the Bridge. If you did drink the soup, you'd forget everything from your previous life.

River of Forgetfulness. Meng Po. The next life. Would I really forget everything?

"If there was tomorrow, how do you want to make up your face? If there was no tomorrow, how would you say good-bye?"

PART 2:

THE RIVER OF
FORGETFULNESS

CHAPTER 12

October 11, 2004.

A BMW 760 drove into the Number One Elementary School on Longevity Road. The narrow entrance gave way to two rows of school buildings, beyond which lay a sports field. The principal had been waiting for a long time. When the car stopped, he opened the door and said with humility, "Ms. Gu, welcome to our school. Please help advise us."

Gu Qiusha carried a limited-edition designer bag as she struggled to step out of the car in her awkward high heels. The principal escorted her along meandering paths into a small quad. A kindergarten was on the left side of the yard, and old-fashioned houses sat on the right. There were robust stands of bamboo and fig trees. Boys must have liked to play hide-and-seek there. In front of them stood a three-story building, its walls painted white and pale blue. Through the open windows came the sounds of schoolkids reading.

She spoke softly, "May I sit in on a class?"

The principal walked her into the third-grade Section 2 classroom. He introduced the VIP and had the teacher continue with her lesson. Gu Qiusha found an empty seat in the last row. With great formality, the principal sat next to her.

The word "Chrysanthemum" was written on the blackboard. Gu Qiusha frowned, and the principal seemed embarrassed.

The teacher began writing beneath the word:

Chrysanthemum surrounded the poet Tao Yuanming's home
I was admiring the chrysanthemum outside the fence
Until the sun almost set
I did not love chrysanthemum best, but there were no better
  flowers to be seen after chrysanthemum

Gu Qiusha tried to remember the poet's name. As she thought, "Yuan Zhen" was added to the blackboard.

The teacher said, "Yuan Zhen was a great poet of the Tang dynasty. His middle name was Weizhi and his hometown was Luoyang. A descendant of the Northern Dynasties' Xanbei ethnic group, he was good friends with poet Bai Juyi. Together, they were called Yuan Bai. They introduced the New Yuefu Movement, and they compiled the movement's anthology."

The teacher was nervous with the principal and the VIP sitting in on the class. She'd read the text very deliberately, then to lighten the mood she hurried to ask, "Has anyone heard of this great poet?"

Third-graders usually knew of Li Bai or Du Fu, but Yuan Zhen was rarely known. The class sat in silence. The principal seemed irritated at the teacher's lack of knowledge.

Suddenly an arm raised high. The teacher was excited to be rescued. "Si Wang, you can answer."

A boy stood up. His seat was in the back of the class, but Gu Qiusha could see his profile. He had a proper face, his eyes were not big, but he looked refined, like one of those kids who could do very little and still be favored. His clothes looked inexpensive. He recited:

No water could measure up to the sea
No clouds looked the same as those on Wu Mountain
No flowers were worth lingering over
Meditation and missing my dead wife was all I could do.

"This was the fourth poem in Yuan Zhen's *Five Poems About Longing*," the boy continued. "It was written as an ode to his dead wife, Wei Cong. He was only twenty-four years old and a lowly clerk when he married Wei Xiaqing, the daughter of the imperial tutor. Wei was from a royal family, but she never looked down on her impoverished husband. She kept his household, and they were happy together. Seven years later, when Yuan Zhen was promoted to investigating censor, Wei died. Yuan Zhen wrote the poem as he grieved—and it is still very popular today."

The boy's answer was so thorough, and he delivered it with such a serious air, that it was as though he'd seen the events with his own eyes. Gu Qiusha couldn't believe it. Would a third-grader have known that someone would be sitting in and prepared beforehand? She'd only come on a whim, though. There was no way that all classes in this building had done their homework. Plus, the boy said everything so naturally. It was obvious that he understood the poem and wasn't just reciting it by rote.

The teacher was stunned. Not even she knew the backstory. She mumbled, "Right, very good."

"I actually don't like Yuan Zhen," the boy continued. "Within six months of writing this, he took a concubine in Jiangling. Then he met the famous courtesan Xue Tao in Chengdu. She was eleven years older, and he wrote poems to flirt with her. His *Book of Yingying*, also called *Book of Huizhen*, was a way to justify how quickly he moved on. No one could have guessed that it would later lead to the classic play *Romance of the Western Chamber*. So his so-called 'No water could measure up to the sea' was just a shortcut to getting promoted by marrying up."

The whole classroom was quiet. None of the other kids understood what their classmate was saying. Even the teacher was confused.

Gu Qiusha looked like she'd been stabbed in the heart. She lowered her head uneasily, as if she felt that all the students were watching her.

"Si Wang, please sit. We'll talk more about the 'Chrysanthemum' poem."

The teacher was eager to move on and started reading her teaching manual at random.

The end-of-class bell rang. Gu Qiusha whispered to the principal, "I want to talk to that kid."

The teacher brought the boy to Gu Qiusha, who'd been waiting in the yard with the principal. The boy was skinny. His arms and legs seemed as if they were all the same length, and his back was as straight as a soldier's. Unlike a lot of kids who played too many computer games and wore thick glasses or were hunchbacked, his eyes were refined. His only flaw was the peach fuzz on his forehead. He looked calm and collected in front of the principal and the VIP, exuding a natural sense of nobility.

Gu Qiusha leaned down and said, "Hello. What is your name?"

"Si as in 'general,' Wang as in 'lookout.'"

"Si Wang, I really liked that poem you read. Where did you learn so much about poetry?"

"I read a lot, I also use Baidu."

"Did you know Yuan Zhen also wrote the famous 'Three Poems on Grief?'"

"I do." The boy didn't flinch, and his gaze made her heart beat faster.

Gu Qiusha still had doubts. She needed to test him again. "OK, can you recite one of them for me?"

"She was Mr. Xie's favorite daughter, she had nothing being married to me. When I had no clothes, she looked all over to help. She sold her hairpins to buy me wine. She had no complaints eating wild vegetables, nor did she mind using leaves as firewood. Now my salary is more than 100,000, but I could only burn paper money for her."

Gu Qiusha was stunned. This was one of the few Tang dynasty poems she had memorized.

The principal couldn't resist applauding the student.

The boy recited another poem right away: "Life after death already came, the future is already here. I gave away your clothes, but not your sewing supplies. Looking at your servants made me sad, I actually want to send you money in the afterlife. I know everyone grieves sometime, but an impoverished couple suffers the most."

"That's enough," the principal said, but the boy started the last poem in the series:

"You died so early, now I know sharing a hundred years is a luxury. A kind man like Deng You never had kids, Pan Yue could not find the words to grieve for his wife. I hope to be buried with you, and be together again in the next life. I will keep my eyes open all night to honor your dedication."

Gu Qiusha and the boy said the last two lines in unison. Gu backed away as an uneasy feeling spread through her entire being.

She asked, "Do you know what 'I hope to be buried with you, and be together again in the next life' means?"

"It's hard for a couple buried together to begin with. And even if there was an afterlife, it would be difficult to meet again."

The boy had no expression on his face. His gaze held a nuanced maturity, and a coldness.

Gu Qiusha breathed hard. She reached out her delicate, bony hand and stroked the boy's pale face. He unconsciously backed away, then stayed still, allowing her to touch him.

The class bell rang. She rubbed the boy's nose and said, "Great answer! Time to go back to class now."

Si Wang ran up the stairs with the other kids, showing none of the jadedness he'd displayed earlier.

"I hope to be buried with you, and be together again in the next life."

When she'd first learned of her fiancé's death nine years ago, Gu Qiusha found a letter from Shen Ming. He'd copied down this very poem by Yuan Zhen.

The principal asked Si Wang's homeroom teacher about the boy. He had mediocre grades, was quiet, didn't speak up in class, and never really seemed outstanding.

"Is his family very intellectual?" Gu Qiusha added. "Are his parents university professors?"

"Si Wang's father is a factory worker. For some reason, he went missing two years ago. His mom works as a postal clerk. His family is not very prestigious."

"Please find out more about him. I want a kid this gifted to be well educated. Do you understand me?"

The principal kept nodding and walked Gu Qiusha to the car. Advertising on the street showed a large mural for the Erya Education Group. Some child prodigy was quoted as saying "Choose Erya. Choose a Better Life."

Gu had long stopped working as an editor for the Education Publishing House. She was now the GM of a private education company, ranked nationally in the top ten. A few years earlier, her father Gu Changlong had retired from his university president position and used his savings to start the Erya Education Group. Thanks to a wide professional network from years of working with government agencies, the company exploded in size in just a few years. They offered language classes for students going abroad, preschool education, and senior classes, too. They had bought and built many private elementary and middle schools.

The company covered every stage of life, from the cradle to the grave. Gu Qiusha had helped with the company since the beginning. When her father recently retired as the GM for health reasons, she succeeded him.

Gu Qiusha was back at her suburban mansion in an hour. She kicked off her heels and scrubbed off her thick makeup by the dresser mirror. Her reflection showed a thirty-four-year-old woman. Her skin was well maintained with almost no wrinkles or liver spots. When she primped, she still seemed very attractive— or at least she looked that way in front of the camera. Everyone would take a second look. But nothing really turned back the years. She always remembered the time when she was twenty-five, when she was about to be a bride.

Although her father was retired, he kept busy, and currently he was attending a meeting abroad. Dinner was a collection of simple dishes cooked by the maid. Gu finished eating alone, drank a small glass of French red wine, and then went into the bedroom to watch a Korean soap opera.

A few minutes later, a man entered the room. He was also in his thirties. There wasn't one whisker on his face, and a faint bruise marred his forehead. He slowly shed his suit and tie and walked out again.

Gu Qiusha was used to evenings like this. She uttered the word "moron" at her husband's back.

His name was Lu Zhongyue.

CHAPTER 13

Gu Qiusha met Shen Ming for the first time in the fall of 1993. She never told him that was also the day she broke up with her ex-boyfriend.

Her ex had attended the same college, and was tall and handsome. He also came from a good family. They started talking about marriage soon after college graduation. But Gu Qiusha had a secret she'd kept from him for as long as possible.

"I never dared to tell you this before," she finally told him one night. "I hope you won't think less of me. In my junior year of high school, I went to the hospital for some pains. We got the best OB-GYN to examine me, and I was diagnosed as infertile. There was no treatment, and I can't have kids. I am still a normal woman, and we can have a marital life—plus, we can always adopt."

Before she'd even finished, his face grew cloudy. He wanted to break up right away. There were plenty of girls who wanted to marry him, some of them were even socialites. Why marry a barren woman? And adopting was unthinkable.

That was how Gu Qiusha's first relationship had ended. She cried on his shoulder and had to watch him leave. That afternoon, she rode the bus home in a daze, and she was pickpocketed. Shen

Ming stood up for her and was injured as a result of his bravery. When she looked at him in her gratitude, she saw his crystal-clear eyes, his clean-cut face, and his shyness and hesitation. She fell for him right away.

Shen Ming taught Chinese at the prestigious Nanming High and was a Peking University graduate. He never mentioned his parents. His long-term residence at the school also confused her. When she was about to ask around privately, Shen Ming told her voluntarily that, when Shen Ming was just seven, his father had poisoned his mother and was sentenced to death. Raised by his grandmother, Shen Ming had no other place to live. He had always lived at the school, ever since he'd been a student.

Gu Qiusha understood that was why he could only work as a high school teacher, regardless of his résumé and ability. He didn't have an upper-class background, and their families could not be more different. Before Shen Ming learned about Gu's father, she told him her secret.

"I've always wanted to marry someone I love and have a cute kid together," Shen Ming admitted. "But marriage is about more than procreating. If I really wanted to marry someone, I would tolerate all of her flaws. Besides, infertility is a health issue and has nothing to do with someone's character. People can be tall or short—that is all decided by fate. We can always adopt."

The next day, Gu Qiusha took her boyfriend home. Shen Ming learned the identity of his new girlfriend's father—President Gu was always in the papers. Her father liked him, surprisingly, and they had a great chat. Shen's daring ideas about education reform were especially well received.

That was the summer of 1994.

During the summer vacation that followed, Gu's father transferred Shen Ming to his office for a three-month secretary position, which made the elder Gu like his future son-in-law even more.

The following year, a grand engagement ceremony was held for the couple. With President Gu's blessings, city Education Bureau leaders talked to Shen Ming and issued a memo to promote him from Nanming High to the Youth League Committee. Shen Ming's future was set, and he would become the Youth League Committee secretary in just two years, which was the fastest way someone could succeed.

In 1995, during the last few days of May, Gu noticed that Shen Ming seemed troubled. He was always distracted during the apartment renovation inspections. She asked him why, and he tried to hide behind excuses, blaming things like the pressure from his students' upcoming college entrance exams.

She asked at school and learned Shen Ming was rumored to be having an affair with a girl in the senior class. There were rumors of him being born out of wedlock, too. She couldn't believe what she was hearing; she was about to marry this man. They'd already had the engagement ceremony—and even the wedding invitations had been mailed. What could she do? As they got closer to the exams, Shen Ming—who was in charge of the senior class—stayed late every night to work with his students. He claimed he couldn't be with her even on weekends. Gu Qiusha grew more and more concerned.

The evening of June 3 was their last night together. Gu and Shen left the new apartment and went to see the Arnold Schwarzenegger movie *True Lies*.

Gu Qiusha asked him, "What lies have you told me?"

Shen Ming looked his fiancée in the eyes, and after a long silence answered, "Someone wants me dead."

He admitted that he'd been born out of wedlock. His stepfather had killed his mother when Shen Ming was seven. When he was ten, his last name was changed to Shen on his residency registration, his biological father's last name. He'd wanted to hide from his fiancée and future father-in-law the shame he'd carried with him since birth.

He vehemently denied having an affair with a student.

Gu Qiusha believed him initially, but she couldn't sleep at night. She felt wronged. She'd been nothing but honest with him. She'd given him everything, including a secret no one could know. Yet Shen Ming had lied to her about the circumstances of his birth. He didn't tell her the truth until the news was all over school. He was dishonest. Considering all this, even if he said there was nothing between him and the student, could she believe him?

"Don't believe anyone, not even the one you love the most."

Her father uttered those words right before their engagement ceremony—his advice for her marriage.

Were those words from just three months ago an omen?

Gu Qiusha tossed and turned all night.

Two days later, Shen Ming's high school friend Lu Zhongyue found her to tell her that Shen Ming was in trouble. Liu Man, a high school girl, had been killed with poison. Shen Ming was in great danger because someone had seen him alone with the girl the night before. The police had a search warrant. Could her father help?

Gu Qiusha broke her teacup as she started crying. Her first reaction wasn't to save her fiancé; instead she imagined the worst-case scenario. Did he kill the girl? Had there been an affair?

Shen Ming called her that evening, but she refused to meet with him.

She couldn't sleep. Her mind overflowed with images from their relationship: their first meeting, first dinner, first date, first hug, first kiss, first . . .

Every detail was like a vivid movie, except that his face became blurrier and blurrier. His nose seemed more hawkish, and his eyes went from calm to angry.

Did he really love her?

Did he date her because of her father? Did he have anyone else? Along with the high school student, were there other girls?

Why did she like him? Because he got her wallet back? His courage while fighting the thief? His hidden talents? The poems he wrote for her every week for the last two years? His calm yet bold attitude?

The next day she heard the news about Shen Ming's arrest. The police had found the poison in his room.

She couldn't go to work that day. Her father was angry. He tossed a letter at her. It was from Shen Ming and addressed to his college friend, He Nian. The friend had stayed in Beijing to work. In a calculated move, he'd given President Gu the letter since it involved him and his daughter.

Shen Ming wrote that he was about to be married and embark on a political career. But the letter contained some sinister information that scared Gu Qiusha. Shen admitted to his friend that he'd researched Gu Qiusha and followed her for a long time before they met. That's why he was on the bus the day she was pickpocketed. His actions had made her fall for him right away, and he then manipulated the situation so her father would value and promote him.

The only positive aspect of the letter was that Shen Ming had not revealed the secret of her infertility.

President Gu was furious about the end of the letter. Shen Ming wrote: "My future father-in-law, well, he is a hypocrite. If I am a thief, then he is the biggest thief. One day, his despicable secret will be revealed."

Her father locked the letter in his safe and told her not to mention it to anyone.

The postmark told Gu Qiusha that Shen Ming had written the letter six months earlier. When He Nian made a serious mistake at work and was demoted back to the city Education Bureau, he was assigned to the Youth League Committee. He Nian learned that Shen Ming would be named the next committee secretary—jealousy infected everyone, especially among college friends. After graduation, someone like Shen Ming with no connections had only gotten a high school teaching job, while He Nian secured a prestigious job in Beijing. How could He Nian stand being Shen Ming's underling now?

Gu Qiusha had her doubts about the letter's authenticity. People loved to kick someone who was down, as her father often said. But whether the letter was real or fake no longer mattered. Shen Ming was already down and could not get up.

She changed the locks on their new apartment, and her father canceled the wedding.

When Shen Ming was in jail, Huang Hai went to Gu Qiusha twice to get more information. She told the policeman the facts, including how Shen Ming had been acting oddly.

Huang Hai asked, "Ms. Gu, do you trust your fiancé?"

"First of all, I trust no one. Second, he is no longer my fiancé."

She'd said this calmly, not caring how it would affect the police investigation. Huang Hai's face stiffened, and he left without saying anything more.

It only took a week for President Gu's insider connections to make the Education Bureau terminate Shen Ming's teaching position and Party membership.

On June 16, Lu Zhongyue visited the Gus. He told them Shen Ming had been released—that he'd been acquitted by the police and needed their help. President Gu was nervous. The terminations couldn't be reversed or undone. Shen Ming must know about them already; he would probably look for them that night. President Gu canceled all work appointments. He had the driver take him and his daughter to the airport so they could depart for a seven-day vacation to Yunnan province's Dali and Lijiang.

June 19, 1995—10 p.m.

While Gu Qiusha and her father enjoyed the sights and sounds of Yunnan, Shen Ming died underground on a thunderous night.

Who killed Shen Ming?

This question had plagued her for the last nine years. True, she'd long ago married someone else, but she had never forgotten her former fiancé.

Gu Qiusha wanted to find out more about that boy, Si Wang.

CHAPTER 14

October 12, 2004. Tuesday. Longevity Road. Number One Elementary School at 4:00 p.m.

Gu Qiusha sat inside the BMW. She rolled down the window to watch the kids leaving school. Many parents waited for their children, their cars idling in a long line. Si Wang walked alone behind a group of chattering kids. No one greeted him. He wore the blue school uniform. His heavy book bag was covered in sand and his red school scarf had holes.

Gu Qiusha opened her door and blocked his way. Si Wang looked up at her. His face was expressionless but he spoke politely. "Ma'am, excuse me."

"You don't remember me? I was in your class yesterday."

"I do." The boy tugged at his clothes. He knew to keep up appearances in front of ladies. "You like Yuan Zhen's poems."

"Where do you live? I can take you home."

"It's OK. I always walk home. I don't need a ride. But thank you for the offer."

The way he spoke, neither proud nor bashful, seemed familiar. She was glad that she'd worn flats today. "OK, I'll walk with you."

Si Wang didn't want to refuse again, so he allowed this stranger to accompany him. Suzhou River ran behind the school, and the small path along the riverbank was a shortcut. It had been too long since Gu Qiusha had taken a walk. The scent of river clay rose up; some dead leaves floated down. Fall was in the air. The river burbled along, exposing the riverbed's foundation of mud and trash, and maybe some animal bones. A boat motored by, its wake crashing against the shore. After the quiet shortcut, sparrows sang in the dusk. Feral black cats clambered on the walls outside the factory. The walls' shadows stretched tall: one red, one blue, one tall, one short.

"Si Wang, I have a question. How does no one know how smart you are?"

He kept walking quickly but didn't answer. Gu Qiusha continued. "I saw your exam papers. I noticed that you intentionally answered some questions incorrectly. You wrote the right answer and crossed it out to write in something wrong, something ridiculously wrong. Your handwriting seems bad—but it's unnaturally bad, like you faked it."

"If I get everything right, I'm afraid someone might pay too much attention to me."

"Finally, an honest answer. Your teacher said you have no friends and don't go on play dates, either. No one has been to your house. Why are you such a loner?"

"My home is small and shabby. I don't want anyone to see it."

"So you're hiding yourself? Then why did you surprise me yesterday?"

"The teacher wanted to talk about Yuan Zhen, but no one answered. I was afraid she would get in trouble with the principal. She is always good to me, so I helped her out. Someone had to answer. I was familiar with Yuan Zhen anyway."

The kid's gaze seemed very sincere. Gu Qiusha's doubts dissipated.

"Do you also like novels?"

"Auntie, are you testing me?"

She crouched down and rubbed his adorable face. "You can call me Ms. Gu."

"OK, Ms. Gu."

"Have you ever read *Jane Eyre*?" The book was a bit mature for a kid his age, but Gu Qiusha wasn't testing him for that.

"Of course I've read it."

In English, Gu Qiusha effortlessly recited the beginning of Jane Eyre's speech to Rochester.

Do you think, because I am poor, obscure, plain, and
little, I am soulless and heartless? You think wrong!

She didn't think the boy could meet this challenge. It would be amazing if he even knew the Chinese translation, let alone recognize it in English.

But shockingly, Si Wang picked up where Gu Qiusha left off to recite the rest of the impassioned speech—and he did so in English:

I have as much soul as you, and full as much heart! And
if God had gifted me with some beauty and much wealth,
I should have made it as hard for you to leave me, as it
is now for me to leave you. I am not talking to you now
through the medium of custom, conventionalities, nor
even of mortal flesh; it is my spirit that addresses your
spirit; just as if both had passed through the grave, and we
stood at God's feet, equal, as we are!

As Si Wang finished, Gu Qiusha was afraid to look into his eyes. Ten years ago, she'd given Shen Ming an English copy of

Jane Eyre. Her father had brought it back from a trip to the US, and she remembered Shen Ming trying to memorize the passage.

"Just as if both had passed through the grave."

She couldn't resist repeating the lines in Chinese.

Si Wang lowered his eyes, hiding his gaze behind long lashes. "Sorry, but I have read the original—and I remember this speech."

"Si Wang, do you understand what it means?"

"Yes, I do."

"Like you have lived it?"

He paused and shook his head, saying, "I don't know."

She, too, was at a loss for words. The pair walked silently. A dilapidated vintage jeep sat on the road by the quietest part of the Suzhou River. The vehicle seemed familiar to her. Two of the four wheels were flat, and the front of the car had almost completely fallen off. There were no car registration stickers, only an out-of-state license plate tucked into the back. A red rose among white skeletons was spray-painted on the back window.

Si Wang said, "The car has been here for two years. I remember it from when I was in first grade and my grandfather walked me."

Technically, this was a corpse of a car. A rotting corpse.

Someone was calling a name. Gu Qiusha turned around in a panic. She hadn't noticed anyone else in the area. She got closer to the car. The doors were locked and the windows were securely shut. Thick dust had settled on the handles. She bravely put her ear next to the window. Her heart was still beating too fast. She wanted to hear that name again. She quivered and looked around. There was nothing but the quiet, barren land, a freezing river on one side and a factory wall on the other.

Plus, a strange boy.

Dusk—5:00 p.m.

No one else passed by. She leaned against the windshield and tried to look in through the dark windows. She made out some debris on the empty seats: newspapers, instant noodle cups, some mysterious and disgusting stains.

She smelled an odor so bizarre that it freaked her out. Was it from this car? Gu Qiusha wanted to break into the car. She knew that she needed to know its secret—just like an autopsy was necessary to reveal someone's actual cause of death.

She circled the jeep twice and thought the trunk looked like it could be opened. Maybe years of rain and sleet had rusted the lock? She found a steel bar from nearby and located a gap in the seam of the trunk. Using the bar and all her strength, she began trying to pry it open.

"What are you doing?"

Si Wang was finally acting like a normal schoolkid, confusedly watching her crazy behavior.

"Can you help me?"

Gu Qiusha wasn't strong enough, but luckily the boy was eager to help—though he looked around nervously, afraid to be taken for a car thief.

The trunk opened.

The intensity of the odd smell inside almost knocked them out. Gu Qiusha covered her nose and looked into the open truck. Flies as big as butterflies flew out and listlessly fell at their feet.

The wind picked up, blustering Si Wang's red neckerchief.

There was a thick roll of carpet in the trunk. The third-grader did something most adults would never dare—he lifted the tightly wound carpet.

"No!"

Before Gu Qiusha could stop Si Wang, he'd exposed a body. Technically, it was a decomposed, almost skeletal male corpse. The remains were riddled with maggots. A leather loafer indicated the victim's gender. He'd been dead for at least two years.

Gu Qiusha ran and hid behind a tree. Si Wang seemed very calm, however. Gently, he closed the trunk so as to preserve the crime scene. The boy acted like a seasoned detective. He looked around carefully, not touching anything so as to avoid leaving fingerprints. It was hard to believe he was only nine years old.

Gu Qiusha already knew who the man was.

CHAPTER 15

"The medical examiner confirmed that the dead man is He Nian," Huang Hai said. "He's been missing for two years." Huang Hai was in his forties now, and his voice was husky and dull. The past nine years had leathered his skin, though he was still big and imposing. He sat inside the GM's office at Erya Education Group, studying everything in the room.

Gu Qiusha had not forgotten this man. He'd talked to her twice in 1995 while Shen Ming was jailed as a murder suspect.

"When I saw the rotting jeep by the river, I thought of He Nian. Very few people drove cars like that, plus it had an out-of-town plate. Then there was that rose and skeleton art on the back. I was sure it was his car."

"Can you tell me what happened? Why did you leave your car to walk with that student?"

"I'm sorry for getting that kid involved. I was just curious, and now he's seen a scary dead body. I am worried about what this will do to him." Gu Qiusha sighed, and crow's feet appeared around her eyes. "Si Wang is a genius. I've never met anyone like him. Kids like that are priceless, and very rare."

"I understand. Can you tell me more about the victim?"

"He Nian worked as the vice GM at our company. He was the Youth League Committee secretary for the city Education Bureau. He resigned a few years ago to start his own business. He was one of the first bureaucrats to go into the private sector. I worked with him for two years. He was quite capable. His personality was a bit off, but he never had any enemies."

Huang Hai said, "The autopsy determined that he died in December 2002, back when he went missing. The body was so decomposed it was hard to pinpoint an exact cause of death. But it appears that he was stabbed in the back. The killer wrapped him in the rug, locked the body in the trunk, and dumped the car. Very few people walk along there, and the winter slowed the decomposition process. By the next summer, all the trash made the whole area smell bad, so no one paid any attention."

"When he went missing, we thought he went to work for a competitor," Gu Qiusha said. "We ran missing person ads online and in newspapers, then we filed a report with the police. We never imagined that he'd been killed."

Gu Qiusha was still shaken by the whole experience. Something had made her discover He Nian's jeep.

"There is one other thing," Huang Hai said. "According to He Nian's file, he also graduated from Peking University in the class of ninety-two, a Chinese major. I think you know what I'm getting at."

Gu Qiusha was prepared for the policeman's fierce look. Calmly, she said, "Shen Ming."

"It was quite a coincidence. When I interrogated Shen Ming in 1995, he said he was being transferred to the Education Bureau and had been internally chosen to be the next Youth League Committee secretary. He was killed a few days later. Instead, He Nian got the job and was transferred to the Bureau just a month before Shen Ming's death."

"What are you saying? He Nian's death had something to do with Shen Ming? Or the other way around?"

"Anything and everything is possible."

Gu Qiusha's heart beat rapidly. She thought of that letter from Shen Ming, the one He Nian had given to her father. He Nian had betrayed his college friend and gotten the secretary's position.

She avoided Huang Hai's gaze. "I don't know."

"Thanks for your cooperation. If you think of anything else, let me know."

Huang Hai left a business card before leaving. Her hands were sweaty from keeping the secret about the letter from nine years ago. As far as she knew, her father still had it in his safe. If he wanted to keep it a secret, what good were her words?

Gu Qiusha was restless. She called her driver to take her to Number One Elementary School.

Another crowded school pickup. She saw him walking out of school.

His vision was good enough to pick hers out among the many cars. He walked up to her BMW and said, "Ms. Gu, did you need something?"

"I wanted to apologize for what happened."

"The body in that car by the river?"

"You are just a nine-year-old. How could I have let you see something that horrific? It was all my fault." She opened the door for him. "Please come inside."

Si Wang was timid and shook his head. "I don't want to dirty your car."

He had obviously never been in a fancy European car before; boys knew all about cars these days. Gu Qiusha smiled. "It's OK! Just come in."

The boy frowned. He gingerly entered and checked out the car's interior. "Ms. Gu, don't worry about that body. I won't have nightmares because of it."

"Really?"

"I've seen dead bodies. My grandfather passed away last year—and my grandmother, too, this year. I saw their bodies going into the cremation chamber."

She hugged him. "Poor baby."

The boy's breath was warm next to her ear. "Everyone dies. Life is just an endless cycle. Birth and death go round and round."

"Si Wang, you must also like philosophy, and not just Chinese and English."

"Do you know of the Six Realms?"

"Tell me."

"The Heaven realm, Human realm, Asura realm, Animal realm, Hungry Ghost realm, and the Hell realm. Humans are forever in the Six Realms. Bad people become animals, Hungry Ghosts, or even go to Hell. Good people reincarnate as humans or go to Heaven. Only Asura, Bodhisattva, and Buddha can get out of the Six Realms."

"Well, that is a Buddhist theory. I am a Christian," she replied, taking out the cross she wore around her neck.

The third-grader looked at her strangely, as if lemon juice had been squirted into his eyes. He retreated to the car door and said, "Do you really believe in Jesus?"

"Why would I lie to you?"

"Do you believe a soul exists after death, that we're all waiting for Judgment Day, and that someone who believes in Jesus will be saved and go to Heaven and others go to Hell?"

"I . . ." Gu Qiusha was stumped by the question. She'd only started going to church after Shen Ming died. "I do!"

"Some books say death is only a stage between this lifetime and the next. On Judgment Day, every dead person will reincarnate and be judged. If you believed in the right thing and did good, you would go to Heaven and live forever, otherwise you would go to a fiery Hell."

"Little genius, have you read all religious books?"

Si Wang kept talking. "Maybe only Taoism is exempt. They value life and look for eternal life. But the ghost world is parallel to the human world. Have you seen a ghost?"

She stayed silent, unable to answer.

The boy added mysteriously, "I have."

"OK, you won. Can we not talk about this anymore? I will take you home."

He muttered an address. The ever-patient driver stepped on the gas.

Ten minutes later, the BMW turned on to a narrow street. It took a lot of honking for the sunning elderly men and women to move and let the car pass, just barely fitting between the bicycles and motorcycles. If his boss hadn't been there, the driver would have gotten out of the car to cuss at the crowd.

"Just park here." Si Wang pointed at a shedding locust tree. He hopped out, said "Thank you," and snuck inside an old three-story building. What types of families lived inside such greasy, peeling walls?

CHAPTER 16

One month later.

Si Wang became the new spokesperson for Erya Education Group. The principal told him he was needed for some school-promotion photos and took him to a photography studio. Si Wang was only later told it was for a commercial. Gu Qiusha's assistants found his mother, his only family. They paid the woman 100,000 yuan on the spot to sign the contract.

Gu Qiusha invited Si Wang to her home for dinner. Wearing new clothes from a children's clothing sponsor and walking into a basketball-sized living room, the boy blushed. In Gu Qiusha's eyes, it only made him more adorable. She led him to the dinner table and introduced him to the family.

"This is my father, the chairman of Erya Education Group. He used to be a university president, Professor Gu Changlong."

In his sixties now, Gu Changlong had dyed his hair a shiny black. He smiled and said, "Si Wang, I have heard about you. You are extraordinary—a genius, I think. Thank you for being our spokesperson."

"Professor Gu, thank you for the opportunity. Hope you enjoy good health and appetite," the boy said, using proper etiquette and very much pleasing Gu Qiusha.

Next, she introduced him to the man across the dinner table. "This is my husband, Erya Education Group's CEO, Mr. Lu Zhongyue."

"Hello, Mr. Lu."

Lu Zhongyue seemed uncomfortable. He nodded awkwardly without saying anything.

Gu Qiusha said, "My husband is not very talkative. He used to be an engineer—you can ask him any math or science questions."

"Great, math and science are my weaknesses. I need all the help I can get!"

"Let's make a toast." Gu Qiusha raised her glass of red wine. The maid had already brought out a lavish dinner made by the chef catering the party.

The boy toasted with juice. The dinner was a success. Gu Qiusha and her father peppered Si Wang with all kinds of questions, but nothing fazed him. Astronomy, geology, history, philosophy— he knew it all. Lu Zhongyue posed some military questions about German tanks in World War II, and the boy had answers for those, too.

Finally, Gu Changlong asked about the economy. The third-grader said, "In the next three years, the global economy should stay prosperous. Chinese real estate prices will double. If you want to invest cash wisely, buy real estate."

"What else would anyone need with a son like this?" The old man sighed and looked at Lu Zhongyue. The younger man paled and lowered his head.

The boy didn't linger after the meal. "Ms. Gu, I need to go home. I promised my mom."

"You're such a good kid."

Gu Qiusha liked the boy more and more, and she couldn't resist kissing his cheek. She asked the driver to take him home.

Watching Si Wang get into the car, she touched her lips. It was the first time she'd kissed him, but it felt somehow familiar.

The mansion felt lonely; her father had already gone to bed. She'd forced both him and her husband to attend the dinner.

Feeling lost, she went up to the second floor. She saw her husband in the hall.

With a cold stare, he said, "That cop, Huang Hai, came looking for me today. He had questions about He Nian's death."

"Why ask you?"

"Because of *him*."

She knew what he meant.

"You went to high school with him, and He Nian went to college with him."

"You are also my husband. He Nian worked for our company before he was killed, and I found his body."

"So now I am a suspect?"

"Nothing will happen to you, so relax." She was about to leave but grabbed his arm and asked, "Why were you so cold to the kid today?"

"Is he your child?"

"He may as well be."

Lu Zhongyue shook his head. "That is your right. It has nothing to do with me."

He shook off her grasp, went into his study, and started another long night of playing *World of Warcraft*.

Back in her bedroom, she sprawled out on the spacious bed and stroked her lips and neck. The room didn't smell like a man lived there at all. In fact, Lu Zhongyue hadn't slept in this bed for three years.

They'd first met in March of 1995 at Shen Ming and Gu Qiusha's engagement ceremony. Lu Zhongyue was sitting at Shen Ming's table and was quite drunk. Shen Ming dragged her to the table to make a toast, but Lu Zhongyue couldn't handle more drinking. He vomited all over the place.

Gu Changlong, like many of the guests, noticed Lu Zhongyue because of this incident. Gu Qiusha's father was a comrade of Lu's father. While the elder Gu was at the Education Bureau, the elder Lu worked in the county government and became an influential department chief. The two men had a good relationship. Gu Changlong often visited the Lu family and remembered Lu Zhongyue.

Lu Zhongyue majored in the sciences and after graduation worked at the steel factory on Nanming Road, just meters away from his old high school. He was the youngest engineer at the factory. But when the factory closed down, Lu had nothing to do. He met with Shen Ming to watch games and drink together. And since Shen Ming had very few friends, whenever he needed someone to hang out with, he'd grab Lu. That's how Lu had become friends with Gu Qiusha. When they renovated the new apartment, Lu often came over to help, which made Shen Ming feel indebted to him.

In June of 1995, Lu Zhongyue was the one who told Gu Qiusha what had happened with Shen Ming. The Gu family had gone to Yunnan to get away from Shen Ming after the rumors and the trouble with the police. When they returned, a red-eyed Lu Zhongyue was waiting for them at the door.

He told them all the details, including how the police had found Yan Li's body on Nanming Road. It was confirmed that Shen Ming had killed Yan Li, because the weapon was still stuck in the victim's body—and it was covered in Shen Ming's bloody fingerprints. Shen Ming escaped to the factory's abandoned underground warehouse and was stabbed in the back by someone.

Gu Qiusha cried profusely, collapsing on Lu Zhongyue's shoulders and soaking his shirt with her tears.

She felt so guilty.

Could she have saved him? What if her father hadn't terminated his job and Party membership? What if she had tried to help him, or even just visited him in jail?

But she'd done nothing for him except project disappointment and desperation.

Gu Qiusha had known that her and her father's actions would change Shen Ming's future—that he'd be crushed, and robbed of ten years of experience. But she never thought he would choose to kill someone. She also could never have predicted someone killing him. Who was Shen Ming? What kind of hate did he have in his heart? If killing Yan Li was revenge, Shen Ming must have hated her and her dad just as much. If Shen Ming hadn't been killed, would there have been more victims of his hatred? She went from feeling guilty to afraid.

Gu Qiusha was sick for a long time. After she got better, she went to Lu Zhongyue out of guilt. Lu was understanding. He missed his old friend, but he also said death was irreversible and one had to say good-bye to the past. Lu Zhongyue also admitted his frustration with life; compared to hard-studying and high-achieving Shen Ming, Lu was always the straggler. His job after college was arranged by his father through his government connections. He was unhappy as a factory engineer.

One summer day, she invited Lu Zhongyue to meet her at a bar. The two drank beer, then wine, and finally whiskey, until they were both very drunk. She woke up in a hotel room with Lu Zhongyue sitting in front of her, looking guilty. How could he have touched his friend's woman? She didn't blame him, however; she only held him and said, "Don't ever mention Shen Ming again."

Gu Qiusha married Lu the following year.

Gu Changlong readily agreed to his daughter's decision. Not only was the Lu family old friends, but his daughter was still reeling from the past. It was necessary for her to overcome the pain, and marrying quickly seemed like the best way for her to heal.

But she never told her secret to Lu Zhongyue.

She was no longer that naive girl. Lu and Shen were different types of men. If Lu knew that his wife-to-be was infertile, he might not have pledged his eternal devotion. She needed to get married first.

Four years after the wedding, Lu became suspicious of his wife's not becoming pregnant. When he insisted on a checkup, she finally told him about her condition. Lu Zhongyue picked a huge fight, but nothing came of it. Just two years earlier, his father had been investigated for corruption and fired from his job. If Gu Changlong hadn't helped his in-laws smooth things over, the elder Lu would have been sentenced to at least ten years in prison. Plus, Nanming Steel Factory was still closed and Lu had no job.

It was the same year that Erya Education Group opened its doors. Gu Changlong appointed his son-in-law as CEO.

She and Lu were estranged, though they still faked intimacy in front of people. He was still respectful toward her father and he still worked diligently. Yet everyone called him a kept man, especially those who were resentful of his position.

Gu Qiusha often thought of Shen Ming on nights she couldn't sleep.

CHAPTER 17

December 2004. A weekend.

The weather was getting cooler. The lone locust tree standing in front of the cluster of three-story gray buildings had lost all of its leaves.

Gu Qiusha stepped out of her car and told the driver to wait. She walked into the building's dark foyer plastered with ads. Almost choking on the heavy cooking odors, she made her way up the narrow staircase, finally arriving on the third floor, where there was a common kitchen and bathroom. She knocked on a door and was surprised to see how young the woman who answered it looked. She had a face like a Chinese movie star.

"Is this Si Wang's home?"

"I'm his mom. Who are you?"

"Hello. You must be He Qingying. I'm Gu Qiusha with Erya Education Group." She tried to seem confident and aloof. Dressed in Hermès, she really stood out compared to the woman in casual house clothes.

"Ms. Gu. Wow, it's you. Please come inside." He Qingying nervously put down the sweater she was knitting and looked at her home as though she was seeing it for the first time. "I'm sorry for such a shabby home. Can I get you anything?"

"I'm glad Si Wang could be our company's spokesperson. I know in the past, you've only been in touch with my assistant, but I wanted to visit myself and bring you some Christmas gifts."

She took out a set of Chanel makeup. Si Wang's mom shook her head. "No, I can't accept this."

"Ms. Gu, you're visiting?" Si Wang came into the living room. Every time she saw this boy, it felt like a rainy day was being chased away by the sun. She smiled. "I'm here to see you."

"I didn't ask you to visit." He lowered his head shyly and busied himself with tidying the sofa and table, making a place for her to sit.

"Don't worry about it. I'm not staying long." She noticed a small bed next to the window and the locust tree right outside. "Is this Si Wang's bed?"

"Yes. My bedroom is inside," He Qingying answered awkwardly.

The woman had a great figure, and although she might have seemed inferior in front of the guest, Gu was jealous. Before coming to visit, Gu had read He Qingying's file. The two women were the same age. Si Wang had gotten his mom's looks. No wonder he was so gorgeous.

Suddenly, two thugs walked in and sat down like they owned the place.

"You have company?" one of them said.

Si Wang and his mom were shocked. The boy retreated into the bedroom. In a panic, He Qingying said, "I'm sorry, can you come back in half an hour?"

One of the men noticed the gifts and shouted, "You can afford Chanel? Where is the money you owe *us*?"

"Stop it! This isn't mine." He Qingying eyed Gu. "My old school friend was just showing me some of her things."

Gu Qiusha took back the gifts and without missing a beat said, "How dare you trespass on private property. I could call the cops on you."

She acted powerful so they would stop their intimidation. It worked. They left, promising they'd be back.

He Qingying shut her door, looking very troubled. "Thank you so much. I am so embarrassed."

"Please let me know if I can do anything to help." Gu Qiusha left her business card and returned the gifts to He Qingying. "I think this would look great on you."

She was about to leave when Si Wang charged out. In a low voice he offered to walk her out. Then he said to his mom, "Don't be afraid. Wang Er will be here in a bit. If those two come back, don't open the door."

Walking downstairs with Si Wang, Gu Qiusha thought about his amazing maturity. Stroking his face and smiling, she said, "Now I know your nickname: Wang Er."

"My mom's the only one who calls me that."

They stopped at the bottom of the stairs and Gu Qiusha looked him in the eyes. "Si Wang, you walked me out for a reason. Do you have something to tell me?"

"Please." He looked around and lowered his voice. "Please don't come here anymore."

"I understand. Will you come to my house then? I will send my driver."

He nodded, serious beyond his years. Watching him caused in Gu Qiusha a pang of jealousy.

"You're a good son to love your mother so much."

"Since my grandparents died, she is my only family."

"Your mom is a good woman."

She looked up at the third-story window. Judging by her looks and manner of speaking, He Qingying seemed like an educated woman. She must have married the wrong man, and now she was paying for it, living in squalor with her genius son.

"Ms. Gu, are you going back?" Si Wang asked, pointing to her car and the napping driver.

"I don't want to leave you." She couldn't resist touching his cheek. Some people had everything but precious children; some people had nothing except for priceless kids.

A horrible thought entered her mind, one she wanted to resist—to stamp out before it was too late. But staring into his crystal-clear eyes, she knelt down and whispered, "If I had a kid like you, everything would be different."

Si Wang looked at her, baffled. He jumped away and ran back upstairs like she'd just given him an electric shock.

CHAPTER 18

Spring was late to arrive in 2005.

Gu Changlong felt tired all the time, and he needed to use the bathroom two or three times a night. It was hard to believe how fragile humans were. One seemed to age dramatically overnight, or even die out of the blue. He had never thought about death before.

Gu Qiusha walked into his study. Winter was still outside. Had she gained weight?

"Dad, I need to talk to you about something."

"Is it important?"

"I want to adopt Si Wang."

"Are you joking?"

"No, I am very serious. I've thought about this for two months. I've considered everything. I have to adopt him. I love him."

Recognizing her determination, Gu Changlong sighed. "Qiusha, you're still so willful. Do you remember how you had to marry Shen Ming?"

"Please don't mention him."

"Fine. How about how you had to marry Lu Zhongyue? No regrets?"

"I don't regret it."

Gu Changlong knew his daughter's marriage had gone bad long ago. He said, "The boy must be nine already. He won't see you as his real mom. Why not adopt a two- or three-year-old?"

"He turns ten this year." Any mention of Si Wang brought joy to Gu Qiusha. "It's easy to adopt a baby, but who knows how a child might turn out. If he became another Lu Zhongyue, then what's the point? Si Wang is different. He's a fine piece of jade. He's smart and understanding. Most adults can't compete with him intellectually or emotionally."

"Adults, indeed. Well you're an adult. I won't interfere. Did you discuss it with your husband?"

"When I told him I couldn't get pregnant a few years ago, we talked about adopting. He wasn't against it." Gu Qiusha approached her father and touched his shoulders. "Dad, I want a child so badly."

"The one you want has someone else's genes."

"Do you really want your son-in-law to take over? Dad, I know you have a lover. If you could give me a younger brother, I won't complain."

Gu Changlong was embarrassed and angry. "Shut up!"

"This kid is my last chance. Since the first time I saw him, I've felt close to him—like he was the person I loved the most in a past life. I can't be without him. It keeps me up at night. I wish I could hold him right now."

"You're crazy." Gu Changlong paced back and forth. "Adopting is not just up to you. Doesn't he have parents?"

"I've investigated Si Wang's family. His dad, Si Mingyuan, was an unemployed factory worker who went missing three years ago. The man's residency was just canceled—so, legally, he is dead. His paternal grandparents died within a year of each other. His maternal grandparents died before he was born. His mom, He Qingying, is the only guardian."

"She would give her son to you?"

"I think she'll agree to it in the end. She worked as a postal clerk, making two or three grand a month. They're in a lot of debt. Loan sharks hassle them every day. She was just laid off last month. So with no job, she won't last very long."

"So he's just a poor kid, dying to have money. Maybe that's why he approached you. Qiusha, you're too naive. Do you really want to go through the same thing that happened with Shen Ming?"

"I told you not to mention his name," she screamed, storming out of the room and slamming the door.

For ten years, speaking the name Shen Ming had been forbidden in the house.

He felt short of breath again. Hurriedly, he put on a pair of reading glasses, then opened the drawer and found his tablets—which he gulped down with some water. Shen Ming's face occupied his mind, just as it had in so many nightmares during the summer of 1995.

Shen Ming had been such a poor bastard with a tragic family story, and he'd undoubtedly brought bad luck to the Gu family. Gu Changlong never would have let his daughter marry him if not for his daughter's previous heartbreak, and then Shen Ming's role in some unfortunate business instigated by Gu Changlong.

Gu Changlong's secretary had been on maternity leave during the summer of 1995. Shen Ming was temporarily transferred from Nanming High to the University President's Office, where he worked hard and wrote amazing speeches for Gu Changlong. The students treated him like a legend after graduation. Thanks to his surprising fluency in English, Shen Ming also greeted foreign guests for the president. In fact, every task assigned to him was flawlessly executed, from hotel reservations to travel plans. People loved him.

Gu Changlong decided to have Shen Ming solve a problem. He gave him a small package, telling him it was a talisman from Putuo Mountain used for warding off evil. Vice President Qian had been a professor and was uncomfortable with politics. For two years he'd been plagued by bad luck and was often sick. Gu Changlong believed that placing this talisman in Qian's big living room vase would erase all of Qian's troubles—and luck would return to all corners of his life. But Qian was a scientist and stern materialist. He had no regard for matters like feng shui and other ancient traditions. If the gift had been given to him in an obvious fashion, Qian would have refused it. So Gu Changlong told Shen Ming to hide the package inside the vase to secretly help Qian. As always, Shen Ming did as he was told. He paid a visit to Qian and successfully completed the task.

A few days later, the ethics committee disciplined Qian, and he was brought up on corruption charges. The reported violation was a bribe worth $20,000 hidden inside a vase in his home. As a stubborn intellectual, Qian couldn't take such humiliation. Using his pants, he hung himself in jail.

Shen Ming didn't learn the truth until later. Vice President Qian and President Gu had never gotten along. Qian had accused Gu of taking kickbacks from the school cafeteria's subcontracting deal. Qian reported it to the university's board of directors. Gu found himself in a desperate situation and took this drastic measure. He couldn't do it himself, and Shen Ming was the easiest one to deceive and use.

So Shen Ming and Gu Qiusha's marriage received his blessing.

The following year, as his daughter's wedding got closer, all sorts of terrible news arrived about Shen Ming. The final straw was when he became a murder suspect. It was around this time that He Nian gave Gu a letter from Shen Ming. Gu was terrified, knowing full well the secret Shen Ming mentioned. He refused to be his son-in-law's puppet, so he personally ensured the destruction of Shen Ming's career.

Upon returning from their Yunnan vacation, Gu Changlong heard of Shen Ming's death. Instead of feeling disheartened, he was relieved. He'd disposed of the time bomb, and his secret would die with him. What scared him lately, though, was that he'd started dreaming of Shen Ming again.

Gu Qiusha was inviting Si Wang to dinner more and more often. She taught him to play tennis, which he enjoyed. It was fun for him. Afterward he'd be fed a good meal and then taken home.

If Gu Changlong was sitting in the living room, Si Wang would spend time with him, doing everything from playing chess to chatting about national affairs. The boy took a great interest in the ancient books lining the living room walls, like a copy of the *Book of Huizhen* signed by Jin Shengtan. As a former university professor, Gu Changlong loved smart kids, so he gave Si Wang an illustrated *Six Geniuses of the World*.

Shen Ming had befriended his father-in-law the same way ten years earlier.

One weekend, Si Wang and the older man were playing a word game in the study. Gu Qiusha and Lu Zhongyue were both out, and the maid was running errands. The two of them were alone in the mansion. The boy was solving puzzles that stumped adults, and Gu Changlong was marveling at the boy's intellect.

Suddenly, his chest tightened and he felt dizzy—it was a heart attack. Gu Changlong fell to the floor, gripped by pain. His forehead was sweaty and he couldn't talk. With a shaky finger he pointed to a drawer.

Panicked, Si Wang opened the drawer to find it filled with bottles of imported drugs covered in foreign words. He didn't know which one was for a heart attack. Gu Changlong couldn't help, as he was almost gone. In those crucial ten seconds, Si Wang looked at all of the bottles, understood the words, and found two tablets for Gu to take. He also unbuttoned the man's shirt and resuscitated him. Si Wang saved the old man's life.

That night as he recovered, Gu Changlong agreed to the adoption plan.

CHAPTER 19

Grave-Sweeping Day 2005.

He Qingying visited the mansion for the first time. Her son clutched her hand and sat her down on the leather sofa. He was very familiar with the house: He knew where the bathrooms were, how to turn on the lights, and how to use all the electronics.

Gu Qiusha welcomed them warmly. She gave He Qingying a set of limited-edition Dior perfumes. He Qingying wore relatively presentable clothes, her hair was done, and she even wore makeup. Any man seeing her like this would take a second look. But her face was wan and when Gu Qiusha looked closely, it was clear that the woman's eyes had become more shadowed in the past few months.

Gu Qiusha's father and husband also greeted them. Seeing the whole family there flustered He Qingying. She couldn't stop thanking the hosts.

After the pleasantries, Gu Qiusha got right to the point about why the two had been invited for dinner.

"Ms. He, please let us adopt Si Wang."

"Are you kidding?" He Qingying's face changed. She turned to her son, who was eating imported fruits.

"No, I am quite serious. I know this seems abrupt and rude—after all, you are his mother. You sacrificed a lot to raise him. But with your circumstances, his genius can't be fully developed. Don't you think it's a shame? I can give him a good life, the best education. Isn't that what every mother wants?"

"Wang Er!" He Qingying slapped the fruit away from her son's mouth. "Did you agree to this?"

He shook his head. "Mom, I won't leave you."

Relieved, she held Si Wang tight as she answered Gu Qiusha. "We have to go home now. Please don't meet with my son anymore."

"Ms. He, Si Wang really likes it here. I will give you one million yuan to guarantee that he has a wonderful future. Even after the adoption process is complete, you won't lose your son. He will still call you Mom, and you can see him whenever and wherever. You and I can even become friends. If you want to work, I'll do everything I can to—"

"Good-bye."

Gu Qiusha stumbled after them as He Qingying dragged her son out the door.

Lu Zhongyue said, "Forget about it. What kind of mom sells her son? Don't be crazy."

"You will agree to adopting Si Wang," Gu Qiusha said, "or get out of my house."

She didn't see Si Wang for the next two weeks. Her home and life suffered from an emptiness marked by a graveyard silence.

Even Gu Changlong asked her, "When is he coming to play chess with me?"

At the end of the month, He Qingying called Gu Qiusha. "Ms. Gu, please forgive what I said when last we spoke. I need to know. Would you really treat Si Wang like your own?"

"Of course!" Gu Qiusha was ecstatic. "Please don't worry. I will treat him like my own. I won't love him any less than you do!"

"Can I still see him?"

"We will sign a contract, and a lawyer will be your witness. You'll be able to see him whenever you like."

He Qingying started sobbing. Gu Qiusha comforted her for a while, and as soon as the phone call ended, she rang the lawyer, instructing him to start the legal proceedings right way.

Gu Qiusha had never doubted that she'd receive this call. She, too, had more than one secret. Using her formidable resources, Gu Qiusha had located He Qingying's debt collectors and told them to use even more despicable methods to ensure their payments, going so far as to suggest that they issue threats against Si Wang. The loan sharks sent members of their crew to "protect" Si Wang on his way home. The past two weeks of nightly harassment had driven He Qingying to the verge of a breakdown.

He Qingying didn't want to give up her son, but sending him to live with a rich family was better than being threatened by thugs. At least now he would be safe. If anything happened to her, he would be cared for. As He Qingying saw it, she didn't really sell her son, it was just a temporary separation. Her sacrifice would protect him. She believed Gu Qiusha truly loved Si Wang and would do as promised. Plus, no matter where Si Wang lived, he would always be the son of Si Mingyuan and He Qingying. A ten-year-old would never forget his mom.

He would be back.

Gu Qiusha believed differently.

Three weeks later, the paperwork was finalized. Si Wang's residency registration was transferred to the Gu family. He was now Lu Zhongyue and Gu Qiusha's son.

They changed his name to Gu Wang.

CHAPTER 20

"Wang Er, come meet the professors."

Gu Qiusha took the boy's hand and led him to meet the various famous scholars. The old men all adored the kid. They listened to him recite Bai Juyi's "Song of Everlasting Sorrow," had him read a few hundred bronze scripts and inscriptions on oracle bones, and heard his theories on Manicheism and Gnosticism.

One renowned scholar held the boy and exclaimed, "He will do amazing things! The revival of Classical Chinese studies has hope!"

"I think he is better suited to studying Western religions," another professor insisted. "I want to make him my PhD student."

"You're all wrong," yet another said. "The kid understands both Eastern and Western schools of thought, but he doesn't need to be stuck in an ivory tower. The accumulation of all knowledge will lead to a grand life. I think he should be in a Buddhist temple. President Gu will have great karma with a grandson like him!"

In May, Wang Er moved in and for the first time in his life had his own bedroom, as well as a private bathroom and the latest gaming system. It took him a few weeks to adjust to the house, though he was most agreeable about the new situation. He accepted his new name and he called Gu Qiusha Mom, and Gu

Changlong Grandpa. But he didn't call Lu Zhongyue Dad, and Lu was happy to have nothing to do with the kid.

Wang Er was sometimes sad. Gu Qiusha knew he missed his real mom and worried that she was lonely. Gu Qiusha had invited He Qingying over a few times, and the three of them even vacationed in Hainan to make up for the separation. She didn't care that her son still called He Qingying Mom; she had completely redeemed the woman. After He Qingying received one million yuan, she paid off all her debts and then some.

But Gu Qiusha's sixth sense told her that He Qingying acted strangely every time they were all together. She seemed odd in front of Lu Zhongyue, like she wanted to avoid him. Perhaps He Qingying was worried that this stepfather wouldn't like Wang Er and would make things difficult.

Lu Zhongyue was the same as ever. He hardly spoke to his wife, and he only talked to his father-in-law about work. He was also very cool to this new "son" and seemed paranoid. Unsurprisingly, Wang Er remained polite and would greet Lu and even ask him science and math questions, to which he never got any answers.

Gu Qiusha watched her husband's every move, but she didn't want to make him act differently. The man was completely destroyed; he just didn't know it.

She had another secret.

A few years earlier after telling him about her condition, she learned that he'd taken a mistress—though she had no proof. She didn't want to divorce him. She didn't mind the idea of being divorced, but it would elicit pity and sympathy from everyone. As the heir to Erya Education, she needed a husband for appearances. Plus, with no evidence of Lu's infidelity, a divorce could result in him receiving half of her inheritance. So Gu Qiusha had come up with a more sinister way to get revenge on her husband.

When she'd gone abroad to see doctors, she brought back a batch of the illegal LHRH, which stimulated the pituitary gland into releasing the luteinizing hormone. The synthetically created LHRH made the pituitary suppress the release of luteinizing hormone and decrease testosterone levels. Ultimately, the lowered testosterone levels would result in chemical emasculation. It was an unnoticeable castration.

She'd been adding LHRH to her husband's food for three years—she'd even begun adding it to everyone's food. As a woman, she had no problem with the hormone. Her dad was in his sixties, so a lower sex drive would help him live longer. Finally, she doctored the drinking system in her house.

Gu Qiusha's "chemical castration" of her husband was irreversible, and it would lead to a permanent loss of sexual function.

In just the past year, Lu Zhongyue had seen many doctors, and by examining his banking records, she knew he only saw doctors who specialized in sexual and reproductive dysfunctions. Lu knew he'd lost something, but he couldn't determine the reason. The problem had no cure. The doctors theorized it was either a result of environmental conditions or genetics. In fact, "Many men suffer from the same ailment these days" was something he heard often.

Every time Gu Qiusha saw her husband's sagging face, hairless chin—and how he took forever in the bathroom—she hoped he'd stay with her until he died. She had sentenced him to life in prison.

If Lu Zhongyue ever learned what she'd done, he would kill her.

CHAPTER 21

June 6, 2005.

Screens on a speeding subway train showed a news story broadcast by the American television network ABC. A boy called James had been found to be a reincarnation of a naval aviator who'd died in World War II, and who also happened to be his grandmother's brother. Since birth, the boy had possessed an aviator's knowledge with a special focus on World War II–era machine parts and aircraft carriers.

He watched the news silently and calmly. When the story ended, he turned to the window and saw his reflection.

The subway's Line 3 reached the station at Hongkou Stadium. He got off the train, walked past narrow residential roads, and then turned onto a tree-lined block. He stopped at an old house with gray walls and a red roof and lightly pressed the doorbell.

A tall, thin man in his sixties, his hair all white, opened the metal door. "Who are you looking for?"

"Is this Liu Man's house?"

The man made a weird expression with his face. "Liu Man? You're looking for Liu Man?"

"I'm sorry. I came here on behalf of my older brother. He was her classmate, and he has been sick in the hospital. He asked me to visit her."

The man took some time to study this good-looking boy of about ten years old with memorable eyes. The boy's steady gaze made him feel slightly afraid.

"Your older brother was her classmate? You probably weren't even born yet the year she died."

"My brother and I had the same dad but a different mom."

"I see. I'm Liu Man's father. Please come in."

The living room was dim, and the old mahogany furniture looked repressive. This was where Liu Man had grown up.

Today was the ten-year anniversary of her body being found on the roof of the Nanming High library.

A black-and-white photo of eighteen-year-old Liu Man sat in a prominent part of the living room. It had been taken during a school field trip to the zoo, right before exams.

The old man gave the boy a can of soda, which he gulped down. He nodded. "Yes, my older brother told me to come today and light three sticks of incense for her and pray she would rest in Heaven."

"Thank you. I can't believe anyone still remembers her after ten years."

The man started crying as he talked. He took some incense from a drawer and gave it to the boy. There was already a cauldron and some fruit in front of the memorial. The boy stood in front of it with reverence, looking at Liu Man's eyes in the photo before adding the incense to the cauldron.

As smoke swirled around, Liu Man's image looked like she was glaring at him!

The boy asked, "Has there been any progress in the past ten years?"

"None." The man sighed and sat down. He pulled out an album full of black-and-white photos. They were of a young couple with a little girl who looked to be three or four years old. "You have no idea how much I adored her. This was her mom. We divorced when Liu Man was seven. I pretty much raised her, so she was a bit odd. After she died, my ex-wife became very depressed. She's been suicidal for years. She's in a treatment facility now—it's like prison."

He flipped through more of the album, all of which was adorned with photos of Liu Man, from kindergarten through junior high. It was strange to know that she had been dead for so many years. The last photo was from her senior year. Everyone posed on the school's playing field, right in front of the vivid oleander flowers. It had been late spring, or early summer, and all the pink-and-white flowers were in bloom. Back then, Liu Man would have had no idea that the flowers behind her would play a role in her death.

Homeroom teacher Shen Ming was also in the photo, standing in the middle of the first row. His face and body were slim and his hair was the longest a male teacher was allowed to keep. Even though his face was blurry, his gaze exuded a confidence that appeared to mask anxiety and sadness.

A few days after the photo was taken, Liu Man died on top of the library. Two weeks later, Shen Ming was killed in the Demon Girl Zone.

"Where is your brother?"

"Right here," the boy said, pointing to a random face in the photo.

"He was a good-looking kid. Please thank him for remembering my daughter. When Liu Man first died, some said that she'd poisoned herself, but I didn't believe she'd committed suicide. Then the police told me it was a murder, that she'd been forced to drink poison. The attic was locked from the outside, so she couldn't get out. She was in pain. She opened the window and got to the roof. But the poison was already working and she couldn't crawl any farther or call for help. She had to lie on the roof and watch the moon as she waited to die. The medical examiner said she struggled for at least an hour. Poor child! One hour. For sixty long minutes, she was alone with no one to help her. God knows how much she cried, how much she hurt. Sorry—you're still a kid. I shouldn't speak to you about things like this."

The boy politely handed the man some tissues.

Still gripped by sorrow, the man said, "My wish hasn't changed in ten years. I want to catch my daughter's killer—and kill him."

The boy left not too much later. Death had been a palpable presence in the home. His cell phone rang.

"Wang Er, where did you go?"

"Mom, my teacher was talking to me. I'll be home soon."

CHAPTER 22

June 19, 2005—10:00 p.m.

Gu Changlong had gone to a lakeside spa, and Lu Zhongyue was out, too. Gu Qiusha knew that her husband wasn't out partying. Maybe he'd gone to Nanming Road? Gu Qiusha couldn't sleep. She noticed black smoke and ashes rising past the window, and then flames jumped toward her window, like eyes watching her.

As she opened the window to see what was going on, her heart beat quickly. In the far corner of the backyard a small shadow was burning foil inside a pan.

"Wang Er," she screamed from the second-story window. She ran downstairs and into the backyard. When she reached him, she grabbed his arm and took away the foil he was holding. The cool night wind became hot from the flames, scattering the ashes. Some specks got into her eyes, making her cry. With a hose she doused the burning pan, causing more smoke to rise. Coughing violently, she ushered Wang Er inside.

"What were you doing?"

"I don't know."

The boy looked innocent, and his expression was enough to generate sympathy. She was about to scold him but instantly softened and kissed his cheek.

"Wang Er, you mustn't play with fire. You could burn down the house!"

"Mom, do you have someone you love the most in this world?"

"What a question!" She wiped her tears and washed her face. "The person I love the most? You, of course."

"Besides me?"

"My father and mother, who have passed."

"Besides them?"

Normally, a husband would be next on the list. She shook her head and frowned. "No one else."

"Really?"

She didn't want to mention *that* person tonight. "Let's start a bath before bedtime."

A few weeks later, there was another incident with Wang Er. He had the driver take him shopping downtown. While the driver was distracted, Wang Er disappeared into a store. It was raining hard that night. Gu Qiusha was worried, so she went to He Qingying's home. He wasn't there. She feared a kidnapping. Rich kids were often targets of criminals. She called the police. But at 10:00 p.m., he came home. Angry and frightened, she demanded to know where he'd been. He said he got lost, had no money, and was too shy to borrow a phone, so he snuck onto buses and trains to get home. Gu Qiusha wanted him to eat some dinner, but he said he wasn't hungry and went straight to bed.

That summer, the Gu family hired an economist to be his home tutor. Six hours of classes a week at 10,000 yuan per hour. Wang Er learned all about finance and economy, including world trends. The curriculum was close to that of an EMBA. The economist said he'd never met anyone this smart. The boy understood new concepts immediately, and he effortlessly applied them to other fields. Homework assignments about the stock markets—using real-world examples from the US and Hong Kong exchanges—were all done extremely well.

Gu Qiusha had never liked managing a large company; she'd always preferred being an editor. The daily meetings and financial reports gave her headaches. She wanted to use her time for workouts, traveling, shopping, and relaxation. Yet Wang Er was able to see the exact problem with each of her executives and analyze the risk for every project. She told her father about it, and he was also impressed. The company was growing rapidly, and cash was tight. Wang Er recommended that she hire a GM assistant. The person had to be an excellent manager and know how to deal with banks.

It didn't take long to find the new hire.

CHAPTER 23

July 15, 2005—8:00 p.m.

Ma Li parked his car and took out his cell phone. "Classmates, July fifteenth is our tenth reunion. Dinner will be at Wu's Hotpot on Longevity Road. We'll go dutch. See you there!"

The message had come from a Nanming High classmate, and had been posted on Renren's class page, too. Ma Li had waited a few days before replying that he'd be there.

He grimaced while walking into the busy restaurant. He stopped to check a mirror and straighten his hair. He wondered if his mustache made him appear jaded.

Ma Li's classmates had already started eating. He had to search deep into his memory for the name of the husky man who was now at least 90 kilograms, his belly drooping over his belt. The two had been roommates. It was amazing what ten years could do to a person. Ma Li despised people who let themselves become fat and sloppy.

Everyone was excited about Mal Li's presence, especially the female classmates. People quickly made room for him at the table.

"I'm sorry to be late. I'll do three shots now!" He said it with a manly air and a deep voice, and true to his word he downed three shots. Everything about him made it seem like he was comfortable in all sorts of situations—and that his life didn't lack women.

"We haven't seen you much since you were accepted to Tsinghua," the class president said, sounding jealous.

Ma Li didn't notice, however. He was too busy passing out his business cards.

"Wow, a senior partner. You're the boss now," another classmate exclaimed.

"I went into venture capital three years ago. I'm just behind the scenes."

His practiced smile lacked warmth but still made one comfortable.

The classmates caught up on each other's lives. Some had wedding rings; some had thinning hair. Some pretty girls were still single. Many people dressed better. A few people talked about their kids. The most shocking thing was how some kids were old enough to be in school. It was like another lifetime ago.

"Wait, where is Ouyang Xiaozhi?" someone mumbled.

"The transfer student? I was her roommate," one of the women replied.

The class president scratched his head. "I heard she got into the Teaching University, and then we lost touch."

"Has anyone noticed that kid eating hot pot by himself?" the fat man asked quietly, indifferent to the class gossip.

The ten-year-old seemed extra pale behind the steaming hot pot. His eyes were pretty, and although his clothes had childish cartoons on them, he exuded a special power just sitting there.

"Yeah, no grown-ups there."

"Kids nowadays aren't like we were. Don't be so surprised."

Ma Li shook his head. The boy paid no attention to them. He was busy eating beef meatballs.

Suddenly, one gossipy classmate said, "Remember Liu Man?"

The table turned quiet; the only sound was that of the boiling hot pot, like the Hell where evil people burned.

"Do you think Mr. Shen killed her?"

"Isn't it obvious? Liu Man seduced the teacher. He was about to be married, so he had to kill her. He got the oleander juice, lured her to the library attic, and poisoned her."

"Mr. Shen was the first one to see her body that morning."

"I remember. It was so scary. I had nightmares for a week!"

"Someone saw Liu Man alone with Mr. Shen the night before. They were talking in the self-study room. Then they found a bottle of poison in his room."

"After they arrested him, the police released him for some reason."

"The teaching director told everyone that Mr. Shen was fired. Who knew Mr. Shen would kill the teaching director?"

"Then Mr. Shen was killed, too! What a weird case. They found his body in the Demon Girl Zone."

The silent Ma Li finally interrupted the chatter. "Stop it! I don't believe Mr. Shen was the killer. Please respect the dead. He was our teacher after all. Didn't everyone love him back then? All the girls said he was hot. The guys loved his high energy and how he was down to earth. He always played basketball with us. He was the advisor to the literary society, too. He knew all sorts of poems."

The speech stunned everyone. No one had seen Ma Li so emotional before. The whole restaurant watched, including the boy at the next table, who stared at Ma Li with an odd expression.

"Never mind all of that." The class president tried to make peace. "It's all in the past, so no need to get upset."

"Mr. Shen was online a few days ago," one of the guys said mysteriously.

The girls screamed.

"Was it a ghost?"

Ma Li asked, "What happened?"

"I saw it, too," someone else said. "He posted on our class page on Renren.com. You can see for yourself."

"It must be a prank."

After that, no one dared to mention Shen Ming again. The classmates finished their meal and started leaving, dropping their share of the bill on the table.

By 9:30 p.m., the restaurant was closing. The female classmates had all left. Ma Li was smoking. He stroked his mustache, his gaze dull and despondent.

The waiter asked the boy, "Hey, kid, did your parents pay yet?"

The kid fumbled in his pockets for a long time and took out a few twenty-yuan notes. "Sorry, this is all I have. Can I go get money from home?"

The waiter called for his manager. A brutish man came over and said, "You think you can eat for free?"

The boy's eyes turned red and misty. The waiter and manager didn't know what to do.

Ma Li stepped in and offered to pay for him, throwing down 200 yuan. It wasn't until later that Ma Li realized that the boy was a great actor.

The manager took the money and made change. "Your kid?"

"I don't know him. I just feel friendly."

The boy sniffled and wiped away his tears. He shakily thanked Ma Li, whose face remained serious looking.

"Kid, go home." He turned to his remaining classmates. "Don't drink anymore—it's time to go."

It started pouring. When Ma Li got into his car, the boy rushed to his window and knocked on the glass.

Ma Li lowered the window. "What's wrong, kid?" he said.

"Can you drive me home?"

"Why?"

"I want to pay you back."

"It's OK."

"It's dark out, and I'm afraid of going home alone. I don't have an umbrella, either."

Seeing the boy's terrified expression, he frowned and opened the front passenger door. He touched the boy's skinny wrist with a hand that felt as cold as a corpse's. The stereo played the theme from *A Chinese Ghost Story*; in high school, Ma Li had idolized Leslie Cheung. A poster of Ouyang Feng from *Ashes of Time* used to hang over his bed.

Summer rain spattered across the windshield. The boy gave his address in the rich suburbs. *Why couldn't he afford a hot pot?* Ma Li was intrigued. He started driving and lit up another cigarette. The boy watched him while pretending to look out the window. He glanced at the boy, too, but averted his gaze when their eyes met.

"To not go home when rich is like wearing a lavish gown in secret," the boy uttered.

Ma Li wondered: Was that expectation or sarcasm? He was a bit shaken. He looked right at the boy, but the kid seemed calm, like he'd said nothing at all.

Ma Li sped through the night, arriving at the mansion in just half an hour. The boy got out of the car and said, "Wait here, I'll bring you the money."

Ma Li finished another cigarette and tossed it out the window. He felt like he was in a daze and drove off before the kid returned.

An hour later, Ma Li got back to his apartment, a cluttered rental. The only clean and ordered section of the apartment was the closet because his clothes mattered the most to him.

Ma Li went online to look for Nanming High Class of '95 on Renren.com. He saw many familiar names, though not everyone was online. He found the post from Shen Ming.

Shen Ming: I'LL BE BACK.

Anyone who'd seen *The Terminator* would understand the reference. A few people had posted replies.

Anonymous 6953: Didn't Mr. Shen die a long time ago?
Hin Lau: Who's doing this?
Nanming High 95: So pathetic!

Ma Li registered with his real name and replied, too:

Ma Li: Mr. Shen, if you are still alive . . .

If you are still alive . . .
Three days later, someone friended Ma Li on QQ. The new friend's name was Shen Ming, and he left a message.

Shen Ming: Ma Li, do you still remember Mr. Shen?

Ma Li saw that the person was online and replied.

Ma Li: Who are you?
Shen Ming: I am Shen Ming.
Ma Li: Don't scare me like that so late at night.

According to the computer's clock, it was 1:40 a.m.

Shen Ming: Still not asleep?
Ma Li: Working late! Doing an investment report. I have an early meeting at the bank tomorrow morning. It'll be an all-nighter.
Shen Ming: Why work so hard?
Ma Li: I like to.

Ma Li felt weird saying so much to someone online. The person was probably a prankster or mentally ill.

Shen Ming: You seemed tired at the reunion. Take time to rest.
Ma Li: Reunion? Hot pot? Who are you?

He typed a few names, all of which the other person denied.

Shen Ming: If you don't think I'm Shen Ming, why did you accept my friend invitation?
Ma Li: I don't know. I just miss him.
Shen Ming: I didn't die.

Ma Li's fingers shook on the keyboard.

Ma Li: I saw your body at your funeral.
Shen Ming: How did I look?
Ma Li: You had a crystal casket. You looked weird, very pale. They said you needed really thick makeup to cover your decaying face. The school forbade us to go since you'd killed the teaching director. I secretly went. Some middle-aged guy paid for all of it. He cried so hard over your coffin, and I tried to comfort him.
Shen Ming: Thanks very much for that, Ma Li!

Wind shook the shadows of the trees outside the window as a few raindrops fell. Ma Li continued typing.

Ma Li: I saw you going into the cremation chamber. That middle-aged guy took out your ashes by hand. I cried a lot. Why am I telling you this? You're not Mr. Shen!

Shen Ming: If I wasn't Mr. Shen, how would I know that you helped a classmate cheat in junior year, charging him ten yuan per question? When I found out, you came to my room at midnight, knelt in front of me, and begged for mercy.

Ma Li's hair stood on end. No one else knew about this.

Ma Li: Mr. Shen must have told somebody!
Shen Ming: Do you really think I would tell anyone? You cried and swore that you'd never do anything like that again. I promised not to tell. Remember how I even paid a visit to your family's home and saw that your dad was a drunk and your mom pushed a street cart? You worked every summer to make money, to help your family. I don't think you told anyone at school about any of this.
Ma Li: Stop!

Ma Li would never forget that visit. Afterward, Mr. Shen gave him fifty yuan every month out of his own pocket. He refused to accept it at first, until the teacher said it was lent to him and to be paid back when he got a job. Mr. Shen helped him through the hardest months of his life. He would be forever grateful to his young homeroom teacher.

More from Shen Ming appeared in the QQ chat window.

Shen Ming: In senior year, you came to me and said you lost a notebook in the library. You'd filled it with all sorts of complaints and insults about classmates and teachers. You were afraid someone would find it, so you asked me to take you there in the middle of the night. You knew I had the library key. We went in and found the notebook. It was really windy that night. The attic door was blown open. We were both curious, so we went up there. It was dusty and filled with old books. You took a copy of

Hugo's *Les Misérables*. The moon hung above the skylight, and a black cat crossed the roof and stared at us. I remember you telling me, "This cat looks possessed. It's not a good omen. Someone will die here."

Ma Li would never forget that night, either.

Ma Li: That copy of *Les Misérables* was hiding in my drawer. I burned it after you died.

Shen Ming: You always read the book with a flashlight. You said there were old student love letters in the book and it had to be kept a secret. But Ma Li, now I have a secret for you. I actually looked through the book. Someone scrawled in bad handwriting next to the Battle of Waterloo illustration, "Everyone who reads this book will be doomed. They will die, either by knife or needle!"

Ma Li: Mr. Shen, I told you not to touch my book. When I first read that curse, I was so scared. I regretted taking it from the attic. I figured some student probably wrote it as a joke. I hid it and didn't think anything more of it. But a year later the curse became true. You were stabbed in the Demon Girl Zone!

Shen Ming: Yes, I died of a knife wound.

Ma Li: So I burned the book. Ever since then I've been terrified of needles. Just the word makes me feel nauseated. I wouldn't go to hospitals if I were sick. If I had to go, I'd tear up the prescription for an IV drip.

Shen Ming: I take it you're not married?

Ma Li: I've had plenty of girlfriends. Some rich ladies have tried to seduce me, too, but no one has stayed with me.

Ma Li suddenly felt crazy for sharing all of this.

Ma Li: Mr. Shen, are you really dead?

Shen Ming: Didn't you see me cremated?

Ma Li: But if you were turned to ashes, how can you be on QQ with me?

Shen Ming: Ma Li, I'm right next to you.

Ma Li: No, it's an illusion. I must have imagined you. I must need some meds. Get out of my head!

For the past few years, Ma Li had been plagued by insomnia and nightmares. Doctors had even prescribed antidepressants for him.

Shen Ming: You think this is a horror movie?

Ma Li: This must be a hallucination. I need to take my meds, take my meds, take my meds, take my meds, take my meds!

The screen filled up with the words "take my meds."

Shen Ming: What drug do you take?

Ma Li: We'll talk in person.

Ma Li's fingers sweated as he typed those words.

Shen Ming: OK.

Ma Li: How will I know it's you?

Ma Li was totally confused. Was he actually trying to confirm that he was talking to a dead person?

Shen Ming: Only I can tell you all your secrets.

Ma Li: Tomorrow at four, in front of Future Fantasy Plaza.

And with that, Shen Ming's ghost disappeared from QQ.

The rain came down harder. It made Ma Li think of that thunderous night when Mr. Shen was killed, June 19, 1995.

That black mourning banner once again flapped in his memory, and he heard the somber mourning music, played to respect the dead. Mr. Shen was in his crystal casket, looking just like he always did, only paler under all the foundation and makeup applied by the mortician. It made Ma Li sick to see his teacher, and friend, like that. Only he was brave enough to touch the cold casket, and the dead body's face. Suddenly, Mr. Shen opened his eyes and bit down on Ma Li's finger . . .

What a scary dream. He woke up covered in sweat. The sky was brightening as he started writing his letter of resignation.

At 4:00 p.m., Ma Li arrived at Future Fantasy Plaza. Someone tugged his shirt, but when he turned he didn't see anyone—until he looked down. It was the kid from the hot pot restaurant.

"Hello, Ma Li!"

Looking at the boy's tranquil face, Ma Li had to fight to speak. "You? You are—"

"Four o'clock at the Future Fantasy Plaza, right? Just like you said."

"No. Where is he? Did he hire you to come here?"

Ma Li pushed aside the boy and looked around anxiously, as if he might find a ghost hiding among the busy crowds.

"Stop wasting time. It's me!" The boy remained calm and said, "What meds do you take?"

Ma Li was stunned. He squinted and backed away two steps. The boy talked like Shen Ming. Even his pitch sounded like him.

"Wait, what did you say?"

"Everyone who reads this book would be doomed. They would die, either by knife or needle!"

"Shut up!" Ma Li's lips turned purple. He looked around and uttered, "Come with me."

The two went to Starbucks. Ma Li ordered lemonade for the boy and coffee for himself. Then he said, "Tell me, who is making you do this?"

"Shen Ming."

He rubbed his chin and started his interrogation. "Kid, what is your name?"

"Death. I mean, Si Wang. Si as in 'general,' Wang as in 'lookout.'"

"What a weird name. How old are you?"

"Ten. I'll be in fourth grade after the summer."

"You weren't even born when Mr. Shen died."

Si Wang answered with poise. "Correct. I was born six months after he died."

Ma Li sat there in disbelief, unable to think of another question.

The boy leaned in and whispered into his ear, "I am possessed by Shen Ming's ghost."

"What nonsense."

"Ma Li, please tell me the background for the essay 'In Memoriam of Liu Hezhen.' Ma Li, want to play basketball? Ma Li, are you collecting the test papers today? Ma Li, why do we study? We study for the rise of China! Ma Li, have you forgotten about Dead Poets Society?"

"Stop talking, I beg you, Mr. Shen!"

Ma Li made like he was going to jump away from the table. He covered his ears and he looked like he was in pain.

Si Wang kept speaking with Shen Ming's voice. "Ma Li, I'm sorry. I didn't want to hurt you. I just wanted you to believe me. I've never left you, my dear student."

"Shen Ming, what happened? Who killed you?"

"If I knew, I wouldn't be a ghost now."

Ma Li wrinkled his brow. He looked directly at the boy, first nodding and then shaking his head. He felt regret. He sipped some coffee to recover his composure. "Have you been a ghost all these years?"

"Yes. I floated from Nanming Road. I saw a schoolkid a few years ago and decided to hitch a ride. You see, this kid's a hunchback, and he was crushed by me."

The boy lowered his head painfully as though being forced.

"Mr. Shen, please don't scare me like this!"

"Sorry, but if I'd met you at night, you'd be even more afraid." The kid was now Shen Ming. His gaze looked like a grown man's, and even his smile seemed out of place. "When I need to take a break, the Si Wang kid comes out. When I need to talk, I control his brain."

"How long are you going to stay with him? Will you just wander around forever if the killer is never found?"

"I guess so."

"I think Si Wang suffers too much like this."

"We are fated to be together, in the same way that you and I are fated to help each other."

Ma Li's face darkened. He knew he was talking to a ghost. "Yes, I've always wanted to avenge your death, but I couldn't find anything."

"How have you been?"

"I just resigned today. I can't take the pressure of being in finance." Ma Li grabbed a tissue off the table and wiped his sweaty face.

Si Wang tapped on the table. "Anything I can do to help? You know that ghosts are all-powerful!"

"What can you do, kid? Can you cure my depression?"

"How about a new job?"

Ma Li noted the boy's serious expression. He smiled bitterly and said, "Don't tell me. I can be a home tutor."

"Yes, for China's largest home-tutoring company—Erya Education Group. You can be the GM assistant, annual salary is six hundred thousand yuan."

"Stop joking."

"Do I have to make the headhunter show up to make you believe me?"

Half an hour later, Ma Li and Si Wang walked out of the plaza together. A BMW 760 picked up the kid and sped away.

It was dusk and Ma Li watched the surging crowds. Everyone was in a rush. No one knew they were speeding toward death—and with countless ghosts surrounding them.

CHAPTER 24

After the summer vacation, Gu Qiusha arranged for Wang Er to attend an elite private school known for cultivating industry leaders. It was funded, of course, by Erya Education Group. He refused, wanting to stay in public school, though he had no friends at the Number One Elementary School. After a few fights about the matter, Gu Qiusha worried that Wang Er would go back to his birth mother, so she relented. Even so, the driver continued taking him to school, where he also continued receiving special treatment. Many people wanted to see the genius in action, but security locked them out. Not even his classmates were allowed to randomly talk to him.

Wang Er loved to paint, so Gu Qiusha built a studio at the house. She filled it with plaster sculptures and paint. Every week he churned out a few new sketches and watercolors.

One late night that fall after Gu Qiusha had taken a shower, she walked past the studio and noticed the light was on. Wang Er was still up. He stood in front of the easel, furiously drawing with a pencil. He shook like he was having seizure. His sketch depicted a dimly lit space. It looked like a nineteenth-century copper-plate engraving. Dirty water dripped everywhere; the background was a cobweb-covered wall. A man lay face down on the ground with a knife in his back and a few mice crawling over his neck. His hairstyle and face made him seem to be in his twenties.

Gu Qiusha stood frozen in amazement. She recognized the shirt worn by the figure in the painting. The striped logo on its sleeve was the same as the one on a birthday present she'd picked out for her fiancé ten years ago.

He'd died wearing that shirt.

She charged into the studio, dragged the boy away from his work, and stared into his eyes. "Wang Er, are you sick?"

He was very pale and had beads of sweat on his brow. Shaking, he said, "I had a dream."

"You drew what you saw in the dream?"

"Yes."

The drawing depicted her nightmare, too. Every night, as dawn approached, she would dream that same scene. It showed how the police had found Shen Ming.

She burned the nightmare sketch the next day. Whenever she looked at Wang Er, she thought of Shen Ming. The boy always kept his eyes down, and he seemed weak. His refined face was pale. His big, black eyes often seemed lost in thought, while sometimes flashing with hatred.

Gu Qiusha was afraid to look too deeply into his eyes.

Some nights when they slept in the same bed, she'd wake up to Shen Ming's face and jump up in horror. Wang Er would ask why and, not sure what to say, she always chalked it up to having nightmares.

On frigid nights, his eyes had an odd light. He didn't look like a kid at all. He'd sidle close to her and hug her neck from behind like a long-lost lover. He tenderly kissed her cheeks and head, blowing warmth into her ears like a kitten. This boy had brought her dead heart back to life. She'd returned to her twenty-five-year-old self.

And she realized that she still loved *him*.

One morning, she heard soft cries and saw Wang Er sobbing into a pillow. The sheets were drenched and he was still asleep, lost in a bad dream. She'd never seen him so sad. She resisted waking him but pressed her ear to his mouth to hear his murmurs.

"I don't want to die. I don't want to die. I don't want to die, Xiaozhi."

CHAPTER 25

"Who are you?"

Lu Zhongyue had produced a full ashtray of cigarette butts. His eyes were bloodshot, and he was still drinking black coffee. His watch read 1:00 a.m. He liked to stay in the shadows to conceal the birthmark on his forehead.

"Someone like you."

Ma Li sat near the window. He could see the top of Jing'an Temple. The waitress delivered a fruit tray and glanced at him again.

Three months ago, Ma Li had become the GM assistant at Erya Education Group. It only took him a month to bring in tens of millions of yuan in investment capital. As a result, he now had the power to fire any executive. Some gossiped that Gu Qiusha favored him for his looks, that he was her secret boyfriend.

Naturally, Lu Zhongyue hated people like Ma Li. The two never spoke at work; seeing Ma Li shamed him.

What Lu didn't know was how they'd both graduated from Nanming High. Ma Li had graduated seven years after him, in 1995, the year Shen Ming was killed.

For the last ten years, Lu Zhongyue had tried hard to forget Shen Ming. But even now, every cold and wet dawn, Shen Ming's eyes hovered above him, just like he was still in high school being woken up for breakfast. They'd been roommates back then and had liked playing games together. Lu favored offense, and Shen was a more defensive player. They won against other teams at least 90 percent of the time; they were the duo to beat.

Lu's other hobby at school was fighting crickets. In the early fall, he stowed pans of crickets under his bed. The other roommates hated the noise. But Shen Ming had helped him grab a spotted cricket near the school. That cricket never lost, until it died that winter. Lu cried so hard. Lu had other hobbies, too, but studying wasn't one of them. Shen Ming helped him cheat on every test, and was the sole reason he graduated.

Lu Zhongyue and Shen Ming had been the best of friends for twenty years. No one could have predicted the friendship. But by late fall of 2005, Shen Ming had already turned to ashes, and Lu Zhongyue felt that he'd been left to suffer all of these years.

Now, he stared at Ma Li. "You asked me to meet just to tell me this?"

"Mr. Lu, there is something neither Ms. Gu nor her father knows. The company you started in Hong Kong seems to have nothing to do with the main company, but is actually transferring its assets."

"How do you know?" Lu Zhongyue rubbed his bare chin, and his face showed his surprise.

"Ms. Gu is clueless about finance and management, and President Gu is old. I feel lucky for you that no one has noticed yet."

"Are you blackmailing me?" Lu Zhongyue stubbed out his cigarette.

Ma Li wasn't shocked by his directness. "I told you—we're the same kind of people. We want the same things. I don't need petty perks."

"I don't understand."

"Mr. Lu, you hate your wife and father-in-law, right?" Ma Li noted Lu's stiff gaze, then added, "So do I."

"Tell me why."

"That's my secret. It has nothing to do with you."

"Fine, let's talk frankly. Erya has many secrets. As my wife's assistant, you must know all of them."

"If anyone knew what I knew, it would be lethal. A lot of people want this evidence."

Lu lit another cigarette. "Ma Li, do you want to make a deal with me?"

It only took ten minutes for the two men to make their arrangement.

Satisfied, Lu Zhongyue puffed smoke rings, but his feet were shaking and goose bumps covered his back. "Honestly, you're a scary person."

"Is that a compliment?" Ma Li feigned sophistication. "You should be grateful to Gu Wang."

"That kid?"

"Mr. Lu, didn't you adopt him?"

"Since we're partners now, I might as well tell you." Lu Zhongyue opened a button on his shirt. He looked around to make sure no one was listening. "Every time I see that kid, every time I look into those eyes, it scares me to death. I can't say why, but I have a feeling he wants to kill me."

"You're mistaken. Gu Wang doesn't want to kill you."

Alarm showed in Lu's eyes. "Are you working for him, too?"

"No, I work for myself. I just think you should treat him better. That would be better for you."

Everything Ma Li said seemed rich in meaning. Lu nodded, lost in thought. "OK, I will."

"Good." Ma Li tossed a pill bottle to Lu.

"What is this? I can't read the words."

"It's in German. You should have someone translate it. LHRH suppresses the luteinizing hormone," Ma Li said. He smiled as he got up to leave, and he asked the waitress for the bill.

"Wait!" Lu grabbed his arm. "What did you just say?"

"Mr. Lu, I recommend that you check your drinking system at home. Don't let your wife know."

CHAPTER 26

Christmas Eve 2005.

The giant Christmas tree shined brightly in the mansion's garden. He Qingying stood outside, her coat and scarf barely protecting her from the wind. Her hair was tied up in a knot, but a few strands escaped and fell in front of her eyes.

Two hours ago, she'd watched the BMW return with Gu Qiusha and Wang Er. They must have been at Mass. Hiding behind the trees, she was able to look into their window undetected. She was alone, just like a few days ago. They hadn't invited her to Wan Er's birthday party, so she'd had to watch from afar.

Wang Er had been born on December 19, 1995, at Zhabei District's Hospital. The searing pain of childbirth was enough to make He Qingying want to faint.

"It's a boy," whispered the nurse as the newborn cried.

He Qingying cried, too. She was weak and tried to open her eyes under the white light, saying, "Let me see."

Crying and barely cleaned of blood, his face seemed murky. His eyes opened a bit to stare at his mother. He Qingying had a strange thought. What was he thinking about? Why was he crying so hard? Was he born already holding an unspeakable grudge?

Though he was born premature, he didn't need to stay in the NICU for too long. All the nurses said the kid was fortunate to be so healthy. Si Mingyuan, Wang Er's father, couldn't stop kissing his newborn son. He registered his son's residency at the police precinct. He Qingying chose the name. She looked out every day while pregnant, as there seemed to be a voice calling her, so she picked Wang, which meant "lookout": Si Wang.

The three of them moved in with Si Mingyuan's parents, where there was just enough room for them to squeeze in. Her maternity leave lasted four months, and then she went back to work at the post office. She earned more than her husband. She dressed well and was smart. The row of Zhang Ailing books on her bookshelf wasn't simply for decoration.

Si Mingyuan worked at the Nanming Steel Factory. Each day he left for work at 7:30 a.m. and came home right before dark. He had few social engagements other than drinking with coworkers. He only smoked Peony brand cigarettes. He read nothing but the newspaper. His tall, muscular build could seem brutish. He Qingying wondered whether it would be inherited. They had a domestic color TV and a Japanese VCR, which he used to watch violent and explicit movies from America and Hong Kong.

He Qingying didn't bother much with him; all her attention was on her son. She rarely contacted her side of the family. She seemed to have become part of her husband's family and had a pleasant relationship with her in-laws.

Wang Er was a cute, healthy boy. When he was three, He Qingying sent him to day care. The new kids always cried, and she was reluctant to drop him off. But he adjusted, and the day care teacher, a young woman, often complimented Wang Er. He liked being held by the teacher, lying on her soft shoulders and smelling her fragrant hair. She occasionally complained to He Qingying about how much he kissed her, embarrassing her.

The locust tree in front of their house dried up and grew robust again several times over. The inhabitants of the hidden nests woke them up every morning. Si Mingyuan grew night-blooming cereus on the windowsill, which only bloomed for a few hours every year. The precious petals were tucked under their son's pillow, helping him sleep. His small bed was in a corner of the living room. Around it the floor was littered with toys and children's books. He rarely read and didn't like watching cartoons—except for *Slam Dunk*. He Qingying was puzzled about why a young kid loved watching that show. He also liked a vintage cartoon called *Legend of Sealed Book*; he cried uncontrollably every time Yuan Gong was recaptured by Heaven.

In 2000, Wang Er turned five. He was over a meter tall and his face grew even more handsome. He still looked like a young boy, but everyone said he was gorgeous. He wasn't a picky eater, which was rare among kids his age, though He Qingying always tried to make him food she knew he liked.

Si Mingyuan's factory filed for bankruptcy that same year. His severance was only about 30,000 yuan. He was now one of the many laid-off workers. He was happy at first, day-trading and watching movies. But soon his stocks fell from eighteen to eight yuan. With a much thinner wallet, he could only afford to window shop toy cars with his son. Someone got him a job working security. He only worked a few days before quitting, saying it was too embarrassing. He went out every night to play mah-jongg and didn't come home until early morning. He'd wake up his son and start yet another fight with his wife.

Her husband had no income, and her in-laws' health worsened. Every expense was now He Qingying's responsibility. Her postal worker's salary was barely enough to live on.

Si Mingyuan frequently took Wang Er to ride a bike in Jingjiang Park. He'd always been patient with him, even playing games with Wang Er, who excelled at chess and beat everyone.

But after a time, Si Mingyuan began to alienate his son little by little. Instead of holding him, he'd chain smoke alone by the window, not even bothering to clean out the ashtray. When he'd had a job, he never drank at home, but now he did, downing liquor with every night's dinner. When he shouted in a drunken stupor, staring at his son with an icy gaze, He Qingying was disgusted.

Did he see his son as an enemy? Was he afraid of him?

Maybe he'd seen too many American horror movies. One movie starring Gregory Peck was about a normal family discovering that their son had extraordinary abilities that no adults could match. They became slaves to their child. The kid was a mutant born with such evil inside him that he could summon endless power, causing tragedy for his parents, and all of humanity.

One rainy night, He Qingying was working late. Si Mingyuan went out to drink and play mah-jongg. When he came home, his son was watching *The Shawshank Redemption*. He slapped the boy.

Upon her return, He Qingying saw the red fingerprints on Wang Er's cheek. Si Mingyuan stood off to the side, dejected. She slapped her husband and clutched her son, rubbing his swollen cheek. Saying nothing, Si Mingyuan ran out, loudly slamming the door behind him. She cursed him as she watched him run away into the rainy night, and he shouted something unintelligible under the streetlights.

When her son was seven, something terrible happened.

Si Mingyuan went missing. It happened before dawn on Chinese New Year, ruining the holiday. He Qingying reported it to the police. Her father-in-law's hair went white, and he had to go to the hospital. She took good care of her in-laws. People thought she was the daughter, not the daughter-in-law.

Endless debt collectors visited. Her husband had accumulated debts she had no idea about, many of them owed to loan sharks. It would take many lifetimes to repay them all.

Si Mingyuan never came back.

September 2, 2002—Monday. Wang Er's first day of school.

It was raining. He Qingying held a big umbrella and tightly held her son's hand on their way to Number One Elementary School on Longevity Road. Her hand was soft and warm and she carried his backpack, inside of which was a new Disney pencil case. Most of the parents were there with their children for the opening ceremony and to meet the teachers. She didn't leave until she saw Wang Er sit down in class.

Two weeks into first grade, He Qingying found a slip of paper in Wang Er's backpack. Li Yu's "Joy in Meeting" was written on it: "Silently going to the Western pavilion. The moon like a hook. Loneliness locked inside a fall courtyard. Parting sorrows can't be contained. Unspeakable feelings in my heart." The words were in pencil, but the handwriting was neat, even for an adult's. She asked him about it, and Wang Er told her he'd found it on the street and kept it because he liked the way it looked.

The following summer, the SARS crisis was the big news. He Qingying sent her son to a drawing class at the Feifei Art Academy. The teacher was a man with long hair and an artistic temperament. He taught Wang Er to sketch and to paint with watercolors. He recognized the boy's talent.

To reward this talent and his matriculation into second grade, He Qingying bought him a computer—an Intel Celeron. Wang Er excitedly played with the keyboard and mouse while watching the Windows XP flag fly by and installing all the programs. Broadband wasn't widespread yet, so they relied on a modem. He Qingying noticed how quickly her son became addicted to going online. He would sit in front of the computer all day. She rarely scolded him for anything, but she did for this, until she herself was crying. The boy actually comforted her.

One day while Wang Er was out with his grandparents, He Qingying turned on the computer. She'd added child-monitoring software and saw that her son was using Google and Baidu to search for very specific information:

1995. Nanming Road murder case.

1995. Nanming High murder case.

1995. Body found at Nanming Steel Factory.

1995. Murder victim Shen Ming.

When He Qingying turned on the computer a few days later, Wang Er had already reformatted the desktop and deleted everything.

Wang Er's grandfather died that fall. His death was sudden. By the time they got him to the hospital, his heart had stopped. His wife was traditional and insisted on bringing the body back to the house to have it lie in state for a few days. With the family crammed in to the narrow space, his grandfather lay on the bed, dressed in the burial clothes his uncle had bought.

He Qingying got time off work for the memorial. Her son sat with her the whole time, and Grandma and the other relatives took shifts sitting with the deceased patriarch. Sometimes it was just the two of them watching a dead body at 2:00 a.m. Worried about the smell, she didn't let her son get too close to the body. But Wang Er just stared at the corpse, unafraid of the flies. His eyes scared her.

Everyone thought the missing Si Mingyuan would be back for the funeral since he was the eldest son. But he didn't show, not even when the body went into the cremation chamber.

The next year, He Qingying's mother-in-law died, too. As her health had declined, her own kids rarely helped. He Qingying was the one who changed her and gave her baths. She also helped the most during the funeral, yet all the relatives hated her and made snide comments.

Wearing a mourning sash around his arm, hearing the things being said about his mother, Wang Er said, "How dare you?"

The memorial fell quiet.

He Qingying no longer owed the Si family anything, and her son had nothing more to do with them.

This was at about the same time that Wang Er began to change.

There was no hot water at home, so He Qingying always took her son to the bathhouse at work. One day, after coming out of the bath, her still-wet hair made her look more tantalizing than usual. A middle-aged man leered at her, eliciting a sinister glare from Wang Er.

The man said with embarrassment, "Is this your son?"

"Yes, chief." He Qingying squeezed out a smile. She pulled her son's sleeve. "Wang Er, stop looking at him like that. He's the Post Office chief. Call him Uncle!"

Wang Er shook his head stubbornly. "Tell him to control his eyes."

Not wanting to cause a scene in front of her boss, He Qingying just sighed and hurriedly ushered her son away. From that moment on, Wang Er didn't allow anyone to get close to his mother.

During the October First holiday, He Qingying had to work. One night, the chief made her stay late and go to dinner with him. He got her drunk, saying that he knew how hard her life was: missing husband, single mom, loan sharks at her door. He claimed he wanted to promote her to the leader of the counter team—and that her income would go up. Maybe she could pay off some debts. He complimented her beauty. She didn't want to refuse right away. She was dizzy. He suggested that they go to a hotel to rest. When she tried to leave him, he stopped her.

She didn't get home until midnight. Her hair was a mess, and her clothes reeked of alcohol. Her lips were bruised and her face pale. Wang Er had stayed up, anxiously waiting for her. He helped her into bed and brought a cup of warm water.

"Mom, what happened?"

"I'm OK. Just go to bed."

He covered her with a thick blanket. He was about to turn out the lights when he noticed one of the bruises on her face.

"Was it that bastard?"

"It's grown-up stuff. You're a kid. Don't worry." Tears filled her eyes.

"Mom, anything that happens to you happens to me."

He held his mom so tight that she almost couldn't breathe.

"Wang Er, it's not what you think, I didn't—"

He kissed her forehead. "Mom, don't worry. I will make money to support us!"

He Qingying lay in bed with a fever all the next day. She didn't know about the incident at work until the day after that. Her coworkers told her that Wang Er had charged into the post office, demanding to see the evil chief. When he found him, Wang Er grabbed an abacus and hit the man in the head, making him bleed all over the place.

At first she yelled and hit her son with a broom. But then she held and kissed him.

"Wang Er, I know you love me the most. But don't you ever do anything like this again!"

Of course she was forced to resign from the post office.

Soon after, Gu Qiusha paid her a visit, stealing her son.

Now it was Christmas Eve, and for the past three hours He Qingying had been hiding in front of the mansion. Her legs were numb, her cheeks frozen.

A curtain suddenly parted on the second floor. Her son's young face appeared, reflecting light like a ghost's. The scene would have scared anyone, except He Qingying.

After seeing him, she rushed off. Like a ghost escaping back into the grave.

CHAPTER 27

In 1995, when Shen Ming and Gu Qiusha's new apartment was almost ready, they tested their new water heater. The two of them squeezed into the tub and painted each other's faces with bubbles. They watched the steam rise around them, wanting the moment to go on forever.

"Qiusha, what is desperation?"

"Desperation?" She stroked her fiancé's whiskers, which had been softened by the hot water. "Why are you asking? Our future is full of hope."

"I had a nightmare last night. It felt like a bad omen."

"Shen Ming, the worst thing is losing the person you love." Qiusha kissed him deeply. "For me, that's you."

A month later, Shen Ming was dead.

When Wang Er first came to live in her home, Gu Qiusha gave the boy baths. She'd found a pale mark on the left side of his back and carefully cleaned it with a washcloth. Its shape was odd: a two-centimeter slit that looked like a knife wound. Gu Qiusha remembered a myth she'd heard when she was young about how a birthmark is the mortal wound from a previous life.

Her heart started to hurt, enough to make her clench her teeth and want to scream. She held Wang Er, stroking his chest and pressing an ear to his heart, listening to his rapid heartbeats.

"What's wrong, Mom?"

Enjoying his relaxing bath, Wang Er had looked at her foamy face with confusion.

Gu Qiusha held him tight and said, "I want you to live for a long time!"

Half of her body was submerged in water. She was in a daze, remembering the way she and Shen Ming had taken a bath in the apartment they never got to live in.

January 2006.

It was a chilly morning. Wang Er got up at 6:00 a.m. and turned on the entertainment system to play a DVD. The gloomy prelude started, the symphony reverberating in the mansion like dark tides. The repetitive bowing of the cello sounded like moving oars, like the rowers were risking their lives to get close to a barren island.

The music woke Gu Qiusha, and she rushed downstairs in a robe. Wang Er sat alone in the living room, staring at the TV; five paintings rotated on the screen. Each one showed a small desolate island—oddly shaped rocks protruding out of the water. Under the steel-gray skies, a small boat rowed by a mysterious man in white neared the island.

"Wang Er," she screamed, blocking his view and shaking his shoulders. "What are you listening to?"

"The symphonic poem *Isle of the Dead*."

"This early in the morning?" She touched his clothes. "Aren't you cold?"

The boy shook his head.

She wanted to turn off the music, but she couldn't find the remote. The sounds of it pulsed throughout the house, piercing the air like a knife. She searched for the power cord so she could unplug it.

"The man on the boat represents death."

"Turn that off!"

"Qiusha, do you know what Hades is?" Before she could reply, the boy answered his own question. "When someone dies and wants to enter the underworld, he needs to pass Hades, but he needs to pay or be tossed in the river by Charon. The water of Hades is lighter than water in regular rivers. Humans need their boat to cross. Even ghosts would melt in the Hades, according to Greek myths."

"What are you saying?" Gu Qiusha said, a shudder wracking her body.

"In the painting *Island of the Dead*, Charon in the boat represents men, and the isle represents women. The sea is the womb that nurtures all. The cypress trees are used to make crosses. Between 1880 and 1886, the artist Arnold Böcklin did five paintings about this. He was obsessed with death."

"Wang Er, stop talking like this."

"The music you're hearing was inspired by the *Island of the Dead* painting—it's from the Russian composer Rachmaninoff."

Finally, she found the power and unplugged it.

A few hours later, Gu Qiusha went to work with trepidation. She'd wanted to call the doctor but found her account had only a few hundred yuan in it.

The procuratorate had sent people to raid her company and seal all the accounts and files. The next day, all their training centers shut their doors. Newspapers reported Erya Education Group being involved in insider trading and bribery.

Seven days later, Erya Education Group filed for bankruptcy.

All of the Gu family properties became frozen as bank assets. Lu Zhongyue asked Gu Qiusha for a divorce, which she agreed to right away. After the divorce, she learned about his shell company in Hong Kong. In the two months before the crisis, he'd arranged for 50 million yuan to be transferred as investments to his company via many offshore accounts.

As Lu Zhongyue was leaving the mansion, Gu Changlong grabbed his collar. "How did I miss seeing you for what you really are?"

"I'm sorry, President Gu, but you're not my father-in-law anymore."

The older man had stopped dyeing his hair, and his silver hair and haggard face made him look elderly. He slapped Lu and said, "You ungrateful bastard!"

Lu stroked his face. "President Gu, everything happens for a reason. I'll see you at your funeral. Good-bye."

He shoved the old man aside, causing him to tumble to the ground, and sped off in a new Mercedes.

Light snow began to fall. The snowflakes looked like shreds of foil and paper money on Gu Changlong's white hair.

It was the day before Chinese New Year.

Gu Qiusha rushed to help up her fallen father. The wind mussed her hair, making her look like a bewildered middle-aged woman. She had no words for her father. All she could do was give him a coat. She'd already dismissed both the maid and the driver. The Gus needed to move out by tomorrow, and they'd already sold anything valuable.

Wang Er walked out in his puffer coat, his cheeks rosy from the cold air. The ten-year-old boy had grown bigger and more handsome. He carried a medium-sized backpack, ignoring his adopted family struggling on the ground.

"Wang Er." Gu Qiusha grabbed him by the leg. "Where are you going?"

With a tinge of sadness in his eyes, he looked down at her. "I'm going home."

"We're not moving until tomorrow."

"I'm going to my mom's house."

"I'm your mom."

Gu Qiusha let go of her dad and tried to hold on to Wang Er. He struggled out of her grasp. "Sorry, Qiusha."

"What did you call me?"

"It's getting dark. I need to make the last bus into the city." He looked up at the dark, snowy skies, his face expressionless. "I'll be in touch in a few days."

As her tears melted the snow on her face, she couldn't stop thinking: *Why did he call me Qiusha?*

CHAPTER 28

A chilly morning in the early spring of 2006.

The shabby corridor was crammed with people. The police had cordoned off the entire fifth floor, and the medical examiners were on the scene.

Gu Qiusha had not worn makeup for three months. Her black hair had grown long, and she was afraid to look into the mirror, scared others would think she was Sadako. She panted as she climbed up the stairs to get to the crime scene, shoving aside the throng of gawkers.

Officer Huang Hai blocked her way. "Sorry, Ms. Gu, we haven't finished our investigation. You can't go in."

"Where is he?" She couldn't care less about how she appeared. She screamed, "Where is he?"

His face was as still as stone. Gu Qiusha wasn't going to overpower him.

A few minutes later, they removed the body from the room. The police had been holding her back, but she pushed through and grabbed at the stretcher. The white sheet fell, revealing a twisted, old face.

When Shen Ming had died in 1995, she never went to see his body. She hadn't known what a murder victim looked like.

Now she did. This corpse was fresh. The skin had cooled, but the muscles weren't yet stiff; the joints could still move. The face was horrific—filled with shame, regret, anger, shock, and desperation.

It was Gu Changlong.

His chest was stained with blood, and a deep wound was visible on the left side of his ribs. He must have been stabbed in the heart.

Huang Hai pulled her away. She turned around and slapped him. His only reaction was to say, "I'm sorry for your loss."

"Who did it? Did you catch him?"

She kept her head lowered as she wiped away the tears, not wanting the policeman to see her vulnerability.

"You don't know where you are?"

"What do you mean?"

"Your husband, Lu Zhongyue—"

"*Ex*-husband."

"This is where he lived."

"Karma!" Gu Qiusha spat out the word.

After Erya Education Group went bankrupt, Lu Zhongyue's good life lasted only a month before his account was frozen. His Hong Kong company was also shut down due to illegal operations. Some debt collectors came out of nowhere. The courts seized his new house and car. He became poor in just a few days and had to move to a bad neighborhood.

The door opened and a cop wearing a white coat stepped out. He held an evidence bag, and another cop held a heavy black bag. He whispered to Huang Hai, "We found the weapon."

"It's pretty clear now." Huang Hai leaned against the wall and lit up a cigarette. "The building surveillance showed your father coming here at around 1:00 a.m. He knocked and went into Lu Zhongyue's room. After an hour, a frantic Lu left with a travel bag."

"He killed his own father-in-law?" Gu Qiusha felt stupid as soon as she said it. When did Lu Zhongyue ever treat Gu Changlong as his father-in-law? Plus, they were divorced.

"The tapes showed no one else coming in or out as of this morning. A neighbor lady who was up for her morning exercise complained that it was really loud last night. She heard two men fighting. Security pulled the tape from the surveillance cameras and called the police, then we found the body."

"But why did my dad come here in the middle of the night?" Gu Qiusha felt more and more afraid. She pulled Huang Hai's arm. "Can I see the weapon?"

The cop opened the evidence bag to bring out a large Swiss Army knife, the kind that could be lethal. The blade and the handle were covered in blood.

"I know this knife. I brought it back last year from a vacation in Switzerland. It was a limited-edition knife. It's not sold here yet."

"Did Lu Zhongyue take it with him?"

"No, I gave the knife to my dad as a gift. I saw him holding it and staring outside just a few days ago. I was worried he'd do something crazy like this."

"So, your father took the knife with him to look for Lu Zhongyue, maybe to talk about something, or maybe to kill Lu. Now he's dead and Lu has run away. The weapon is still at the scene. The medical examiner will confirm if the knife was the weapon."

She crumpled to the floor. "My dad was sixty-five, in poor health, and heavily medicated. How could he kill anyone?"

"It's simple. Erya Education Group's bankruptcy was rumored to have been caused by an insider—and that is the son-in-law, right?"

"I wish I could have killed Lu Zhongyue!"

"We're monitoring the whole city. APBs went out to the airports, and also to the train and bus stations. We're searching for him everywhere. Do you have any idea where he might have gone?"

"I don't know. Even before the divorce, we rarely talked. I have no idea where he could be." Gu Qiusha looked bewildered. "Officer Huang, he is very dangerous. He might come after me."

"I'll catch Lu Zhongyue." Huang Hai's curt statement was calm yet forceful.

What went through Gu Qiusha's mind was the eleven-year-old boy who'd just dissolved their legal relationship.

He'd changed his name back to Si Wang.

CHAPTER 29

Gu Changlong's funeral was sparsely attended. All the people who used to visit just to kiss up to him were nowhere to be found now. Even his relatives shied away, fearing trouble. Everyone knew the sordid details of his death and that the killer was still at large.

The night before he was killed, he had a long talk with Gu Qiusha. He said living with nothing in his old age was worse than dying alongside the man who caused the scandal. She tried to talk him out of it, even though she was just as bitter. She also mentioned another name.

"Shen Ming?" Gu Changlong jumped up angrily. "Are you still thinking of him?"

"What if you'd saved him? If you hadn't fired him, you could have given him another chance. Would he still have tried to kill someone? Would he have died underground? If you hadn't done those selfish things, Shen Ming would still be my husband. He accepted me. We would have lived a happy life. We wouldn't be like this today."

"Shut up!"

"Before our engagement ceremony, Shen Ming told me all about how you made him frame Vice President Qian. You have no idea how guilty he felt. He thought he was a killer, that he'd caused an honest man to kill himself. He didn't dare expose you, because we were becoming family. He said he would wait for karma, an eye for an eye. Dad, you used Shen Ming and tossed him aside like a sick dog. You're a despicable man."

"I gave him the best payment. I let my precious daughter marry a poor kid like him!"

"Go to hell."

Gu Changlong ran out of his home in shame. Gu Qiusha didn't know he had the knife.

Did I cause my father's death?

Even after Gu Changlong had turned to ashes, this question haunted Gu Qiusha. She could cry no tears.

After the ashes were put away, Huang Hai was waiting for her. His strong features made her think of the Japanese movie star Ken Takakura.

"Ms. Gu, we've confirmed the Swiss army knife as the weapon that killed your father. We found Lu Zhongyue's fingerprints on the bloody handle. We've officially identified him as the killer."

"Then catch him," she said coldly, walking out of the funeral home.

Huang Hai followed her. "Lu Zhongyue may have gone to another city. The manhunt is nationwide, but we need your help."

"You think this is more than just a regular murder?"

This made him pause. "You know perfectly well that we've been watching your place ever since He Nian's body was found."

"He Nian, me, my father, and Lu Zhongyue. We all had something to do with Shen Ming's death back in 1995."

The four of them used to be Shen Ming's closest friends, but they betrayed him at his most perilous time. They all were plagued by inescapable guilt.

"Since 2002, two have died of unnatural causes, and one is on the run as a killer. I believe none of this is a coincidence. They all can be traced back to Shen Ming."

"I'm the only one left, so I guess I'll be dead soon."

"I'm sorry." Huang Hai showed some expression for the first time. It was regret.

"If you really wanted to solve this, go investigate Si Wang, a fourth-grader."

"The boy you adopted?"

"I think he must have known Shen Ming even though he was born after Shen Ming died."

"I don't understand."

"Me, either. Why did I meet him? How did he come into my life, make me love him, and then destroy me?"

Huang Hai nodded and said coolly, "I'll investigate him."

"The boy has a mark on his back."

"What is it?"

Gu Qiusha didn't want to linger. She walked out of the funeral home and left in a taxi.

There were so few friends and family at the funeral that she had to cancel the memorial dinner. She observed the cold city from the backseat of the car.

In just three months, she'd lost her company, her wealth, her power, her home, her husband, her father, and her most precious son.

She had never dared to think about how Shen Ming must have felt ten years ago after being jailed under false charges, robbed of his beloved teaching job, losing everything he'd worked for—and even losing his bride. How pained and desperate he must have been.

Just like she felt now.

Shen Ming?

If there were another life, who would you be?

Were you that foil-burning boy in the backyard last June?

Wang Er?

As the adopted son of the Gu family, he knew every secret. Gu Qiusha's oversight enabled Lu Zhongyue and Ma Li to have all the power at work. She had looked into Ma Li's past and found that he'd lied on his résumé. He did graduate from Tsinghua, but his high school was Nanming High. He'd graduated in 1995, and no doubt he was one of Shen Ming's students.

Si Wang—Ma Li—Shen Ming.

How terrifying could a fourth-grader be?

The taxi stopped on a narrow street—not where Gu Qiusha rented an apartment, but in front of a blooming locust tree.

Spring was finally here.

She stared at the third-floor window. Women's and kids' clothes were hung out to dry. She looked through the mail—there were letters for He Qingying, but most of it was junk mail. They still lived here.

Gu Qiusha didn't want to go up, so she had to hide. Day after day, night after night, she would keep watching until she had evidence, until she discovered the secrets the boy held.

She was more afraid of the boy, someone who used to call her Mom, than of Lu Zhongyue, who killed her father.

As she turned to leave, a voice sounded.

"Ms. Gu, I'm glad to see you again."

It was a warm female voice. She turned to see He Qingying. She still had a pretty face and trim figure. Her shopping basket held some fresh ribbon fish, Si Wang's favorite.

"Oh, hi. I was just in the neighborhood."

Gu Qiusha avoided eye contact. A year ago, she'd had the upper hand, but now their fortunes had been reversed. They were the same age, but Gu Qiusha looked a lot older.

"Is everything OK?" He Qingying said, pointing at the black mourning sash on Gu Qiusha's arm.

Gu Qiusha smiled bitterly. "I have nothing."

"What happened?"

"Stop acting so innocent," Gu Qiusha retorted. "I was just at the funeral where my dad was turned to ashes."

"I'm sorry." He Qingying backed away, staring at Gu Qiusha.

"I must be wrapped in the stench of the dead. Don't get too close!"

"I'm . . . sorry about your loss. I'm grateful for the help you gave us in the past. Do you want to come up?"

"No need. I don't want to disturb Wang—" She caught herself. "Si Wang."

"Classes are over. I don't know if he's home yet."

"Ms. He, I need to say something. Your son may be a genius, but don't you think he's really odd?"

"What do you mean? Wang Er is definitely extraordinarily smart, but he's still just a kid. He needs warm clothes when he's cold, he needs the doctor when he's sick, he likes my cooking . . ."

He Qingying's expression made it clear that she was lying.

"Do you believe in reincarnation?"

"Ms. Gu, what are you talking about?"

"At birth, every kid has past-life memory, whether it was a long and happy life or a hard and short one. All happy, sad, conflicted, or painful memories are stuck in the infant's brain, which is why they cry so much. They gradually forget, until nothing is remembered. Their brains are wiped clean as a toddler." Gu Qiusha looked up at the window. Her mind was filled with images of that man and how they met. "Maybe, many years later, they would meet someone from a past life. They think they remember, but it was a lifetime ago."

Visibly rattled, He Qingying said, "People have to forget. Isn't it better to forget?"

"Do you know someone called Xiaozhi?"

It was a name Si Wang had murmured in his sleep. He Qingying shook her head.

"If you haven't found his secret, either, you'd better be careful. The kid is cursed. He'll make everyone around him suffer—including my family, your husband, and you."

"That's enough. Don't you think you're being out of line?"

"I'm sorry, you're a mom. I'm a woman, too. I don't want anything to happen to you. I hope you think about what I've said before it's too late. Good-bye."

Gu Qiusha turned and left. She didn't get home until after dark. Her apartment wasn't too awful, and the rent was only 5,000 yuan a month. She had some money tucked away, thanks to the jewelry she'd sold, so she was able to live comfortably.

As she walked into the apartment, she heard a noise behind her. But before she could turn around, she felt a freezing pain in her back. The stab pierced her heart before she could struggle or scream.

The last thing Gu Qiusha saw was the photo of her and Si Wang on the wall.

"When you kill someone, everything changes. Your life changes. You'll live the rest of your life in fear."

In 1995, she and Shen Ming watched a tape in bed. A month later, he died.

PART 3:

BRIDGE OVER
TROUBLED WATER

CHAPTER 30

Do you believe in reincarnation?

Humans have souls. Souls and breathing have a subtle and intertwined relationship. Sleep is a temporary separation of our souls and bodies; death is a permanent separation. Animals and plants also have souls. Souls can move from one life to another.

The ancient Egyptians believed in reincarnation. In The Republic, Plato said that he believed in reincarnation. Pythagoras was the first philosopher to deeply study the concept. Judaism believes in reincarnation of the body. Jesus Christ reincarnated.

In the Song Dynasty Novel Anthology, Liu Sanfu remembers three lifetimes. He was a horse in his previous life. He was happy whenever he saw a stable, and his heart hurt when his hooves were damaged. So as a human, he always slowed down over rocky roads and took care to remove pebbles from horse's hooves.

Buddhism believed that after death, the Seventh Awareness leads the Eighth Awareness out of the body—that happens after Zhong Yin, the intermediate existence between death and reincarnation, is reached. The soul can reincarnate as human, animal, ghost, or god, as in the Six Realms. Some reincarnated souls have memories of past lives.

Zhong Yin is a transition from the end of the current life to the next one. The Zhong Yin body has special abilities and can see worlds that human eyes can't. The forty-nine days after death make up the Zhong Yin phase, which is why the Chinese have the 49th-Day Ceremony for the dead. The Zhong Yin in Hell is parched like burnt wood; Zhong Yin in life is like smoke; Zhong Yin in the Hungry Ghosts realm is like water; Zhong Yin in the Desire realm has a gold color; and it is bright white in the Color realm.

Human Zhong Yin can take the form of children . . .

"What nonsense!" Huang Hai abruptly changed the radio station in his police car, unable to take another moment of this philosopher's lecture.

Grave-Sweeping Day 2006.

The police car stopped at Number One Elementary School on Longevity Road. Huang Hai entered the schoolyard and stood behind a boy who was watching a dead sparrow being buried by sand.

"Are you Si Wang?" His hair was grayer now, but he was still solidly built, and his voice was still low and husky—which made many people remember him.

The boy stepped on the sand to flatten the bird's grave. His face was pale. Without the sand on his nose, he would have seemed very mature.

"Mr. Policeman, that's me. Do you need something?"

"You were the one who found the body in the jeep two years ago?"

Si Wang dusted off the sand. "That was so long ago. Why are you asking now? I wasn't the only one there."

"The other person was Gu Qiusha, who became your adoptive mother last year. But you two ended the relationship a few months ago."

"The car had been there for two years. She was the one who wanted to break into it."

"She is dead."

The boy looked caught off guard before frowning. "How did she die?"

"She was murdered in her home on the night of her father's funeral. The killer hasn't been found."

"OK. I hope you solve the crime soon."

"You're awfully calm."

The boy stood and started to leave the schoolyard. "Mr. Policeman, I need to go home."

Whether out of habit or intention, Si Wang took the small path next to the river. Huang Hai stuck to him like glue.

"Kid, don't take this road anymore. It's too isolated—there may be bad people around."

"Isn't it your job to catch the bad guys?"

"Yes, and there are no bad people I can't catch."

"Really?"

Huang Hai didn't know how to answer. He used to catch every criminal. But in the eleven years since 1995, there had been five murders he'd been unable to solve.

Standing there next to the Suzhou River, he grabbed the boy's school bag. "Wow, kids' backpacks are really heavy these days!"

"Mr. Policeman, why are you following me?" Si Wang asked as the two continued walking.

"Before Gu Qiusha died, she asked me to check on you. She said you were a genius, that you know many secrets."

"I'm just a fourth-grader. I don't know your name yet."

"Huang Hai, like the Yellow Sea. Ever take geography? China has four large seas. I've forgotten the names. You're a genius, you would know."

"Mr. Huang Hai, I'm a member of China's Youth Vanguard. I can help you solve the crimes."

Huang Hai stopped and pointed to an empty lot. "This is it."

He Nian's body had rotted away here for two years. The jeep was gone, and the ground was now covered by trash and dust. Nothing seemed recognizable.

The boy was afraid to walk into the empty lot.

"Mr. Huang Hai, do you believe in ghosts?"

"No, not at all." He lit a cigarette in the wind and hastily added, "There are no ghosts in this world."

"I think the dead person in the trunk called me."

"Nonsense!"

"You don't believe me? I've seen ghosts."

His cigarette ashes fell to the ground. He grabbed Si Wang's arm and dragged him away from the lot.

Ten minutes later, they'd arrived at the boy's home.

"Just drop me off here. It would scare my mom if you went upstairs."

Si Wang grabbed back his school bag. Huang Hai handed him a business card and said, "Kid, if you think of anything, call me immediately."

Huang Hai leaned against the tree to watch the boy go upstairs. He lit another cigarette, thinking of Gu Qiusha's corpse.

She wasn't found until three days after she'd died—and she was only found then because of a water leak in her building. The neighbors asked the maintenance office to check it out, and her body was discovered face down, her limbs spread out. Water was everywhere, making the body a bit bloated. The lethal wound was in the back, going almost straight into her heart. The weapon wasn't found at the scene. There was some cash in the place, but no money or jewelry was missing. There were no signs of sexual assault. It wasn't a money- or sex-based crime. It was a revenge killing.

The killer took care cleaning up the scene—no fingerprints or hair. Elevator surveillance didn't catch anything. It was hard to tell whether the killer was a man or a woman. Only the time of death was known—three days ago, the day of Gu Changlong's funeral. Huang Hai presumed that the killer had come up via the stairs, gone inside when Gu Qiusha opened her door, and stabbed her once in the back.

The most bizarre part of the case was that he'd seen her at the funeral home just hours before she was murdered. The saddest moment in that woman's life. He'd wanted to comfort her. He couldn't forget what she'd said: "I'm the only one left. I guess I'll be dead soon."

She'd sentenced herself to death.

This was an ultimate embarrassment to a seasoned detective.

Then she asked him to pay attention to Si Wang.

The next day, Huang Hai returned to the school.

When Si Wang walked out, he said, "Let me walk you home."

"I can walk home by myself."

"Kid, you know both Gu Qiusha and Gu Changlong are dead. I'm worried about you. Get it?"

He brusquely grabbed the boy's school bag and walked toward the street. Si Wang was like a prisoner who had no choice but to obey.

A couple of schoolkids whispered among themselves: "Is he arrested?"

Si Wang untied his red neckerchief and complained. "Please don't walk me home in front of people. They'll think I did something wrong."

"Let them talk."

"Did you solve the case?"

"Which one?" Huang Hai turned to look at him.

They passed the Muslim temple on Changde Road; someone was selling lamb skewers. Si Wang looked as if he was drooling. Huang Hai bought ten skewers, gave four to the kid, and told him not to eat too much. Si Wang heartily ate the skewers and seemed more relaxed.

"Aren't you afraid to spoil your dinner?"

"It's OK. My mom is working late. I'll just microwave some leftovers."

"Where is your dad?"

Huang Hai knew the answer. He had researched Si Wang's background.

"My dad—he went missing four years ago."

Huang Hai said solemnly, "Si Wang, come have dinner at my house."

"No, I'd rather go home."

"Come with me." His words sounded like an order.

He lived near the Muslim temple in an old high-rise, almost right next to the precinct. When he opened the apartment door, a musty odor wafted out. His face reddened. "Sorry about the mess!"

He fumbled to open the windows and tidied the cluttered living room. Instant noodle cups littered the kitchen table and cigarette butts filled the ashtray. It was a true bachelor's pad.

Si Wang was cautious in the stranger's house.

With some difficulty, Huang Hai found the boy a place to sit and then poured him a glass of milk. The boy politely took a sip. Huang Hai turned on the television, which was showing the popular children's program *Detective Conan*.

After much struggling in the kitchen, he found a pack of noodles and some frozen beef in the fridge.

"How about some beef noodles?"

Ten minutes later, when Conan used the needle to defeat Mouri Kogorou, piping-hot noodles arrived on the dinner table. Huang Hai's noodles weren't horrible, though they were the only dish he made well.

Si Wang finished every last strand, including the broth. Huang Hai gave him an odd smile. The boy scrambled up but was pushed down to sit again. "Had enough?"

"Definitely—I'm hiccuping. You're not eating?"

"I'm not hungry." His voice was as heavy as the sound from the bottom of a jar.

"Mr. Policeman, are there no criminals you can't catch?"

"Of course not."

"You swear?"

"I . . ." Huang Hai was about to light up again but decided not to. "With a few exceptions."

"Murder cases?"

Huang Hai's gaze turned icy. "Why are you asking?"

"I think your taking on the Suzhou River case—and the Gu Qiusha and Gu Changlong cases—has something to do with your other unsolved cases."

"Why does a schoolkid need to know so much?"

Si Wang no longer bothered with pleasantries. He was about to leave when Huang Hai stopped him. "Wait."

"It's getting dark. My mom said I shouldn't go to strangers' houses."

"When were you born?"

"December 19, 1995."

"Two unsolved cases happened before you were born."

"Also in 1995?"

"Yes." Admitting this made him despondent.

Calmly, Si Wang said, "The Nanming Road murder case?"

Huang Hai's face turned ashy and he clutched the boy's collar to lift him off the floor. Si Wang's feet dangled.

"Let me go!"

"How did you know?"

"The Internet."

Huang Hai's big hands could have easily crushed him, but he put him down. "Sorry, kid."

"They said three people died at Nanming High that summer?"

"I'm sorry, I'll take you home."

As he exited Huang Hai's car at the end of the ride, Si Wang asked, "Can you do me a favor?"

"Tell me."

"Can you find my dad? He went missing on Chinese New Year in 2002. He's called Si Mingyuan. We reported it to the police."

"I'll do my best."

From that point on, every few days he'd pick up Si Wang at school and they would go eat lamb skewers—or sometimes he fed him at home.

By May, Gu Qiusha had already been dead for a month, and there was still no progress with the case. The police had temporarily identified Lu Zhongyue as the main suspect and continued looking for him.

Huang Hai agonized over it and decided to pay Si Wang a visit at home. It was a weekend.

Si Wang wore a look of astonishment while opening the door. "Why are you here?"

"Are you doing something bad?" Huang Hai walked into the narrow room, where the TV was playing *The Grudge*. "You're home alone?"

"No, my mom's home."

This made him pause. "Does your mom know about me?"

Why would she? No mom would want a cop hanging around her fourth-grader.

As Huang Hai was deciding what to do, He Qingying came out of the bedroom. She was wearing something new, and her hair was done up.

She said, "You are?"

"Uh—" He was used to dealing with bad guys, but a pretty woman made him tongue-tied.

"This is Mr. Huang Hai, a policeman."

"Wang Er, what did you do?" she said, glaring at her son.

"Ma'am, please don't misunderstand. I came here uninvited because Si Wang asked me to help with something—his dad." Huang Hai noticed her eyes flickering at those words. "I heard your husband has been missing for years. Your son wants me to help find him. I was just looking up the records at the police station."

"Thank you!" she said.

"Sorry, I haven't been able to find him yet, or find any hotel records of him locally or in other cities. And there were no train or plane ticket records, either. But I've promised Si Wang that I will keep looking."

To be polite and as a gesture of respect, He Qingying made tea for the cop. He clumsily uttered thanks and sipped the tea, almost burning his lips.

She changed the topic to her son's education. "Si Wang is very smart. You know what happened last year. Ms. Gu gave us an opportunity for him to see more of the world. But now he's back to the way he was. His grades are mediocre. He rarely talks to his classmates, and even the principal ignores him now."

The policeman nodded and gently told her all about how he frequently walked the boy home, treating him to lamb skewers. The boy blushed and hid in the bedroom.

Huang Hai asked, "You mentioned Ms. Gu—you know she's dead, right?"

"What? When?"

"You hadn't kept in touch, then? She died a month and a half ago." He resumed his stern expression. "When was the last time you saw her?"

"It was around Chinese New Year, when we dissolved the adoption and changed his residency registration."

"Not since then?"

"No."

"Great, thanks for your cooperation. I'll be going now, though I might visit again soon."

Once he was downstairs, he couldn't resist looking up at the third floor. His mind was filled with He Qingying's face.

Was she lying?

CHAPTER 31

It was spring.

Er Hu had been a security guard for two years, and he always passed this house during his patrols. The big Christmas tree had made everyone in the neighborhood envious. Who knew the family would go bankrupt right after Chinese New Year? Everything had been moved out. An old man used to sit near the front gate and cuss until a strange woman took him back inside.

He heard everyone in the family had died.

What he remembered the most was the boy in the family. He was about ten, a good-looking kid, with shining but expressionless eyes. He often walked alone in the garden or stared out the windows. Whenever Er Hu passed the house at night, he'd see the ghost-like boy standing by the second floor window, his face so pale that it looked scary—like he was playing a joke.

It was the same every night.

Er Hu's hometown myth said that someone like this was usually possessed.

As the family went bankrupt, the boy disappeared. Er Hu was relieved, though he still saw the boy in his nightmares.

The mansion was now being prepared to welcome a new owner. Er Hu was surprised to see that strange woman again.

Dressed in black, she looked like a recent college graduate, demure and low-key. Her hair was in a ponytail and pinned with a white flower, as though she was in mourning. She was beautiful, with snow-like skin and alluring eyes. She looked like a beauty from an ancient painting.

Before the Gu family scandal, Er Hu had seen her a few times. He remembered her face and wanted to follow her. She always paced in front of the mansion to look in, and she hid whenever anyone came out. He tried to question her, but she said nothing as she left.

Her hair was fragrant.

On this day, she stood in front of the renovated mansion. A woman in her thirties with an unfashionable perm approached. She had a boy with her, a third- or fourth-grader. They had luggage and seemed to have traveled a long way. They looked like a mother and her son from a small town.

"Is this Lu Zhongyue's house?" asked the woman with the child.

The attractive woman turned around and answered with a frown. "Not anymore. He went missing a while ago. Why are you looking for him?"

"Oh, no, what am I gonna do?" The woman almost fainted but for her son's help. "Sorry, who are you?"

"I'm Lu Zhongyue's cousin. I'm here to deal with the house."

The frazzled woman with the son looked at the younger woman with pleading eyes. "Can you help me?"

"And who are you?"

She dragged the boy to her side. "This is my son, also Lu Zhongyue's son."

"What are you talking about? My cousin doesn't have children."

"Ten years ago, I was his girlfriend. He wanted to dump me after I got pregnant. He gave me some money for an abortion back home. I knew he had someone else he wanted to marry. I cried like crazy and went back home. The doctor said the fetus was too big to abort. If I insisted, it would be dangerous. I didn't want to let the baby go, so I gave birth. Thank god my parents were reasonable, and they helped me with the baby. So now here we are."

"My cousin had no idea?"

"He was cruel to me then, and I was too busy hating him. I had the money he gave me, plus we were thousands of miles apart. I never looked for him again." She became more embarrassed as she talked. She pointed to the boy's forehead. "See, he has a birthmark here, just like your cousin. Trust me, this is his flesh and blood. There are tests now, right? I can run a test."

"Stop it. I'm not doubting you."

"Last year, the boy's grandparents passed, and our savings are almost all gone. I want to work, so I need to give the kid to Lu Zhongyue. It took me a long time to find this place. I heard he's rich, so if he's not going to acknowledge his son, at least the boy will be fed." The woman started crying as she said to her son, "Tell Aunt your name."

The boy seemed very docile. "Aunt, I'm Lu Jizong."

"I'm sorry, but you have to go for now. I want to find him, too, but he's a wanted man. The police are looking for him."

"The bastard. It's karma! But what are we gonna do?"

The younger woman opened her wallet and handed 3,000 yuan to the mother. "Take this for now. Use it as traveling expenses."

"I can't accept this."

"I'm his cousin, so his problems are my problems. I'll fix the mistakes he made. But I can't find him. If I hear of anything, whether he's in jail or whatnot, I'll tell you right away. Let's swap numbers. I'll get in touch soon."

"Thank you so much!"

The single mom tucked away the 3,000 yuan. After exchanging phone numbers, the younger woman added, "If you hear of anything about him, let me know. This might save his life."

"Don't worry, I will."

The out-of-towner left with her son. She turned around often to look back. Er Hu was being scolded by the security chief. How dare he let someone like this inside the neighborhood gates.

The waning sun shone on the black-skirted woman standing by herself. She looked like a frozen flame. The oleander trees by the road were about to bloom.

Her name was Ouyang Xiaozhi.

CHAPTER 32

Christmas 2006.

Huang Hai brought Si Wang home. He'd bought a lot of prepared foods, as well as two bottles of rice wine for himself and a large bottle of Sprite for the boy.

Icy rain fell.

Si Wang's face had matured some. His eyebrows were bushier now. In a few years he'd be a teenager.

The policeman intentionally took the boy to a bathhouse, and saw what he expected, a knife wound–like birthmark. He frowned but didn't say anything.

Si Wang had been visiting Huang Hai's apartment often. He was allowed to explore every part of the place except for one small room, which was always locked.

Huang Hai drank by himself and chain-smoked until the boy's coughing made him stop.

"Huang Zhiliang died two years ago." He touched the boy's nose with a shaky finger. "It's like a dream."

"Who's Huang Zhiliang?"

Huang Hai took out a framed photo from a drawer. It showed him and a young boy in the People's Park. Lots of balloons lined the park garden for June First Children's Day. The boy looked a bit like Si Wang.

"He was my son, only a year older than you. Four years ago, he was diagnosed with leukemia. I took him to hospitals across the country for a bone marrow transplant, but there were no matching donors. Huang Zhiliang stayed in the hospital for a year. Chemo made him lose all his hair. He died in my arms. He was ten."

"You must miss him a lot."

"I cried all the time that year—until I met you, kid."

The middle-aged man held the boy, stroking him like his own son was still alive.

"What about his mom?"

"We divorced a long time ago. She ran off with a rich guy and moved to Australia. She's not been back since our son died."

"It's not your fault." The boy touched the man's wrinkled face. "You can call me Huang Zhiliang from now on."

"He's dead, and he won't be back, kid," Huang Hai said quietly.

"Death is a dream, and so is being alive."

"Here you go again, talking like a grown-up." He downed a whole cup of wine.

Si Wang pulled on his arm. "Enough! You're drunk!"

"Don't try to stop me!"

The boy helped the man to the sofa as Huang Hai mumbled, "Huang Zhiliang, don't go. Huang Zhiliang!"

He became nauseated and started vomiting. Why couldn't he hold his liquor tonight? While cleaning up, he noticed the door to the always-locked room was open. He looked for the key, realizing the boy had taken it. Huang Hai rushed into the musty room. The boy stood like a statue staring at the wall, which was covered in yellowed papers and photos—so dense they looked like memorials at a funeral: barren wilderness, fallen walls, smokestacks, a run-down factory, rusted machinery, stairs to the underground, a metal hatch with a round handle.

The Demon Girl Zone, according to Nanming High mythology.

Si Wang didn't realize it, but his lips were bitten through and he had blood trickling down his chin.

The photos were from the June 1995 crime scene, with big portable lights illuminating the black background, all the dirty water, and gross reflections.

Si Wang saw Shen Ming: twenty-five years old, bushy hair, wearing the shirt his fiancée got him stained to black. The red-dotted mourning sash was hard to recognize through the large patches of blood. His face was still submerged in a puddle.

In the next photo, the body was flipped over. A deathly pale face exposed under the lights.

Si Wang turned away, but it was too late. He began to cry.

Huang Hai covered the boy's eyes.

Shen Ming was unrecognizable. He'd been killed and had lay there soaking in water for three days. Three days of gradual decay.

Si Wang pushed away the man's hands and stared at a photograph of the mortal wound: a red line less than two centimeters long. It was enough to split the heart in two.

There were no photographs of the weapon.

After the body was removed, the police continued to inspect the crime scene. The water was pumped away, and all evidence was gathered. There were no graves or bones as rumored, just some weird letters and symbols on the wall.

Huang Hai still remembered the knife that killed Yan Li. Made by a military factory, fifteen centimeters long, it used special-grade steel and had a blood reservoir. It looked like a weapon the special forces used. It was sharp, maintained its hardness, and resisted corrosion really well. It was hard to find on the market. At the time, only certain government agencies had access to it.

One of the room's walls showed countless red lines connecting people in the case. The bright-red writing looked like blood.

Shen Ming's name was at the center.

Surrounding it were eight lines, each pointing to a name accompanied by a photograph of the individual: Liu Man, Yan Li, He Nian, Lu Zhongyue, Gu Qiusha, Gu Changlong, Zhang Mingsong, and Ouyang Xiaozhi.

Liu Man, Yan Li, He Nian, Gu Qiusha, and Gu Changlong's names were crossed out, indicating their deaths.

Only three people remained.

Lu Zhongyue was in hiding. That wasn't an easy life, and it wouldn't last forever.

Pointing at the wall, Si Wang asked, "Who are Zhang Mingsong and Ouyang Xiaozhi?"

"Zhang Mingsong taught math at Nanming High." Huang Hai was reminded that he had not followed up on those two in a while. "Ouyang Xiaozhi was the girl who said Shen Ming might be at the Demon Girl Zone."

"Did they all have something to do with him?"

"I drew up this chart a month after he died. The most suspicious person was Lu Zhongyue. He married his dead best friend's fiancée. He worked at Nanming Steel Factory, and was on the graveyard shift that night. It was less than 200 meters from his office to the crime scene. His dad worked for the district government. But he claimed to be asleep during his night shift, and there was no evidence connecting him to Shen Ming's death. I've watched him all these years. When He Nian's body was found two years ago, I talked to him. Who knew he'd actually become a killer. He's now wanted all over the country."

"Do you put all your files here, and don't let anyone in, because this is your secret zone and your shame as a cop?"

"Stop the crazy talk." He rushed Si Wang out of the room and poured a cold cup of water over his head. "I let you in on too many secrets tonight. If your mom knew about this, she'd never let you come here again."

"Do you feel better now?"

"I'm OK, I just think you can be frightening, sometimes. You're not like a kid at all."

"Everyone says that."

"Why do you care about something that happened in 1995? You weren't even born then."

"For you."

The answer surprised Huang Hai. He looked at the flickering Christmas tree outside the window. "You're a freaky kid."

The doorbell rang. Who would visit on Christmas Eve? Huang Hai locked the small room, and Si Wang opened the door as if he was the host.

A man in his fifties with salt-and-pepper hair stood hunched in the door way. His face was wrinkled, thin, and tired. He frowned and looked at the door number again. "Kid, is this Officer Huang Hai's home?"

"Yes."

"Sorry to bother you. Is your dad home?"

"He is."

Huang Hai pushed the boy behind him and brusquely said, "Mr. Shen, I told you not to look for me at home."

"Sorry, Mr. Huang. Your line was busy, so I just came over. It's too important."

"What is it?"

"Last night, he bought a book—*The Da Vinci Code.* I've read it so many times. It's about religion, history, art, and murder. It also has Knights Templars and the Priory of Sion monastery."

"What?"

"Priory of Sion!" The man actually said the English words fluently.

"Mr. Shen, you're too old to say foreign gibberish to me."

Si Wang looked at Huang Hai with a strange expression and then pulled on his shirt. "Let him in."

He rubbed the boy's head. "Go wait in the kitchen. This is grown-up stuff."

Si Wang sighed and did as he was told, knowing he could eavesdrop through the door.

"Sit," Huang Hai said before making tea for the uninvited guest.

"I followed him," the excited man said. "On the subway he was reading *The Da Vinci Code* and making notes, drawing crosses and other weird marks. He was mumbling something, maybe their organization's secret code."

"Did he see you?"

"Don't worry, I was careful. I wore a surgical mask like I was sick, and a hat. He couldn't see my face."

Huang Hai scratched his head and lit a cigarette. "Damn it. I was afraid that he'd call 1-1-0 again or complain to our bureau chief. The chief's daughter is taking her college exams next year, and he's been tutoring her."

"That's too dangerous. Tell your chief that he can't be allowed near kids. I think he's part of the Priory of Sion or the Rosicrucians, or at least with the Fraternal Order." The man drank some tea before continuing. "You're a cop. I'm a prosecutor. We both know that people with something to hide never get away with it for long. I can guarantee that he's not just a math teacher."

"Well, he's an elite teacher in the city—of course he's more than just a teacher."

The prosecutor seemed more and more excited by the minute. "There's evil in his eyes! I know everyone thinks he's a good guy, a model citizen, but you have to trust my instincts. When Shen Ming was killed and you guys couldn't solve the case, I went to the library a lot to read about forensic and criminal investigation. I ran into him at the library and told him who I was, and my relationship to Shen Ming. I asked him about the books he was checking out and he hid them from me. I asked about what happened at the school after Shen Ming's death. He told me the principal was fired and the teachers and students were under a lot of pressure. Then he just ran off. He was obviously hiding something. I used my connections to look up his library records. He checked out theology books about symbols, detective novels— like *And Then There Were None* and *Murder in Mesopotamia*— and even forensic books."

"Mr. Shen, stop for a second."

"Don't interrupt me. When he killed my son, he was already over thirty years old. So now he's forty-something. But he's not married. A guy like that has no trouble finding a wife. He must be a pervert."

"That's pure speculation."

"Also, I dug deeper into the pervert's background. Know what I found? His grandfather worked with foreign missionaries, like Opus Dei in *The Da Vinci Code*. In 1949, his grandfather was executed as a foreign spy. He said a bunch of things before he died—supposedly a curse in Latin—condemning everyone at the rally. Mr. Huang, do you get it? His grandfather was in a cult. It makes sense that his grandson would be, too. Twenty years ago, his father committed suicide in a really strange way. He locked himself in a stone hut and burned himself to death. I think it was some kind of self-sacrifice."

"Mr. Shen, you're an experienced prosecutor. Listen to yourself. You know you need evidence. I appreciate your efforts, but for the past ten years I've been hearing these clues and leads, over and over again. I've investigated them, too. They lead nowhere. They're nonsense. You keep calling me and going to my office, and now you're stalking me at home."

"Last night's discovery was very important. It proves he was connected to the secret society in *The Da Vinci Code*."

"I think you should go home and rest. Stop doing these dangerous things. He must know you're following him. He's already called the police so many times. I don't want to have to arrest you."

"There's one more clue. The last one. Listen to me. He may be an elite teacher, but he never joined the Communist Party. Or the Democratic Party. He's a suspicious character."

"Now you're making stuff up. Is this the Cultural Revolution? Good thing I'm only a detective and have never taken bribes or mistresses. You'd have something on me, too. Ten years ago, you thought he was suspicious. I listened to you and I looked into it. He had a good alibi. On June 19, 1995, he was at an academic conference, staying at a hotel on an island. At least forty people verified this. It was raining hard that night, and the island's only boat couldn't leave. He shared a room with the Education Bureau chief. He couldn't have done it."

"I've read a lot of detective novels over the years. Even the seemingly perfect alibi can be faked. I can't believe that you let him fool you."

"The night Liu Man was killed, he was tutoring two senior boys until 2:00 a.m. He couldn't have killed Liu Man, either. He never married, but there are always women after him. He's from a good family and is a Tsinghua graduate. He's picky, so he stayed single. It's pretty common."

Shen Yuanchao's voice shook. "I've followed him for ten years. No one in the world knows him better than I do. Mr. Huang, I don't blame you. I know you've looked for the killer all these years, too. I'm grateful. But I'm Shen Ming's dad. I can feel that his soul never reincarnated. He's still around me. This morning, he was in my dream. I saw him standing next to a river. He still looked twenty-five, and he had a thick bowl of soup. He wanted me to avenge him. He told me that I'm right about the killer."

A dream? Huang Hai couldn't believe it. "Please leave, Mr. Shen. Take a good rest. I guarantee I will catch the killer. Unless I die first."

The policeman opened his door and made Shen Yuanchao leave. Waiting for the elevator, the prosecutor turned around and shouted, "Remember to search his house. You know where he lives. There's a yard. If you dig around, you'll find a lot of bones."

Huang Hai made sure the prosecutor got on the elevator before closing his door. Si Wang had come out of the kitchen.

"Were you eavesdropping?" Pissed off with everything about the night, he shoved the kid aside.

Si Wang looked at him with an innocent expression, like he was terrified. "Who is he?"

"Si Wang, we were just playing games." He bit back a curse and said lightly, "He's . . . an old friend."

CHAPTER 33

Christmas Eve.

Shen Min was in bed. Many stars hung in her bedroom; it was like sleeping under a starry sky snuggled up in a thick comforter. One of the headboard lamps was on so she could read the Christmas cards from her classmates.

One boy wrote: "Shen Min, I like you. Can we be friends?" The fifth-grader giggled and tossed the card under the bed.

Cold rain hit the window. Anxiously, she looked at the clock. Why wasn't her dad home yet? Was he still interrogating prisoners?

Finally, she heard his key in the lock. He looked more like a tired grandfather than a father. When he came into her room, she felt the cold mist that followed in behind him. As soon as he saw Shen Min, he went from serious to happy. Stroking her hair, he said, "Little Min, go to bed. You don't want to be late for school."

"Dad, where did you go?"

"I went to see an old friend." Her father turned off the light. "Good night."

Shen Min had to take two buses to get to Number One Elementary School on Longevity Road. She was in Section 3 of the fifth grade, and her classroom was in a secluded yard, in a blue-and-white building.

She had almond-shaped eyes, luminous skin, and dark, glossy hair—and she wore a thick white cotton skirt.

After school, she liked to play badminton with some other girls in the neighborhood until it got dark. She hit their shuttlecock into a thicket the kids couldn't climb into. As they worried about what to do, a boy emerged from the bushes.

He was around Shen Min's age, and though they were in different classes, they often saw each other at school. The boy's face was memorable because his eyes always seemed sad. At school it was rumored that he was a genius. But nothing he did made him stand out, and the teachers ignored him. He had no friends and was always by himself. Shen Min couldn't remember his name. She needed to find the shuttlecock.

The boy wiped off some leaves and dirt and then showed the girls the shuttlecock before placing it in Shen Min's soft, cool palm.

"Thanks! Are in you Section 2? What's your name?"

"I'm Si Wang, Si as in 'general,' Wang as in 'lookout.' You?"

"Shen Min. Shen as in 'applying,' Min as in 'agile.'"

"Shen Min?" he asked, shocked.

"What's wrong?"

"Our last names are pretty rare, right? I bet no one else in the class has your last name."

She naively nodded. "Do you also live here?"

"No, I was just passing through."

"We can play together."

When Si Wang picked up the badminton racket, they both discovered a cut on his hand. He'd gotten it rooting around in the bushes.

"Oh no, you've hurt yourself. That's my fault."

"It's OK." Si Wang used his other hand to press on the cut and stop the bleeding.

Shen Min wanted to take him into her apartment and put ointment on his hand, but she was afraid of her dad seeing her.

"Wait here—don't go!"

The girl ran upstairs. In less than two minutes, she was back with ointment, bandages, and alcohol swabs. She grabbed Si Wang's hand and cleaned the cut before sealing it with a bandage.

The other girls snickered. The boy ran out of the neighborhood.

Si Wang had finally made friends. During recess he would play badminton, hide-and-seek, and hopscotch with the girls. He didn't care if the boys laughed.

During the second semester of fifth grade, when all the students were cramming for their tests, Shen Min was loving music class. In the warmer weather of May, she dressed in a light blouse that showed off her lean neck and arms. The piano teacher accompanied her as she sang, "Let's paddle our oars, the boat is sailing in the waves, a beautiful pagoda is reflected in the sea, green trees and red walls surround us. The boat is floating and gliding in the water, a cool breeze comes toward us. Our red kerchiefs face the sun, the sun is on the water, the fish are watching us, listening to our happy singing."

One girl in Section 2 was really rich. An Audi was always waiting for her after school. She often tried to tempt Si Wang into a ride. One day, Shen Min hid behind a tree and watched the girl tugging on Si Wang's shirt. "I have two tickets to *Harry Potter*—you want to go?"

The boy awkwardly turned to run and bumped into Shen Min. The two laughed and took a walk around the school garden.

"You know why they call me a genius? I have superpowers."

"What?" Her eyes went round. "Superpowers? I don't believe you."

"I know your dad's name—it's Shen Yuanchao."

"Yeah, but that's easy to find out."

"You have an older brother. Not a cousin, a brother. I bet you didn't know that."

"How do you know this?"

"Go home and ask your dad."

She thought of her living room, where there was a black-and-white photograph of young man beside a photograph of her mom. Dad never mentioned who he was.

"Let's change the subject," Si Wang said. "How is your mom?"

"She died."

"I'm sorry."

"She had me when she was over forty. The doctors told her it would be risky, but she insisted on having me. The day I was born, she died after a lot of bleeding." Shen Min started crying. "I killed my mom."

"When is your birthday?"

"December 20, 1995."

Si Wang used his fingers to count. "Ah, so she was already pregnant that day."

"What are you talking about? What day?"

"You'll have to call me older brother. I was born on December 19, a day earlier than you."

"I won't!"

"Fine, do you know when your older brother died?"

"No. What are you talking about?" She wiped off her tears and stared at him in confusion.

"June 19, 1995." Si Wang lowered his head and started crying.

"Why are you crying?"

"I got something in my eye."

"Don't move—stare straight ahead."

The girl licked his eye.

"My dad told me girls can cry but boys can't." She looked proud as she said this.

He nodded. "He's right!"

"Are you going to cry again?"

"No, I promise." The boy wiped his tears and turned around. "I need to go home now—bye!"

Two weeks later, the school year ended. From there, Si Wang and Shen Min went to different junior high schools, never to meet again.

Sometimes she fantasized about going on outings with Si Wang. They would row a boat on Yinchu Lake in Changfeng Park. The sad boy would sit across from her, their oars moving in sync as they hid in the shadows of the Tiebi Yin Mountain, gazing at the setting sun.

CHAPTER 34

Fall 2007.

"Kid, do you know why I told you the secret about that room last Christmas?"

Huang Hai and Si Wang were playing Xiangqi. Anyone looking in might have thought they were father and son.

"You were drunk."

"Nonsense! I can hold my liquor. I wanted you to know. You must have your own secret about Shen Ming's death."

"We want the same thing."

"So let's do a trade. I told you what the police know. Why don't you tell me what you know? You learned Gu family secrets at their place and must know more about Lù Zongyue."

Si Wang was about to swoop in for a win, but he pulled back his piece. "Can I not say anything?"

"No. I still have lots of secrets, too. If you don't tell me, I won't tell you."

"You lose." The boy took a deep breath. "Let's start with Gu Qiusha."

"OK."

"She had a medicine cabinet in her room with a locked drawer. I stole her key and opened it. There were tons of imported drugs, a lot of them not in English. I copied the letters and relocked the drawer so no one would know. I went online and saw they were German. I found out that they were for suppressing human luteinizing hormone—they made testosterone drop."

Huang Hai scratched his head. "I'm confused."

"In other words, chemical castration: making someone a eunuch with drugs."

"That's vicious."

"They were for Lu Zhongyue. I pieced together why she only let me drink bottled water at home, never water from the tap."

"No wonder Lu Zhongyue always seemed off." Huang Hai lit a cigarette, stood up, and paced by the window. "If Lu found out, he must have hated Gu Qiusha. It makes sense that he would want to kill her."

"For the past year I've been terrified that he'd come looking for me. I'm always reminding Mom to lock the windows and doors, and that if a stranger knocks, to not open the door, no matter what."

"Kid, if only I had a son like you." Huang Hai tapped the boy's nose. "Don't worry, as long as I'm around, you guys will be safe."

"Really?"

"I guarantee you that the minute the guy shows up, I'll catch him." The cop looked at the time. "Go home now—your mom will call if you're not back soon."

After the boy left, he went into the small room. He looked at his wall of connections, touching Shen Ming's name tacked up in the center of the chart.

In June of 1995, a week before he was killed, Shen Ming was still in jail, and he demanded to see Huang Hai. He said he had some major clues. So in the middle of the night, Huang Hai left home—where his one-year-old slept—and cycled to work.

Sitting there in the interrogation room, Shen Ming looked more like a ghost than a person. He anxiously pulled at his hair, his calm high school teacher demeanor all gone. He knelt down and pleaded with Huang Hai, "I didn't kill anyone . . . I didn't kill anyone."

"What proof do you have?"

"Mr. Huang, there are two rumors about me at school, and one of them is true."

"You were seeing your student Liu Man?"

He wiped away some tears and his lips trembled. "No, I was born out of wedlock."

"Your birth father wasn't the man who killed his wife and then got executed?"

"No. That guy's last name wasn't Shen, so people said I wasn't his kid." Shen Ming coughed violently. "My real dad is a good guy like you, with a respectable job and social standing. I once swore to him that I would never tell anyone."

"I see. If he has nothing to do with this case, I respect your secret."

"I was named Shen Ming at birth. My mom got married when I was three, and I took my stepdad's last name. That man was an animal. He had other women but used my mom to support him. I wasn't his kid, so he took his anger out on me. He'd beat me when my mom wasn't home. He was careful not to leave marks. I told my mom, but he denied it. My earliest memories are of crying and screaming. Every time he walked toward me, I'd shake so hard and hide under the bed. I was only five or six."

Huang Hai had heard a lot of similar stories before, but he still muttered, "Such evil."

"When I was seven, my stepdad poisoned my mom, killing her. He was arrested and executed after I reported it to the police. My grandma was my only family. I couldn't bear to keep the wicked man's last name, so we changed it back to Shen Ming."

"I wondered about that when I read your file."

"My grandma wasn't educated. She worked as a nanny all her life, and for the same employer most of the time. You know Serenity Road? I stayed in a basement there from first through ninth grades. It was damp, dark, and full of rats. I grew up like a lost ghost. I look geeky now, but I got in fights every day back then. Kids ganged up on me—they'd throw stones and try to pull down my pants. They'd even pee in my face. I would fight back and go home with bruises. But I won in the end. No one could beat me anymore, and they scattered as soon as they saw me. They said I would turn into a thug—or a murderer like my step-dad. But I did good in school, using old textbooks and materials donated by the family my grandmother worked for. I made it into Nanming High."

"Shen Ming, I have sympathy for you, but it doesn't change how I feel about the case."

"I have to tell you, though. My stepfather is now ashes. He was executed, but he still haunts me like a drunken black shadow, his heavy footsteps always coming closer and closer."

Huang Hai, a new father, grew sad. "Enough."

"Let me finish! I dreamed of seeing him in jail. I saw that dirty face getting close to mine as he squeezed my neck. He wants revenge on me for telling the police. Without me, they'd have believed that my mom died from an illness. He wouldn't have been sentenced to death. Time after time, I wake up after being strangled to death."

"I've had nightmares like this, too, dreaming of criminals I executed." Huang Hai wanted to slap himself. Why was he sharing his fears with a suspect?

Suddenly, Shen Ming's hand reached across the guardrails and seized Huang Hai's sleeve. He said with trepidation, "Last night I dreamed that I died. A knife stabbed me in the back and I turned into a boy."

Twelve years later, there were more wrinkles on Huang Hai's forehead. He added a name to the wall and drew a new line—from Shen Ming to Si Wang.

CHAPTER 35

In 2007, Si Wang was attending May First Junior High School.

He Qingying had an uneasy feeling this year, maybe because it was her son's zodiac year. She vowed to spend more time with him, so she decided to open a store he could hang out in. Having paid off all of her debts, she still had about 100,000 yuan in savings leftover from the Gu family's adoption compensation.

In the summer, with Huang Hai's help, He Qingying opened a small bookstore across from the May First Junior High School.

Si Wang named it Deserted Village Bookstore.

In the scorching summer heat, He Qingying went to the wholesale market in order to stock their store. They chose Si Wang's favorite literature and history books—and also reference books, which would help the bookstore survive. He Qingying also selected copies of Guo Jingming's *Sadness into a River,* Han Han's *One City*, and suspense and thriller novels since kids liked to read those.

They opened on the first day of school. Huang Hai brought some of his colleagues to celebrate. Seeing all those cops in one place made it seem like there'd been a murder at the store.

By 8:00 a.m., the firecracker ceremony had ended, so He Qingying took her son across the street to school. Si Wang wore a red kerchief, and he begged his mom to go back to the store. She was a bit sad to realize that her son no longer wanted to be seen at school with his mom.

The junior high was on Longevity Road, very close to night-clubs. Luxury cars congregated by them and call girls went in and out. The school had a moderate-sized yard with oleander trees. The classroom buildings were clustered in a horseshoe shape, with a small patio in the middle. A two-story building sat across the playing field, looking like a barren island. This was the infir-mary and the music classroom.

Si Wang adapted faster than anyone else. If he hadn't been intentionally trying to do badly, he'd have been the best student in class. He still had almost no friends, and all the teachers fig-ured him for a loner. Since the Erya Education ad campaign had disappeared long ago, no one knew what had happened to him in third and fourth grades. He talked more at the bookstore and brought over his classmates, promoting all sorts of bestsellers and the *Zui Novel* magazine. He also made sure everyone knew that they sold reference books and textbooks for cheaper than the school did. He Qingying gave all the students 20 percent off.

The following year in spring.

The Nude Picture Scandal was all over the Internet, and many kids saw the photos. He Qingying was worried but couldn't bring it up to her son, so she let it go.

Si Wang's last baby tooth fell out, and his permanent teeth grew in. Unlike other kids, he gave all his baby teeth to his mom, who stored them in her bottom dresser drawer.

"Wang Er, your hair and teeth are precious. My suffering gave them to you. I must take good care of them."

Si Wang was a student at the junior high school—seventh grade, Section 2.

His dad had been missing for six years now. They were used to a life without him. He could have been a part of their past-life memory even if their family photo still stood by the bed.

At the bookstore, business was good. He Qingying and Si Wang were more like partners than mother and son. In their first year they even made a small profit. Huang Hai's protection meant they weren't hassled by the Industry and Commerce Bureau, the Tax Bureau, or the Municipal Inspectors. She worked in the store every day. She only brought in outside help when there was an emergency.

When she had trouble sleeping, she would stroke her son's back. Si Wang said he never wanted to grow up; he didn't want his Adam's apple bulging or his voice changing. He wanted to keep holding his mom at night when he slept. The light glowed through the curtains, illuminating He Qingying's face. The Taiwanese movie star Lin Chi-ling was only four years younger than her—there must be men who found her attractive.

Si Wang had his thirteenth birthday on December 19, 2008.

He had never celebrated a birthday at a restaurant. Usually, his mom brought home cake and the two would sing birthday songs. This time, Huang Hai brought gifts. He really wasn't good at gift giving. He brought ham and salted fish, and an ugly set of stationery, but the gesture was appreciated. He helped her cook but kept spilling spices and seasonings. The brutish cop tried to talk about household matters with He Qingying, and that amused her. The two of them had fun joking around.

When she turned around, she saw Si Wang's cold eyes watching her.

Before they blew out the thirteen candles, Huang Hai rushed to say, "Wait, let me make a wish."

He Qingying could guess his wish, but Si Wang blew out the flame before he could say it. She held her chin and watched her son. What was *his* wish?

After the birthday celebration, He Qingying took a walk with Huang Hai. When she got home, Si Wang was watching a horror movie, his eyes full of disappointment. He may have been hard to read sometimes, but she knew him well enough to realize that this had not been a fun birthday.

Three years later in winter.

Rain blurred the view out the windows as He Qingying took her son to do grave-sweeping. The car passed Nanming Road. Si Wang closed his eyes and didn't open them again until after they left the area.

This was the grave of Si Wang's paternal grandparents. Quiet streams and robust pines enclosed the area. The names of the dead were written in black paint and the names of the living were in red. Si Wang's name was in red, as was Si Mingyuan's, the oldest son. He Qingying laid out their offerings at the gravesite. They knelt and then burned incense for their ancestral spirits to enjoy.

An hour later, they arrived at another cemetery. She bought some joss paper and had Si Wang hold a bouquet. They found the worn-looking grave in the crowded cemetery, where there was a photo of an elderly couple.

"Bow to your maternal grandparents."

Si Wang properly bowed three times. He and his mom burned joss paper until the smoke hurt their eyes.

It started snowing on their way home.

"Mom, where do you think Dad went?"

"I don't know."

Her frosty answer made it sound like she was talking about some irrelevant dead person.

CHAPTER 36

Yi Yu first saw Si Wang when she was in Section 2 of ninth grade at May First Junior High. It was late fall 2007.

She walked alone past the coal cinder track and noticed the boy in the sandbox, carefully building a castle and mumbling like a crazy person. Yi Yu paced around him until he turned to look at her.

"What do you want?" he said.

"This is my turf." The fifteen-year-old girl had a beautiful voice, but she was sounding rude on purpose.

"Why? This is for everyone to use."

That's when she slapped him. The twelve-year-old boy hadn't gone through puberty yet, making him scrawny like a monkey. He fell and ate a mouthful of sand. She was bigger and much taller, and he was no match for her. So he ran.

Yi Yu always wore blue sweatpants, a white school jacket, and black running shoes. No one had seen her in a skirt, not even anything bright. She hardly seemed feminine. She was almost 170 centimeters tall, her hair as short as a guy's. Her eyes were large and bright. She didn't play with girls, or boys. Everyone treated her like an ogre. None of the boys liked her, especially since she frequently beat up the younger ones. Some said she was a lesbian.

But she didn't like girls, either. Her grades were great—she always ranked number one on the end-of-semester tests. She was as good at history as she was at calligraphy. Her skills seemed to show decades of experience, enough to compare to master calligraphers. The school principal actually hung one of her pieces at home. To the English teacher, she once recited Yeats's "When You Are Old." She remembered every word and pronounced it perfectly, though she'd never been abroad.

One day after school, Yi Yu ducked into a small alley and checked behind her to watch the boy from the sandbox. He'd been following her. Two thugs jumped out, but their target was the boy. They backed him into a corner and were about to rob him when he screamed for help.

The passing grown-ups rushed away, pretending they didn't see anything.

Yi Yu ran back and hit one of the thugs. They were useless and couldn't retaliate. Each of them took a few blows and ran off.

"You're amazing," Si Wang said.

"It's nothing." She brusquely patted her hands like she was flexing. "Hey, why were you following me? I can beat you up."

"Because you're a weird person." The boy didn't seem scared. He puffed up his chest like a man. "Yi Yu, I saw how on your history exam you wrote in traditional Chinese."

"I've always liked to write that way. The teachers don't care. What does it matter to you?"

"Your handwriting is gorgeous. Not like a girl's." Then he got to the point. "Can I be your friend?"

Surprised, Yi Yu looked at him solemnly and spoke like a teacher. "Classmate, are you joking?"

"I'm like you."

"What?"

"I'm as lonely as you are."

The boy seemed as cool as a grown-up.

"I don't understand. But we can be friends," she said.

"I'm Si Wang, Si as in 'general,' Wang as in 'lookout.'"

"OK, I'll call you Younger Brother."

The following year, the 2008 Beijing Olympic theme song played all over the city. "Beijing welcomes you . . ."

Yi Yu was in the second semester of the ninth grade. She was two months away from the high school entrance exams, but she didn't study at all. She still ran around like a boy all day long. She carried around *Crime and Punishment* and *My Name Is Red*. The teachers didn't demand anything of her because they were sure she'd make it into an elite high school. If she hadn't been so odd—and wasn't a member of the Communist Youth League— they would have sponsored her for early admission.

Thirteen-year-old Si Wang was 160 centimeters tall but still as skinny as ever. He often attracted thugs. Yi Yu became his protector, making sure no one bothered him on his way to and from school. She knew martial arts, though she'd had no training. Still, no one could best her. An old guru from the athletic society said it was as if she'd practiced with Huo Yuanjia, the martial arts master.

She and Si Wang discussed Chinese fiction and poetry, as well as the world's literary classics. Everything from *Les Misérables* to *The Red and the Black*, *The Gadfly*, and *Anna Karenina*—as well as Kafka, Borges, and Haruki Murakami. Yi Yu bragged that Mo Yan would win the Nobel Prize in Literature in four years.

One day on their way home from school, they passed an Alexander Pushkin statue in a garden. Yi Yu stopped and said a bunch of Russian. Si Wang didn't understand a word.

She explained, "This poem is called "Should This Life Sometime Deceive You."

"Yi Yu, where did you learn Russian?"

"That's a secret."

"Fine, but I have secrets, too. How about we share?"

"No."

The wind rustled her short hair. Her manly gaze hid some glamour.

Si Wang recognized the Changde Apartments building. He whispered, "Hey, did you know Eileen Chang lived here? She met and married Hu Lancheng here."

"Pfft!" Yi Yu smirked at him. She slung her book bag over her shoulder and looked at one of the terraces. "Hu Lancheng? That bastard!" She actually spit on the ground.

Si Wang backed up a step. "Why are you so upset?"

After a pause, she stroked the address on the doorway. "Actually, I used to come here when it was called the Eddington Apartments."

She grabbed Si Wang's hand and charged into the dark hallway. Her hand was cold like a corpse's. She seemed to know every step. They arrived at a door.

"It was here," Yi Yu said. "Eileen Chang lived here for years. There were so many books—Chinese books, foreign books, art books from Europe, plus a cheap sofa and a rattan lounge chair. That famous photo of hers was from that chair. The place wasn't too messy. Sometimes after she got paid a lot for one of her books, maids came. Should I go on?"

An old man's voice rang out. "Who is it? Kids shouldn't play here!"

"Let's go!"

They ran downstairs and back out to the street. It was getting dark.

"I think I understand now." Si Wang breathed heavily and stared at her eyes. "You're definitely extraordinary!"

Yi Yu bought two cups of bubble tea at a street cart. Drinking in big gulps, she said, "'I'm not wary of hurting myself. I don't want to pretend. Life used to be carefree, I don't want to mislead you. Things are different now, so many are hurt and gone. There is no use crying, the old vanguard is helping the new regime.' I like Yu Dafu the most out of all the poets from back then. He was a real man. Although his marriage to Wang Yingxia was never as wonderful and romantic as people thought."

"You've met him?"

Yi Yu laughed like a man. "I've drunk, fought, and chased girls with him. You believe me?"

As expected, Yi Yu's test grades came out, and she was number one. She got into the elite Nanming High.

When they said good-bye to one another, Si Wang said, "We'll see each other again."

CHAPTER 37

Mid-July, 2009. Zhong Yuan, Chinese Halloween.

The city didn't look like it was celebrating the holiday. Few pedestrians knew of Zhong Yuan. She was an exception. She still looked young. Most would have guessed her age incorrectly. She went into the subway from the Yaxin Square stop. Dressed in a long white skirt, her slim ankles showing, she walked in black flats. Long dark hair, light makeup, a bit of color on her lips, a simple purse.

She was Ouyang Xiaozhi.

A pair of eyes from the nearby escalator watched her as he got closer. The boy was leaving the station via the escalator, and Xiaozhi was going into the station. A wind gust lifted her long silky hair and brushed it against the boy's hand as they passed each other on the escalator.

He was fourteen or fifteen years old; good-looking, tall.

Was it him? She couldn't resist looking back. The boy had turned around and was almost stumbling in his haste to reach her. Xiaozhi rushed forward to avoid him, weaving through the throngs of people. A train entered the station, and she quickly ducked inside.

He was still pushing forward, shoving people to make way. The exiting passengers were his roadblocks, and their curses rang out behind him. A man hit him in the back, angry about being pushed, and the boy lost his balance and fell.

"Wait," he yelled watching her disappear into the crowded subway car. Back on his feet, he rushed for the doors, but they closed just as he got there.

As the train pulled away he pounded on the glass like a crazy man, chasing after her for more than ten meters until he was finally left behind. Some subway workers stopped him. Their large hands held him down, pressing his face against the cold ground.

"Ouyang Xiaozhi."

She'd seen him pound on the train's window and had wanted him to be careful. But now she was deep inside the tunnel. She couldn't hear her name being called, but she knew—it was him.

Rush hour, summer. A rampant sweaty odor. A ghost seemed to be hiding behind every person. Today was their holiday, Zhong Yuan—*ullambana* in Sanskrit—meaning "saving those who were upside down."

She left the subway half an hour later and took a bus to Nanming Road.

Various new buildings had long ago replaced the dilapidated factory and forest. Giant billboards lined the roads, advertising Carrefour and Printemps. Instead of domestic trucks and bicycles, imported cars clogged the road. The bus stop was still in the same place, though the original sign had been replaced by an ad for *Twilight*. Nanming High sat across from the bus stop, unchanged in the past fourteen years. Many brass plaques adorned the school's entrance, including some new awards from the Education Bureau. The convenience store was gone, replaced by an expensive apartment complex.

She stood across the street, separated by traffic. Students came out now and again, likely on their summer break. Boys and girls played and flirted. Soon they would be saying good-bye to one another.

Ouyang Xiaozhi observed from afar. Suddenly, she noticed a face that wasn't youthful like the others—it looked jaded, and she was awestruck.

Zhang Mingson: His eyes suggested he had the potential for being a psychopathic killer.

He carried a briefcase. In his early forties, his hair was neat. He had a well-trimmed beard, straight back, and purposeful eyes. As he left the school, students all nodded in respect. It appeared that he was worshipped by students. He was the most well-known math teacher in the district. He charged high fees to tutor students at home, and many were willing to pay. Ouyang Xiaozhi figured that his prices must have quadrupled by now. She watched him get into a black Datsun Bluebird and drive away.

She walked ahead for a few hundred meters and found an overgrown path, the path leading into the Demon Girl Zone.

One of the construction projects had blocked the tall chimney. There was a temporary wall, but the gates were left open. The factory ruins looked more run-down than before. She touched the factory walls; the rough concrete and exposed bricks felt like decaying skin and flesh. She tiptoed into the factory, stepping on trash. The smell of shit crept out from the dark corners, likely from migrant workers and the homeless. She got to the underground entrance, walked down, and entered Hell.

As soon as she took one step, an icy sensation traveled from her toes to the top of her head. She sprang back as if electrocuted, taking deep breaths against the wall. When anyone entered the Demon Girl Zone, a knife would pierce that person's heart.

She felt a pain in her heart for no apparent reason, and she had to kneel down and wait it out, sweating profusely.

In 1988, when she was just eleven, she had been here and faced that round hatch door.

Twenty years later, the color of that memory had not faded in the least.

It had been noon and a few Nanming High guys, one of whom had a birthmark on his face, had been hanging out. They crossed the road in front of the school and ate lunch in the shade of the trees on the perimeter of the forest. A starving girl followed them. She had not had meat for days. She drooled as she stole a drumstick from one of the lunchboxes.

She fled deeper into the woods, eating the chicken as she ran. The boys gave chase and finally caught up to her in the abandoned factory. All the girl had to show was the leftover chicken bone.

They punished the thief by locking her inside the Demon Girl Zone.

Endless blackness. Desperately, she pounded on the hatch door, hoping someone would hear. Maybe the boy with the birthmark would take pity on her and let her out?

She was locked inside a grave.

Hoarse from shouting, she passed out by the door. Time was interminable. In the deathly quiet, she didn't know how much time had passed. Was it night or day? Had anyone noticed she was gone? Would anyone look for her? She was so thirsty that her throat burned.

A blinding light crashed into the dark basement. She cowered and shielded her eyes with her hands, having no idea what she'd have to face next.

She saw just a blurry shadow at first; she was hardly able to open her eyes in the light. A man approached and stroked her dirty, knotted hair. She faintly made out his eyes when he lowered the flashlight; they were like dim candles and didn't reveal his thoughts. His face was very pale, his features strong.

"There really is a little girl here."

She couldn't summon a reply.

"Are you OK? Are you mute?"

She shook her head.

"You've been down here for two days. Poor thing, come with me!"

He tried to help her stand, but she had no strength. He squatted to lift her and carried her out of the dark factory. It was midnight. Stars lined the breezy sky, and the factory still puffed out some smoke, like it was burning a pile of bones.

"Don't be afraid. I go to Nanming High. I'm a senior in Section 2."

She used her last bit of strength to hold on to him. The young man's back was cold, but his heart beat quickly. His neck smelled clean, and a thick fuzz grew behind his ears. Her head drooped against his cheek, the only warm part of his body. She wanted to keep going like this forever, even if it meant starving to death.

He mumbled as he walked, knowing the trees would never whisper a word of what was said. "Lu Zhongyue said they locked a little girl in the Demon Girl Zone because she stole his drumstick. I asked if they'd let her go, and they said they all forgot. Didn't they know you could have died? What were they thinking? If I hadn't broken in, they would have been murderers!"

He walked along Nanming Road to some illegal huts. He knocked on a homeless guy's place to get some food and water. Once he saw that she would recover, he ducked into the night, probably in a rush to get back to school.

She would never forget his face.

Now it was 2009 and she'd returned to the devastated Demon Girl Zone. For all that had changed around it, time remained frozen here. Noises like cries filled her head. Were those her cries from 1988? Or those of Shen Ming's ghost?

There was also a putrid smell. Ouyang Xiaozhi charged down until she got to the hatch door.

The door wasn't shut.

A man's shadow came at her.

She screamed as the shadow collided with her—a collision of bones. She fell backward and her head hit the cold wall. She tried to catch the shadow's arm but was pushed away.

The shadow disappeared as quickly as it had appeared.

Her shoulders and head hurt so much that she thought she might have a concussion. She struggled to get up but stumbled. She'd never be able to catch up.

Out of nowhere, she smelled thick cigarette smoke.

She remembered her flashlight and shined it on the Hell-like space. It was only about twenty square meters, with dirty water on the ground. The same water from fourteen years ago? Some odd lettering had been carved onto the wall, saying something that looked like "Tian Xiaomai."

A sharp pain radiated along her back. She swore she'd return to the Demon Girl Zone one day.

Back outside, the sun was setting. She took a deep breath and felt reborn. The monster-like factory, the shaky chimneys, the tall buildings being built—it was like seeing past lives and the present.

Who was hiding in the Demon Girl Zone?

CHAPTER 38

Christmas 2009.

Shen Yuanchao wore a black coat, his white hair messy from the wind. Most of his whiskers were white, too. He stubbornly looked up at a window. Three years ago, he'd been in this exact same spot.

A young man walked in front of him. He was tall, thin, and pale with a quiet, loose expression, suggesting he'd attract a lot of attention from female admirers. It was curious that he wasn't at a Christmas party.

"Who are you looking for?"

The old prosecutor was startled out of his thoughts. He stepped back and carefully examined the boy who'd asked the question. He recognized the face. "Oh, you're Huang Hai's son?"

"Yes, did you need to see him?" said Si Wang, now fourteen.

Puberty was in full swing, and he had the whiskers and deeper voice to prove it. His appetite had doubled and he'd grown almost as tall as his mom. In a few years he'd be as tall as Huang Hai.

"He didn't answer my call. Is he home?"

"I'll take you up."

Si Wang took Shen Yuanchao to the apartment and pressed the doorbell with familiarity. Huang Hai opened the door, his groggy face making it obvious he'd been asleep thanks to a rare day off. He saw the young man first and hugged him as if he was his son, then he looked at Shen Yuanchao.

"Why'd you bring him?" The policeman's face changed, and he looked at the prosecutor with confusion.

"I retired early. I wanted to have a chat."

Huang Hai ushered his visitors inside and uttered, "Kid, did he do anything to you?"

"No. Hear him out."

Shen Yuanchao took out a small gift box from inside his jacket. "Merry Christmas!" This was the first Christmas gift he'd ever given.

Si Wang thanked him, accepting the gift for Huang Hai without reservation.

"What are you doing?" Huang Hai felt the urge to stop the boy, but he'd already unwrapped the gift, a hardcover edition of Hemingway's *The Old Man and the Sea.*

"I couldn't decide what to get you. I've been reading this lately," Shen Yuanchao said. "It's suited my mood. I guess I'm like that old man, stubborn and refusing to believe in fate."

"Hemingway?" Huang Hai frowned. "I think I've heard of him."

Si Wang poked him lightly. "It's a great book. I've read it. Accept it."

"Fine." Huang Hai took the gift and placed it on a dresser and turned to his unexpected guest. "Mr. Shen, please believe me, the police will find the killer. Don't do anything stupid."

"Are you talking about the math teacher Zhang Mingsong? The guy bought a car six months ago. It's harder to follow him now, but I won't give up."

He noticed there was a copy of *The Da Vinci Code* on Huang Hai's bookshelf. He was certain that Shen Ming had been killed by a psychopath obsessed with human sacrifices; only knowing the killer's knowledge and psyche would help catch him. Shen Yuanchao used to love reading, going so far as to earn a bachelor's degree in literature. But he'd only read world classics like *Anna Karenina* and books by Lu Xu, Mao Dun, and Ba Jin. He knew nothing about religions and iconography. That's why he researched *The Da Vinci Code*. In his theory, because the book had sold sixty million copies, at least 1 percent of the population were potential killers.

Everyone thought he'd lost it, but he was committed to his quest.

"Mr. Huang, please don't misunderstand me. I'm just here to thank you. I want to thank you on Shen Ming's behalf, for the years you spent looking for my son's killer!"

Si Wang piped up. "The killer will be caught."

"Quiet," Hang Hai said. "What do you know about such grown-up business?"

Shen Yuanchao pointed to the copy of *The Da Vinci Code*. "This book would be great for your son to read, too. Good-bye."

Shen Yuanchao was still thinking of the boy's face and his flickering eyes; were they sending a message?

Shen Yuanchao returned home late, still thinking of Huang Hai's son and his flickering eyes. Had they been sending him a message? His daughter had waited up. She was a beautiful fourteen-year-old who looked older than her age. For some reason she'd turned down all the invitations she'd received to Christmas parties.

She'd just had her birthday a few days ago, which was also the anniversary of her mother's death.

Shen Yuanchao first found out about his wife's pregnancy on June 17, 1995. It was the last time he saw Shen Ming.

He remembered the feast his wife had made for his twenty-five-year-old illegitimate son that day. He knew his son was in trouble, but he did nothing to help him. Shen Yuanchao was more worried about who knew of their relationship. He was afraid if the news got around, his job as a prosecutor would be jeopardized.

Now, he regretted his behavior on that day. The only consolation was that he'd actually hugged his son before they parted ways.

Neither of them could have known that parting would last forever.

When he came back after seeing his son out, his wife told him, "Yuanchao, I'm pregnant."

He didn't know what to do. They'd been married for more than a decade, but doctors had said his wife couldn't conceive. He never blamed her; he just became a workaholic. He spent his days catching corrupt criminals, and rarely spent time at home. He was grateful that his wife tolerated him, especially about the illegitimate son.

But when she did get pregnant, his wife wanted to keep the baby, even though it was high risk.

Five days later, Huang Hai came around with his stern face and told him that Shen Ming had been murdered.

He expressed no emotions. He just nodded and provided what information he knew. He was a cold-blooded man facing his problems. He returned to work and acted normal; only late at night, when he was alone, did he kneel down and sob.

Six months later, his daughter was born. His wife died of a hemorrhage during childbirth.

Holding her lifeless body he couldn't help but think of the devastating losses he'd been made to suffer that year. Did any man have a worse fate?

He named his daughter Shen Min.

He was a middle-aged widower whose duty it was to raise his daughter and find his son's killer.

When it was late, after his daughter went to bed, he was always exhausted but couldn't sleep. He often thought of Xiao Qian, Shen Ming's mother.

Shen Yuanchao met her when he was twenty. Xiao Qian was a maid's daughter who'd dropped out of school after only a few years. She sold food on the street, and he bought rice cakes from her for breakfast. As the rice cakes turned golden in the wok, he watched her beautiful face. Every time she blinked, her big eyes made his heart flutter.

That summer, he took her fishing in Suzhou River. He took her to shows at Daguangming Theatre, and they kissed on park benches in People's Park . . . which led to Shen Ming.

A few months before Shen Ming was born, Shen Yuanchao left the city to go to the Great Northern Wilderness as one of the educated youth. There by the border of China and Russia, he couldn't receive letters or calls. He was stuck in the deep snow and faced the Russian soldiers across from the river daily. He didn't know he had a son until he visited home the following year.

He accepted his son as soon as he held him, but he couldn't marry Xiao Qian, and he couldn't let the secret get out. If it did, he'd lose his chance to join the Communist Party. So he abandoned his girlfriend and their son and returned to the Great Northern Wilderness.

Seven years later, the esteemed Party member Shen Yuanchao was given the chance to return to the city. He returned to his parents' side like a released prisoner and was awarded the job at the procuratorate.

Xiao Qian was dead by then. In order to support her son, she'd married the bastard who poisoned her.

Shen Yuanchao came to realize that his son was looking more like him all the time. The boy's name was changed to Shen Ming, but they had to keep their secret in order for Shen Yuanchao to keep his position at the procuratorate. Once a month, he visited his son and gave the boy's grandmother twenty yuan—half his earnings back then. The money he gave increased every year until Shen Ming went to college.

Eventually, he was able to achieve his dream and become a People's Prosecutor. The woman he married was from a more respectable background. And he became the incorruptible Prosecutor Shen.

Within a year of their wedding, his wife found out about Shen Ming. He admitted to his mistake and was prepared for a divorce. But after crying for a bit, she never mentioned it again. When she found out she was unable to conceive, she wanted to meet Shen Ming—she even wanted him to move in. But Shen Yuanchao refused. He was afraid of people finding out.

Now his daughter was in the eighth grade.

Shen Ming had been dead for fourteen years. Shen Yuanchao often fantasized about seeing him again, but he had no idea what he'd say if he did.

If Shen Ming had another life, would he still remember his so-called father?

CHAPTER 39

Late fall 2010.

It was the weekend. Yi Yu came looking for Si Wang. She still wore a blue tracksuit and still kept her hair short like a man. Si Wang came downstairs; he was taller than her now.

"Wow, you have whiskers! You're looking more and more grown-up."

She punched him in the chest, but he was prepared to take the blow.

Yi Yu had been at Nanming High for two years. She still scored best on all of the tests, but she didn't kiss up to the principal. The teachers weren't nice to her, either. The only thing she liked about the school was going to the library. Once she snuck into the attic and found a stash of old books. She'd heard the story of how a student had been poisoned with oleander juice and the killer was never found. Her math teacher was Zhang Mingsong. She noticed that he read bizarre books about iconography and history; was obsessed with American, European, and Japanese suspense novels; and was a rabid fan of zombie movies.

Si Wang asked her to help him find someone: Lu Zhongyue. He showed her the police photo and shared what he knew.

"This guy killed at least two people," she said. "He would be long gone by now. Why would he hang around here?"

"It's what my gut tells me."

He was serious, so Yi Yu promised to help. "Can you come with me?" she asked.

The two rode bicycles down a secluded path. There was a brick wall with a fence. An old-style house could be seen through the black iron gate. They locked up their bicycles and pressed the doorbell. The door opened.

The small yard was full of plants, and golden leaves fell from everywhere like rain. The two-story house was a bit dilapidated, but the staircase and sculptures in the entryway indicated previous glamour.

"What is this place?"

Yi Yu didn't reply. They walked into a cold, damp living room with mosaic tiles on the floor and peeling walls—though it wasn't dusty and there weren't any cobwebs. A corridor smelled like dried orange peels. A stream of light poured out of a half-open door. They tiptoed inside. It was a room with three floor-to-ceiling bookshelves packed with very old books.

They found a woman in there, too. Though it was hard to think of her as a woman, just like it was hard to think of Yi Yu as a woman.

She was wrapped up in a thick scarf. Her skin was paler than most and lined with deep wrinkles. Her droopy eyes still hinted at previous beauty. Her teeth were all gone, her mouth shrunken. It was hard to tell her age, but she was definitely very old.

Yi Yu was familiar with the place, and the old lady treated her casually. But Si Wang's presence did surprise her. Her murky gaze briefly flickered.

"Don't be afraid." Yi Yu went behind the old lady to massage her shoulders. "He's my good buddy. We went to the same junior high."

"How are you? I'm Si Wang, Si as in 'general,' Wang as in 'lookout.' I'm in ninth grade now."

"Si Wang—what a great name. You can call me Miss Cao."

She spoke classic Mandarin. But her speech was garbled from her lack of teeth, and her voice was hoarse. She spoke very slowly, as if she was pulling the words out of a deep well.

"Finally, Yi Yu, you have a friend now. This is wonderful, I'm very happy for you."

Yi Yu kept massaging the old lady as she said, "I hope you like him, too. He may seem dumb, but he actually knows a lot!"

The old lady lifted a shaky twig-like hand to touch Yi Yu's hand. The two hands were on top of one another; one was about to pass on, the other was youthful, but the moment they touched, they seemed to belong to the same person.

"Child, you look like you have stories," Miss Cao said.

The old lady turned to look at Si Wang. There was something witch-like about her. She could have been two hundred years old.

"No—no, I don't."

"Any friend of Yi Yu's would have stories. I'm almost ninety years old—I've heard them all."

"We don't need to put him on the spot." Yi Yu picked up an antique-looking wooden comb to brush Miss Cao's white hair. She said a long string of French. The old lady replied. They looked like a great-granddaughter with her great-grandmother, but they sounded like good friends.

Miss Cao closed her eyes, clearly enjoying having her hair brushed. "All these years, you've always come this time every week to comb my hair. When I die, you'll be combing someone else's hair."

"Don't worry, you'll live for another twenty years at least. I'll be old then, too."

This made Miss Cao smile. She said to Si Wang, "Child, Yi Yu is a good person. Don't be alarmed by her. Treat her as a real friend. She'll help you with any problems you have."

"OK, Miss Cao, this will be our secret."

"There are no secrets." She sounded like a sage mountain telling Si Wang that he was just a child who hadn't even found the path yet.

Yi Yu started boiling water and organized some boxes of medicine. She unpacked some vegetables and prepared a very good mostly vegetarian meal.

"Eat." As usual, she bossed around Si Wang.

Yi Yu, Si Wang, and Miss Cao sat down like a family in a restaurant. An old painting hung behind them.

The old lady picked up her chopsticks. "Aye, my teeth are bad now. I really miss the Ba Bao Spicy Paste from Rongshun Restaurant."

After eating, Yi Yu got up and said, "We have to go now. Please be careful here on your own."

"Don't worry, I'll not die here by myself."

"Don't say such nonsense." Yi Yu took the old lady's hand and held it like she never wanted to let go.

"Time to go you two." Miss Cao turned to Si Wang. "Child, when water from the pipes runs into the ocean and is refiltered, it is not the same water that went past your hand."

"Oh?"

"You'll understand one day."

They walked out of the house and into the night. As soon as they got back on their bicycles, it started raining.

"Should we go back in and wait out the storm?"

"We've left already—let's not bother her."

The fifteen-year-old boy and the eighteen-year-old girl quietly sat on their bikes under the shadows of the fence. Random raindrops fell and chilled their cheeks like needles.

"So you used to be a man?" Si Wang asked, breaking the silence.

"She was the last woman who ever mattered to me." Yi Yu sounded like an old man just then.

"You didn't answer my question."

"Fine, we're best friends. I don't want to lie to you. I still remember what happened in my previous life. But my former life was too long, so I was so happy to die and be set free."

Si Wang looked back at the trees inside the fence. "You're lucky she's still alive and you can see her."

"I had many women in my past life. Everyone left me. I was like Don Quixote. Only she was left."

"Was she your wife?"

"I never wanted that, except when I wanted just that."

"I don't understand."

Yi Yu laughed bitterly at the sky, sounding especially maudlin. "You'll understand in another twenty years. Men and women, parting and separation, waiting and the end of waiting. It is too late. Soon after we met, I was sent into the desert of the Tsaidam Basin. We were apart for thirty years. When I got back, I was almost too old to walk."

"So it was a tragedy."

"Every life is a tragedy."

Yi Yu reached out to feel the raindrops on her hand. She put on her hat and rode out of the lane.

The street was quiet. The wheels rolled over the golden ginkgo leaves. The street sign read Serenity Road.

Si Wang followed her and yelled, "Do you know this street well?"

"I spent the last twenty years of my previous life on this block."

"With Miss Cao?"

"No, she lived on the east end, and I lived on the west end. There were four hundred meters between us. I'll show you."

One minute later, they rode up to a big mansion. The three-story building had lights on; a lot of people lived there. There was a half window by the ground, probably for the basement.

"I lived on the first floor." Yi Yu pointed to the spot right in front of her. Sounds from a soap opera came from a TV inside.

Si Wang looked at the basement window. "Do you still have any family from your past life?"

"How would I know?" She sighed from her bicycle. "Maybe none from this lifetime, either."

"Endless traveling toward a far land, countless tents with lights at night. Wind howled, snow fell, why did my homeland never make such noise?"

"Nalan Xingde's 'Eternal Longing'? What made you think of that poem?"

He didn't answer. When he brought his bicycle around, he noticed a row of houses across the street. They stood ominously in the rainy night. Roof tiles were missing, the paint was peeling, and weeds grew out of the windows.

Yi Yu came up right behind him and said, "A murder happened there. It was years ago. No one could figure out who owned the house, so it's been empty since then."

"A murder?"

"Let me think. I remember stuff from my youth easily but not so much from later. Yes, it was 1983, also a rainy fall night. The owner of the house was a well-known translator who hung himself in the late seventies. The house was taken over by a Cultural Revolution rebel faction leader who died in 1983 when his throat was slashed by broken glass. There was lots of speculation that the ghost of the translator had killed him. Some said it was a revenge killing by his victims' family members. The police investigated for a long time and never found anything."

Si Wang pushed his bicycle up the stairs. He touched the building all over, from the rusty iron doors to the rotten wooden mailbox and drooping door sign.

Number 19 Serenity Road.

Yi Yu had a sensation that something in this house related to her friend.

Si Wang's hand fell away as if electrocuted. He quickly rode away from Serenity Road.

The rain came down harder, but Yi Yu followed him until they got to the locust tree outside his house.

"Go home," Si Wang shouted.

"Wait, I have something to tell you."

He ducked inside the doorway and nervously looked around. Was he worried about being seen by neighbors?

"Si Wang, remember how you asked me to look for Lu Zhongyue? You were right! There's a tiny DVD store on Nanming Road, right by the new shops. It was closed the first few times I went there. But one time it was open. It only sells old movies like Hong Kong action movies, romantic comedies from the eighties, and spy dramas from Russia and Eastern Europe. The store owner is just some guy. I can't tell you anything special about him. He has a face that would get lost in a crowd. But he had a light birthmark on his forehead. I got a copy of *Battle of Moscow*. He didn't even count my money, just gave me change. He smoked nonstop. He had at least two cigarettes in just a few minutes, there was a huge ashtray full of cigarette butts."

In the cold night, Si Wang couldn't help sneezing.

Yi Yu kept talking. "Most people get music and movies online now, so no one else was in the store. I have no idea how it stays open. One night when it was raining hard, I was walking around by myself. You know that guys aren't even as brave as I am. There was no one on Nanming Road, but I saw someone coming out of the store. He had a big umbrella and was walking toward the old factory. I followed him. The rain helped hide me. It was the owner of the store. He knew the place well and didn't get lost. He got to the Demon Girl Zone and went underground. I stayed outside for at least an hour. He never showed up again. It was like he time-traveled to Qing dynasty. I was really hungry and tired, so I finally left."

"Did he see you?"

"I don't think so." Yi Yu ducked into the shadows. "I know the art of invisibility."

CHAPTER 40

Throughout 2010, Huang Hai had felt cursed.

He stood in line for two hours for IMAX *Avatar* tickets during Chinese New Year.

He'd asked He Qingying to the movies. He had always been calm and collected dealing with criminals, but he stuttered with her. Luckily his biggest worry didn't come to pass—she never mentioned Si Wang. She must not have told him about the date.

When he held her hand, she resisted a bit before giving in. Her hand was cold, like touching a corpse's. They chatted amicably at first but then stopped. They didn't look into each other's eyes, but their shoulders inched closer and closer.

For the past three years, Huang Hai had helped with He Qingying's bookstore. He looked in on her daily. If anything went wrong at her house, he was the first one there. He even fixed her television.

Si Wang's relationship with him became strained, however.

After the Chinese New Year, he took Si Wang to the Muslim temple. Someone was selling sliced fruitcake. He bought the boy a small piece and thrust it into his hand. Back in the car, he said, "I need to ask you something."

"A new case?"

"No, all recent cases are solved. I wanted to ask you . . ." Huang Hai didn't know how to say what he wanted to say so he just spit it out. "Si Wang, I don't know when your dad will be back. Would you be OK with me being your dad?"

The boy hit him and jumped out of the police car. He spit out the half-chewed fruitcake and ran toward the Suzhou River.

It was so cold.

Huang Hai didn't see He Qingying alone after that.

Fall arrived.

Sunday. Light rain fell. The endless high-rises on Nanming Road made it hard to think of the murders fifteen years ago, even though Nanming High hadn't really changed.

"Kid, who told you there was anything?" Huang Hai gripped the steering wheel. Wipers swept away the water. A long road stretched ahead of them, making it seem as though they were heading toward a paranormal dimension.

"A secret informant. I have to protect her identity." Si Wang sat in the front passenger seat. "Trust me, I'm not a normal person. You know what I mean."

They were in an unmarked police car. Huang Hai had driven back yesterday after catching a murderer out of town. He'd only slept for three hours before Si Wang knocked on his door, claiming to know where Lu Zhongyue was. But he didn't share any further details.

"Your not being normal only makes sense to me."

The car stopped in front of the nameless DVD store. Tucked between a foot-massage place and a hair salon, it would be easy to miss if not for the movie poster for Leslie Cheung's *Happy Together*.

The rain fell harder.

Huang Hai wore plain clothes. He told Si Wang to stay in the car, no matter what happened. He knocked on the door and pushed inside.

The thick cigarette smoke suffocated him, making the lifelong chain-smoker cough. He held his breath to scan the store: He saw old Hong Kong movies on the right-hand side, and on the opposite side were posters for Japanese movies introduced to China in the eighties. The covers featured stars like Ken Takakura, Komaki Kurihara, and Tomokazu Miura.

Huang Hai watched the only other man in the store turn around slowly.

"Lu Zhongyue?"

The man escaped through the back door.

Huang Hai crouched and took out his QSZ92 handgun. He kicked open the back door. The rain was still coming down hard. He ran out, mud flying everywhere. Huang Hai chased the man. It was impossible to see his face clearly; even his back was blurry.

In his low, booming voice, Huang Hai ordered the suspect to stop.

The man ran into a construction site.

Frantic footsteps echoed in the dark corridors. He followed the man to the sixth floor while watching out for exposed steel bars. He finally caught sight of the man again, and the guy actually jumped out of an unfinished window.

There was another building across from the window. Huang Hai didn't hesitate to jump, either.

"Stop!"

Where did the noise come from? The fifteen-year-old's voice was hoarse, and swallowed by the rushing rain.

Huang Hai didn't make it. The forty-eight-year-old man disappeared into the space between the two buildings.

It was a fifteen-meter free fall. A twisted body lay on top of a muddy construction site.

Si Wang screamed and ran down to his friend.

The QSZ92 fell a few meters away.

Si Wang fell upon the man. All of his limbs were broken. His hands were bent behind him like a puppet with broken strings. He lifted up Huang Hai's head, which was covered with rain, blood, and mud. He was still alive.

Si Wang shook the man's head and slapped his face. "Don't die! Hold on! An ambulance will get here soon!"

The kid hadn't even called 1-1-0 yet.

Huang Hai was fading; his eyes were half-closed, blood spurted out.

"Huang Zhiliang—"

"I'm here," Si Wang cried, shouting so as to be heard over the din of the rain. "Dad, I'm here."

Si Wang or Huang Zhiliang, what was the difference?

The boy clutched Huang Hai's hand, trying to pass on his own warmth. He pressed his ear to Huang Hai's mouth. He heard some faint sounds.

Huang Hai breathed out the boy's name. His eyes were open under the steel-gray sky as the rain washed out his bloody eyes.

Just before dying, Huang Hai faintly saw the fifteen-year-old boy trying to give him CPR. Si Wang swallowed the man's blood. Burning tears fell on his face and blended with the thick rain.

Huang Hai's soul floated up and he saw his broken body, and the sobbing teenager.

Si Wang wiped away his tears. He looked calmly cruel in the falling rain.

CHAPTER 41

Seven days later.

Huang Hai's martyr ceremony was held in the biggest hall at the funeral home. All city officials attended. This was the second line-of-duty death of a police officer that month. He Qingying wore a dark suit and held a bunch of white chrysanthemums, tears swirling in her eyes. She clutched her son's hand and stayed in the back of the crowd. Some of Huang Hai's colleagues had met her. They all tried to comfort her, treating her as the widow.

The police chief finished his long-winded eulogy, and somber music played. Si Wang held on to his mom and they bowed together. Her hand was frozen. She could hear her son say, "Mom, I shouldn't have, I shouldn't have."

"Enough! Wang Er." Her whole body shook. "It's not what you think."

The mother and son straightened. Along with the rest of the mourners, they said good-bye to Huang Hai for the last time.

His body was draped with a flag. Dressed in a perfectly pressed uniform, his hands and feet had been expertly reconstructed. It was impossible to tell that there had been numerous bone fractures.

He Qingying reached out to touch the cold glass, as though touching his face. He'd passed away in Si Wang's arms seven days ago.

The physical intimacy she'd shared with this man had been limited to touches on the forehead and nose. She'd never experienced an iota of desire during the time she spent with the policeman—just a warmth, like a rebirth.

Si Wang never shed a tear.

She took her son's hand and started to leave the hall. She turned to see the mass of policemen. She could feel a pair of eyes staring at her but couldn't see him, or her.

Every policeman at the funeral swore they would catch the criminal to appease Huang Hai's soul.

There were still no clues.

The police repeatedly searched the DVD store. They extracted DNA samples from the cigarette butts. The landlord also gave them a copy of the suspect's identification card. There was no such person in the system. The store hardly had any customers, and the owner rarely socialized, so very few people remembered his face. The police managed to get a portrait of him from the landlord's descriptions.

They showed the illustration to Si Wang and He Qingying.

Si Wang was sure it was Lu Zhongyue, especially because of the birthmark on the forehead. He'd been Lu Zhongyue's adopted son and they shared a home for more than six months. He knew how to recognize the man.

He Qingying insisted that her son stay away from the investigation. She forbade the police to contact him. She even wrote a letter to the police chief, saying Huang Hai had died and she didn't want Si Wang to be next.

The tears she cried during those days were for Huang Hai, and also for her unruly son. She blamed him for his impudence and impulse, and she blamed him for Huang Hai's death.

He didn't dispute this belief and kept mumbling, "I got him killed."

Over the last six months, Si Wang had truly become a teenager. He started paying attention to his appearance, being very picky about what he wore and how he looked. Even if he just wore a school uniform, he'd check himself in the mirror. He'd also joined the Youth League.

He helped his mom open a Taobao online store called Demon Girl Zone. Bookselling had become harder and harder, but with both an online and a brick-and-mortar store, they could make ends meet. The Taobao store also sold textbooks, which generated most of their earnings. He Qingying tried hard to be a great online retailer, even asking customers to please give her a positive rating online. Every weekend, Si Wang would help his mom with customer service, packing, and sending for delivery.

Si Wang faced the high school entrance exams in another six months; he wanted to go to Nanming High.

He Qingying strongly opposed the idea. She didn't want him to board after all these years of just the two of them. Plus, the elite high school was known for its intense pressure. Students committing suicide was common these days. She was worried her quiet son wouldn't adjust, even with his genius intellect. She really wanted him to live a peaceful life. It was easier to apply to a technical secondary school or trade school. Jobs would be easy to find.

"Wang Er, are you going to listen to me?"

The room was dark. He Qingying's hair fell on her shoulders. She still looked much younger than her age. It was no wonder that male students sometimes gave her one hundred yuan to change so they could linger. Si Wang always stared at them and his mom would signal him to calm down.

He flipped over in bed and said to the wall, "Mom, why did you give me this name?"

"Didn't I already tell you? When you were in my belly, I looked out every day and thought I heard someone calling me. So I named you 'lookout,' Si Wang."

"People at school gave me a nickname. They call me Death."

He Qingying grabbed her son and stared at him. "Why?"

"Si Wang . . . siwang . . .*death*."

She covered his mouth. "We'll go to school tomorrow and tell the teacher that no one can call you this!"

"Mom, the nickname doesn't bother me. I like it."

"Why? Why would you?"

"I think I am like death. I haven't had maternal grandparents since birth. Dad went missing when I was in first grade. Who knows what happened to him. My paternal grandparents died when I was in third grade. I found a dead body in that jeep. Then I went to the Gu family and they died. I met Huang Hai; his home was a museum of death. Now I just saw him die. Are they all coincidences?"

He seemed so calm—like he was reading a lecture.

"Don't think that way. No matter what, I will protect you."

"Mom, I've grown up now. I should protect you."

"You'll always be a kid in my eyes."

"Don't all moms want their kids to get into good high schools? If I can get into Nanming, then why stop me? Didn't you name me look out so you could look out at success?"

He Qingying stroked her son's back, her voice soft as silk. "Believe what I say. You're an incredibly smart kid. You have many special secrets. But your dad is Si Mingyuan, and your mom is He Qingying. We were all born poor. This is our fate."

"I never minded us being poor."

"If I die, go look for a rich family."

"Don't die!"

Si Wang held her so tightly she thought she would suffocate.

CHAPTER 42

Three weeks later. It was both the coldest and shortest day of the year in the Northern Hemisphere.

The man looked no older than thirty. He had a tall, lean build and was handsome. His hair was on the longer side, especially for a cop. His eyebrows seemed permanently furrowed above his steely gaze. He rarely displayed any discernible facial expressions, but people liked to avoid making eye contact with him nonetheless. Having transferred to the precinct just three months ago, he hadn't known Huang Hai very well. They'd only met a handful of times. But the bureau chief assigned Huang Hai's old cases to him.

Six murders remained unsolved. Three were deaths from June 1995, fifteen years ago: Liu Man, a Nanming High student; Yan Li, the teaching director; Shen Ming, the one-time suspect and former teacher. There was also He Nian, Erya Education Group's executive, missing since 2002 and later found in 2004, rotting in a jeep; he'd been Shen Ming's college classmate. In 2006, Shen Ming's fiancée, Gu Qiusha, was killed, and her father, Gu Changlong, was killed by Lu Zhongyue. Lu Zhongyue was Shen Ming's high school classmate and had married Gu Qiusha after Shen's death.

Huang Hai died while chasing after Lu Zhongyue.

The new cop had also inherited a set of keys. He unlocked Huang Hai's apartment door. Someone must have been there recently. Wind howled and the room was as cold as a refrigerator.

The usually locked small room was open.

The cop could smell the scent of someone else being in the apartment. He took out his gun and crept to the doorway of the small room, aiming his weapon. Sometimes really daring and perverted criminals would break in to policemen's homes.

He saw a young man's face.

"It's you?" The man's voice was crisp and bright. He put away his gun, recognizing the fifteen-year-old boy.

"Who are you?" Si Wang said.

Even though the man wore a uniform and had a gun, Si Wang was still cautious. The boy crouched by the metal cabinet and tucked something under him.

The cop took out his department identification and showed it to the teenager. He had the same rank as Huang Hai. The photograph matched the face in front of Si Wang. The name next to the embossed photo said the man's name was Ye Xiao.

"Si Wang, you finally came."

"Were you watching me?"

Ye Xiao pulled him up. He'd been sitting on copies of case files for the 1995 Nanming Road murders. He put the files back into the cabinet. "I noticed you at the funeral. You were the one who found the body six years ago by Suzhou River. Huang Hai died on the job because of you, too, right?"

"You're saying I killed Huang Hai?"

"No, not at all. But I'm curious. Why do you have his keys?"

"I came here often, so he gave me the keys to make it easier."

Si Wang looked calm, but Ye Xiao detected something. "For this small room, too? Si Wang, you're lying!"

One of Ye Xiao's colleagues had told him that Huang Hai kept a small office in his apartment, which contained tons of copies of case files and all of his notes. The room was always locked.

After Huang Hai died, the police didn't find any personal keys on him. Now it was clear that Si Wang had taken them in order to access the apartment. The young man was willing to steal from a dead man to find out about the old cases. Why?

Ye Xiao saw the wall, still plastered with shocking photos and files. Another wall had Shen Ming's name written in red letters, with nine thick lines around it. One of the newest lines actually went to Si Wang's name.

Ye Xiao studied the young man carefully, slowly piecing together the case's intricate and confusing details. Si Wang was born after Shen Ming's murder, but for a time he'd been Gu Qiusha and Lu Zhongyue's adopted son, so he had a relationship to the case.

The cop looked at one of the files Shen Ming has been sitting on, which was filled with Huang Hai's messy handwriting. It outlined Shen Ming's background and had taken Huang Hai six months to piece together. Ye Xiao knew most of it, but there was one very puzzling new piece of information. The file contained details of another murder—one from before Huang Hai was a policeman. This case had happened on Serenity Road.

On a rainy fall night in 1983, on the old mansion-lined Serenity Road, a little girl ran into the street and cried for help. Neighbors responded to her shouts, and the cops soon arrived. They found her father murdered.

The dead man was a department chief for some government agency, last name Lu. Someone had used broken glass to slash open his throat. There were a lot of weird things about the case. The victim had had a lot of enemies. During the Cultural Revolution, he'd ruined many people's lives. Everyone was glad to see him dead; the case was closed.

At that time, a thirteen-year-old Shen Ming also lived on Serenity Road, right across the street.

Ye Xiao put away these files and took Si Wang out of the room. He stared at the young man. "Tell me, why are you so interested in Huang Hai's cases? Did the victims have anything to do with you?"

"Sorry, I must have read too much *Detective Conan*. My mom runs a bookstore. We have tons of suspense books. My dream is to be a policeman."

"I thought the killer had broken in. If you weren't sitting there, I might have shot you." He made a gun using his forefinger and thumb and pointed at the young boy's head. "Just kidding, I wouldn't do that." His eyes were very calm, like he was holding a real gun.

Si Wang seemed really afraid, however, and handed over the keys. "Sorry, I won't come here again."

Ye Xiao watched the dark night outside the window. "I'm in charge of Huang Hai's cases now."

"Please promise me you'll catch that evil person. You must avenge Huang Hai's death!"

"It is my job to do so."

"Can I be your assistant? I have lots of useful information!"

"Like that damn DVD store?" Ye Xiao shook his head, his eyes finally revealing some emotion: sad frustration. "Sorry, I'm not blaming you. You did very well. I should thank you for bringing us closer to the killer."

"I already said this many times. A friend of mine told me about it. You guys questioned her, too."

"Right—Yi Yu. I talked to her just this morning."

"Did you scare her?"

Ye Xiao grimaced. "More like she scared me. What a weird kid. She didn't cooperate at all, even though she said all the right things."

"Can I go home now?" The young man walked to the door, carrying his backpack.

Ye Xiao called after him. "Hey, Si Wang, famous detective."

Si Wang stopped and Ye Xiao strolled over to hand him one of his business cards. "If you know of anything, or you ever need any help, call me. Anytime. I'm always working."

Si Wang got into the elevator and took a deep breath. He reached into one of his pockets. It was good that Ye Xiao didn't search him. He'd hidden a strand of necklace that had been in Huang Hai's cabinet.

The necklace was tagged: "June 22, 1995. Evidence from Shen Ming murder scene. Found in victim's hands."

CHAPTER 43

Two weeks after Chinese New Year—Rice Dumpling Festival 2011.

Ma Li hadn't been back in this city for a long time. He streamed *The Walking Dead* on his computer, and felt a real kinship with the show.

His cell phone rang. A voice said, "Hey, this is Shen Ming."

It was a clear, youthful voice—and it didn't belong to either the elementary school student or the high school teacher who'd died sixteen years earlier.

"You—"

"We haven't seen each other for a while. I've missed you."

Panicked silence.

"You there?" asked the voice.

Shen Ming or Si Wang? Ma Li felt trapped. "I'm here."

"I want to see you. Right now."

He paused. It was eight o'clock, and he'd just finished dinner.

Before agreeing, instructions were given. "Let's meet at the bird-and-flower flea market. You know where it is?"

"The old Workers' Cultural Palace?"

"Yes."

Ma Li wanted to say more, but the other person hung up.

Half an hour later, the moon was hanging low. People said the Double Seventh Day was Chinese Valentine's Day. But according to tradition, two weeks after Chinese New Year was the real lovers' day. In ancient times, single people could only meet at this time.

The bird-and-flower flea market sold plants and pets. Tonight it was decorated with flower lanterns. Ma Li had aged well and still looked good with a clean shave and longer hair. He stood alone by the entrance, watching the teenagers coming in and out and feeling unsure about everything.

"Ma Li."

Alarmed, Ma Li turned around to find a good-looking young man. The boy was unrecognizable. He'd grown up and looked completely different. His chin had whiskers and his Adam's apple bulged. He no longer needed to look up at Ma Li.

Ma Li wondered if he should call the young man Shen Ming or Si Wang. They hadn't seen one another for five years. In early 2006, Ma Li had helped the boy complete his revenge against the Gu family and helped strip Lu Zhongyue of illegal assets. As a result, he'd made tens of millions of yuan himself and gone abroad to start a business.

As far as he knew, Si Wang's and He Qingying's accounts hadn't grown by one cent.

Ma Li had been scared to contact the boy again. Whether or not the kid was possessed by Shen Ming's ghost, he was afraid to get more involved. Everything he made could disappear as easily as Lu Zhongyue's money had. He could have been killed.

"As you've seen, I'm still looking for Lu Zhongyue. The truth is a lot more complicated."

It was him. A young man's face but talking like a grown-up—virtually the same as Mr. Shen.

The two walked past a stone bridge. Groups of couples were trying to guess the riddles on the lanterns. Fireworks flew overhead, and bits of those would fall and illuminate all the happy faces.

"Sixteen years ago, this was still the Workers' Cultural Palace," Si Wang said. "There was a stamp market right where we're standing. If you were a stamp collector, you could buy random stamps and hope they'd appreciate. But usually they were worthless the next time you came to the market."

"I remember borrowing twenty yuan from you to buy a set of *Romance of the Three Kingdoms* stamps," Ma Li said. "I don't know what happened to those after I graduated high school."

Si Wang nodded in a way that was beyond his years. "Kids today have no idea what stamp collecting is. That summer day in 1992 when I first became a teacher, you also reported to Nanming High. You were wearing a gray shirt, blue track pants, and Saint Seiya stickers on your backpack. I found out later that your favorite was Dragon Shiryu. You were tall and had big eyes. All the girls liked you."

"I almost forgot. It was so many years ago."

A biting wind blew. Ma Li watched puffs of hot air escape from his mouth and rise in the night sky, joining the fireworks.

"The army training was on the hottest days of the summer," Si Wang said. "I remember the intense sun. The oleander trees were the students' only shade. Everyone went to the shade during the breaks, but they still sweated so much, especially with those uniforms. You had heatstroke. I carried you to the hospital. You didn't have enough money to be admitted."

The conversation made Ma Li touch his cheek unconsciously. "Now I'm too pale."

"You were the first student to discover the Demon Girl Zone."

"In eleventh grade, there was a girl from another class who drowned while swimming. Everyone ran to that abandoned factory at midnight and burned all the stuff there to memorialize her. Everyone bought a stack of joss paper. They said the place was haunted and that the dead could get blessings and the living could stay protected. That was the Demon Girl Zone's only purpose for us."

"It's where I died."

Ma Li seemed lost in his memories. "I had a stack of books by my bed, all sorts of reference books and an Einstein biography. After dark, I'd go to Mr. Shen's room and talk about relativity and the origin of the universe. We'd talk about everything in the Milky Way, black holes, white holes, worm holes, neutron stars, quark stars, soliton stars, dark matter, dark energy."

"I knew you were an odd kid back then. You studied like crazy before the college entrance exams. You studied with Zhang Mingsong. Your dream was to attend Tsinghua University, which wasn't easy to get into. But Mr. Zhang graduated from there, and he was an elite math teacher. One night you were crying in the study room. I asked you what was wrong. You only said, 'I don't want to go to Dead Poets Society anymore.'"

"Shut up!" Ma Li acted like he wanted to cover Si Wang's mouth.

"I'm Shen Ming. I've been sitting on this boy's shoulders for the last sixteen years, and I've been watching you!"

Another blast of fireworks filled the sky. Si Wang was like a fighting dog. He stared at Ma Li until the grown man lowered his head in fear.

"Don't look at me. I'm no longer Ma Li the student. But you're still Mr. Shen. I'm envious."

"You envy me? For what? For being murdered when I was twenty-five? For wasting away in the Demon Girl Zone for three days? You envy me for being a lost ghost, living through Si Wang? Do you think I will leave him now and possess you?"

"No—"

"You're still afraid of me? Ha!"

"To be honest, I used to dream of the dead Mr. Shen. But now I dream of the ten-year-old Si Wang."

The young man stroked his face. "Am I that scary?"

"In 2005, you manipulated so many people and arranged to bring down a family. You gave me their secrets, telling me about insider trading and bribing officials. I was terrified that I'd be destroyed. But you were so confident, like the Gu family was already sentenced to death."

"They're the ones who betrayed me sixteen years ago. I swore I'd have revenge the day I was born. I had a list: Gu Qiusha, Gu Changlong, Lu Zhongyue, Zhang Mingsong."

Ma Li tensed. *The list included Zhang Mingsong?*

"So from the first day you met Gu Qiusha, you'd planned all this?"

"I used everything I knew about Gu Qiusha to make her fall in love with me, like I had romanced her in my last life. After I was adopted, I discovered all of their problems and figured out all their weaknesses, including Lu Zhongyue's."

"Like the pills you had me give Lu Zhongyue. He was really destroyed."

A cruel look passed the young man's face. "I was trapped in the body of an elementary school student then. I needed a helper I could trust. Someone who could control the situation, and make Lu Zhongyue act a certain way to help destroy the Gu family. Lu couldn't escape, either. I thought about it and decided you were best."

"Did you plan the school reunion and all the online chats, too?"

"Too bad Long Zhongyue still got away. I underestimated him."

"You hate him that much?"

"After the Gu family went bankrupt, I figured out the combination to Gu Changlong's safe. There was a letter from 1995. The letter faked my handwriting to look like a letter from me to He Nian—my college classmate. He Nian worked at the Education Bureau and then Erya. He went missing for two years before his body was found by the river. Maybe it was jealousy, but He Nian backstabbed me with that letter. The only person who could have faked my handwriting was Lu Zhongyue."

"Lu Zhongyue and He Nian plotted against you?"

"I didn't want either of them to die. It's too late for He Nian. But I want Lu Zhongyue to live and suffer. That's how he can pay for what they did to me."

"Mr. Shen, you're scaring me right now."

"Humans are like animals. When everyone around you is cruel, your killer instinct comes out."

They returned to the flea market entrance. Ma Li took out his car keys and said, "Let me drive you home."

He had a black Porsche SUV. The young man got into the front passenger seat and buckled up. The stereo was playing Leslie Cheung's "I."

Fireworks rose above the car. Neither man spoke another word.

CHAPTER 44

June 9, 2011.

Nanming High hadn't changed much, except for all the high-rises around it, creating an expansive and cluttered skyline.

She signed in with the doorman and crossed the familiar sports field. It was almost summer break. The students were preparing to go home, but they turned to look at her as she passed in her white dress. Her face was as even as ivory. Her old-fashioned bangs and shiny almond eyes made her look like a goddess whose real age was impossible to guess.

The fence at the edge of the sports field was still lined with rose bushes. She stood by them and petals falling on her face turned the scene into a simple, beautiful watercolor. She plucked a few petals and crushed them into a red ball, then ground that into the dirt.

"Fallen like mud and ground like dust, only the scent remains." She whispered this line from the poet Lu You, and remembered a day from sixteen years ago: June 19, 1995.

It was the rainy season, and it always rained after lunch. She was in Section 2 of the senior class. Pacing by the sports field, she ran into the dazed Mr. Shen. The man who had just lost everything looked at her with an unreadable expression. He backed away.

"Don't talk to me . . . don't come any closer." Shen Ming avoided her eyes. "I'm not a teacher anymore."

"I heard you'll have to leave. When will you go?"

"Tonight—eight o'clock."

"Can it be later? I'll wait for you at 10:00 p.m. at the Demon Girl Zone."

"Demon Girl Zone?" He looked at the petals at his feet.

"There's something I need to tell you, but it'll be better to tell you later."

She looked around, careful of eavesdroppers. Why ten o'clock? Because she needed to go over the school's fence. Part of it was low and easy to flip over, but people would see her if she did it any earlier.

"Fine, I promise you. I need to tell you something, too."

The eighteen-year-old girl went deeper into the bush, brushing back her hair. "Ten o'clock, Demon Girl Zone."

That was the last time she saw Shen Ming. He had been so preoccupied. Thinking about it now, she wondered if it was because he'd been thinking about the murder he ended up committing that night.

She was Ouyang Xiaozhi.

He went to the Demon Girl Zone.

Then he died.

Sixteen years later, she was still here. But where was he? In another life? Or was he a ghost?

Ouyang Xiaozhi straightened her hair and walked to the teachers' building, heading for the top floor. She knocked on an office door.

"Come in."

Sitting behind the desk was Nanming High's most famous teacher. Most people would be flustered by her stunning beauty, but Zhang Mingsong seemed unaffected.

"Mr. Zhang, I'm Ouyang Xiaozhi. I'm here to report for my first day."

"Ms. Ouyang, welcome to Nanming High. I got your file from the Education Bureau."

She nodded at Mr. Zhang politely and looked outside at the multipurpose building. "It's great being back at the alma mater as a teacher!"

"You graduated in 1995, right? I think I remember you. It doesn't look like you've changed much all these years later."

Zhang Mingsong spoke in an official manner. He'd aged well and didn't seem much older. A giant bookshelf stood behind him. She remembered his face from the college entrance exams.

"You were always my idol. I've wanted to be a teacher ever since attending high school here. I went to the Teachers' College as a Chinese major. Then I went to Xihai as a volunteer and taught six years of high school Chinese at a remote village there. After that, I worked for another six years at a city high school. I've been a teacher for twelve years now."

"That's all very admirable." His voice darkened. "Now, Ms. Ouyang, I read your old school file and I see that your homeroom teacher was Mr. Shen."

Xiaozhi frowned. "Yes, that's correct. Everything about that was so sad and awful."

"Let's not talk about the past anymore. I'll take you to the administrative office so you can complete all the paperwork."

Half an hour later, Ouyang Xiaozhi had finished all of her first-day procedures and was ready to be Nanming High's Chinese teacher.

Zhang Mingsong seemed a bit standoffish. As they parted, he coldly shook her hand and walked away without another word.

She exited through the school gates and crossed the busy Nanming Road. She didn't leave right away; instead, she thought back to twenty years ago. The building behind her disappeared—concrete, steel, and tiles flew into the sky. It was like the end of the world. After the universe of dust and mud fell away, the impoverished huts that used to line the road were all that remained.

June of 1988, not long after she first saw Shen Ming.

Fire.

An unassuming match turned into a ball of fire. Black smoke and dust fanned into flames. It only took a few minutes for the fire to turn uncontrollable, destroying everything in its path. Flames lit up the forest like it was day-night.

Coughing, yelling, cursing, screaming, crying, sounds like firecrackers . . .

She was just eleven. The lethal fumes filled her nose and mouth. She always thought people burned to death in a fire, but now she realized they actually choked to death from the smoke. She instinctively tried to stop breathing in, coughing as she ran. Tears streaked her face, partly from the smoke, partly from regret and guilt.

The smell of burning flesh. The illegal huts made from cardboard and wastepaper were very flammable. The smell of burning rubber tires sickened her. Just as she was about to lose consciousness, that man appeared again.

He rushed to her like a ball of fire. In fact, he charged right into a ball of fire to get to her. He held her tight and ran through the flames.

She leaned against his chest, listening to his heart racing and wishing she could melt with the fire.

He carried her out of it.

She opened her ash-streaked eyes. The night sky was bright with the fiery glow. Stars still twinkled, and the moon looked even more beautiful.

As she regained her breath and took in some fresh air, she recognized her savior. It was the same man who'd rescued her from the Demon Girl Zone.

"We're still alive," eighteen-year-old Shen Ming said.

She looked at his smoke-smeared face, his slightly burned face and scalp. She fought herself to say, "I didn't mean to do this."

She felt his heartbeat speed up. He shook his head sadly. "Remember, don't say anything!"

Twenty years had passed since then, and she'd never again mentioned what happened.

Their secret.

June 19, 2011—almost dusk.

Ouyang Xiaozhi returned to the scene of the fire. Brand-new buildings stood behind her, Nanming High sat across from her, and the Demon Girl Zone lurked a few hundred meters away.

Just as she was about to head to the bus stop, she saw a teenage boy. He didn't look like he belonged at Nanming High.

His face seemed familiar, like someone she'd seen two years ago at the Rice Dumpling Festival.

CHAPTER 45

June 9, 2011.

Yi Yu arrived at the bus stop across from Nanming High. Dressed in a white school uniform and wearing a black backpack, she looked like a tomboy who could no longer hide her femininity.

Sixteen-year-old Si Wang was waiting for her.

Yi Yu casually strolled toward him. "You looking for me? How did you do on your high school entrance exams?"

"I'm waiting for the results. I hope they're high enough for Nanming High so I can be your classmate." Passing girls checked him out as he leaned against the bus stop, his open collar fluttering in the wind. "What's up with you?"

"Just had my college entrance exams a few days ago. Think I'll go to Hong Kong soon."

"What? Why didn't you tell me?"

"I applied to Hong Kong University. I already passed the interview." She swept back her short hair, looking like a wanderer, someone who'd never fit in. "I'm not suited to colleges here. Even if I got into Beijing or Tsinghua University, I'd be forced to drop out. Might as well go to Hong Kong where there are fewer rules."

"Then I can't see you anymore?"

"I'll come back and visit plenty," she said, patting his shoulders. She leaned next to him and let the sun shine on her face. More and more of the passing students, especially pretty girls in dresses, looked at them with curiosity. How did a famous tomboy get together with a good-looking teenager?

He lowered his voice. "Ever been to the Demon Girl Zone?"

"Please! Let me tell you, this was one big cemetery back in the day. Ruan Lingyu's grave was right under the Demon Girl Zone. She was Cantonese and buried at the Guangdong Public Cemetery. It was called the Lianyi Cemetery then, though it was so luxuriously landscaped it was more like a park. There was a bridge after the gate and a lot of classical Chinese architecture. Some of the burial plots had coffins, some had offerings to gods. Most graves were made of stone and really classical. There were stone tables, benches, horses, and sheep, and the round graves were surrounded by a stone wall. Some tried to look like emperors' graves, some had secret passages. Luckily, it was the Republic of China era, or they would have been in trouble. Ruan Lingyu's grave was the shabbiest. The tombstone was just a meter high. The whole cemetery was destroyed during the Cultural Revolution, and schools and factories were built in its place. All those precious lots for rich families with good feng shui—gone! Nanming High's library was where people made offerings to the dead." Yi Yu was proud having rattled off the history.

"Did you say that someone died there?"

"That's normal! Who doesn't die? I don't want a lavish funeral myself. Much better to toss my ashes into the sea."

"How do you know so much about Ruan Lingyu's grave? Only someone who was there would know. Didn't you say it was all destroyed during the Cultural Revolution? How did you see it? Were you at her funeral?"

"Yes."

"And another thing—you said that in your past life you lived on Serenity Road in 1983. There was a murder across the street—and that house is still empty today?"

"Yeah, what's it to you?"

"Remember a kid? He was around thirteen. His grandma was the maid. They lived in the basement of your house."

"Aunt Yun's grandson?"

"Yes."

"Aunt Yun was my maid. I wasn't rich, just eighty-something and really sick. The government assigned her to help me with day-to-day stuff. She was in good health and did everything. She only had a daughter who was killed a few years earlier. Left a son. I took pity on them and had them stay in the basement. I forgot his name, I just remember he was really good at studying and actually got into a good high school."

Si Wang listened quietly as Yi Yu kept talking.

"I watched him go from elementary school to junior high. No parents around to nag him, yet he was disciplined. I often saw him in the basement doing homework by the lamp. He loved to read. I lent him a set of *Strange Tales from a Chinese Studio*. No kid on Serenity Road liked to play with him. He was beat up a lot. Aunt Yun was superstitious and always worried he wouldn't live a long life because his face didn't seem blessed."

This conversation depressed Si Wang, so he changed the subject. "I've been cramming science books lately. I don't think reincarnation exists. It's just that some people are born with supernatural abilities, like having all the memories that once belonged to someone who's passed on."

Yi Yu's face changed, showing an elderly person's skepticism. "Fine, let's say I have a man's memory. Someone who was born in 1900."

"Did you say 1900? When the Eight-Power Allied Forces invaded Beijing?"

"Yes, the twenty-sixth year of the Guangxu era—the Gengzi Incident."

"You still remember it?"

"C'mon, now, I was just born that year." She watched the deepening dusk. Nanming Road was about to be covered by shadows from the towering buildings. With closed eyes she recited, "Where did the old powers go, here I am back again."

"That sounds familiar."

"It was from *A New Account of the Tales of the World* by Liu Yiqing. Two men called Liu Chen and Ruan Zhao went up to Tiantai Mountain. In a valley they met two young women who invited them home. The men felt like they'd found paradise. They stayed the night and the women made them forget all their troubles. They remained there for six months and finally went back after missing their hometown. When they returned to it, their village was nothing like they remembered. No one knew them. It was already the Jin dynasty, about two hundred years later. Their families were in their seventh generation. It was rumored that they got lost in the mountains and didn't return. Later on, they left and were never seen again."

"Sounds like a Washington Irving story."

Yi Yu patted his shoulders. "Kid, you know me so well. Liu Yuxi was demoted to the borderlands in the Tang dynasty. When he returned to Xuandu Temple in Chang'an for the second time, everything was different. That's why he was saying 'here I am back again.'"

"You're an exile, too?"

"I was born into a poor intellectual's family in the early twentieth century. Luckily, I had a businessman uncle who gave me tuition money. On May 4, 1919, I was on that square. I helped set fire to the Zhao Mansion. But I went to Japan the following year."

Yi Yu laughed at the confused look on Si Wang's face. "Hey, have you ever heard of Sola Aoi? I'm a woman now and not interested in these things anymore. But in my past life, I had a doomed relationship with a Japanese girl. There was a girl called Anna from my Nagasaki school days. She actually died for me. I don't remember her original name. She was Catholic, so I just remember her given name."

"You were quite the womanizer!"

Yi Yu blushed, lowering her head in shame. "I left Japan after that and went to school in France. First to Paris, where I stayed in Montmartre, and then Provence, in the lavender-scented Grasse. I was friends with Sartre in Paris. I ran into Hemingway, James Joyce, and Ezra Pound at the Shakespeare and Company bookstore. Ever read *The Sun Also Rises*? I read the first draft in front of Hemingway. I stayed four years in France. What a crazy place. I didn't want to waste my life there, however. So I made the trendiest and most hot-blooded choice for back then. I went to frozen Moscow. I crossed Europe to get there. I saw Lenin's memorial on Red Square, and I was so excited to see the red star on top of the Kremlin. I was awed and so inspired. I got into Moscow's Sun Yat-sen University and met my idol. In the 1930s, I was involved in an incident and was deported. The university closed because of that, too."

"So you came back to China?"

"Yes, but I had to stay anonymous. I lived in the concession zone. If the Nationalist Party had caught me, I'd have been jailed or shot. I couldn't join the revolution, either. They thought I was a traitor and a lap dog for Chen Duxiu. I could only hang out with the intellectuals and artists and spend my time writing poems and drinking. I worked as a teacher, reporter, and editor—and I wrote martial arts serial novels for newspapers. I edited Xiao Hong's *The Field of Life and Death*. I also read her *Tales of Hulan River*. We only met a few times, but I really liked her. She was a real Northeastern girl. I've always wanted to write a book called *The River of Life and Death*."

"Is that so?"

"Yes, plus *The River of Forgetfulness* and *Meng Po Soup*! When civil war broke out, I went all over the country: Wuhan, Chongqing, Chengdu, even the remote Kunming. I was like the exiled Liu Yuxi. Southwest Associated University didn't want me, because I was too much of a rebel. So I went over the hills to the Tibet region. I lived in the real wilderness for years before coming back to inland China. I was already in my forties. Then I met her."

"Miss Cao?"

"She was extremely smart. That's why I fell for her. But she was married to a bureaucrat. She didn't love him. In 1949, her husband abandoned her to go to Taiwan. She had a chance to find him via Hong Kong, but she chose to stay here."

"Because of you?"

"I was a so-called traitor. She was the wife of a Nationalist Party official. She stayed for me, but we were apart for thirty years. When we met again, she was in her eighties. Her father had left her that house, and the government gave it back to her. We stayed on the same street but hardly saw each other. It's just as well—less heartache. I've loved a lot of people and hated a lot of people, but I married no one and had no children. That was my biggest regret from my past life."

"You want a kid?"

"It's better than being reincarnated. A kid can carry your genes to your children's children. Your life never ends. My old age was sad and long. Miss Cao was the only one I could talk to. Some foreign reporters would interview me to gossip about people I knew from back in the day. But I was sick of it. I wanted to die early. I lived to ninety-two and died in bed."

"Living too long made you desperate? What if you'd died young?"

"Si Wang, you wouldn't understand!"

"Last question. Did you ever finish writing *The River of Life and Death*?"

"I wrote it when I had lots of free time in Qinghai. It took me thirty years. Then I burned it."

"Why?"

"I was writing this book with every minute of my life. So are you!"

The young man thought a while before relaxing. He pressed his hands together like an ancient scholar. "Brother Yi Yu, I may not know your name from your past life, but we became friends anyway. We were fated to meet somehow. I don't know when I'll see you again, but please take care."

She also made the same gesture. "Brother Si Wang, I'll go back and pack. Until we meet again."

"If only we had two shots!"

"Ninety years ago, when I was leaving home, Li Shutong had just become a monk at Hangzhou's Hupao Temple. My uncle was his good friend. Before we left, Li Shutong came to see us off. He'd written a song."

Yi Yu sang:

By the temple, next to the road, grass connected with sky
Night wind, sounds of the flute, setting sun on the mountains
Corner of the world, end of time, so many friends leaving
One cauldron of wine marks our good-byes, dreams get colder
The song ends, and we part.

She said nothing else, just gave a smile. She looked beautiful.

Yi Yu walked toward Nanming High but stopped to turn around and look once more at Si Wang.

He shouted in alarm, "Watch out!"

A dump truck barreled toward her like a bull. The brakes screeched, but the truck didn't slow down at all.

It was as though the dust cloud picked up Yi Yu and flung her through the air until she landed right in front of Si Wang.

Students screamed. He was in a daze but knelt to pick up her soft and distorted body.

Blood spurted out of her mouth, covering her beautiful, knowing face.

PART 4:
MENG PO SOUP

CHAPTER 46

The last day of July, 2011. The hottest day of the year.

The sun was up at 7:00 a.m. Cicadas chirped loudly from the locust tree. Using bookstore earnings, He Qingying had bought a new shirt for her son from a Taobao designer store. She straightened his collar and forced him to shave his long hair. She took his new wallet and put in it the money for tuition, room and board, and handling fees—a total of 2,990 yuan. She nagged him about being sure not to lose it.

Ever since kindergarten, she'd always accompanied her son to the first day of school, but not today. She just walked him to the nearest subway station.

Si Wang had been accepted to Nanming High.

Last night, she reminded him that because of all the work being done to the natural gas lines along Nanming Road, buses had been rerouted, and the easiest way would be to take the subway.

Watching his descent into the station, she shouted, "Wang Er, I'll be at the parent-teacher meeting."

He had to change lines to get close to the school, which left him with a ten-minute walk. He was already running late.

A sedan drove up, and the driver rolled down his window. "Hey, you going to Nanming? Ten yuan each, flat price."

He got into the back seat of the gypsy cab and covered his wallet. Just as the car was about to pull away, a girl in a white dress opened the door. Si Wang scooted to the left, making room for her.

"Nanming High." Her voice was soft as she apologized to Si Wang. "Sorry, can I share this ride with you?"

He was speechless when he got a good look at her face. She wasn't a girl but a woman in her thirties. The years had left no marks on her. She could have passed for a college student. She must have been growing younger, like some mythical creature.

Ouyang Xiaozhi.

She recognized the sixteen-year-old young man.

"Are you a new student?"

He nodded clumsily.

"Are we leaving, or what?" the driver said, eager not to be ticketed for idling in front of the subway station.

"I'm sorry," Xiaozhi said, looking at her white ceramic watch. "Just seven minutes left—we really can't be late!"

She lowered her head awkwardly, her pale face kind of flushed. Sweat beaded below her hairline, thanks to having rushed out of the subway station.

Si Wang avoided her gaze and said nothing. He looked everywhere but at her.

Five minutes later, the car arrived at Nanming High via a shortcut.

Xiaozhi paid the driver before he could. He followed her out of the car and said, "Hey, I still owe you five yuan!"

"Don't worry about it. Thanks for sharing the cab."

Summer morning. There was construction dust everywhere on Nanming Road. Her smile accelerated the heart rates of many male students.

Luckily, they weren't late. New students accompanied by their parents gathered at the gates. Si Wang was the only one alone. Whole families showed up, many of them arriving in private cars. It didn't take long for the road to look like a parking lot.

The sports field had been converted to an admissions office, and signs showed where the new students needed to go to pay the various fees. Xiaozhi walked past the oleander bush. The red flowers bloomed even brighter now.

She walked into the teachers' building. At the floor-length mirror by the staircase, she ran her hands over her hair and clothes. Her makeup was light, and her conservative outfit seemed indifferent to the steamy weather. Her skirt covered her knees, and she wore flats.

Xiaozhi noticed the student with whom she'd shared the taxi.

All the new students either stood on the sports field or went to first-floor classrooms. All of them except for the young man following her.

She turned, wearing a serious expression. She was used to the attention from male students. She needed them to see her as untouchable.

Si Wang stood in the corridor until his cell phone rang. It was his mom making sure he got to school on time. He told her everything was fine, then he went downstairs and out onto the field to pay his fees.

An hour later, the new students and their families went to the assembly hall for a ceremony. Si Wang stood away from the crowd. He was exposed under the bright sun, and sweat drenched his new shirt.

Looking at the school library, where Lianyi Cemetery's memorial hall once stood, he uttered, "I'm back."

CHAPTER 47

The sun was fierce.

It was as hot as the Sahara—at least 40 degrees Celsius. Heat waves crushed the young students standing on the playing fields. Girls and boys alike made up excuses to escape the heat, everything from menstrual cycles to fainting. Only he stood straight under the sun and watched the training instructor. His pale skin was now so tan it looked ready to peel.

The military training lasted five days, ending before Indian Summer. The instructor complimented his willpower. No one would dare pick on him now.

When the new students finally moved into the dorms, He Qingying insisted on helping her son settle in. He got his school uniform, a number of black tracksuits. The girls clearly admired him and He Qingying teased him about that.

There were more parents than students in the dorms. The kids needed all the help they could get organizing their beds and luggage. When He Qingying finally got everything done, she left reluctantly, reminding him to call home on a regular basis.

"Mom, I'll be fine."

Si Wang kissed her forehead. Students snickered. He didn't care.

He spent his first overnight at school. All Nanming High students boarded there. They were allowed cell phones to make calling home easier, but they weren't to use them during class. Si Wang's roommates made fun of his knockoff phone. They used iPhones, and two of his roommates had iPads. They all obsessed over *Plants vs. Zombies*.

He carefully looked at the windowsill—twenty years of etchings blended together. Among the names and years and symbols, "Dead Poets Society" was scrawled in a corner.

Cicadas chirped outside the window, and the wind carried the scent of oleander flowers, helping cool the night. He stared at the library across the dark playing field.

A light went on in the library attic.

Si Wang continued to stare from his fourth-floor dorm room, wishing he had binoculars.

It was lights out. One of his roommates told him to get in bed and another one pulled shut the curtains without a word. Si Wang had been sitting on the seat by the window for the past two hours. Everyone already thought he was weird.

At that moment, far away in Guangzhou, Ma Li received a text: *"I'm back at Nanming High. My bed is the top bunk in your old room."*

Si Wang heard from his mom the next morning. She was anxious to know how he'd slept and eaten. He said everything was fine and asked how she was. She said that she couldn't sleep at all without him at home.

First day of class.

Section 2 of tenth grade was on the third floor of the white building. There were thirty-two students—seventeen guys and fifteen girls. Si Wang was one of the taller students; he sat in the fifth row and was about ten meters away from the blackboard. It was a good spot for goofing off. He shared a desk with an outgoing guy who kept chatting with everyone. Two girls sat in front of him; one had short hair, one had a ponytail, and both of them were average looking. They were friendly to Si Wang. He only answered when asked, and never initiated conversation.

The teacher walked in. In his forties, he carried a thick file and wore a perfectly pressed white shirt; a gold pen poked out of his chest pocket. He had the build of a young man, just with less hair. His assertive gaze swept the room, filling every student with his confidence and pride.

"Hi, class. I'm your homeroom teacher, Mr. Zhang Mingsong."

He turned to the blackboard and wrote his name. For a math teacher, he had excellent handwriting. The students whispered. Mr. Zhang was on TV a lot.

"I've not been a homeroom teacher for ten years. The school asked me to do it, and coach you all the way to graduation. I considered carefully before agreeing. I chose this class, Section 2."

Some students actually clapped. A few of the geekier students thought that having the famous Mr. Zhang as their homeroom teacher was like winning the lottery. It was the same as having an in-home tutor for free, and it got them closer to a top university.

Zhang Mingsong was already immune to all praise. He didn't chitchat before starting his math class, which was dry and foreign to many of the students. But everyone stayed focused. Zhang Mingsong received another ovation at the end of class. He solemnly surveyed the room before locking eyes with Si Wang.

He frowned, as if scared by the teenager's gaze. The bell rang, signaling the end of class. Zhang Mingsong didn't say good-bye before walking out of the room.

Si Wang didn't move during the class break; he waited for the next bell. Zhang Mingsong had already chosen the classroom leader, a chubby girl with glasses. She instructed the class to stand and greet the next teacher.

It was now Chinese class, and Ouyang Xiaozhi was the teacher.

"Hi, class!"

She bowed deeply and then walked to the podium. Her every gesture was friendly. Students noticed she wore no rings, not even a wedding band. She wrote her name on the blackboard.

A girl in the front row loudly whispered, "Wow, Ouyang Xiaozhi, too! Did you read those books?"

Xiaozhi smiled in a way that made everyone pay attention. "You can call me Ms. Ouyang or Ms. Xiaozhi. Know why I'm called Xiaozhi? It's the name of a flute." She elegantly smoothed her hair from her shoulders to her back. "I'm honored to be your Chinese teacher. This is my first class at Nanming High. I graduated from the teachers' college and taught Chinese for twelve years. I just transferred here two months ago. Oh no, now you know my age!"

The words relaxed the class. Another girl whispered, "I thought she was in her twenties!"

Ouyang Xiaozhi didn't mention that she'd graduated from Nanming High.

"Please open your textbook to the first essay, 'Spring in the Garden: Changsha,' by Mao Zedong."

The teacher started reading the poem, her voice was as gentle as before: "In the peak of youth, passion reigned . . ."

Forty-five minutes later as class ended, Xiaozhi announced the topic for the next day and said good-bye to the students. She walked out of the room feeling confident about how well the first session had gone.

Xiaozhi returned to the teachers' lounge, which was filled with dozens of desks. The teachers chatted and shared snacks.

At dusk, as she was preparing to walk out, she ran into Si Wang again. He backed away shyly.

"Hello," she said. The wind picked up her hair, showing off her face even more.

The teenager took his time to answer. "Hi, teacher."

"I remember you. My first day here was the first day of class. We shared a ride."

"It was OK." His voice was so low even he couldn't hear it.

"You're Si Wang, right?"

"Yes."

She said good-bye and turned down the road, heading for the subway station. The construction never seemed to end.

When Ouyang Xiaozhi suddenly turned around, the awkward student was gone.

CHAPTER 48

"She's in Hong Kong," Si Wang said as he brought a cup of warm tea to Miss Cao and opened the box of moon cakes.

"She never mentioned it to me."

"She was trying to surprise you."

"This isn't a . . ." She paused to look outside at the overgrown plants. Primrose scented the air. She took her time finishing her thought with, "surprise."

"Don't worry, she called me today and asked me to visit."

A moment of noncommittal silence. She raised the tea cup for a sip. "Fine, thank you, Si Wang."

"Not having any moon cakes?"

She opened her toothless mouth.

"I'm sorry!"

Si Wang slapped his own face. He sliced open the cakes and scooped out the fillings. The elderly woman took one piece and held it in her mouth to savor the taste. "Thank you! The last time I had moon cakes was in 1948!"

"Yi Yu never had moon cakes with you in all these years?"

"Moon cakes are to be shared with family. We're always alone. You won't understand, child."

"No, I do." His expression was serious.

"Tomorrow is the Mid-Autumn Festival. I almost forgot how moon cakes tasted. But they haven't changed since last I had one." Miss Cao looked a bit tired. It was hard to imagine how sixty years ago her face drove men crazy. "Is she really in Hong Kong?"

"Yes!"

Yi Yu was still alive.

Three months ago at Nanming High, Yi Yu said good-bye to Si Wang after the exams. Just after parting ways a dump truck hit her. She'd been seriously hurt, and after three days and nights in the ER, she was pulled back from the verge of death. But she hadn't woken up since.

"But the phone hasn't rung," Miss Cao said, pointing to the phone.

"Hong Kong University is very strict. She's a good student and always studying."

Lying to the elderly was like lying to kids.

"As long as she's doing well."

Finally, Miss Cao smiled at him. She picked up another piece of the moon cake. Her appetite was good today.

"No worries, she won't forget you."

"Hah, I wish she would forget me! Then she could be a normal girl and not waste her time with me!" The kind woman's rough yet warm hand stroked Si Wang's palm. "It's getting dark. Your mom is waiting for you."

"Miss Cao, take care of yourself! I'll be back. Call me if you need anything."

He left the ivy-covered house and returned to the dark Serenity Road, slowly pedaling his bicycle. The road was so quiet it was creepy. The moon moved between lotus flower–like clouds. The streetlights elongated his shadow, almost stretching it across the road like taffy. There was Yi Yu's house from her past life: Its mailboxes were stuffed full of today's paper and junk mail. A lot of people still lived there. The half window from the basement apartment was right next to the sidewalk. Si Wang got off his bike and crawled up to the window, staying as flat as possible. He spit in his hand before wiping off the dusty window. He took out a flashlight, but the light wasn't enough to penetrate the dust. There seemed to be a lot of junk inside.

He looked across the road at the dark old murder house. If the first floor lights were on, he could tell what was inside, be they people or ghosts.

Si Wang stood up again. He took a deep breath. The road remained empty.

A single leaf fell in front of Serenity Road Number 19. He touched the rusty plate on the door and pressed his ear against the door. He could hear the sound of falling dust, and something else, like wind moving through the roof, or snakes crawling on the ground.

He used his knuckles to tap on the murder house door. Dull echoes came from within.

The front door was locked, but he noticed a small yard to the right hidden behind a squat wall with bushy willow leaves. Si Wang flipped himself over the wall, landing on the patio. Leaves, trash, and cat feces littered the space. There were two broken windows on the side of the house. He easily opened one of the windows and checked out the inside of the house using his flashlight. It smelled of decay. Most people would have been scared to enter, but he crawled right into the house.

He waved his flashlight's beam across the empty room. Most of the furniture had been removed as part of the crime scene back in 1983. Either that or it had been stolen once the police investigation was completed. A few chairs were left in the living room, covered in thick cobwebs. He held his breath, not wanting to inhale too much mildew or toxic dust. He didn't see a body shape marked on the floor. That only happened in American movies.

But he saw some symbols and lines left by the police, marking where the body was found.

He stood in front of the living room window and used a dirty washcloth to clean the window. Now he could better see the moonlit Serenity Road and the basement window across the street. The stairs creaked as he walked upstairs, like they could collapse at any second.

There were three rooms on the second floor. The bathroom had a filthy toilet. Large white tiles had turned the color of coffee. There was a brick tub seen only in old-fashioned homes. Another big room with a corpse-like big bed, barely upright with rusted metal. Mice scurried underneath. He covered his nose before backing out and opening the door to the last room.

A small bed sat inside, the wooden frame almost completely rotten. Clusters of roaches crawled past. The mirror on the wall was inside an oval black frame. Si Wang got closer and saw his blurry reflection.

Sixteen-year-old Si Wang stared back at him. He was afraid to clean the mirror. He could tell that it was haunted.

He turned around and saw a shabby chest of drawers and some toys on the floor. He picked up a doll, the kind many little girls played with back then. The naked doll's large, dusty, time-worn eyes stared ahead like she was alive.

Si Wang put back the doll, feeling the need to leave this haunted place. The flashlight reached a corner, where he saw a black hole in the wall. At some point it had been covered by a board, but years of neglect had rotted away the wood.

With some trepidation, he reached in and found a square-shaped cookie tin. After wiping away the dust, Si Wang appreciated the box's quality. There were hand-painted illustrations of ancient beauties Xue Baochai, Miaoyu, Wang Xifeng, and Li Wan. The words on the tin said "*Dream of the Red Chamber*'s Twelve Girls of Jinling."

In the old days, many homes had boxes like these. They were used for storing candy and snacks. Usually, they were just brought out for the holidays.

He used his fingernails to pry open the lid, releasing an odor that smelled like someone's musty ashes. He reached inside and found a few cards. One was of General Guan from *Romance of the Three Kingdoms*, and another one was of the battle between the three warriors and Lu Bu. Kids today had no idea that cigarette packages once included free trading cards. Scenery or characters on the front, descriptions on the back, they had nothing to do with cigarettes, really. Some street vendors also sold them independently. Many boys collected them, trying to get all the warriors of *Outlaws of the Marsh*, *Romance of the Sui Tang Empire*, and *Generals of the Yang Family*. Kids played by putting two cards together on the floor and slapping them together. Whichever one flipped over was the winner.

This was obviously a girl's room, belonging to the victim's daughter, and the crime's only witness. But cigarette cards were a boy's game.

Si Wang dumped out all the contents of the tin. A pair of tarnished hair clips tumbled out, something a twelve- or thirteen-year-old girl would use.

There was also a cassette tape.

Training the flashlight on the tape, Si Wang could see the year 1983 written on Side A, along with the following: 01. "Alone on the Western Pavilion"; 02. "Eternal Love"; 03. "Melancholy"; 04. "No Love Lost"; 05. "Deep Is the Night"; 06. "Who Knows My Heart."

All of the songs were from the Teresa Teng album *Tender Love*. It was a pirated copy since the real release wasn't available in China back then. The album had twelve songs and used ancient Chinese poems as lyrics. The song "Melancholy" used a poem from Li Yu. Songs on Side B used Li Yu's "Rose tears making one drunk, regret forever lasting in my life" and Ouyang Xiu's "Last year this time, the holiday fair was bright, the moon rose above the willow, and we met after dusk."

The six songs on Side B were 07. "Rose Tears"; 08. "Everlasting Sorrow"; 09. "Meeting After Dusk"; 10. "Looking at You Through Tears"; 11. "Unspoken"; 12. "Missing You."

Nothing else but rat droppings was in the hole in the wall.

Standing in this girl's bedroom that had been untouched for thirty years, Si Wang breathed in the scent of decay.

Suddenly, his cell phone rang.

It was his mother, wanting to know why he wasn't home yet. He told her he was on the way.

He tucked the metal tin back into the wall. Whether or not it had anything to do with the crime, the police definitely hadn't found this hiding spot.

Si Wang rode home, with the moon casting a long shadow behind him.

CHAPTER 49

A sixteen-year-old girl's shiny black hair framed her doll-like face. Her eyes were so bright that boys were afraid to stare into them. She'd just entered high school and was listening to Teresa Teng's "Eternal Love." She was staring out the window, waiting for the moon to rise. It would be another two hours. Her dad was worried she had a crush on someone.

The doorbell rang.

Her dad was cooking in the kitchen, so she ran out to open the door. A stranger stood outside. He was about her age, taller than her by half a head. He looked at her shyly.

"Who are you?"

She should have asked this question, but the boy said it first.

"Shen Min," she blurted out. "Sorry, do I know you?"

"I'm here to talk to your dad."

"Hold on." Shen Min frowned and closed the door. Where had she seen this face before?

Shen Yuanchao was sixty-one and retired. He had gray hair and a lean face, but his eyes were still piercing. He went to the door. "You are?" Staring at the young man, he tried to remember why he recognized him.

"Prosecutor Shen. How are you? Huang Hai was my father. We've met before. I'm Huang Zhiliang."

"Huang Zhiliang, yes. Please come in!"

The young man nodded politely and offered a box of moon cakes. "Happy Mid-Autumn Festival!"

Shen Yuanchao was used to turning down gifts, but since it was from a high school student he accepted it. Shen Min came out of the kitchen with some hot tea. Shen Yuanchao offered some to their guest, but he declined.

"I heard about your dad last year," Shen Yuanchao said. "He died trying to find my son's killer. I regret making trouble at your home and upsetting him. I'll never forget something he told me: I'll catch the killer—unless I die first. He was such a good cop. I misunderstood him."

"It's all right. My dad solved lots of crimes, all except the ones surrounding the 1995 Nanming Road murder. He told me that if he died, I'd inherit his mission. We have to solve those cases, and I need your help. I'm here to help you, too."

"I had no idea he felt so strongly about it. But you're still in high school. I doubt you can help me."

"It's OK. I'll get into the Police Academy."

"Such dedication—like father, like son. It's been three years since last I saw you. You're so handsome now. You remind me of my son, Shen Ming. If he were still alive, he'd be forty."

Moon cakes had been placed on the small pedestal standing underneath the portraits of Shen Ming and Shen Yuanchao's wife.

"May I light some incense?" The young man stood up with a solemn expression. "For my dad."

With tears in his eyes, Shen Yuanchao found three sticks of incense and called to his daughter, "Min, help him light these."

She looked at him dubiously, like he was a mental patient, but ultimately she obeyed him. Si Wang bowed three times to the portraits, lit the incense, and turned around like he was a ghost, looking at Shen Yuanchao with such bitterness.

"Kid, what's wrong?"

"Mr. Shen, if you ever run into new clues, please let me know." Si Wang jotted down his cell phone number. "I'll help you find the killer."

"You're too young to be thinking about such things. Catching killers should be left to grown-ups."

"I'll wait for your call," Si Wang said, watching Shen Min, who was hiding behind the sofa and blushing.

His gaze lingered on her face. He left the living room, put on his shoes, and walked out the front door.

He rode his bicycle in the setting sun until he arrived at the dirty street where he lived. Greasy takeout joints and hair salons staffed by heavily made-up women lined the block. High-rises seemed to go up everywhere except here. His neighborhood had become a slum. Many of the buildings seemed ready to collapse, thanks in great part to all the illegal construction. A two-story building turned into a five-story monstrosity. The older residents had mostly moved to the suburbs, renting out their places to migrant workers; five or six people stayed in one room. Ever since Huang Hai died, He Qingying worried about safety every night. She cautioned Si Wang not to go out because of all the fights. Calling 1-1-0 was useless.

Si Wang came in late. He Qingying had prepared dinner and wanted to know why he hadn't returned home earlier. Now forty-one, He Qingying had left beauty behind. No one took a second look anymore.

It was a holiday, but she was in a bad mood.

Si Wang asked what was wrong.

"Didn't you see the sign? They're making us move. I don't know how much money they'll give us. Everyone's saying it'll be a big amount. I don't know what to do."

"I don't want to move."

"Wang Er, you were born here, so you're used to the place. But I've always wanted to get us a better home. You lived well with the Gu family."

Si Wang hugged his mother, saying, "Mom, let's not mention them anymore."

The moonlight outside was so bright that it hurt his eyes.

CHAPTER 50

Dear Xiaozhi,

Reading my letter is like seeing me.

I never told you how I once saw a ghost.

You know how there used to be a large forest by the steel factory near Nanming High? In 1988, when I was a senior, I often played soccer there. Whenever the ball got kicked over the factory walls, I'd go get it. One day, it was very late. When I got over the wall, everyone else had left. Days get dark early in winter, and it was windy. There was no one around me, just the Demon Girl Zone and the woods.

Supposedly, it was easy to see ghosts at times like that.

I saw her.

She came out of the wild reeds. She wore a tight Mandarin dress, and the cold weather didn't seem to bother her. She looked at me oddly. I was just seventeen. She actually spoke to me in Cantonese. I remember the soft sounds of her voice, but I don't remember what she said. I didn't feel afraid. I walked with her among the ruins and watched night fall. The moon rose above the run-down chimneys. I saw the sadness in her eyes. Her twenty-five-year-old self was frozen in that wasteland, never changing or getting hurt again.

Time turned into thick dust.

My young self stood alone. I was holding a soccer ball. The reeds sang next to me, rustling in the wind.

She smiled at me, but she didn't take me away.

I grew up, just like other people. I went to college, had a life. I didn't change the world; it changed me.

I changed so much that she would never recognize me again.

I was old then.

She was born in 1910; she died on March 8, 1935. She was buried in a public cemetery for Guangdong descendants. The graves turned into a factory, and her remains became part of the Demon Girl Zone.

Would I die like her at twenty-five?

Your teacher,
Ming
March 8, 1995

Fall of 2011.

Ouyang Xiaozhi sat alone in a corner of the Nanming High library. She smoothed out the sixteen-year-old letter; Shen Ming's neat handwriting filled the yellowed paper.

It was the last day of school before the October holiday break. As a student, Ouyang Xiaozhi spent countless hours in the library, indifferent to the haunted attic. She believed back then, as she did now, that every book was precious. She sometimes became so immersed in a book that she'd forget to eat.

The library had been renovated since she'd been a student. The reading room was still there, just with new desks and chairs. Many more books were available, both old and new. She walked among the shelves and found that copy of *The Rise and Fall of the Third Reich*. The blue cover had a drawing of Hitler. She flipped to the last page, where the checkout card was kept. Shen Ming's name was among the many who'd checked out the book. She put the card to her lips, almost smelling the scent of a past life. So many people had borrowed the book, but no one recognized the secret. Someone had drawn a pencil sketch of her face on the back.

Why this book? Because no girls read it.

There was a Japanese movie from 1995 that showed a similar scene.

Someone else entered the library. Ouyang Xiaozhi put away the letter and returned the book to the shelf.

She hid behind the shelf to watch the newcomer. It was him again.

The tenth-grader Si Wang walked around the library with familiarity, his fingers gliding over the spines of the books, until he stopped on *The Rise and Fall of the Third Reich*. He plucked the book off the shelf, flipping to the last page. He took out the checkout card and put it to his lips.

Ouyang Xiaozhi couldn't believe it. He couldn't have seen what she'd done earlier.

Si Wang spent a long time with the book. Before he left, he took a quick but focused look up at the attic.

Once she knew he was gone, Ouyang Xiaozhi let out a deep breath. From the library's second floor window she watched him walk across the sports field.

Half an hour later, she went back to the teachers' lounge. No one else was around. Some of the teachers were in the cafeteria, while others had already gone home. Stacks of homework sat on her desk. Her computer's screensaver was the poster for the Japanese movie *Love Letter*. Fatigue hit her. She absentmindedly rolled the mouse, making the screensaver disappear.

She found a note that had been tucked under the mouse. Someone had written a few lines of a poem.

Missing our enchanted meetings, you are now out of reach
The night is not the same, who am I yearning for
Longing coming undone like silken threads, unrequited in my
heart
It may be the same time next year, but my longing has turned
the wine bitter.

During the Qing dynasty, Huang Zhongze wrote that verse as part of his *Sixteen Poems on Longing*.

Not only did she know the poem, but she recognized the handwriting. Ouyang Xiaozhi's heart pounded as she took out the old letter. Comparing the handwriting, she was sure it was the same person.

She reached for her teacup but knocked it over, spilling rose tea. Using napkins she scrambled to clean up the mess. The note was damp. Would the writing be lost forever? She put the note on the windowsill, under a paperweight to dry.

Ouyang Xiaozhi rushed into the hallway, frazzled. Students and teachers passed. Anyone could have gotten into the teachers' lounge.

Anyone could have been possessed by Shen Ming's ghost.

The night is not the same, who am I yearning for.

CHAPTER 51

Late fall. Serenity Road.

Miss Cao's yard was littered with leaves.

Sixteen-year-old Si Wang arrived on time with food suitable for the elderly. In the last few months the two had become friends. They met almost every weekend.

During their last visit, she'd asked him bluntly, "You are like her, aren't you?" Miss Cao never called Yi Yu by her name. "Who were you in your last life?"

"I was just an ordinary person who died at twenty-five. I didn't have a crazy life like she did, so I envied her—just like I envy you, Miss Cao."

"Twenty-five?" Her wrinkled lips shook as she waved her hand. "Child, come closer."

He had become like her great-grandson; he lay in her arms and listened to her slow, dull heartbeat.

"I was married but never had kids. I miscarried from all the running during the war," she said, stroking his hair. "I wanted a kid so badly. My husband went to Taiwan and became an important person. He married and had kids there. In the eighties, he came back and saw me once. After that we never saw each other again. I read about his death in the papers. I've seen so much death. You might want revenge, but it is often too much to ask for. Do you understand?"

"But—"

"Time is like a river. One can never go back." After uttering these words, she fell asleep.

Si Wang walked into the study, thinking about how she looked weaker than usual. The folds, sags, and marks of aging on her skin seemed more obvious than ever.

Still looking like she was sleeping, Miss Cao reached out a skeletal hand and hissed the words, "Is—she—dead?"

"Who? No. She's in Hong Kong. Don't think crazy like that!"

"You're lying."

"No, I just wrote her a letter."

"I dreamed about her again last night."

Another dream? Had Yi Yu really died in Hong Kong?

Miss Cao said, "She told me she was dead." Tears fell down her cheeks. With a great deal of effort, as if she was using the last of her breath, she recited a poem: "No water could measure up to the sea. No clouds looked the same as those on Wu Mountain."

Si Wang added the last two lines: "No flowers were worth lingering over. Meditation and missing my dead wife was all I could do."

When he visited Miss Cao a week later, the door was locked. Trying to peek in, he met a neighbor who told him that Miss Cao had died seven days ago, the night he'd been there.

Si Wang knelt by the stairs and bowed three times.

He rode to the other side of Serenity Road with tears in his eyes. The old three-story building once had a mysterious owner who lived there in the eighties. The man lived through the tumultuous twentieth century.

He asked Policeman Ye Xiao about the owner of the house.

"The last Trotskyist of China." Ye Xiao watched Si Wang's expression. "Why are you asking?"

"He saw the young Shen Ming."
"But he died in 1992—when he was ninety-two."
"I know. He was my only friend."

CHAPTER 52

Christmas Eve 2011. Saturday.

Using binoculars, Ma Li looked down at the street from his balcony on the twentieth floor. It was a festive sight: twinkling Christmas trees, young couples walking together. He noticed a man in a dark jacket and a beret walking toward his building. He looked like a professional killer.

Someone buzzed Ma Li's apartment from the front door. Ma Li looked at the surveillance screen and saw that it was the man. But he'd taken off his hat, revealing Si Wang's sixteen-year-old face.

"It's you?"

"Ma Li, it's Shen Ming."

"How did you find me?"

"I have your phone number and license-plate number. It was easy to find the address."

"You knew I was home?"

"I had a feeling."

Ma Li let in the boy. He hadn't been out for days. About a minute later, Si Wang was at Ma Li's door.

"Merry Christmas," the young man said in English.

Ma Li shook his head in a daze. He fumbled around a pile of slippers for adults and kids, looking for a pair for Si Wang.

"You got married?"

"Divorced," Ma Li said, relieved.

Si Wang walked across the polished wood floor into the spacious living room. Expensive ceramics lined the wine cabinet and there was a real leather sofa.

"How old is your kid?"

"Four." He took out the child's photo. "A girl. She lives with her mom in Guangzhou."

"Do you miss her?"

"I'm used to it. She visits once a month, but she doesn't really know me." Ma Li poured him a glass of milk. "Why did you need to see me?"

"Two things. One, I'm back at Nanming High. Two, you still haven't told me everything."

"You should go." Ma Li grabbed the glass and pushed Si Wang to the door. "I must be crazy! You're not Shen Ming. You're a deluded teenager. Why did I let you in?"

But the young man didn't want to leave.

"I'm sorry, I've done enough for you. I've done too much for you. Don't make me call security."

"You forgot what you carved in the windowsill for Dead Poets Society?" Si Wang returned to the living room and started reading:

A word is dead
When it is said,
Some say.
I say it just
Begins to live
That day.

"I don't remember that."

"It's by Emily Dickinson, an American poet. I first read this poem in the Nanming High library, about seventeen years ago tonight. The only people there were you, Liu Man, and Ouyang Xiaozhi."

Ma Li stopped himself from saying something. He got a can of beer from the fridge and took a big gulp. Foam covered the edges of his mouth.

"Thank you for not throwing me out," Si Wang said.

"Are my words still on the windowsill?"

"Yes."

"What a miracle."

"My homeroom teacher is Zhang Mingsong."

Ma Li shook his head and took another gulp of beer. "I wouldn't have guessed."

"Some people said he killed me."

"Not possible."

"Do you know who did?"

Ma Li grabbed at his hair and mumbled, "God, am I dreaming? Why did I have to run into Mr. Shen's ghost?"

"Think of it as a dream."

Ma Li pushed Si Wang aside and opened the window to take in all of the glitz of Christmas Eve. He took out a pack of cigarettes and lit one. The wind quickly carried away the blue smoke. "Kid, are you schizophrenic? You think there's a ghost on your shoulder? Let me tell you something. You're living a fantasy. Everything you're talking about never happened! There is no Zhang Mingsong, no Liu Man, and no Ouyang Xiaozhi!"

His face turned cold. He flicked the cigarette out the window.

"I'm not a kid. I'm your high school homeroom and Chinese teacher. I'm Shen Ming. If I were still alive, I'd be forty-one."

"It's too cold!" Ma Li closed the window.

"You're saying I made up Ouyang Xiaozhi? I see her every day. You can see for yourself when you go to Nanming High."

"No. I never want to go back there."

"Ouyang Xiaozhi is my Chinese teacher."

"Why is she teaching? Why did she return to Nanming High?"

"She came back this year. I don't know why."

"Xiaozhi doesn't know you're Shen Ming?" Ma Li heard himself and changed his phrasing. "Or doesn't know that you claim to be Shen Ming?"

"I haven't told her yet. I might soon." Si Wang paced back and forth in the living room until he noticed a limited edition copy of *Farewell My Concubine*. "You still watch this?"

"I took it out this morning. I was going to watch it if I got bored tonight."

Ma Li remembered that when the school organized a viewing for the film in 1994, Mr. Shen left the theatre crying.

"I want to watch it again." Si Wang almost sounded petulant. He fed the disc into the DVD player. Ma Li turned off the lights and the two sat on the sofa and watched the movie. An arena appeared on the screen; the emperor and his concubine, wearing Peking Opera makeup, went in together.

Almost three hours later Ma Li and Si Wang walked out of the building together. They got to the garage; Ma Li still had the same Porsche.

On the drive home, as they got to the Wuning Road Bridge over Suzhou River, Si Wang shouted, "Stop the car!"

"We can't stop here!"

"Stop!"

Ma Li always listened to his teachers. He hit the brakes and pulled up to the bridge railing.

"Thanks." Si Wang jumped out of the car and waved. "Goodbye!"

"You OK?"

Standing under the bridge light, Si Wang smiled. "Don't worry! I'm not going to jump."

The Porsche sped away to join the other cars zooming over the bridge.

Si Wang watched the quiet Suzhou River and screamed.

CHAPTER 53

The last day of 2011.

"I'm a ghost."

"Fine, can you please just stop watching *Detective Conan*?"

"Officer Ye Xiao, I'm serious."

"Si Wang, it's late, and you should head home. Or your mom will call me again." Ye Xiao shaved in front of the bathroom mirror.

Another face was in the mirror, a sixteen-year-old's face. A calm and untamed light came out of his eyes. In a few years, he would be more handsome than Ye Xiao.

"I'm Shen Ming."

Ye Xiao turned off his razor. The world quieted. Half of his face was unshaven. He looked at Si Wang.

"Thank you for letting the police know. Now we can solve all of these cases."

Ye Xiao lived on the twenty-eighth floor of a building across from the never-dark Future Dreams Plaza. There was a military sniper rifle leaned up next to the window. Si Wang picked it up curiously.

"Careful," Ye Xiao shouted, "that's a real gun!"

"Who are you trying to kill?"

Ye Xiao put away the rifle and warned him not to tell anyone.

"I'll keep the secret." Si Wang bargained with the policeman. "But you've got to believe what I'm saying."

Ye Xiao was a bachelor who lived in a one-bedroom apartment. His place was neater than Huang Hai's. He didn't smoke or drink, but there were still plenty of instant noodles and junk food. He was good at suppressing his desires.

"After Shen Ming died in 1995, his ghost didn't go away. It's been hanging around this city for the past sixteen years, and using the body of Si Wang."

"You ambushed me at home to tell me this? You've kept the secret for this long—why tell me now?"

"I'm afraid I won't live to see eighteen."

"Anyone threatening you?" Ye Xiao looked out the peephole on his door. "I'll protect you."

"No, but I've been having nightmares lately. I'm always dying in them—getting my throat slashed, getting hit by a car, or falling from a building."

"You're afraid if you die, this secret will die with you, and you won't have your revenge?"

"Ye Xiao, you're very smart."

"If you're really Shen Ming's ghost, why don't you just go kill the killer?"

Si Wang smiled bitterly. "I don't know who he is. He got me from behind, so I never saw the person's face."

"I *will* catch him."

"Any leads? How about the guy who ran the DVD store? I'm the only one who can help you. I'm Shen Ming. I know a lot of things others don't. Ever since I was born as Si Wang, I swore I'd find the killer. I helped Huang Hai and I'll help you."

"All right, but you're a killer, too. You killed the teaching director, Yan Li—right?"

The question made Si Wang shake, and his expression turned dark, like he was back at the murder scene. "Yes."

"You know, I thought you had someone hidden inside you. I see the shadow of loss in your eyes. Only someone who has been through pain has that look. I get it, because we're the same."

"You've lost someone you loved?"

"It was devastating."

"But you don't know what it's like to be killed. It wasn't about the physical pain. It was turning into someone else after you die. You have to say good-bye to everyone you knew and start over as a baby, wasting all the years you lived before."

"I don't believe in ghosts. But tell me everything you know—real or fantasy. Go ahead, ghost detective."

"Why did Shen Ming go to the Demon Girl Zone on June 19, 1995? That's the biggest question."

"Right. If we knew why, maybe we would be a lot closer to the truth. So are you going to tell me?"

"It's a secret."

Ye Xiao shook his head and opened the door. "You can go home now."

"Wait—about Zhang Mingsong?"

"I've talked to him. He said Huang Hai interviewed him many times back then. He was even taken to the precinct. The Education Bureau management bailed him out. Is he a killer? I can't tell."

"Why can't you search his house?"

"There is no evidence. We couldn't get a search warrant." Ye Xiao redirected the conversation. "We got off track. I still have no reason to believe what you've told me."

"If you don't believe me, you'll regret it."

Ye Xiao thought of Shen Yuanchao. He decided to give the young man another chance. "Let's talk about Shen Ming's biological dad, Shen Yuanchao."

"I was Shen Yuanchao's illegitimate son. This was his biggest secret. He was terrified that others would find out about me. He wasn't a heartless guy. He did pay my living expenses every month. When I lived in the basement, he gave me books—everything from comics to classics. I especially remember *How the Steel Was Tempered.* He had a deluxe hardcover copy, and Pavel Korchagin was in a color engraving on the cover. Pavka rode a horse and wore a Red Army cap, looking stoically into the distance. I read that book at least ten times and almost wore off the cover. I memorized Nikolai Ostrovsky's words. I still remember the Chinese soldiers who fought for the Red Army against Symon Petlura. I wrote that quote in red ink on the title page: 'The most valuable thing for a person is his life, we only live once. We should live our life so that when we look back, we won't regret how we wasted our lives, nor be ashamed of why we didn't achieve anything.'"

"I saw this book at Shen Yuanchao's house. It was on his bookshelf. He retrieved it from Shen Ming's dorm room after Shen Ming died."

"Wow, he actually kept it for me."

Ye Xiao watched the young man's face. It had the expression of a much older man. If he was faking it, his performance was Oscar-worthy.

Ye Xiao took out a pen and some paper and asked, "Can you write it now?"

Si Wang nodded shakily and wrote:

The most valuable thing for a person is his life, we only live once. We should live our life so that when we look back, we won't regret how we wasted our lives, nor be ashamed of why we didn't achieve anything. When he dies, he should be able to say, "My entire life and all of my energy was devoted to the most glorious mission in the world—liberating all of humanity."

Ye Xiao closely watched him finish writing the quotation.

"Why did you become a cop?" Si Wang asked.

"Fate."

"Like how I turned into Si Wang after I died?"

"Maybe."

"You believe I'm Shen Ming's ghost?"

Ye Xiao shook his head. "There are no ghosts. I can help you, though—but you'll have to help me, too."

CHAPTER 54

The coldest month of the year—2012.

The Nanming Road construction project had dragged on for too long, causing students and teachers to complain. Everyone knew it was because of corruption. Ouyang Xiaozhi took the subway to work. Once again, she was close to being late. Someone got into a black taxi; she ran up, waving and shouting for them to wait for her.

Si Wang opened the door.

Xiaozhi got in the car and smiled awkwardly. "Si Wang, I'm sorry!"

Xiaozhi was so cold she kept rubbing her hands. Si Wang asked the driver to turn on the heat.

"You'll be there before the car heats up."

"It's fine, I can handle it." Xiaozhi's face was pale, but puffs of her hot breath and the scent of her shampoo reached him.

They rode the rest of the way in silence. When they arrived Xiaozhi whispered, "Being late is not good. Please don't let the other students know."

Mr. An, a handsome unmarried political science teacher, saw her and called out sweetly, "Xiaozhi."

The greeting embarrassed her. Everyone, teachers and students, called her Ms. Ouyang now.

"Morning, Mr. An."

"Did you have breakfast yet?"

He'd brought breakfast for her.

"Oh, thank you. I am a bit hungry."

She accepted the food and the two of them walked into the school together. Si Wang still stood outside the entrance in the chilling wind.

Xiaozhi turned around and said, "Si Wang, get inside now, don't be late!"

The whole school knew about Mr. An's crush on Ouyang Xiaozhi. The male teachers were jealous, while the female teachers wished her well. Xiaozhi looked young, but she was 35 and needed to be married. Mr. An was from a good family who lived in a high-end development near Nanming Road. Supposedly, he was related to the principal.

The first class was political science. Mr. An found Si Wang staring into space so he called on the boy. Everyone thought Si Wang would be humiliated, but Si Wang answered perfectly. He described the difference between Marx and Hegel, and brought up Spinoza's ideas about monism, as well as Kant's discussions on "What is man." Mr. An was stunned, and all he could squeeze out was, "Si Wang, you read a lot of extracurricular books."

The literary society met in the afternoon as usual even though finals were coming up. Ouyang Xiaozhi was the advisor. Shen Ming had been the advisor in 1995. One year, he gave her a book of poems by Li Qingzhao because he knew she liked Yi'an-style poems. That was the first gift Xiaozhi received from him.

"Si Wang, are you paying attention? Don't be nervous—we're a literary society, not a class. I've heard from other students that you know a lot of classic poems. Know any by Li Qingzhao?"

"Deep is the pavilion, clouds gathering nearby. Spring is here, but he's gone. So much has happened, we're old and nothing is the same. Who is here to sigh with me? No point in doing anything."

Xiaozhi looked down at the book. Not even she had memorized the whole poem. She was impressed. "Very nice!"

After the literary society's meeting ended, Si Wang was about to rush out of class when Xiaozhi asked him to wait for her. They walked out on the playing field together. There was a thick layer of frost on the ground; no one was around. He had nothing to say to his teacher, so he just kept walking.

"Where are you going?" she asked.

They stopped at the corner of the field. The wall where roses bloomed was now barren.

"Si Wang, you're a really odd kid."

Everyone agreed on this. Tenth grade was almost over, but he was still a loner, and had nothing to say to anyone. Supposedly, some girls texted him about movie dates, but he never replied.

"Please tell me—what does your dad do?"

"He's just a regular person," Si Wang answered. "He's not very educated, and he's always traveling."

"Your mom?"

"She runs a bookstore."

"No wonder you know so much poetry."

"It's a small store right across from my junior high."

By the time they reached the school gates, it was dark. Another cold wind gust swirled, and snow flew everywhere.

"Si Wang, you'd better head back. I'm going home, too."

Mr. An appeared, eager to talk to Xiaozhi. Si Wang backed away.

"Xiaozhi, have you decided?"

"Sorry, I want to go home early today. We'll have dinner another time?"

"Oh, that's a shame. I already made reservations at that Japanese restaurant."

Disappointed, Mr. An looked around, probably wanting to see if anyone was picking her up.

He saw Si Wang and turned back to Xiaozhi, smiling. "It's OK. Take care getting home."

The wind was stronger than before, the snow, too. Xiaozhi stood up her collar to tuck in her hair. A red Elantra stopped in front of her. It was the unlicensed cab driver from before. Xiaozhi was about to get in when Si Wang called for her to stop.

She looked back in surprise. "What is it?"

"Don't get in!"

"Why not?" She was confused, shocked that a shy kid like him would grab her arm so brusquely.

"Instinct, it doesn't feel right."

He looked at the driver; the man was the picture of innocence. Another teacher came out wanting the ride. Xiaozhi backed away and gave up the car. "Mr. Wang, go ahead."

"Thanks."

The teacher looked at her with a weird expression; she was holding hands with a student.

The taxi sped away, leaving her and Si Wang in the snow.

"Sorry." He finally let go of her hand.

Xiaozhi hugged herself, and coldly said, "What were you doing?"

"Didn't you think that driver was dangerous?"

"Yes, taking unlicensed cabs is bad. It's illegal and affects the market, and it's risky, too. I wasn't acting like a teacher. I promise you, I'll never take an illegal cab again." Xiaozhi rubbed her arms. "You really grabbed me."

"I—"

"Forget it. Just don't anything like it again." Xiaozhi puffed out a ball of white air. "Si Wang, thank you for looking out for me."

They stood by the dirty, empty road.

"I might as well walk to the subway station. Bye!"

She took a few steps before Si Wang stopped her, insisting that he walk her to the station.

"It's fine. You'll miss dinner at the cafeteria."

"It's not safe around here. I don't trust you walking by yourself."

The words made her feel awkward, but she didn't know how to refuse.

Nanming Road looked different at night, desolate but littered with construction equipment. Si Wang said nothing. Snow flew into their eyes and blurred their vision. Thankfully the streetlights were still on, casting their shadows on the white ground.

They were on the same path to the Demon Girl Zone; stuck between two construction zones, the abandoned factory lay ahead of them. Xiaozhi stopped and she could almost see the abandoned chimneys. She couldn't take another step.

"What are you looking at?"

"Oh, it's nothing," Xiaozhi said.

"I heard there's a place there called the Demon Girl Zone."

It was the first time Si Wang said those words to her. Xiaozhi's face turned from a frozen pink to a deathly white.

"You—" She adjusted her expression. "You heard this from older students, right?"

"I know that a teacher died there in 1995."

She was afraid to face him so she turned to look at Nanming Road. "I went to Nanming High in 1995, too. The teacher you mentioned was my homeroom teacher."

"You've been there?"

"Don't ask questions like this. He was killed."

"Who killed him?"

"I don't know. I don't think they ever solved the case. Si Wang, please don't mention this place or walk here again. I want you guys to be safe, OK?"

She kept walking forward, not lingering at all. Si Wang walked next to her. His nose was running from the cold wind.

"Go back. You don't want to get sick."

"It's OK, I'll walk you to the subway station."

"Si Wang, I need to ask. Why do you never call me Ms. Ouyang, and just Xiaozhi instead? It's not very polite."

"Sorry, Xiaozhi."

"Maybe I should be apologizing. You're a special kid. You obviously express yourself differently than other children do. I can't force you to talk like everyone else, and maybe you think using polite names for teachers is a meaningless formality."

They reached the subway. By now a layer of snow covered the ground.

"Thank you, Si Wang!"

CHAPTER 55

Second semester of tenth grade.

Zhang Mingsong was almost fifty. Despite his thinning hair, he still looked young. Some said he was a playboy and had a lot of girlfriends—that he didn't want to be tied down to a wife.

Mr. Zhang arrived at school early each day so he could clean the office meticulously. He also jogged at school to stay in shape. He'd worked here for over twenty years. He knew every inch of the property, from where the weeds grow to how to look into girls' dorm rooms.

Si Wang often used the sports field. He used to be as skinny as a soybean. He exercised intensely every morning: two laps, forty push-ups, twenty pull-ups. He boxed, practiced martial arts and Thai boxing. In the cafeteria, he often requested raw eggs. Students were afraid of him. The boys said he was crazy and the girls joked that he was a muscle freak.

Si Wang behaved as if he had an enemy, as if he would be killed if he didn't work out.

One day in February after the last class, Zhang Mingsong stopped him. "Si Wang, please come to my office."

His office was on the top floor of the teachers' building, in a room reserved for elite teachers. It was spacious but dark. The window was open only a crack and covered with a thick curtain. With utter seriousness, Zhang Mingsong said, "Sit. No need to be nervous. Know why I asked you here?"

Si Wang shook his head no. He sat on a chair in the corner of the room. Awards flags given by past graduates plastered the wall behind him, as well as teaching awards from the city and even national organizations.

"I don't normally get involved in things like this. I like to think of myself as just a math teacher. But since I'm also a home-room teacher now, I need to help everyone."

"What did I do?"

Zhang Mingsong had a DSLR camera on his desk, and photos lined the glass tabletop. He put away the camera and looked at Si Wang. "I'm worried about you. You're too quiet and have no friends. You act weird. Some students say you scare them."

"I don't know what others think. I've always been like this."

"You jog alone every morning. I noticed a few girls watching you. I talked to them. Some people said you don't like girls?"

"I'm just shy around them."

"That's not a reason." Zhang Mingsong showed a dubious smile. "You're not telling me everything."

Si Wang put on an innocent expression.

"You stand out in my class, maybe even in the whole school."

"I like to read too much. I'm just a geek."

"A boxing geek?"

"I live in a bad neighborhood. Thugs are fighting in it all the time. I work out to protect my mom and me."

"Si Wang, I looked at your file. Your family is moving soon. I understand." Zhang Mingsong took a sip of tea. "Your dad went missing when you were in elementary school, and you grew up with your mom. Your father doesn't even have a residency registration anymore, even though your mom tells us he works in other cities."

"Mr. Zhang, these are private matters. Please don't tell anyone—not even other teachers."

"Don't worry, I protect all my students." He noticed Si Wang's eyes weren't on his face but on the giant bookshelf behind him. "What are you looking at?"

The bookshelf didn't seem like a math teacher's. They were volumes of history, religion, semiology, and criminology: Gnosticism, Carl Jung's autobiography, the Holy Grail, medieval witches, summoning spirits in ancient China, Tibetan mantras, psychiatry, and introduction to medical examiner techniques. There was also a copy of *The Happy Prince and Other Tales*, as well as *The Picture of Dorian Gray* and *Salomé*.

"Sorry, I was just curious."

"These are my favorite books. I·can lend you some if you want."

"Can I go now?"

After sending off Si Wang, Zhang Mingsong leaned back in his chair, deep in thought. He went to the other side of the teachers' building after it was dark.

He unlocked the file room. Aside from him, only two other teachers had access. Rows of dusty metal cabinets were labeled with categories and dates. He quickly found the files for the class of 1988—Shen Ming's high school class.

Zhang Mingsong had been his math teacher.

The thick file was untouched; it contained everyone's registration card, a student handbook, test scores, and teacher comments. The class was small that year, just 100 students in three sections. Shen Ming was in Section 2; he started in 1985. Lu Zhongyue was in the same section.

He opened Shen Ming's registration card. Under the flashlight, the black-and-white photo was blurry. Shen Ming's gaze was moody in the picture; he bit his lips like he was trying to hold back something. Even today, he would have been a teen heart-throb.

The file showed Shen Ming to be an excellent student. He scored between 85 and 90 for Chinese. His English, political science, history, and geography scores were amazing as well. He did well in physics and chemistry; his math was weaker, but he still scored in the eighties. His homeroom teacher gave him high marks, saying he was a well-rounded student. He was also in the Youth League Committee; he represented the school at district-wide meetings, and won all sorts of awards.

In June of 1988, a month before the college entrance exams, there was a serious fire at the squatters' huts across from Nanming High. Zhang Mingsong was the teacher on duty that night. He would never forget the towering flames. Shen Ming had charged into the fire and didn't come out for a long time. Just when everyone assumed he was dead, he emerged shrouded in fire, appearing like a god in the night sky. As people came to his aid, they realized he was holding a little girl—one of the homeless children who lived in the huts. The fire killed sixteen people, including her parents.

There was always an awards ceremony for heroes after every disaster, no matter how many people had died. Shen Ming was recognized as a brave youth. Combined with his academic excellence, he was able to get sponsored admission to Peking University.

That was twenty years ago. But was Shen Ming really dead?

CHAPTER 56

Early spring 1994.

She walked into the Nanming High teachers' building for the first time. It was raining slightly. The teachers' lounge was damp. Even though she was wearing thermals, she shivered.

Six years had passed. Shen Ming was already a grown man, a respected high school Chinese teacher. Ouyang Xiaozhi remembered his face.

She was no longer that dirty, hungry, homeless eleven-year-old girl. She had a black backpack and her white sweater was long enough to cover her knees. She had long hair, which was rare for girls back then. Only Hong Kong movies showed hairstyles like this. Her pale skin almost made her look malnourished, but it was her eyes that made people remember her. Her beautiful nose and lips were striking. She looked like a teenage version of the movie star Joey Wong.

Judging by appearances, this seventeen-year-old seemed to be from a good family.

Her enrollment was unusual. With the exception of a few bureaucrats' children, no one transferred into this elite school.

"Good morning teacher, I'm Ouyang Xiaozhi." She spoke gently and bowed, her manners soothing.

Shen Ming had never seen a student so courteous. He spoke a bit awkwardly. "Welcome, I'm Shen Ming, Section 2's homeroom teacher and also your Chinese teacher. Let me introduce you to your classmates."

No one else was in the teachers' lounge, and he didn't seem to want to be alone with this female student.

They got to the chilly classroom. Xiaozhi bowed again. "Classmates, good morning, I'm Ouyang Xiaozhi."

Shen Ming assigned her to share a desk with Liu Man.

Ma Li sat behind her. He admired her hair, which looked like a black waterfall. Several boys craned their necks to catch a glimpse of her slender fingers as she took out a pencil case and books and arranged them on the desk. Liu Man, dressed all in red, was very warm, helping her new classmate clean up her desk.

Busy rain fell on the window. A few early-blooming camellia shivered in the spring chill.

Shen Ming started his Chinese class. The lesson was on Lu Xun's "In Memoriam of Liu Hezhen." He wrote on the blackboard: "Showing my biggest sorrow to my enemies, making them rejoice in my pain, this would be my meager offerings to the dead, my dedication to the martyrs."

Ouyang Xiaozhi suddenly turned around to nod at the male students ogling her. She opened her mouth, but no sound came out. She was mouthing, "I hope we get along."

She assimilated to the school quickly and was friendly with a few girls, especially Liu Man. The boys tried to kiss up to her, but Xiaozhi was always coolly rebuffing them.

Shen Ming seemed to always avoid her. Xiaozhi was worried he had recognized her. Was it her eyes? But girls developed so much while growing up. In six years, she'd changed completely. Except for the class discussions, Shen Ming hadn't spent any time with her. He did get along with other students. Liu Man came to him with questions all the time; he also played basketball with Ma Li.

The friendliest teacher was a young and pretty music instructor. She'd just started there after graduating Teachers' College. Music classes weren't taken seriously then, and they were rare after the second semester of eleventh grade. Xiaozhi's impressions of music class were limited to memories of her teacher playing the piano. Her last music test was singing along with the piano. Some students sang pop songs or "Love Song of the Mandarin Ducks." The teacher played accompaniment for all of these popular tunes, but she chose "My Country" from the textbook. Xiaozhi had thought then that it would be wonderful to be a teacher.

Ouyang Xiaozhi never mentioned why she transferred to Nanming High. A teacher revealed the secret—her father was an army colonel who'd died in the Sino-Vietnamese War. He was awarded the martyr honor. Xiaozhi and her mom were left all alone. She was a dedicated student who'd been going to a good high school in the city but had to transfer to a boarding high school for some reason. Since her family had martyr status, the Education Bureau sent her to Nanming High.

Actually, her dad wasn't a martyr.

Early spring, 2012.

She wasn't that high school girl in a white sweater anymore. She was a high school teacher in a white coat and knee-high boots.

It was a clear, starry night; the oleander had not bloomed.

Xiaozhi crossed the sports field heading for the multipurpose building. She opened a door on the fourth floor, which led to the roof balcony. As a student she'd come here often. Very few students knew of this place now.

She looked down. Mr. An was pacing on the sports field. The man kept asking her out. She'd already turned him down twice, but he kept at it. This was the only spot on campus where she could escape him.

The moon was bright. Wind howled across the roof, mussing her hair. She turned around suddenly, sensing someone else's presence.

"Si Wang, what are you doing here?"

"Shh!" He put his finger to his lips. "He'll hear us!"

Xiaozhi nodded. He walked to the balcony railing and looked down.

"Why is he hassling you?" He kept his voice low, afraid that the wind would carry it.

"Don't get involved in teachers' business."

"I was worried for you."

"Si Wang, please call me Ms. Ouyang." Her expression stayed strict, but she kept her voice low per Si Wang's wish. She almost breathed out the words, which made her sound comical.

"Fine, Xiaozhi."

"Why aren't you sleeping at this hour?"

"Can't sleep."

"Were you following me?"

"No, you just showed up on the sports field, and Mr. An was chasing you. I was afraid he would try something."

"But how did you know I was here?" She patted down her skirt and looked behind her in horror. "No one else knows about this door."

"I do." He put a finger to his lips to shush her. Under the dim light, Mr. An could be seen walking out of the school dejectedly.

"Who are you, Si Wang?"

"I've been here," he said, stroking the balcony railing, "but it was many years ago."

"Just how old are you? How can you even say 'many years ago'?"

"Seventeen years ago, you were standing here, too. You were shaking and almost fell. If someone hadn't grabbed you, you'd have fallen and died."

"Shut up!" Ouyang Xiaozhi's face changed. She started walking away but turned back, as if wanting to say something.

"You were trying to kill yourself."

She lowered her head to hide her eyes. "I just . . . wanted to get some fresh air. I wasn't looking and almost tripped."

"That's not what you said! You said that ever since you got to the school, people were spreading rumors about you. They made up lies. You were a good girl, you were afraid to talk to guys, and you never associated with thugs. You were being harassed, right?"

"Yes, I did say those things. How do you know all of this?"

"In 1995, you said a lot of things on this roof. If people just said things about you, you would have taken it—you were used to it. But by the second semester of senior year, even uglier rumors started. They even involved your parents. You couldn't let them go. As long as you stayed here, you'd never get away. You were a transfer student about to take the college entrance exams. You couldn't transfer again. You had nowhere to go."

Back in 1995 she'd struggled like a wounded kitten on this roof. The two of them fell to the ground; his hand held her waist. Xiaozhi stopped fighting. Her cheeks were cold with leftover tears. They looked at the stars, both of them breathing deeply. She turned to look at her teacher.

Shen Ming explained how he'd been on night patrol and seen her shadow on the roof. He'd suspected someone was about to jump and ran up.

All of these years later, she still remembered their conversation as if it had happened yesterday.

"Xiaozhi, there's no need to kill yourself," Shen Ming had said.

"Why?"

"I almost died saving you from that fire seven years ago. If you kill yourself, I'd have saved you for nothing."

"You recognized me?"

"I thought you looked familiar, but you seemed different, so I've secretly been watching you. You always stare at the wilderness across from the school, and you go to the Demon Girl Zone alone. It made me remember that little girl."

"Mr. Shen, I thought you'd never recognize me."

"I still have the gift you gave me."

"This is the third time you've saved me. I don't know how I can thank you."

"The best gift would be for you to live every day happy."

Ouyang Xiaozhi's smile turned into laughter so loud that the whole school could have heard her.

The next day some students said they'd heard a ghost the night before.

Now all of these years later, on an equally chilly spring night, Xiaozhi was once again standing on this balcony. The moonlight illuminated her tears.

"Where did you hear these stories?"

Si Wang pointed at his head.

"Did you leave that note with the Huang Zhongze poem on my desk?"

"Yes."

Standing there shaking in the cold wind Xiaozhi slapped Si Wang. "You're despicable! Sick! Do you know what you're doing? Are you crazy?" she screamed. "Si Wang, I beg you, please don't bother me anymore! Don't think there is anything between us."

"You're the one who doesn't get it," he said, his eyes unwavering, the shape of her palm visible on his cheek.

"I'm sorry, I had to slap you to wake you up." She stroked his face with her ice-cold slender fingers. "I'm your teacher, Ms. Ouyang. I'm thirty-five; I'm not much younger than your mother.

299

You're just seventeen and so handsome. You could have any girl you wanted."

"None of that matters."

"Listen, kid! Everything you said happened after you were born. Do you know that the teacher who saved me has been dead for a long time?"

"He died at 10:00 p.m. on June 19, 1995." Si Wang's calm declaration of Shen Ming's hour of death sounded like he was answering a test question.

"Stop it!"

"Are you afraid?"

"Si Wang, you think too much. Have you been researching everything about me since coming to Nanming High? Did you read his diary? Copy his handwriting?"

"He didn't write diaries."

"You talked to Ma Li?"

"You really don't talk to any of your old classmates?"

"Stop acting like a grown-up. Don't get close to me. Don't like me. I'm—I'm poisoned!"

"Poisoned?"

"Any man who gets close to me dies."

"I believe you."

Her tears had dried in the wind, and under the crisp moonlight her face looked like a ghost's. She choked out the words, "It's lights out. You have to get back to your room. Please don't violate school rules."

Xiaozhi ran off, leaving him alone on the balcony.

Across the sports field, the light in the library attic was on again.

CHAPTER 57

Grave-Sweeping Day.

In the seventeen years since Shen Ming's death, Shen Yuanchao had studied all kinds of killers. He was no longer afraid of dead bodies, coffins, or graves.

It was a rainy day. Bright-yellow rapeseed flowers surrounded the cemetery. Above the words "Martyr Huang Hai" was a serious photograph of the man embedded on the tombstone. He should have been buried in the martyr cemetery, but they obeyed his wish to be buried with his son in the regular cemetery.

Shen Yuanchao held a black umbrella and a bouquet of chrysanthemums. Si Wang was already there. The young man turned around, holding three sticks of lit incense.

"I'll catch that monster," Shen Yuanchao said, "and kill him with my own hands." He had more white hair than before, but his gaze was deeper, more chilling. "You grew taller. I'm here to pay respects to your dad."

"Thank you, Prosecutor Shen."

Shen Yuanchao clutched the young man's cold hands. Staring at the grave he said, "I didn't make it to your funeral. So I came today to see you. I know you thought all the clues I found over the years were dead ends, but I'm really grateful to you."

"My dad heard you. He would bless me to find the killer."

"You're too young."

"My dad often mentioned an American movie. It's set in the 1950s, and it's about an honest prosecutor's son in the racist American South. The protagonist always recited this poem: 'I am the master of my fate. I am the captain of my soul.' It was from English poet William Henley."

"What are you telling me, child?"

"Prosecutor Shen, you're a lot better than I thought. You're a good man."

"I've been retired for a long time. I worked as a prosecutor for forty years. I have no regrets as a Party member. I'll bid you farewell for now."

"Let me walk you out."

Shen Yuanchao took one last look at the grave and was shocked by what he noticed. Under Huang Hai's name, the words "Son Huang Zhiliang," were carved and filled in black ink, meaning he was dead. If Huang Hai had other children, their names would also be listed, but filled with red ink if they were still alive.

Si Wang stood in front of Huang Zhiliang's grave.

Shen Yuanchao may have been old, but he had good vision. He clearly saw the tombstone for Huang Zhiliang, whose birth and death dates were 1994 and 2004. The tombstone photo showed the ten-year-old who'd died from leukemia and had some resemblance to Si Wang.

"You—you!" His teeth chattered.

"That's right, I'm Huang Zhiliang. I died eight years ago from leukemia. I wanted to tell you that reincarnation is real."

CHAPTER 58

Ye Xiao walked into the slums. All around him stood dilapidated houses and illegally built shacks. Many families posted signs against the forced move. Some people were building structures, digging in for a long battle. Red light seeped out of some seedy hair salons. Idle young men squatted on the ground and smoked. He'd dressed in regular clothes so no one could tell he was a cop. His forehead was bandaged, and he sported a big bruise. Every step hurt his back.

Si Wang was waiting for him at the noodle shop. The teenager looked different again: His chest was even broader, visible muscles lined his chest and arms. No one would dare pick a fight with him.

"What happened?" Si Wang looked around. "Who did this to you?"

"Know what happened at Future Fantasy Plaza?"

"Everyone does."

"I was buried almost one hundred meters deep. I almost died."

"If you died, what other cop would help me?" Si Wang spoke to Ye Xiao like they were the same age.

Ye Xiao didn't mind. Each man ordered a bowl of Suzhou-style lamb noodles.

"Why can't we meet at your house?"

"Huang Hai came to my house all the time, then he died. I don't want that to happen to you."

"Not a bad reason. How's your mom doing?"

"Still stressed about the forced move. The money from the developers isn't enough to buy a bathroom. She's always worrying about where we'll end up."

Ye Xiao pointed to Si Wang's bulging biceps. "Where'd you get those?"

"Boxing club. It's a charity club for boxing fans. I don't have to pay to practice. They say it's the end of the world this year, but I'm not worried. I've already died once, so I've got nothing to lose. I just don't want to miss out on catching my killer. I don't want Lu Zhongyue to kill me the next time I see him."

"I won't let you run into him." The wounded Ye Xiao looked masculine inside the loud, greasy noodle shop. "When I get better, we can practice."

"But who knows if I would even remember anything in my next life? I might not after passing through the River of Forgetfulness and drinking the Meng Po Soup. Then there's the Animal realm in the Six Realms of reincarnation. I could return as a cow, a horse, a dog."

The cop's face darkened. "A week ago, I went to Shen Yuanchao's house and borrowed that book with Shen Ming's handwriting—*How the Steel Was Tempered*. I took the book and your handwritten Pavel Korchagin quote to the Police Academy's handwriting lab. The experts said they were written by the same person."

"So now you believe that I'm Shen Ming?"

"Even the best handwriting experts can be wrong. I don't believe in ghosts."

"I'm not a ghost."

"Kid, I'm not debating this with you, I'm here to warn you—don't pretend to be Huang Hai's son. This is not a game. You're disrespecting Huang Hai and his son, and playing a joke on poor Shen Yuanchao. If you were really possessed by Shen Ming's ghost, you shouldn't lie like this."

"He told you?"

"Yes, Shen Yuanchao said he was paying his respects at Huang Hai's grave when he saw the dead son of Huang. That kid has been dead for eight years, but now he's apparently grown up and looking for Shen Ming's killer—as well as his own father's killer."

"I'm sorry, I didn't really think he would believe me."

"Prosecutor Shen believes you."

"I . . ." Si Wang couldn't eat anymore; he put down his chopsticks. "Did you tell him everything?"

"I almost did. But I thought if he knew that a high school student called Si Wang was impersonating Huang Hai's son, he could make trouble for you at school. Then you'd be done. What if your mom found out?"

"Please, no!"

"You should thank me. I told Shen Yuanchao it was his imagination. But he made his daughter, the girl born after Shen Ming's death, prove that she also saw you at their house on Mid-Autumn Festival."

"I'm sorry."

"Don't look for him again. You'll ruin his life."

"He was my dad in my past life. I won't risk his life."

Ye Xiao finished his noodle soup. "Si Wang, you're risking your life, too."

CHAPTER 59

Shen Yuanchao never saw Huang Hai's dead son again.

A month later, the weather turned hot. The rush hour bus reeked of sweat as a high school girl with a ponytail did her English homework by the window. Finals were coming up in a few days.

Colorful sights passed outside the bus. Someone saw her face reflected in the window. She was prettier than before; her white face had rounded a bit and looked youthful and fresh.

Shen Min suddenly noticed him.

The young man wore a track suit. He held on to the pole to avoid falling on the crowded bus.

She remembered him from last year's Mid-Autumn Festival.

There was no place to hide. He greeted her without conviction.

She pretended not to hear and kept doing her homework, though her heart started beating faster.

The bus lurched along its route, drove some more. Si Wang couldn't stay silent. "It's too dark—don't write on here."

Signs for Haidilao Hot Pot went on outside the window. Her ponytail shook, and she put down her pen, but she still refused to look at him. The air on the bus was swampy, and Shen Min's face flushed. She tried to avoid the young man's gaze. Past the countless tired faces crammed together, she noticed a middle-aged man with the typical haircut looking at her. He was unremarkable except for the birthmark on his forehead.

The bus stopped and he suddenly squeezed toward the exit.

"Stop," Shen Min cried.

Si Wang also noticed the man with the birthmark. He shouted, too, and pushed aside two older ladies trying to get to the exit. He was stuck, however, and being screamed at by his fellow passengers. The guy had already jumped off the bus and many more people streamed onboard, blocking Si Wang's exit.

"Don't close the door," he pleaded.

The driver looked back in the mirror, cursed, closed the doors, and merged with traffic.

A scared Shen Min looked out the bus window. The older man stood calmly on the street, watching the bus roll away. She stood up and pushed her way through the pathetic passengers and got close to the out-of-breath young man.

They got off the bus together two stops later.

Shen Min started talking first. "Why did you try to chase him?"

He coughed and said, "I saw him stealing someone's wallet."

"You can catch thieves?"

"I try to do good."

"Thanks."

"For what? He wasn't stealing from you."

"I'm talking about that day when you came to my house and made an offering for my older brother."

"That's something I needed to do. I will catch your brother's killer."

A lot of street vendors were next to the dark bus stop, feeding hungry workers on their way home. Delicious smells swirled up from the stands. They walked to a stand selling deep-fried stinky tofu.

"You hungry?" he asked.

"A little."

Si Wang bought some piping-hot tofu, and the two shared it. Shen Min stared at him as she ate.

He lowered his head shyly. "What are you looking at?"

"You look familiar. I met you when I was a kid. When was it?" She looked at him more closely. "I remember! It was at Number One Elementary School on Longevity Road. You were in Section 2, and I was in Section 3. Lots of kids said you were a genius. I was your only friend."

"Yes, that's right. I can't believe you recognized me. If you showed me a photo of myself back then, *I* probably wouldn't even recognize me."

"I remember you telling me you were Si Wang, Si as in 'general,' Wang as in 'lookout.' But why did my dad say your last name was Huang?"

"Sorry, I lied to you. Si Wang is *siwang*, or *death*."

"So Si Wang isn't your name—it's just an alias?"

"Right, my name is Huang Zhiliang, but I also have a nickname—Little Ming."

She ate the tofu as she said, "Wait, I'm called Little Min!"

"My Ming is *ming* as in 'tomorrow.'"

"Why is Huang Zhiliang also Little Ming?"

"So many questions! But fine, I'll tell you. You know Zhuge Liang, the great historian?"

"Of course!"

"What was his middle name?"

She opened her eyes wide. "Kong Ming! So, Huang Zhiliang is Little Ming?"

"Yep, you figured it out!"

"But my dad said you died."

"Your dad is right. I died eight years ago when I was ten."

"You're lying!"

"Fine, I'm lying."

His mix of lies and truth unsettled her. She backed up two steps. "I need to go home."

"Municipal inspectors are here," someone shouted. Within seconds, the vendors had pushed their carts away into the night.

The young man also disappeared.

Dazed, Shen Min mumbled, "Si Wang? Little Ming?"

CHAPTER 60

June 19, 2012. The seventeenth anniversary of Shen Ming's death.

A new moon decorated the sky. She crossed the path near Nanming Road and reached the space between two construction lots; the abandoned factory was still there. Tall chimneys stood among wild reeds; insects and frogs chirped. She crawled inside the factory ruins. Her flashlight revealed piles of junk scattered all around. She reached the stairs that went underground.

Demon Girl Zone.

One, two, three, four, five, six, seven. She counted seven steps to reach the end of the path. She faced the thick hatch door, the round handle thickly layered with cobwebs.

Deep breathing.

She imagined the body, Mr. Shen's twenty-five-year-old body, decaying in the dirty, bloody water.

She was afraid to open the door.

It was 10:00 p.m. She returned to the factory's ground floor. She crouched down and from her bag took out some silver joss paper that she lit.

The woman burning the offering was dressed in white and her black hair draped her profile. Her slender fingers almost touched the flames. She was neither Nie Xiaoqian, the female ghost of *A Chinese Ghost Story*, nor any ghost or spirit. She only looked like an unearthly creature. No wonder students called her Ms. Goddess.

She always kept her dates, even if it was seventeen years later.

The flames colored her face red. She held her skirt hem carefully to keep it from the fire. Some ashes from the burning joss paper fluttered into her eyes. Her tears sizzled as they fell into the fire.

Someone else was there. She could tell by the sound of crying.

Ouyang Xiaozhi turned around and saw a person entering the chamber.

Si Wang.

She screamed loud enough to scare off any ghosts. She covered her face with her sleeve and mumbled, "Why are you here?"

"Xiaozhi."

The final exams had been administered last week. Si Wang was the only student who had not left school. He crossed the bonfire and slowly approached her, as if he was ready to shed his ghost shell.

"Don't touch me."

He grabbed his teacher's arm. "Don't be afraid! I'm here!"

She looked up and tried to retain her teacher's composure. "It's summer break—why aren't you at home? Why are you here in the middle of the night?"

"Shouldn't I be asking you that?"

Her eyes looked like puzzles drenched in tears. The flames burned out, leaving yellow and black ashes.

"This has nothing to do with you. You weren't even born when he died." She shook her arm. "Let me go."

Si Wang was a lot stronger now. His shoulders didn't even move. His fingers still gripped her like a vise. "Still remember *Dead Poets Society*?"

311

Si Wang's unwavering voice made Xiaozhi's heart beat fast. She looked downstairs and shook her head. "You mean that American movie?"

Shen Ming had played that movie for his students when she was in high school, getting him in trouble with the principal and the teaching director.

"Not just that, did you really forget?" Si Wang said in his youthful voice, "Starting tomorrow, I will be a happy person / Feed the horses, cut firewood, travel the world / Starting tomorrow, I will think about grains and vegetables / I have a house facing the sea, flowers blooming in spring."

She was losing her sense of reality, time, and space. On the eve of Grave-Sweeping Day in 1995, Shen Ming took Ma Li, Liu Man, and Ouyang Xiaozhi over the school walls. They went to the Demon Girl Zone and recited poem after poem by Hai Zi.

This was the Dead Poets Society founded by Shen Ming. It was a secret among the four of them. No one else ever knew about it. Had the school administrators found out, Shen Ming would have been fired.

The Demon Girl Zone didn't frighten the four of them—it was just a place to hold their poetry-appreciation gatherings.

Two months later, two members of the society died: one on the library roof, one in the Zone's underground area.

"The society read two poets the most, one was Hai Zi, the other one was Gu Cheng. They both died. One died by suicide on the railroad tracks. The other one killed his wife with an ax and then himself on a South Pacific island."

"What does that have to do with Shen Ming's death?"

"You dressed the same way on June 19, 1995."

She looked down at her white dress and then stared at him. "Who are you?"

"If I said I was Shen Ming, would you believe me?" The voice came from deep within his chest, and his eyes looked like those of a thirty-five-year-old man.

"No!"

He coolly recited a conversation from the past.

"Mr. Shen."

"Don't talk to me, don't get close to me. I'm not a teacher anymore."

"I heard you won't be at school after tomorrow. When are you leaving?"

"Tonight—eight o'clock."

"Can it be any later? I will wait for you at ten o'clock in the Demon Girl Zone."

"Demon Girl Zone? Is it important?"

"I have some things to tell you. It's not easy to do during the day."

"OK, I promise you. I have some things to say to you, too."

"Ten o'clock, see you by the entrance to the Demon Girl Zone."

June 19, 1995, the last day Shen Ming was alive. They had their final conversation by the school fence.

"Shut up. No. Stop, please . . . don't say anymore . . . please." She covered her ears and kept mumbling.

"Xiaozhi, at ten o'clock that night seventeen years ago, I was here. But I didn't see you." Si Wang let go of her and stroked her hair. "Did you come here that rainy night?"

She couldn't say anything. She just kept shaking her head.

"You didn't come here?" He smelled her hair. "OK, I believe you."

"Leave me alone!"

She crawled out of the dirty factory. The new moon had faded. The night reminded her of a spring night seventeen years ago. Mr. Shen and his students sat in the woods, watching the Lyra constellation meteor showers.

Ouyang Xiaozhi tried to run but Si Wang gripped her wrist.

The seventeen-year-old student ran with his teacher; they rushed to the subway stop, but they had missed the last train.

Xiaozhi hailed a taxi. Si Wang wouldn't let go of her door. She was rattled, but her voice was firm. "Let go. Let me go home!"

June 19, 2012—10:45 p.m.

She left in a taxi. She watched the star-less sky and thought of the Demon Girl Zone seventeen years ago: damp and cold underground, Shen Ming sitting with the members of the Dead Poets Society. The white candles surrounding them made it seem like an ancient rite. Flickering shadows on the walls looked like cave paintings. Ouyang Xiaozhi, dressed in a big white sweater, passionately read a Gu Cheng poem, *"The sky is gray..."*

CHAPTER 61

July 7, 2012. Chinese Valentine's Day.

The school organized a summer trip just for the eleventh-graders. They were going to a nearby island, a well-known vacation spot. On the way to the dock, Xiaozhi ran into anti-Japanese protests. Signs saying "Protect Diaoyu Islands" were everywhere. Cars couldn't move at all, so drivers turned off engines and waited. One protester put up a "Boycott Japanese Products" poster on the car window. She was reminded of Shen Ming from seventeen years ago. He would get indignant talking about modern Chinese history. One day he actually led the class in singing "Blood of the Republic."

She got to the dock at the last minute.

It was the hottest day of the year. The whole class was going on the trip, over one hundred kids, plus the teachers. The school didn't pay for this excursion, but the students' families didn't mind. The kids were just back from vacation and eager to share their stories. Some had just gone to Taiwan, some went to Hong Kong Disneyland every summer, and some had even been to Europe.

Xiaozhi stood apart from everyone, watching Si Wang. He leaned against the ship's railing. Seagulls flew around him; salt scented the air. His eyes were closed, as though he was meditating. Some of the students whispered, "Mental case."

Si Wang left his spot and walked close to Xiaozhi. His face was especially handsome in the sunlight.

"Have you seen the sea before?" she asked casually, her eyes fixed on the murky water.

"I've lived a sheltered life. In seventeen years I've never left this city. Maybe traveling is all about giving you another life. I remember my past life, though. I've already lived twice as much as other people. It's like traveling through time."

Xiaozhi turned around and left without another word.

A few hours later, the ship docked at a fishing island with tall mountains and white sandy beaches. The teachers and students were staying in a homey inn. Zhang Mingsong led the group, taking endless photos with his DSLR. He got shots of all the students, except for Si Wang.

Mr. An, the political science teacher, was like a fly who kept pestering Xiaozhi. She sometimes talked to him, being neither warm nor cold. The wind picked up the hem of her floral-print dress and showed her shapely legs. The boys sneaked a peek while the girls looked on with jealousy.

There wasn't much entertainment on the island. All the students played in the sea regardless of whether they swam. Si Wang's fit muscles were the most eye-catching on the beach, embarrassing the couch potatoes and beanpoles. Girls came over to say hi, but he acted cool, collecting shells by himself.

Xiaozhi didn't even bring a swimsuit, so she sat and chatted with a few female teachers. Many were disappointed.

The refreshing sea breeze made everyone forget about the heat. A lot of people got sick from eating the seafood, including Zhang Mingsong and Mr. An.

Xiaozhi didn't eat much, but she walked around the fishing village. She picked the remote corners of the island, going from the trees to the beach.

A clear moon sat over the horizon.

She wanted to lay down on the beach to remember the sight. The round moon was almost golden between the sea and the sky.

Suddenly, a pair of hands gripped her from behind. She screamed and got away. Another hand reached out. She struggled. Her assailants were local thugs.

"Let her go!" Si Wang came out of the woods, the moon illuminating his face.

Xiaozhi ran to his side. "Help me!"

There were four of them. They told Si Wang to mind his own business. But he crept closer to them and hit one to the ground. His muscles looked ready to explode. The thugs bled profusely after a few Thai boxing moves. Xiaozhi kept shouting for help, but the night beach was quiet and the surging tides covered her voice.

But after about five minutes, two of the men were on the ground and the other two ran off.

Si Wang told her to go. She was sure the bad guys were getting help. Who knew how many more would show up?

Wind blew at them in the dark night. Her hair and skirt flew around her like a blossom of the sea. She couldn't run more than a few steps. Si Wang had to drag her to a hill. Her wrist was so hot it was burning.

Finally they got to the other side of the island. No one would find them on this side.

Moonlight chased their shadows, the seawater kept surging. White foam lapped at their feet and wet the edges of her dress. His forehead and arm bled; the blood dripped onto the sand. He was still standing stick straight.

She took big gulps and mumbled, "Thank you."

"Why were you by yourself?"

"It was too quiet inside. I wanted to listen to the sea."

"The sea?"

"Yes, I could hear it."

Xiaozhi listened with her eyes closed. Si Wang got closer to her, almost close enough to kiss her.

She retreated half a step but stayed close enough to touch his wounds. "Si Wang, listen to me—you can't get into fights anymore."

Her slender fingers caressed his forehead. The blood felt hot on her hand. Her face had a luminous shine in the moonlight.

"Pick the flower when you can, rather than regret when the flower is gone," Si Wang said softly.

She remembered 1995, that spring evening when she and Mr. Shen took a walk in the wilderness. She was reading the classic poem "Golden Gown" by Du Qiu. Ouyang Xiaozhi was depressed at the time. New rumors about her had been circulating through the school. The girls gossiped about it during lunch break and the boys were happy to listen. Supposedly, Xiaozhi's father wasn't a martyr but a deserter. And, supposedly, his commander had executed him for being a deserter in Vietnam, the martyrdom was the result of a bribe, and her mother was a promiscuous widow.

Xiaozhi didn't talk to those girls. Even if she hadn't been so shy, they didn't like her, so she was never going to have the chance to defend herself. Even if she showed her dad's award to everyone, they'd say it was fake.

Boys acted friendly, but she kept her distance.

No one talked to her except for her desk mate, Liu Man.

She had been going to an elite high school in the city, but the neighborhood was rough—thugs harassed her and fought over her. Other students' parents complained about how she attracted a bad element; one of the parents was a city administrator. The school bowed to pressure and made her leave. She was sent to the rural Nanming High to get away from the bad city element. Pretty girls were always followed by gossip. Just like the proverb, "Flies don't stay on flawless eggs," people assumed she was guilty.

Words could kill.

August 23, 2012. Chinese Valentine's Day.

A remote island.

The wind made Xiaozhi's vision blurry. She covered her eyes as though she had a headache. "Sorry, I got confused for a minute. You're not him."

She tried to hide her tears.

Si Wang reached out his hand, still hot from the fight. He held her chin to turn her toward him.

Not all the blood had dried and his fingers smeared blood on her cheek, somehow making her look even more stunning.

"Look at me, Xiaozhi."

The ocean wailed; tears ran into her mouth.

"Walk me back," she rasped into his ear. "If anybody asks about your wounds, just say they're scratches from branches."

Si Wang held on to her face for quite some time. When he finally let go, he tried to clean away his blood.

Later that night, back in her room with all of the other female teachers, she chanted to herself: "He is dead."

CHAPTER 62

Fall arrived.

When news of Mo Yan winning the Nobel Prize in literature was announced, people took Chinese class more seriously. Ouyang Xiaozhi lectured about *Dreams of the Red Chamber*, the part where Lin Daiyu arrived at the Jia mansion, and she brought up the book's fifth chapter where a dream foretold the fates of the twelve girls of Jinling.

"They said it's a match made in Heaven, but I remember another promise I made. I can't forget, no matter what. She is alone in another world. Life is never perfect, we may live together forever, but it's never enough."

A few brown leaves floated outside the window. Xiaozhi recited the poem about Xue Baochai titled "Doomed Life."

"Si Wang."

He stood up quickly. "I was paying attention."

"Since you finished the book a long time ago, I'm curious. Who is your favorite girl among the twelve?"

"'Doomed Life' was about Xue Baochai, but it also mentions Lin Daiyu. People always pitied Lin but complimented Xue. My favorite is Qin Keqin, who died a lusty death. Didn't Jia Baoyu's sexy dream from chapter five take place in her bed?"

Xiaozhi coughed, slightly embarrassed.

"Actually, the Ms. Goddess in Jia Baoyu's dream was probably Qin Keqin. His sexual education came from a young married woman."

"Today's literary society meeting is over. Everyone can go."

It was Friday and the students were out the door in no time, leaving Xiaozhi and Si Wang alone.

"Xiaozhi, why didn't you let me finish?"

"They're just kids, why say so much?"

"Right, we're the only grown-ups."

"What are you going on about?" She teasingly pushed him. "I sometimes think you're not seventeen."

"I'm forty-two—seven years older than you."

The truth changed her demeanor. "Shut up!"

Si Wang walked out of the classroom, fetched his backpack from the dorm, and headed for the school gates.

Ouyang Xiaozhi caught up to him. "I'm sorry."

"It's OK."

As they walked on Nanming Road she said, "Si Wang, I saw your cell phone screensaver—tickets to Jacky Cheung's 1995 concert."

"I went to that."

Her expression was troubled. She hesitated before saying, "There's a Jacky Cheung concert tonight in the city. Do you want to go?"

"You have tickets?"

"No, but there are scalpers."

"I didn't know about it."

Xiaozhi acted nonchalant. "You're busy? Have another date?"

"No, I'm free."

Si Wang called his mom, saying he had a tutoring session that night and wouldn't be home until after ten.

"Do you lie to your mom a lot?"

"Not at all. My mom is the best woman in the world. The prettiest, too!"

The two joked and laughed as they walked to the subway station.

It was dusk, and the train to the city was crowded. Standing there on the cramped train Si Wang looked very grown-up, while Xiaozhi looked younger than her years. They looked more like a couple than teacher and student.

"In 1995, I noticed you copying a poem," Si Wang said. That year, the famous romance novelist Qiong Yao had written a poem for "Ghost Husband," an episode of the hit TV show *The Plum Flower Trilogy*. He now recited this supernatural story, in which the protagonist believed that the man she loved had died, but years later, his ghost communicated to her with poems. She then started to believe in ghosts.

"I just remember the line, 'The bridge over troubled water has endless sorrow.'" Her voice was louder than the sounds of the subway car, but she didn't care who heard her.

They arrived at the stadium well before the concert started, so they headed to the convenience store to buy snacks. Near the stadium, Xiaozhi bought tickets from a scalper; they turned out to be good seats. They were pushed along by the crowd.

She shouted to Si Wang, "I haven't been to a concert in ten years!"

"It's been seventeen years for me!"

Inside the loud concert hall the stage was lit up like a fireball. Si Wang screamed like an excited high school student; Xiaozhi also screamed, surprising herself for acting like such a fan.

The singing sensation came out in a glittery costume. His first two songs were "Li Xianglan" and "I'm Really Hurt."

The two of them had purchased LED sticks on their way in and Ouyang Xiaozhi waved hers back and forth. Most of the crazy fans were in their thirties. Si Wang was among the younger fans, but he sang right along. Xiaozhi laughed at his screechy voice.

When Si Wang wrapped his arm around her back she didn't resist. She leaned into him and her hair covered his face like a silk scarf.

For the next two hours the songs continued—"A Stab in the Heart," "Traveling with You," "I Waited Forever"—and their cheeks remained warmly pressed together the entire time.

Near the end of the show Jacky Cheung sang something that didn't come out until after Shen Ming had died—"She Came to My Concert"—and Xiaozhi held Si Wang's neck and hid her face in his chest.

Did she want to hide her crying or was she afraid to hear the emotional song? She held him so tightly he had trouble breathing.

The final song was "A Kiss Good-Bye." She let go of him, wiped away her tears, and looked into his eyes. Everyone sang along to the chorus, "We kissed good-bye in the crazy night." His lips got close to hers but stopped two centimeters away.

He didn't kiss her.

"You are not Shen Ming." This was the first thing she'd said since the concert began.

Half an hour later, the stadium had emptied out. They stayed in the empty hall. LED sticks, drink bottles, and snack containers littered the ground. They watched the crew dismantle the equipment on stage.

She leaned her head on his shoulders and softly said, "Hi."

"What do you want to say?"

"I—I don't know."

He took off his jacket and covered her lap. "Are you cold?"

"A little." She closed her eyes and took a deep breath. "Do you know, in five years, I'll be forty."

"I'd be forty-seven."

She shook her head bitterly. When she opened her eyes, she saw the night sky. The wind howled and a dry leaf fell on her face.

Ouyang Xiaozhi caught the leaf in her mouth and chewed it to pieces. "When you're rushing at night, don't forget to look up at the starry sky."

He didn't react for a long time.

She stood up. "Go home, Si Wang."

CHAPTER 63

Two days later.

Xiaozhi taught her Monday morning Chinese class as usual. She didn't look at Si Wang, and he avoided her. But by the afternoon, the students were gossiping and laughing; it was a mixture of mockery, envy, and jealousy.

Si Wang threatened one guy and got some of the story out of him. Someone had seen them at the concert.

It didn't take long before everyone on campus knew. The students looked at them like they were the stars of the Nude Picture Scandal.

Xiaozhi heard the teachers whispering. One woman said, "Kids today are something else. They actually date teachers. How disgusting. They watch too many Japanese adult movies."

The whole week passed in a daze. No students stayed to talk to her. Si Wang didn't say a word; when he passed her in the hall he intentionally lowered his head. As soon as classes ended she went home, even though she knew Si Wang was hiding in the oleander trees, watching her. Only Mr. An followed her, but she ditched him, leaving him angrily kicking a tree.

During several political science classes Mr. An called on Si Wang, asking him bizarre questions.

On Friday, he pointed at Si Wang's nose and asked, "Are there ghosts? If you had a ghostly secret, then what is materialism?"

The questions made no sense. All the students knew what he really wanted to ask.

Si Wang didn't back down to Mr. An. "There are ghosts in the world. I have a ghostly secret, so do you. We all do. Only you can't see the ghosts. But I can feel it, sitting on my shoulders and watching all of you, every minute of every day."

The class went wild, enraging Mr. An, who yelled at Si Wang, "Get out of my class you punk."

Si Wang stood very straight and answered calmly, "Sorry, teacher, you have no right to throw me out."

"Then I will leave." Mr. An threw down his books and stormed out of the classroom.

The students were stunned. Si Wang sat down calmly, but he was shaking all over.

Homeroom teacher Zhang Mingsong called him to the office and lectured him. Si Wang was supposed to apologize to Mr. An, but Si Wang shook his head. "Why can't I answer honestly in class?"

"Si Wang, you really believe in ghosts?"

"A ghost has been with me all this time." Si Wang looked like a middle-aged man. "Do you believe me, Mr. Zhang?"

The homeroom teacher seemed shocked. "Well, I'm not as conservative as you guys assume. I've been interested in philosophy and religion for years, and all sorts of paranormal things, including ghosts."

"I see," Si Wang said, pointing to the big bookshelf behind Zhang Mingsong.

"If you really have something unique to share, you can tell me. I'm your homeroom teacher, I won't say anything."

"I'm sorry, I was just mouthing off."

"Fine, but I think you do have a secret. I'll find out what it is."

"Mr. Zhang, can I go now?"

"Apologize to Mr. An and we'll forget about all of this."

Zhang Mingsong never mentioned Ouyang Xiaozhi.

That night, she was in bed when she got a text from Si Wang: *"I'm sorry. I'll apologize to Mr. An. I'll tell him I ran into you at the concert, you fell and I was helping you up, which explains why we were leaning on each other."*

Xiaozhi squeezed her phone so hard she thought she would crush it. She waited half an hour to reply: *"Si Wang, don't lie, no matter what!"*

"Xiaozhi, the whole school is talking about us. It's a crisis. What should we do?"

"Forget them! Don't get distracted. You have to study hard and listen to the teachers."

"Did you ever like me?"

Xiaozhi didn't reply to this text. She assumed Si Wang was up the whole night, just like her.

CHAPTER 64

December. It was so cold that the air almost froze.

Shen Min was now in the eleventh grade, and she'd become even prettier. She looked especially alluring in her school uniform.

She read a new American book called *The Lovely Bones*. The novelist told a tear-jerker of a story about a girl who became a ghost after being killed. The girl's ghost stayed on Earth to watch her killer and her family, feeling powerless about what she couldn't do.

Shen Min's father was no longer a prosecutor, but he was still very stern with her. She was afraid to tell him she'd fallen in love.

The guy went to another high school, though she had never seen him in a school uniform. He had a cool haircut, like one of those singing and dancing Korean celebrities. His cell phone was always the latest iPhone. He knew all the right things to say to charm girls. He got their numbers quickly and got them into bed after only a few meals—not that Shen Min was there yet.

They often met by the street food carts; the May First High School was next door, and Wilderness Books was across the street.

One weekend they went to see a movie. Hand in hand, they walked out. The teenage boy whispered, "Little Min, you must be tired. Let's go to a hotel."

She wasn't an immature girl anymore. Her face stiffened, "No!"

"Fine, you better get home then so your dad doesn't worry."

Shen Min was reluctant to go. Once she was on the bus she waved good-bye.

The teenage boy stayed where he was and made a call. He got some cigarettes from a convenience store, chain-smoking his way through five of them. He never smoked in front of Shen Min. Soon, a teenage girl ran over, the same age as Shen Min but dressed more provocatively, and a lot less pretty. He took the girl into his arms and flirted with her. They kissed for a while before going into a nearby hourly motel.

Around midnight, the teenager stumbled out of the motel with a cigarette and a can of beer. The girl followed him. Suddenly, a muscular young man charged toward them.

Si Wang's eyes were crazed. "Hey, stop!"

"Who the hell are you?" The teenage boy puffed smoke at him. "Get out of my sight!"

The teenage girl also said drunkenly, "Crazy!"

"Young lady, if you don't want any trouble, you should go now."

Under the dim streetlight, Si Wang took away the boy's cigarette. The girl wasn't stupid—she took off.

"What the hell do you think you're doing?" The teenager pushed Si Wang, but he didn't move at all. It was like trying to move a wall.

"I don't want to beat you up. I'm just warning you not to see Shen Min again."

"Oh, do you go to school with her? You like her, but she's not into you, so you're stalking her? Poor loser!"

"I'm her older brother, and I don't call her Little Min!"

The teenage took a swing at Si Wang, who blocked the punch. Si Wang's right fist connected with the boy's nose, and blood spurted out. The boy tried to stand up but was hit again. More hits followed.

He could barely cry for help.

"If I ever see you with her again—"

Si Wang left right away to avoid the police.

The teenage boy managed to disappear from Shen Min's world.

CHAPTER 65

December 21, 2012. The end of the world according to the Mayan calendar.

"If there was tomorrow, how do you want to make up your face? If there was no tomorrow, how do we say good-bye?"

Xiaozhi often felt that this was the song in Shen Ming's head right before he was killed.

From the thirtieth floor of the building, they could look down on half the city. His knockoff cell phone's ringtone was "If There Was Tomorrow." Not the original from 1990 but the mixed duet with Shin and Simon Hsueh. Xiaozhi sat on the windowsill with her legs folded, puffing hot air on the cold glass. He drew on the steamed glass—first a kitten, then some glasses.

"Si Wang, please behave!"

She puffed once again and the mist swallowed the kitten.

"I'm Shen Ming."

"I asked you to come here tonight, not Shen Ming."

They were in Ouyang Xiaozhi's tidy one-bedroom apartment.

Even though they'd seen each other in class, they hadn't spoken for days. Early that morning, however, she got a text from him: *"Xiaozhi, I want to see you. If there was tomorrow?"*

It was Friday. Xiaozhi didn't text him the address until it was dusk. It was the end of the world, the first day of winter, and also the shortest day of the year. Traditionally, people would go to the cemetery on this day because it was a day when the ghosts came out.

Si Wang didn't go home after getting the text. He came out of the subway, turned off his phone, and went up to her apartment.

"Mr. Zhang talked to me this morning. He told me not to have any contact with you, not even in the teachers' lounge."

"Zhang Mingsong?" Si Wang drew a puppy on the window. "Why?"

"The principal talked to me in the afternoon too, saying the same thing. The school Party Committee made the decision."

"Is everyone saying this?"

"All the teachers and students. Your mom will know soon, too."

"What's the point? If there was no tomorrow?"

She added some steam to the glass. "Wouldn't that be great, if tonight really was the last night ever? Sorry, I shouldn't talk like this, I'm a teacher."

"Xiaozhi, why didn't you ever marry? There must have been a lot of men who liked you."

"What do you want me to say? That I haven't forgotten Mr. Shen? That I feel guilty about his death? You're wrong."

"You're lying."

Ouyang Xiaozhi squeezed his nose like he was a toddler. "You'll understand when you're as old as me."

"I'm seven years older than you."

"Shut up—"

Si Wang kissed her before she could finish.

After a slight moment of hesitation Xiaozhi relaxed into him. He breathed out. "I'm sorry."

"I warned you—any man who gets close to me dies."

"Can you tell me why?"

"I gave myself the name Xiaozhi."

"A name doesn't matter. I'm Si Wang, but also Shen Ming."

"I was an abandoned baby. Someone found me in a trash can near the Suzhou River. I don't know who my parents were or when I was born. I don't remember when I started to live with a group of homeless people. We scavenged for food. When I was eleven years old, we got to that slum across from Nanming High. I picked trash and lived in a world no one cared about. I stole a drumstick and was locked in the Demon Girl Zone for it. If you hadn't saved me, I would have died."

"I still remember your face from that day."

Xiaozhi leaned against the window like she was floating in air. "I didn't even have a name when I was locked down there. But for the first time in my life I really wanted to live. I was so grateful you saved me. But when I got back to the homeless people and had to keep picking trash, taking beatings all the time, eating cold and hard buns, I would think, why did you save me? Why didn't you let me die?"

"You wanted to die?"

"I'm sorry, I set that fire. I used a match to light some trash in a hut. I just wanted to kill myself, I didn't think anyone else would be hurt. I was only eleven, too naive to think the fire would spread and get out of control."

Tears squeezed out of her tightly shut eyes.

"I remember watching the fire and hearing the screams. The fire trucks weren't there yet. I wasn't trying to save you, I just wanted to look like a hero, even if I had to die."

"Weren't you afraid of dying?"

"No. It was a few weeks before the college entrance exams. It was so difficult back then. I wanted to be a Chinese major at Peking University, so I had tens of thousands of competitors. I thought I'd get sponsored admission even if I saved just one person. It was a totally selfish act. I'd been fantasizing about a fire or a flood—anything that would put the whole school at risk. Just so I could save someone and get an award. I'm the one who should say sorry."

"No, you did save me. I set the fire and killed people, including the homeless people who helped raise me. I'm a killer, or at least an arsonist. But I never told anyone this. You're the only one who knows."

He looked down at the teeming crowds and smiled bitterly. "I've known your secret for a long time. When I saved you that day, you still had half a box of matches. I put them in my pocket. The way you talked to me, how afraid you were, that told me everything."

"Why didn't you say anything?"

"I didn't want your life ruined. Another selfish reason was, if you weren't a victim but an arsonist, my saving you would be pointless. Who would get an award for saving a killer?"

Xiaozhi stroked his chin. "Mr. Shen, I remember you telling me seventeen years ago, in the woods by Nanming Road, that we were the same."

"Like two meteors coming from outer space to the same blue planet, colliding and turning into ashes."

"Shen Ming, I'm still grateful that you saved my life. It changed everything for me. Everyone heard about the selfless high school hero and the little homeless girl. An army officer adopted me since his wife couldn't have kids. I became an army brat and had everything I needed. For the first time in my life I wore new clothes and ate rice every day. I wasn't looked at with disgust anymore. The day after I was adopted, my adoptive father was called to the front line in Vietnam. When I saw him again, he was already a martyr."

"Xiaozhi, I don't need to know this."

She was talking to the space in front of her. "After that, my adoptive mother started disliking me. She saw me as the orphan who'd brought them bad luck. But she was family to a military man and got a lot of benefits, and I got a lot of opportunities as a martyr's daughter. I was able to go to school. August First School accepted me. I studied really hard to catch up, jumping several grades in a few years, and got into a good high school in the city. When some thugs singled me out and bothered me, I had to transfer to Nanming High."

"Then we met again."

"I didn't think you'd recognize me."

"First in 1988, underground in the Demon Girl Zone, and then in the fire. After six years, you'd turned into a gorgeous young woman. You looked so different—except for your eyes." He caressed her face.

"If anyone knew about me and that fire, I'd go to jail—or at least I wouldn't have the life I have today."

"Liu Man knew."

Ouyang Xiaozhi sighed. "I should have guessed."

"The night before she was killed, she talked to me in the self-study room. She told me she knew about us. She said she was always jealous of you. No one paid her any attention after you came. Every boy liked you more."

"She got close to me and acted like my best friend just to find out my secrets?"

"I think those rumors about you at school all came from her. She said she learned who you really were a few days earlier. She knew you were adopted in 1988, the only survivor from that fire, and I was the one who saved you."

"She imagined the rest?"

"Yes, Liu Man guessed that I liked you. She said we had done things. I denied it of course."

"But we never did anything, I've never even been inside your room, Mr. Shen."

It was hard to tell if she looked relieved or regretful.

"Then I found Liu Man dead the next morning, I—"

Xiaozhi covered his mouth. "Don't say anything else."

After a long time, he continued, "I died thirteen days later."

"That was quite a year for me. After Mr. Shen died, I was accepted at the Teachers' College. After graduation, I went to the poor rural area to teach. I was once like those kids, hungry and uneducated."

"I don't need to know your past. There is only one question left. But I'm afraid if I ask, you'll disappear forever."

Ouyang Xiaozhi covered her face. "I know what you're thinking. Why did I ask to see you that night? Why didn't I show up? Why didn't I tell the school or the police after you died? Why did I lie to everyone?"

Si Wang said nothing.

Xiaozhi looked out the window. The city was full of lights and commotion on this chilly night, but it was a gilded shell.

The phone rang playing, "If there was tomorrow, how do you want to make up your face? If there was no tomorrow, how do we say good-bye?"

When he woke up from dreams where he kept killing people, it was already dawn on December 22. The concrete jungle outside hadn't changed; it was still snowing hard.

There was tomorrow after all.

Ouyang Xiaozhi was standing by the window, wearing a cotton robe, staring at the snow-covered city. He stood behind her, wearing nothing. He was afraid to stroke her shoulders again. He leaned in to smell her hair.

She turned to look at his eyes, their lips once again so close.

She shook her head. "Si Wang, please go. Your mom is waiting for you."

He didn't say, "I'm Shen Ming." He got dressed in silence and went to the door. He looked at her back, she was like a puff of smoke, ready to disappear at any moment.

How do you say good-bye?

Si Wang walked out into the snow. The reborn city felt warm, and his steps became lighter.

He reached Suzhou River and looked down from Wuning Road Bridge. The River of Life and Death melted away all the fallen snow.

He didn't get home until the sun rose. His mom was waiting by the door. She hadn't slept all night, and her eyes were bloodshot. She seemed to have aged a great deal in just one night.

"Where were you?"

Under his mom's menacing gaze, Si Wang took off his coat and poured himself a glass of water, grabbing some bread from the fridge.

"Wang Er, I waited for you all night. I was afraid to call your homeroom teacher. I was afraid he'd punish you if he knew you didn't sleep in the dorms. I went to Policeman Ye Xiao, too, and he looked for you all over. He even went to Nanming High." He Qingying grabbed his collar in her rage, as if she was going to tear apart the sweater she made for him. "If you don't tell me, I'll die in front of you!"

"I was with a woman," he answered nonchalantly, still eating the bread.

After recovering from her initial shock, He Qingying made a call. "Hello, Mr. Zhang? Sorry to bother you so early. This is Si Wang's mother. I'm calling to tell you that my son didn't come home last night. He said he was with a woman."

Zhang Mingsong's shouts could be heard through the phone. He Qingying pressed the receiver to her ear and hung up after a few minutes. Then she walked over to her son and slapped him.

PART 5:
THE SURVIVORS

CHAPTER 66

January 1, 2013.

Ye Xiao sat alone in Huang Hai's apartment, staring at the chart on the wall. The apartment had been on the market for two years, but there had been no buyers. All the files had been moved out except for the wall chart.

The big name in the middle, "Shen Ming," still looked vivid, red like blood.

Ye Xiao had been over all the leads countless times, the same as his predecessor, but none of them went anywhere. Most of them were dead.

Could it be Zhang Mingsong, Shen Yuanchao's favorite suspect? He'd been questioned and had a perfect alibi.

Ye Xiao added a new name—Si Mingyuan.

He was Si Wang's father and went missing in 2002. His residency registration had been canceled. He worked at Nanming Steel Factory before being laid off. Had he returned to his workplace on the night of the crime? There was no evidence for it right now. Ye Xiao didn't think it was worth asking He Qingying about.

Si Wang.

He couldn't have killed Shen Ming, as he was born six months after the murder.

Si Wang and Ye Xiao had become friends. He still claimed to be Shen Ming, and supposedly carried the same memories, personality, and emotions. The two did have the same handwriting. Maybe he never drank the Meng Po Soup?

Ye Xiao didn't believe Si Wang was Shen Ming. Si Wang was an unusual kid, but there was no such thing as reincarnation.

Maybe Si Wang had bigger secrets?

Ye Xiao's cell phone rang. He rushed out of Huang Hai's apartment.

A body had been found near Si Wang's home.

Workers for the forced move were taking apart the neighborhood; bulldozers boomed and homes crumbled. Many people tried to stop the demolition, but they were dragged away amid cries. Onlookers gawked in front of the ruins.

In the rubble of one house that had just been taken apart, some workers found a broken skeleton near the patio. The more they looked, the more human remains they found.

Ye Xiao squatted near the bones. Two deep holes in the skull looked back at him, as if they had something to say.

Who are you?

He suddenly felt someone watching him; he turned around and saw the eighteen-year-old Si Wang.

Though the identity of the body had yet to be confirmed, the medical examiner's report did contain some details. The victim was male, approximately 176 centimeters tall, between thirty-five and forty years old, and he'd died about ten years ago; there was a lethal stab wound near his neck. It was presumed to be a murder. The demolished house had changed owners many times over the years. The police were inquiring into who had lived here ten years ago.

Ye Xiao came to Si Wang's building late that night. Most everything around it had been destroyed already but the single locust tree still stood.

A shadow hopped along the ruins. Ye Xiao watched the movement, all too aware of the thugs who worked these parts. The forced move had just made the area worse. Paying closer attention, however, he was able to make out Si Wang, who was crying under the cool moonlight.

Ye Xiao walked up behind him. "Who are you crying for?"

The teenager jumped up and tried to kick Ye Xiao. He dodged the blow and grabbed Si Wang by the throat.

"It's me!"

"Sorry, I thought you were one of the workers destroying our homes."

"How have you been?"

"Horrible," he said, scrambling around until he found a place to sit on the remains of a brick wall.

It was the first time he'd seen Si Wang so depressed. "What else are you not telling me?"

"Ye Xiao, I will tell you everything. But first you have to look into someone for me. The survivor from that 1983 murder case on Serenity Road. The one who reported the crime, the victim's only daughter."

"Why her?"

"Please."

Against his better judgment Ye Xiao agreed to look into the woman. A week later, surprising results came back. The girl's records had disappeared. Ye Xiao visited the victim's relatives and learned that she'd been adopted by the victim. After the murder, no one else in the family wanted to care for her. Another couple adopted her and she was never heard from again. There was only one photo of her from school, a black-and-white shot taken when she was thirteen.

He gave the photo to Si Wang.

CHAPTER 67

The Lunar New Year came later than usual in 2013.

Lu Jizong was eighteen years old. He'd graduated junior high two years ago and gone on to a private trade school. He was going to work on the assembly line at a Japanese-funded car factory and make at least 3,000 yuan a month. But during winter break it was announced that the principal had run off after embezzling money. The school closed down.

The small southern town where he lived was cold and damp every winter. The narrow streets were littered with trash and it was muddy whenever it rained. Songs like "You Sold My Love" and "Best Culture Show" played endlessly everywhere. Motels with hourly rates, Internet cafés, and hot pot restaurants lined the street near his home. He knew every shop owner's name. He never left town. The only trip he'd taken to a bigger city was when he was eleven.

For the first time, he saw skyscrapers, busy overpasses, and Mercedes and BMWs leaving mansions. His mom told him, "Jizong, your dad lives here, he'll give us a good life."

He had never seen his dad.

From the day he was born, his family had been his mother and her parents. He only became curious when he saw other kids' dads. When he'd ask about him the answer was, "Your dad lives far away and is an evil man who abandoned you and your mom. You'll never, ever meet him."

Seven years later, Lu Jizong found a photocopy of his father's registration card and learned his dad's name. He and his mother went to the address. But the lavish house was empty. Only a young woman was there.

She was his father's younger cousin. Her face was beautiful but a bit cold. His dad was already missing and the house had new owners. No one could help them, even though the woman gave his mother some money.

Disappointed, they returned home.

For years, Lu Jizong's mother ran a food cart on the street. She managed to raise a healthy young man who had a pale birthmark on his forehead.

Now, a middle-aged man watched him from the Guilin Rice Noodles shop across the street. Neither the man's common haircut nor his pale, clean-shaven face was memorable. He would have faded into the crowd if not for the birthmark on his forehead.

The man finished eating his spicy beef-tripe noodles and lit up a cigarette, keeping an eye on the teenager staring at a computer screen inside the Internet café.

Two days ago, the man had taken a long-distance bus to this dirty little city. It was his first time here. He'd hidden among the crowds heading home for the New Year. In the last seven years, he'd not taken a single flight, or a train since the rail companies had started requiring residency registration cards to match the tickets. Every once in a while, he would buy identity cards lost by people who were close to his age and resembled him. He used them to stay at motels and cheap rental apartments. He had seen his wanted poster everywhere; he would get nervous whenever a cop walked by. At least it was easy to keep his forehead covered.

He didn't stay long in any place. What cash he had was now long gone. He'd worked odd jobs and ate only occasionally. He tried to go back to his city, and even ran a small DVD store for a while, but it was just a front for other illegal ventures. Three years ago, a man came in—he recognized the man, Huang Hai. He ran like crazy and when he got to an unfinished building, he saw that the cop had taken out his gun, so he jumped. Being dead was better than being caught. He made it across but Huang Hai fell to his death.

He had another person's blood on his hands.

His name and photograph reappeared on wanted posters in train stations and banks. Years of living on the run had made him as sly as a fox. He wouldn't make the same mistake again.

The one time he took a bus a strange teenager spotted him. They both recognized one another.

It had been a close call. If he hadn't been able to get off the crowded bus, Si Wang would have caught him.

It was Si Wang's fault he was in this predicament.

Si Wang had scared him, ever since first meeting him eight years ago. After he met the boy's mom, nightmares woke him up every night. He never thought the boy would become his adopted son.

Before he turned thirty he'd been an energetic man who could get women pregnant. He didn't know when he'd become a lesser man, until he found out about his wife chemically castrating him.

He'd wanted her dead and had no choice but to follow Ma Li's plan. Together they bankrupted his wife's family business, embezzling tens of millions in assets. Just as he was celebrating becoming rich—he'd even made plans for a corrective operation in Japan—he fell into a lethal trap.

In early 2006, he also went bankrupt.

His ex-father-in-law found him. He won the fight and left the old man in a pool of blood.

Lu Zhongyue started his life on the run.

In his darker moments, he thought back on his life: his girlfriend when he was a teenager; his high school roommates; and the shame, jealousy, and hatred from 1995.

He had considered suicide. He'd stood on roofs and next to rivers, wanting to end it all. So what if he turned to mush and was tossed into a cremation chamber? Maybe the police would know who he was and report the death as a fugitive's suicide.

He would be another warrior in twenty years.

At moments like this, he thought of Si Wang, who'd been renamed Gu Wang. He was probably back to Si Wang now. He would be eighteen.

Lu Zhongyue decided he couldn't die. It wasn't that he lacked courage, but things couldn't end like this.

He had to learn the truth and Si Wang was his only hope. This was the primary reason he decided to keep living.

There was a second reason.

Living in borrowed spaces, losing everything, running here and there, even being caught by the police. None of it mattered. His biggest regret was not having an heir.

He remembered his girlfriend from eighteen years ago. He'd sent her away with a big belly and money for an abortion.

Thinking of it now made him want to stab himself.

If he hadn't kept her address, he never would have come to this small, freezing town. He found their shabby apartment building. The gorgeous young woman he'd adored nineteen years earlier had turned into a plump middle-aged woman. He had to think hard to remember her name: Chen Xiangtian.

Yesterday, the forty-year-old woman had left her apartment with a tall, lanky teenager. The young man looked seventeen or eighteen; his face and features looked a bit familiar, but his eyes were flat and showed no spark. He had a birthmark on his forehead.

He broke into their mailbox and found the teenager's name: Lu Jizong.

CHAPTER 68

Lunar New Year's Eve 2013.

The apartment felt like an igloo. Thankfully the electric cooker was adding some steam to the tiny space. Lu Jizong and his mother had a simple but nourishing holiday dinner while watching the boring New Year's Eve Gala show. A few days ago their mailbox had been tampered with and a letter from the school had been opened. Chen Xiangtian wondered which one of the local bastards had done it.

Someone knocked on the door.

Who would visit on Lunar New Year's Eve?

Chen Xiangtian's face tightened and she mumbled, "Is it him?"

She stood up in a rush, touched her son's face, and quickly checked herself in the mirror, embarrassed for the way she looked. The knocking continued until Lu Jizong opened the door.

An attractive woman in her thirties stood in the dark hallway, wearing a coat and shivering.

The teenager sneezed. He backed up a few steps. "I know you."

"I can't believe how tall you've gotten."

"Jizong!" His mom said anxiously from behind him. "Who is it?"

Chen Xiangtian recognized the woman, too. Her excitement turned to doubt and disappointment. "And you are—"

"I see my nephew still remembers me." The woman walked into the apartment and looked at the second-hand furniture and electronics.

"You're Lu Zhongyue's cousin?"

The woman smiled warmly. "How are you? We met seven years ago."

"Why did you come here on Lunar New Year's Eve?" Chen Xiangtian asked. "Where is Lu Zhongyue? Where did he go?"

"There is still no news of my cousin. I came here to work recently and wanted to see Jizong. I sent you a text. You gave me the address."

"Oh, right. Please make yourself at home. If you don't mind the simple food, we can eat together. You can call me sister-in-law."

"Call me Xiaozhi." She sat down casually, pulling out gifts from her jacket pockets—including a red envelope for Jizong. "How is Jizong lately?"

"This kid is still playing around. His trade school closed down. He's just playing computer games all day."

Lu Jizong stayed silent, picking out dumplings from the hot pot. He looked up at his aunt and said, "I want to go out and work."

"It's just as well, your aunt will help you."

"You'll let me?"

One hour later, Xiaozhi left. Chen Xiangtian and Lu Jizong walked her downstairs. She gave them her new phone number and said she'd check in on them soon.

Xiaozhi spent the rest of Lunar New Year's Eve alone in a nearby motel. Firecrackers crackled around her.

A month earlier, Nanming High had announced that Ouyang Xiaozhi was leaving voluntarily and transferring to teach in a rural southern school.

She left abruptly. Before Si Wang could catch up to her, she had gotten into a taxi. Under the dreary sky, Nanming Road was windy. She was afraid to turn around to look.

She got on a train the next day.

She sent a text: *"Shen Ming? If you really are Shen Ming, then you're the world's luckiest person. Please treasure everything you have now. Forget me. Let's never meet again! I really am very grateful to you. Ouyang Xiaozhi, sent from a faraway place."*

She took that number out of service after sending the message.

Ouyang Xiaozhi decided on this town because it was a mountain away in an impoverished Miao village where she would teach at the middle school.

She'd saved Chen Xiangtian and Lu Jizong's contact information from years ago because she needed to find Lu Zhongyue.

Another seven years had passed, and the monster was still hiding. It seemed obvious that Lu Zhongyue had plotted against his good friend to get everything Shen Ming once had, and that he had killed Shen Ming on June 19, 1995, in the Demon Girl Zone.

Xiaozhi realized that only one person could make Lu Zhongyue come out of hiding, his son, Lu Jizong. He was eighteen, just like Si Wang. They had similar personalities, too.

By early spring, Xiaozhi was teaching in the Miao village. Surrounded by impoverished kids, she could finally put her past behind her, though she could never escape it.

Every night when it got quiet, she would sit in her tent and look out at the crystal clear valley, thinking of the spring of 1995.

Eighteen years ago, Mr. Shen had stood by the oleander trees near the sports field, reading, "In 'The Waste Land,' T. S. Eliot said that April was the cruelest month."

Xiaozhi spoke from behind the fence. "Teacher, is living cruel or is death cruel?"

She surprised him. He shook his head and answered, "Death, of course."

"Yeah, living is great, so great." She realized he was wearing earphones. "What are you listening to?"

Shen Ming put one earbud into her ear, and in a clear Cantonese voice she heard: "Endless seasons, time passing so fast. Finding it and losing it again, never wanting it but having it. Did I ever find it? I can't explain my mistakes. I don't know who to blame. What do we look for in life? Giving up and owning wasted my life. Not getting close before it got away. Can't figure out life in my confusion. Everything I lost was everything I owned . . ."

It was Danny Chan's "What I Wanted"—the theme song for her favorite TVB drama, *Looking Back in Anger*.

"Do you still have the gift I gave you?"

"Yes," he said, sounding mortified.

"Please hold on to it."

"I'm sorry, Xiaozhi, we shouldn't talk like this. I'm your homeroom teacher. We can't meet in private anymore. Other students will get the wrong impression." Shen Ming retreated two steps, as if he didn't want to smell her hair. "You have to give it your all to get into Teachers' College."

"Is it because you're getting married?"

"That's got nothing to do with it."

"Your fiancée must be very pretty."

"What are you saying?"

"I wish you a lot of happiness. We will all go to your wedding, and we'll give the bride a crystal necklace." Xiaozhi was smiling, but her heart was a different matter. She now knew the meaning of faking happiness.

"Yes, Qiusha is a good woman." Shen Ming was troubled. Looking directly into her eyes, he said, "Xiaozhi, you'll get married one day, too."

"No, I never want to marry."

The teacher turned to leave. Xiaozhi shouted after him, "Hope you guys have a baby soon!"

"Who would remember me after I die?" Shen Ming mumbled to himself as he got to the teachers' building.

About two months later, he was dead.

CHAPTER 69

Lunar New Year's Eve.

He Qingying couldn't sleep because of the loud firecrackers. She heard soft crying. It sounded like it came from underground, but it was coming from her son's bed. He was crying under the comforter.

She pulled back the comforter and slid her svelte body into the warmth of the bed. "Wang Er, no one can find Ms. Ouyang now. You can blame me if you want. When I was your age, I also cried in bed—even harder than you're crying now."

Si Wang turned around, his pillow and face drenched. "Mom, do you still miss Dad?"

"Sometimes."

In the eleven years since Si Mingyuan had left, many men had pursued He Qingying. Some had money, some were handsome, and some were divorced or widowed. She turned down all of them, including Huang Hai.

Ever since Huang Hai's death, running Wilderness Books became harder than ever. Kids today didn't read anymore. If not for the reference books she sold from her Taobao store, she would barely make ends meet. Si Wang didn't want to see his mom suffer. He helped out whenever he could and offered to get another job. His mom said they had enough savings for him to finish high school.

There were strange calls every weekend, either at dawn or midnight. He Qingying always picked up first and the person would hang up. Si Wang asked Policeman Ye Xiao to track the call. It belonged to an unregistered cell phone from out of the province. He told Si Wang not to worry about it. He thought it was probably someone involved with the forced move; it was a common tactic the developers used to get residents to move out faster.

For He Qingying and Si Wang, coming home every day was like entering a war zone. Some of the neighbors fought, but most of them just gave up. It only took two meetings and a low-ball financial settlement for He Qingying to agree to move. That was the end of their family home.

"Mom, why did you say yes to those assholes?"

Si Wang missed Huang Hai. If he were alive, the demolition crews wouldn't dare hassle them.

"Wang Er, they're powerful and connected. We're just a widow and a kid. I don't want to fight them."

"A widow and a kid?" He frowned. "Is Dad really dead?"

Si Mingyuan had become little more than a blur in Si Wang's memory.

"Sorry," she said, stroking her son's cheeks. She hadn't aged well over the past couple of years. "You have no idea what they could do. I don't want you getting hurt."

"What's there to be afraid of?" Si Wang backed away a few steps, punching the air a couple of times and doing a Thai boxing kick. "If those bastards bother us, I'll break their legs!"

"Shut up!" She gripped his hand and felt his muscles clench. "Wang Er, I don't want you to become a thug. That's not the life for you. I just want you to live a peaceful life."

"I won't hurt anyone who doesn't hurt me!"

"You're more mature than other kids. Why don't you understand me? I've had enough of this house anyway. It's drafty in the winter and hot in the summer. You never have friends over. I haven't given you a good life. I don't even take you on vacations."

"It's OK, I've been to tons of places!"

"I didn't do a good job. I never could afford to buy a place with the money I make now. I'll rent an apartment near the bookstore so you can have a comfy home. I've wanted that for you for years. The compensation for the move is going to pay for your college tuition."

Si Wang lowered his head. He leaned against his mom and listened to the sound of her blood pumping. In early spring, He Qingying got paid for the forced move. Their place would be taken down just like the others, and in its place would stand a high-end condominium. Si Wang had a hard time letting go of their old place. He loved the cherry blossoms he'd drawn on the walls and the poems he'd carved into the windowsill. Would the locust tree be cut down? The memories of his father were still in this apartment.

By their last day in the place, there wasn't much left to move. He Qingying had thrown out most of their stuff—a lot of it had been her husband's. Si Wang helped the movers and worked tirelessly. Neighbors said he looked more and more like a young Si Mingyuan.

That evening they moved into their new apartment, a two-bedroom near Wilderness Books. It was in good shape and had nice furniture; the bathroom and kitchen were satisfactory, too. It was their dream home. Si Wang had his own bedroom, and his mom got him a new single bed.

A few days later, He Qingying organized clothes in her son's bedroom. Si Wang suddenly said, "Mom, let me comb your hair."

"Why?"

"Let me do it. I've never combed a girl's hair."

When did her son learn to talk like this?

He Qingying sat in front of the mirror, and Si Wang crawled out of bed bare-chested. Just a few clumsy strokes with an ox-bone comb made her yelp in pain. She turned to touch his chest, "Wang Er, aren't you cold?"

"Not at all."

It was probably because he was used to boxing half-naked— and the weather was less chilly these days, anyway.

"Am I getting old?"

'No, Mom, you're still young. Your hair is still thick like a young girl's. Let me make two braids for you."

"That's too hard for you to do. I haven't had braids for thirty years."

"When you were thirteen?"

He Qingying started to speak, then stopped, shaking her head. She never talked about this.

"Why won't you tell me about your past?"

"Stop combing my hair. I need to go sleep now."

As she tried to stand, Si Wang pushed her down and continued combing. He whispered, "Afraid to say anything?"

"Wang Er, you *do* know about my past. My parents died before you were born. I worked at the post office."

"What about before that? Where did you go for junior high? Where did you live? Did any fun stuff happen? Do you still know any friends from back then?"

"Did you go through my things during the move?"

"Sorry."

"If you saw that stuff, then what more is there to ask?" He Qingying spoke evenly, but her heart beat so fast that it could have jumped out her chest.

Her son took out a photo album from under the bed. The red cover was musty. A faded color photo was on the first page: a girl in a dress standing in front of the Postal School.

It was He Qingying at seventeen or eighteen.

Even with the unfashionable clothes and hair, she was a beauty. Slender arms held down her skirt hem so the wind didn't flip it up. Her sad eyes focused on something in the distance. She looked like a young Momoe Yamaguchi.

Family photos followed, most of them of Si Wang's maternal grandparents taken at their old house. There weren't many photos of He Qingying, and there were no shots of relatives or other people, like classmates; Si Mingyuan wasn't in any of the photos. The album was probably made before her marriage.

Si Wang took out a metal tin from under the bed.

"You found this, too?"

"All thanks to the move."

Si Wang opened the tin he'd found at the murder house on Serenity Road. It smelled moldy, and the Teresa Teng cassette was inside.

He Qingying hadn't forgotten the cassette from long ago. As a teenager she secretly listened to it every day.

"Wang Er, this is trash I wanted to throw out. Why did you keep it?"

"I've seen a photo of you when you were thirteen. Ye Xiao found it for me. He didn't know it was you in the photo."

He Qingying's expression changed and she began to shake. "When I was thirteen? Where was I?"

"Nanhu Junior High, seventh grade, Section 2. At the corner of Nanhu Road and Serenity Road."

"You must be mistaken."

"Do you still remember the name Lu Mingyue?"

Goose bumps ran up her neck as she stiffly shook her head. "You're imagining things."

"Don't lie to yourself." Si Wang kept combing her hair. "You know I found your secret. I also found out that you and Lu Mingyue were born on the same day. Your personal files started

357

after 1983. Nothing exists from before that. I learned this from the Archive Bureau."

"Shut up!"

"Lu Mingyue's files stopped after 1983 because something happened to her family that year. Her father was killed. She reported the crime and was the only witness."

"What do you want to say?" He Qingying tried to struggle out of her son's grip. "Go to bed already. Good night."

Her arm was pinned by Si Wang like she was a criminal. "Mom, you never visit your side of the family. I found my uncle's number and called him pretending to be a policeman. He told me you weren't Grandma and Grandpa's biological child."

"Wang Er, listen to me."

"Lu Mingyue!" Si Wang shouted the name. "That's your real name, isn't it?"

She stopped trying to free herself, and her body went limp.

"No. Lu Mingyue was just a name I used to have. I almost forgot the name I was born with."

"Because you aren't Lu Jingnan's biological child, either, right?"

For the first time, Si Wang said the name of the person who was murdered on Serenity Road in 1983.

"Wang Er, why are you doing this?"

"I'm trying to save you." He kissed his mom's neck.

"So you've already been to Serenity Road Number 19? I was born there. My dad, your real grandpa, was a famous translator. He hanged himself when I was four. That's my first memory. Soon after, my mom, your grandma, died, too. Our house was taken over by a bureaucrat called Lu Jingnan. His wife couldn't have children, but she was a kind woman. She adopted me since I had no one. My childhood wasn't horrible. I grew up there. When I turned twelve, my adoptive mother found her husband cheating on her. She killed herself by jumping into a river. No one could protect me after that."

"Mom, are you saying that bastard Lu Jingnan—"

"Calling him a bastard would be too kind!"

"You killed him?"

"Wang Er, please stop asking!"

"I was at Serenity Road tonight. I've studied Huang Hai's files. Lu Jingnan's murder wasn't done by an outsider. Someone tried to make it look like there was a break-in. A window was smashed with a brick, but most of the glass was outside the window, meaning it was broken from the inside. The police debated this for a while, so the case was never solved. But no one realized the victim's daughter—the only witness and the first person to call it in—was the killer!"

"This is just your speculation. You have no evidence. Who'd believe a high school kid who gets into fights all the time?"

"Mom, I'm not going to tell anyone. The case is thirty years old, and the victim was evil. You were just a little girl."

"I admit it," she spat out. "I killed someone."

Si Wang put down the comb, wiped away his mom's tears, and whispered, "The victim was your adoptive father, Lu Jingnan."

"He was an animal! No one knows what he did to me. No one suspected I killed him. He was drunk that night, and I tried to fight him off in the living room. A window broke during our fight. I grabbed a piece of glass and cut his neck. There was blood everywhere. I broke the glass on the floor so there was no weapon. Then I opened the door and sat on the stairs to cry, and when someone passed by, they asked me what was wrong. Soon the cops came."

"No one else was around?"

He Qingying shook her head in a daze. "If anyone saw me, I would have been caught. Wang Er, please, I beg you—don't ask me any more. You've been too cruel to me already."

CHAPTER 70

Grave-Sweeping Day.

Shen Min was eighteen and as adorable as a blooming bud. It rained lightly as her father took her to pay respects at her mother's grave. Afterward, they carried joss paper and flowers to a public cemetery in the suburbs. Her brother, whom she had never met, was buried here.

They were surprised to see a young man squatting by the grave. He was burning joss paper and incense.

"Who are you?" the prosecutor yelled.

The other man turned and awkwardly tried to leave.

Shen Yuanchao grabbed his arm. "Stop! Are you Huang Zhiliang?"

"I'm sorry, I was just . . ."

"Thank you!" Shen Yuanchao was emotional and held the younger man. "Child, you don't have to say anything."

Shen Min was confused. She put down the flowers by the tombstone, which read:

Beloved son, Shen Ming
May 11, 1970–June 19, 1995
From Father Shen Yuanchao

The young man stood stiff in Shen Yuanchao's grasp, then he reached up almost involuntarily to hold the older man. Their hug grew tighter and tighter.

"I'll catch that monster," Si Wang whispered to Shen.

"If only you were my son."

"Dad, stop acting like this," Shen Min said.

The rain was soaking the two mean so she moved the umbrella over their heads. Her father finally let go of the young man. He coughed twice.

"Sorry, I know you're here to pay respects to my son. His spirit in Heaven will protect you."

Shen Min stared at the young man. Last week, as she was heartily eating at the spicy hot pot place near May First Junior High, someone patted her shoulder. It was the young man. In the last few months, she'd become more wary of the opposite sex. She was just about to run when she recognized him.

"You scared me," she'd said.

"Sorry about that. So you remember me?"

"You're Huang Zhiliang."

"Yes, Little Min." He pointed to across the street. "I work at that bookstore every weekend."

"Great, I'll go buy books there."

"Better not, the boss is a mean lady. If you came in to talk to me, she might fire me."

"Fine." She stuck out her tongue.

"How is your dad doing?" The young man sounded older than his years.

"He's retired and reading all these weird books."

"Weird books?"

"Mostly about murders and stuff. I get freaked out by the covers. I think he's going crazy."

"Have you been to your older brother's grave yet?"

"We've been going to Grave-Sweeping Day ever since seventh grade. My dad drags me."

"Can you tell me where it is?"

Shen Min never thought he'd actually show up for the holiday.

Shen Yuanchao shielded his daughter. "Are you—still alive?"

A question you can only ask in a cemetery on Grave-Sweeping Day.

The young man looked at him noncommittally and then looked back at the gravestone. "I'd only go from this world after Shen Ming's killer paid for his crime."

"Huang Zhiliang, am I hallucinating you?" Shen Yuanchao touched the young man's face and hair. "No, this is not a hallucination. Little Min, can you see him? Am I talking to thin air?"

"No, I see him, too."

Shen Min hid behind the tombstone; she didn't want to lie to her father.

"You're alive! If I can see you, then Shen Ming could be alive, too. He would be forty-three this year." Shen Yuanchao was crazed by the encounter; he knelt in front of Shen Ming's grave and lit an offering. "Little Ming, if you're still alive, please tell me."

The young man left the cemetery as father and daughter prayed. By the time they looked up, Huang Zhiliang's ghost was gone.

CHAPTER 71

June 19, 2013.

The eighteenth anniversary of Shen Ming's death.

Zhang Mingsong became more and more agitated as it got closer to 10:00 p.m. His blood seemed to flow faster, as if it would burst from his vessels. He took off his shirt and knelt on the mat, drawing hexagons on his chest and making odd hand gestures—a spirit reincarnation ritual.

For the past year, he had been focused on Si Wang. After the rumor about his dating Ouyang Xiaozhi, she was fired. Zhang Mingsong was forced to make a public apology as the homeroom teacher. At the request of the principal and various parents, he'd started secretly watching the teenager. Si Wang practiced all day at the boxing club, hitting the sandbags so hard his knuckles bled.

The doorbell rang.

Did he have any students to tutor today? He checked his calendar and no one was scheduled. Maybe it was a parent with a gift?

Zhang Mingsong got dressed. He put away the mat and opened the door to a stranger.

A man in his sixties with a grim expression.

"You are?" He remembered that face. One afternoon at the library years ago, many times on subways, near his neighborhood's lawn . . .

June 19—10:00 p.m.

He wanted to scream. Before he could close the door, the other man hit him on the head with a wooden stick.

By the time he woke up, an hour had passed.

Thick curtains covered the windows. Books were everywhere, the floor was surprisingly clean, and there was no dust on the furniture. His hands and feet bound, Zhang Mingsong shrank into a ball in the corner of his bedroom. His mouth was stuffed with a rag, and his forehead throbbed.

Shen Yuanchao, who paced back and forth holding the wooden stick, looked like a vicious old butcher.

"You're awake." He squeezed Zhang Mingsong's neck to make his face turn red. "Listen to me! I know you'll scream for the security guard if I let go, so just nod or shake your head, OK? Don't lie!"

Zhang Mingsong nodded his head in fear.

"You're a serial killer, right?"

When he shook his head, Shen Yuanchao slapped him.

"You have the Fraternal Order symbol here. Who do you think you are? The American president? You're a pervert. You're into witchcraft and other cult stuff, aren't you?"

Another shake of the head, another slap.

"You killed Shen Ming on June 19, 1995, right?"

Zhang Mingsong almost swallowed the rag. The veins on his forehead popped as he shook his head like he was having a seizure.

"You're still lying! I've already waited eighteen years, and I refuse to wait any longer. It's time!" The prosecutor picked up his stick. "You used a knife. I'll use a stick."

Just as Shen Yuanchao was about to deliver the first blow—and Zhang was about to lose control of his bowels—the doorbell rang.

Shen Yuanchao dropped his weapon to the floor and stood as still as a statue.

The doorbell rang three times before he walked soundlessly out of the bedroom to the front door.

A low voice from the other side of the door. "Prosecutor Shen, are you inside? I'm not with the police. It's Huang Zhiliang."

"Huang Zhiliang, what are you doing here?"

"I'm a ghost. I can be anywhere I want. I knew you'd come for him tonight."

"Huang Zhiliang, this has nothing to do with you. Please leave now."

"I said I'd kill the monster with my own hands to avenge my father's death. If you don't open the door immediately, I'll call the cops."

The door opened just a crack. There was almost no light in the small opening, just a blurry shadow. The young man rushed inside and relocked the door.

Shen Yuanchao backed away a few steps. "Child, I won't give up the chance to kill him."

"Thank you. I know you want to spare me the kill so you can take the blame. But I'm the ghost here. I'm not afraid of laws."

"How did you find me?"

"I got a call from your daughter half an hour ago. She said you left this morning and haven't been home since. She also told me about the letter you left her, saying her older brother was killed by a monster eighteen years ago tonight—and that you'd gone out for revenge."

"I didn't say who I was looking for."

"Shen Min is a good kid. She doesn't know where you went, so she asked me for help. She was afraid you'd kill someone. She didn't want to call the police, because you'd be locked up whether or not you killed anyone. I promised her I'd bring you home to her."

"But you know who I was looking for."

"There was no one else you wanted besides Zhang Mingsong."

The young man charged into the bedroom.

Zhang Mingsong panicked when he saw Si Wang.

"You're sure he is the monster?" Si Wang looked back at the prosecutor. He pulled out the rag in Zhang's mouth. He tried to speak, but his voice was too raspy. "Mr. Zhang, sorry I got here so late." Si Wang squatted by Mr. Zhang and checked over his wounds.

"You're here to save him? You know him?" Shen Yuanchao widened his eyes and prepared to hit Si Wang.

But Si Wang stood up and grabbed the wooden stick, slamming it against his own head. His forehead bled. The move stunned both Shen Yuanchao and Zhang Mingsong.

"Yes, I came here to save him." Si Wang let the blood flow into his mouth.

Shen Yuanchao thought back to the night his son was killed. Shen Ming's back must have bled this way, too.

"Child, you're not a ghost, are you?"

"Ghosts can't bleed—only humans do." Si Wang wiped the blood on his face; he looked terrifying, like a demon. "For three years I followed this man you tied up, andI don't believe he's Shen Ming's killer."

"You sound like a cop!"

"I'm sorry I lied to you. Huang Hai's son, Huang Zhiliang, died a long time ago from leukemia. I looked like him, so Huang Hai became my godfather. I'm Si Wang, Si as in 'general,' Wang as in 'lookout.' My dad is Si Mingyuan; my mom is He Qingying. I go to Nanming High. I'll be a senior after this summer. This man here is my homeroom teacher."

"Why are you doing this?"

"For Huang Hai. He was like a father to me. I read all the files. Your son's killer is someone else."

Shen Yuanchao was quiet for a long time before he finally relaxed.

Si Wang untied Zhang Mingsong and whispered, "Mr. Zhang, keep cool and don't do anything crazy."

"Thank you, Si Wang!" He stretched a bit but didn't move from the wall.

"I came here tonight to save him, but also to save you," Si Wang said, still kneeling by his teacher. "If you killed him, you'd be a killer. You'd be sentenced to death. I don't want to see that happen. What would your daughter do if you died?"

"For the past eighteen years, I've thought of my son every moment of every day. The hurt didn't go away but got more intense. I owed him too much in this life. I never repaid him while he was alive, so I need to avenge his death, even if I have to die. You wouldn't understand."

"You're wrong," Si Wang said. "Too much has happened since he was killed. Your memory is jaded. You don't really remember the past. Even if you found the killer, that wouldn't bring back your son. Let it go."

A tearful Shen Yuanchao nodded. "I told myself this for years. Is now really the time to give up?"

Si Wang helped Zhang Mingsong stand up. "Mr. Zhang, he won't be a danger to you anymore. But please promise me something."

Zhang Mingsong shook, grabbing Si Wang as if he was a lifeboat. "I'll promise you anything you want."

"I apologize for what he did tonight. He just misses his dead son too much. Please pretend that nothing has happened. Don't call the police, either. I'll do everything you ask if you promise me that."

"Fine, I promise. I won't hold a grudge."

"Thank you, I'll remember this favor," Si Wang said before turning to the prosecutor. "Let's go!"

With Si Wang carrying the stick and the rope, the two quickly left the seventh floor and then Zhang Mingsong's neighborhood. The security guard didn't pay them much attention; he assumed they were a father and son asking Mr. Zhang for tutoring help.

Si Wang stopped a taxi and gave Shen Yuanchao's address.

It was 10:30 p.m.

Eighteen years ago, Shen Ming was already a corpse.

Shen Yuanchao didn't talk at all. His hair was a mess and he just stared into the night, imagining the pain of being killed and the endless loneliness after death.

"Please promise me not to do anything like this again," Si Wang said. "Leave the revenge to me."

"You're still a kid."

"I grew up a long time ago."

For some reason, Shen Yuanchao thought back to thirty years ago. Maybe the older one got, the more vivid one's memories of youth became.

"Shen Ming was my illegitimate son. He's half brother to Shen Min. His mom died when he was seven."

"I know."

"One year, on May First Workers' Day, when I was still unmarried, I took Shen Ming to People's Park. It was the happiest day of his childhood. He rode the merry-go-round. We bought a balloon for five cents and drank orange juice for twenty cents."

"I didn't forget."

"Child, what did you say?" The old man looked at Si Wang in confusion, the hairs on the back of his neck standing at attention. Si Wang turned to look out the taxi's window, through which the streetlights glared. "Eighteen years ago—forty-nine days after

Shen Ming died—I asked a Taoist monk to do a soul-calling ritual."

"You're a Communist, a true believer in dialectic materialism. You believe in that kind of thing?"

"Someone told me that my son died in a very negative place. Any ghosts would be trapped underground forever. Only a soul-calling ritual would get him out. He could visit me forty-nine days after his death and then reincarnate." Shen Yuanchao looked very serious as he said this. Maybe he was senile, or maybe he believed in different things now.

As he walked Shen Yuanchao up the stairs, Si Wang whispered, "I'm sorry I lied to you for two years."

"It's OK. It would have been great for it to be true. At least I'd have a chance to see my son again."

Standing in front of the apartment door, the young man gripped the hand of the older man, saying, "There are no ghosts in this world. Please don't look for Shen Ming's ghost anymore!"

Shen Yuanchao looked unprepared to face his daughter, but Si Wang rang the doorbell anyway. Shen Min opened the door right away. Overjoyed, she hugged her dad. She ushered her father inside, and Si Wang quickly ran back down the stairs.

Could he really have been a ghost?

CHAPTER 72

It was the summer before the college entrance exams.

All the students were either getting extra help or being tutored at home. Shen Min was a good student, so she wasn't desperate. She saw Si Wang every weekend; he always asked about her dad. To her surprise, after that night on June 19, the rest of the summer was quiet. Her dad didn't go out and make trouble anymore. He exercised in the neighborhood and practiced calligraphy at home. He had tea with former coworkers and read the news with as much fervor as other retired Party members, always holding copies of *Reference News* and *Global Times*.

Shen Min had a crush on Si Wang.

She used the excuse of thanking him for saving her dad to take him out to eat and invite him to movies. She was a dainty beauty, but she was a rabid fan of horror movies; even dumb domestic thrillers made her scream and get close to Si Wang. She would shiver and hold him in the dark theatre, her hair fanning over his face, scaring and distracting him.

One time, after a movie as the two were eating ice cream, Shen Min said softly, "Dad said you're not a ghost."

"I'm sorry I lied to you two. I'm Si Wang, Si as in 'general,' Wang as in 'lookout.'"

"Which story of yours should I believe?"

"Don't believe anything I say."

"Liar!" She slid closer to him.

Si Wang moved away. "What if I really was a ghost?"

"I'm not scared."

"Time to go home."

"My dad is going to the procuratorate tomorrow for a meeting of other retirees. Come visit me." She blushed. This was her first time inviting a guy over.

Shen Min took care to primp before Si Wang's arrival. She wore a pink dress that didn't quite cover her knees and had her hair done. In a few years she would be a stunning young woman.

Si Wang arrived right on time. Shen Min had put out plenty of snacks for the two of them.

"There must be a lot of girls at school who like you."

"No." He was embarrassed and afraid to make eye contact with her.

The truth was, after his relationship with Ms. Ouyang was exposed at school, no girls talked to him. The boys were jealous but still made fun of him.

"You're lying again!" Shen Min pulled him up from the sofa. "Why don't you check out my house?"

He had been staring at Shen Ming's memorial photo in the living room.

"I've never met my older brother," Shen Min said, turning sad.

"Your brother has always been with you."

"You mean his ghost? I'm not afraid."

"If only there were ghosts. Little Min, let me be your older brother."

"Why?" She wrinkled her brow. "You're only one day older than me."

"So I can protect you."

"No." She tried to hold on to his arm, but he just walked toward the door.

He took a deep breath and said, "I should go, my mom has dinner waiting for me."

"I'll take you out to eat next week."

"We shouldn't meet again."

Shen Min's face paled. "Why not?"

"I'm sorry. I still have some important things to finish."

"What are you hiding?" She grabbed his arm. "Si Wang!"

He escaped her grasp and charged downstairs. Looking at the oleander bush in the neighborhood garden, he muttered, "Killing."

CHAPTER 73

September 2012. Senior year.

Zhang Mingsong kept his word: He didn't go to the police or make trouble. He only became more interested in Si Wang. The boy was even more quiet now, avoiding his homeroom teacher whenever possible. One night, Zhang Mingsong asked, "Si Wang, do you play Ping-Pong?"

"A little—why?"

"Play with me."

The Ping-Pong room was in the male students' dorm. Before being renovated it had been Shen Ming's room. Zhang Mingsong opened the door. A thick layer of dust covered the table; no one had been here for a while.

"You ever been here before?" Zhang Mingsong was picking out a paddle.

Si Wang calmly looked around. "Yes, I've been here."

"When?"

"In my last lifetime."

"You're quite a joker."

He quickly hit a ball that Si Wang returned, scoring a point. "You play pretty well!"

The two played for more than half an hour. Zhang Mingsong slowed down first. He sat down, sweating and gulping down soda. Si Wang sweated a lot, too. He took off his school shirt and wearing just a tank top revealed his muscular build.

"Si Wang, I haven't really thanked you for saving my life."

"It's OK, Mr. Zhang. Why didn't you ask how I knew Mr. Shen?"

"Who knows?" Zhang Mingsong sounded nonchalant, but he did want to know.

"He is my dad's good friend. I played at his house all the time. His daughter called me that night, saying he might have gone to your house."

"Then you know what happened to his son."

"Yes."

"Did he think I killed his son? The police did their work. If I was really the killer, would I be teaching you guys today?"

"It's a misunderstanding."

Zhang Mingsong breathed heavily, looking up at the cobweb-covered ceiling. "Did you know that Shen Ming used to live in this room? The students say this room is haunted so no one really plays Ping-Pong in here."

"Has anyone ever seen Mr. Shen's ghost?"

The overhead fluorescent lights started flickering. In the alternating light and dark, with a pitch-black corridor outside, it did seem as if a ghost was present.

"He's here." Zhang Mingsong seemed unaffected. He patted Si Wang's chest. "Get dressed and go back to your room."

The weather had become chilly. Chinese parasol trees shed leaves that slipped through the open windows, littering the blackboard. Students studied as hard as they could. Zhang Mingsong turned down almost all of the tutoring requests. He was the only teacher who dared to approach Si Wang and the two became quite close.

Si Wang's cell phone rang, the ringtone was actually Chang Yu-sheng's "I'm a Tree in Fall."

Zhang Mingsong sighed, "I loved this song when I was younger."

"It has been around since before I was born."

"Yes, but Chang Yu-sheng didn't die until after you were born." The two were walking past the library. Zhang Mingsong put on a serious expression. "Si Wang, your math grades have been slipping."

"I've never been good at math."

"You need some tutoring!"

Si Wang stopped and looked up at the library. "Everyone wants to be tutored by you."

"I'll be grading homework here, but I won't be free until ten. Come to the library then."

Hours later, the librarian had gone home long ago. Zhang Mingsong sat alone in the empty reading room. There was no homework to grade; he started to flip through a copy of *Angels and Demons*.

10:00 p.m.

Si Wang showed up, carrying his math textbook.

Zhang Mingsong grinned. "Great. It's a bit cold here—let's go upstairs."

"Upstairs?"

Zhang Mingsong led him to the stairs and saw Si Wang's hesitation. "You're afraid?"

"No."

Si Wang started up first, and Zhang Mingsong followed. Once they were in the dusty attic the moon cast some light through the murky window.

Zhang Mingsong closed the door. The lock was weird, in that it actually only worked from the outside. If someone followed them, both would be locked in the attic and then the only way out was through the window in the roof.

There were books everywhere and two little stools.

Si Wang looked around before saying, "Mr. Zhang, I heard someone died up here."

"Yes, it was eighteen years ago, a student by the name of Liu Man. She died the night before the college entrance exams. The police said she was poisoned with oleander juice extract."

"Did they catch the killer?"

"Some people said the killer was Mr. Shen, who was killed later. Who knows?"

Si Wang retreated into a corner. "Are we not going to go over math?"

"Let's chat first. You're a unique kid. I've felt that way ever since I met you two years ago."

"Everybody says that."

"I was surprised and disappointed to hear about you and Ms. Ouyang."

After thinking about it, Si Wang said, "I don't want to talk about it. I probably won't ever see her again."

"You're too young. You don't understand that there are many things in this world we can't get even if we wanted to. Sometimes people don't know themselves."

"What are you saying?"

"You don't really know what you want." Zhang Mingsong approached Si Wang, standing close enough behind him to breathe on this neck.

"Mr. Zhang—"

"Si Wang, you're a good-looking guy." Zhang Mingsong's voice was a smooth as velvet. "Many of the girls like you, right? Actually, it's not only girls who like you." Zhang Mingsong's hand stroked Si Wang's face, moving from his chin, to his ears and nose, and then to his lips, until his fingers were in Si Wang's mouth. "You can bite if you want to."

The scent of Si Wang's nervous sweat filled the room as he struggled to get free. He ran out of the attic shouting, "Mr. Zhang, I'm sorry!"

Under the light of the bleak moon, Zhang Mingsong sat down on the floor, feeling lost. He threw a handful of dust into the air. He wiped his fingers with a tissue and put one back in his mouth to see if it tasted of the teenage boy.

He was sure Si Wang would be back.

CHAPTER 74

Winter 2014.

Thanks to air pollution, the atmosphere was hazy this season. It was difficult to see very far from Nanming High. When you looked out from a top-floor office, the library was shrouded in clouds.

Zhang Mingsong felt as though he'd lost sight of Si Wang.

Since their meeting in the attic, the student never avoided the teacher. He always seemed at ease whenever Zhang Mingsong talked to him one on one. In these moments when no one else was around, Zhang Mingsong would touch Si Wang's hand intentionally. At first Si Wang would back away, but then he would allow the touch.

About a month before the exams, he got a text from Si Wang:

"Mr. Zhang, can I come to your house for tutoring tonight?"

"Sure, I'll be here."

Zhang Mingsong went home early to prepare for his guest. He made sure the apartment was spotless, keeping the curtains covered. He took a bath and put on some cologne. He studied himself in the mirror. He thought he looked more like a student than a teacher in his fifties.

The doorbell rang.

Zhang Mingsong opened the door with a smile. "Si Wang, welcome."

"Good evening, Mr. Zhang." Si Wang walked in politely. It was his second time here and he looked around cautiously.

He'd turned nineteen last month so was no longer a minor.

Zhang Mingsong patted his arm. "You're taller than me now."

The AC was set low, and the room was humid. Zhang Mingsong took Si Wang's jacket, asking, "Need a drink?"

Before Si Wang could answer, two cans of beer appeared on the table.

Si Wang pushed away the beer. "It's OK, I'm not thirsty."

Zhang Mingsong walked behind him and took off his shirt, exposing his chest. He whispered into Si Wang's ear, "Let's start the session."

Si Wang punched him in the stomach hard. Before he could fight back, another punch landed on his face. His teeth felt like they would fall out. He blacked out as he fell to the ground.

A few minutes later, Zhang Mingsong was tied up with a nylon rope; all of his clothes had been removed.

Si Wang looked grave, putting one foot on Zhang Mingsong and spitting out, "Mr. Zhang, you were wrong about me."

"Sorry. I'm sorry. I was wrong. Please let me go. This is a private thing. It's always consensual. I've never forced anyone."

"Now I know why Xiao Peng hanged himself in the Nanming High dorms in 1988. You are the reason he had to kill himself."

"Xiao Peng?"

"Do you still remember him? He was short and very pale. He was often mistaken for a girl."

"How do you know about him?"

"Two months before he died, he always went to you for tutoring. It was always at night and he'd come back to the dorm late. He didn't talk much then. We all thought it was the stress from studying for the college entrance exams."

"Who are you?"

"That doesn't matter. What *does* matter is what you've been doing for the last twenty years!" Si Wang opened a drawer. He found an eyebrow-trimming blade and swiped it against Zhang Mingsong's face. "If you don't admit what you did, I'll carve the words on your face."

"No!"

"After Xiao Peng hanged himself, no one stayed in that room anymore. It was empty until Mr. Shen moved in. I remembered his face when you took me to play Ping-Pong. I could see his body hanging in front of me."

"I admit it!"

"Was it in the library attic?"

"Yes, I lured him there with tutoring as an excuse, actually I was—"

"Tell me."

"I promised him that if he did what I told him, he could get better math scores, which would make or break his college entrance exam results. I didn't think he'd be that neurotic and kill himself."

"Xiao Peng was an introverted kid. He couldn't handle that kind of mental abuse. He didn't dare tell us, and not his parents, either. He paid for it with his life!" Si Wang put away the blade. "Who else?"

Zhang Mingsong took a breath. "He was the first one, and the last one."

"I don't believe you."

Si Wang searched the room for half an hour. Finally, he found a hidden compartment in the dresser. There were several envelopes inside, all labeled chronologically. He opened the first one. Zhang Mingsong groaned. There were photos of a naked teenage boy of no more than seventeen or eighteen. Si Wang could tell that the photos had been taken in the attic. The date on the envelope was September 1992.

"Prosecutor Shen was right: You're sick, and this is the proof!"

Si Wang opened another envelope. These photos showed a familiar face: Ma Li. They were taken in May 1995. He couldn't stand to look at the appalling images.

Zhang Mingsong murmured from the floor. "If I hadn't taken those photos, they would have reported me after they got into their top universities."

In the envelope with Ma Li's photographs was a note:

Ma Li:

Last night I hid in the library and saw what happened between you and Mr. Zhang. I can't believe it. You were forced, right? I don't want to see you like this. Please stop. If you don't have the courage, I'll help you put a stop to it.

Liu Man
June 1, 1995

Si Wang read the note three times before returning his attention to Zhang Mingsong.

"You know who Liu Man is?" Knowing he was done for, Zhang Mingsong confessed to everything. "Ma Li gave the note to me."

"Then you killed Liu Man?"

Zhang Mingsong chuckled bitterly. "No, she was poisoned. How could I have gotten to her? I have alibis for the murders of both Liu Man and Shen Ming."

"I get it, you can stop talking."

"Si Wang, you're gorgeous."

Zhang Mingsong was still tied up, but he didn't take his eyes off his captor, smiling at him in his disturbing way. Si Wang watched him with a fierce hatred that could have burned Zhang Mingsong to a crisp.

"You're interested in 1995, right? Let me tell you what else I know. I was really jealous of Mr. Shen then. He was younger and had fewer credentials. I went to Tsinghua, which was just as prestigious as his school. But he was going to be a university president's son-in-law and I was just a high school math teacher."

"You spread the rumors about him?"

"I made up the story about him dating Liu Man. It was a very believable rumor." Zhang Mingsong actually smiled with satisfaction. "Lu Zhongyue was the one who told me about Shen Ming being an illegitimate son."

"Lu Zhongyue?"

"He went to high school with Shen Ming, they were best friends. Xiao Peng was their roommate. I didn't know why he told me about it at the time. But when he married Shen Ming's fiancée, I understood."

"It was him!" Si Wang slammed the wall. He turned to stare at Zhang Mingsong, at his pitiful and despicable face. "Good-bye, Mr. Zhang."

Si Wang looked over the room once more and made sure to collect all the envelopes filled with the despicable photographs. Si Wang left Zhang Mingsong on the floor; he was still tied up and naked.

Zhang Mingsong was afraid to shout. What if a neighbor or the security guard found him like this? He slowly shimmied across the floor, hoping to find a way to untie himself. Not that getting loose would matter much at this point. Si Wang had taken all the evidence with him. His life would be ruined. He'd no longer be a respected teacher. Those boys would come back and prosecute him. He'd be sentenced to prison and forced to live with real rapists and perverts.

Zhang Mingsong wanted to kill himself.

Suddenly, he realized that Si Wang hadn't completely closed the door when he left.

CHAPTER 75

At the same time.

Ma Li came out of the bathroom after a shower. Someone was calling from an unfamiliar number. After a few seconds of hesitation, he picked up.

"Ma Li, it's me—Si Wang."

"It's the middle of the night. What is it?"

"I just left Zhang Mingsong's house."

Ma Li's heart sped up, but he made sure to keep calm. "What's going on?"

"I know the secret."

It started snowing outside.

"What did you say?"

"I know about the secret between you and Zhang Mingsong. He admitted everything. I saw the photos."

That silenced him. He felt naked, like he was kneeling in the snow with everybody watching.

Si Wang added coolly, "I also saw the note Liu Man wrote you."

Si Wang gave an address, and Ma Li hung up.

He took a deep breath and from his high-rise perch he watched the flying snow. He opened his arms to look at the world at night. The evil that had been buried for eighteen years was about to come out.

He really wanted to end it all.

But no, before he did, he had something else he needed to do.

Ma Li got dressed and drove off in his Porsche SUV, roaring along the filthy, slushy streets.

He looked at himself in the rearview mirror; he'd just had his own zodiac year. The last few times he'd gone out to the clubs, he'd made some nice conquests, but there was never a second night with any of the women.

Ma Li was the dream guy for a lot of girls in high school, including Liu Man. She had an unrequited crush on him. She always used the political science class as an excuse to ask Ma Li for help. She also hounded him for math help every evening. The closest encounter they had was in the summer of 1994. She'd invited him to a movie, but he insisted on bringing another roommate. Liu Man had to buy three tickets. She joined the Dead Poets Society just to get close to him, especially at that underground reading in the Demon Girl Zone.

He didn't hate her. He just felt that his body was dirty and not worthy of a pure girl like her.

The first time Zhang Mingsong had offered to tutor Ma Li was during the second semester of eleventh grade. It happened in the library attic. He finally realized that the mythical attic ghost light was always turned on by Mr. Zhang. When his teacher's hand touched him, he didn't know whether to scream or resist.

After it was over, he cried, though he didn't know what it meant. Zhang Mingsong took some photos of him and comforted him with words, as if they were still in class. Mr. Zhang called it a way to relax after so much studying.

"Ma Li, you're the most good-looking boy I've seen. You should have a bright future and be very successful. As long as you listen to your teacher, study hard, follow school rules, and don't make trouble, I'll recommend you for bonus points. You'll be that much more likely to be admitted to the top schools."

Zhang Mingsong's face was especially despicable in the attic light, and Ma Li cowered like a meek lamb in his arms.

Ma Li had one dream since entering Nanming High: Ma Li's only dream had been to get into Tsinghua University and become the best of the best.

Zhang Mingsong had graduated from Tsinghua, too, and had supposedly added bonus points for several students before. Were they all as good-looking as Ma Li? Within the year, Ma Li's bonus points were processed. The price was the weekly midnight tutoring sessions with Mr. Zhang.

One night, Liu Man snuck into the library and crawled on top of the attic. She saw their secret through the little window on the roof.

Liu Man wanted to talk to him in private, but Ma Li tried to avoid her. So she finally wrote him a note.

He broke down after reading the note and he gave it to Zhang Mingsong. With no expression, he said to Ma Li, "You know what you have to do."

Ma Li knew that if anyone discovered his secret he'd lose his chance at getting into Tsinghua.

It only took him a few days to plan the murder. He got the oleander juice from the trees by the sports field, and made it into poison.

On the evening of June 5, 1995, he saw Liu Man talking to Mr. Shen in the self-study room. After she came out of the room, he got close to her in the dark corridor and said, "I'll meet you tonight at ten in the library attic."

Nervous, he waited in the attic until Liu Man finally came up like a ghost.

She asked him to stop seeing Mr. Zhang and even said she would go with him to the police. Ma Li walked behind her, put on gloves, and poured the poison down her throat. Liu Man didn't see it coming, and before she knew what was happening she'd taken a big gulp of the poison and swallowed it. Ma Li ran out of the attic and locked it from the outside. For close to an hour he remained crouched by the door listening to Liu Man pounding, until she stopped.

Before he'd gone to the library he'd lit some incense laced with a sleeping drug so his roommates slept harder than usual, not even noticing that he'd left and returned.

He saw Liu Man on the library roof the next morning at six o'clock.

He couldn't believe it. Was she still alive?

Mr. Shen crawled on to the roof to inspect the body. Ma Li thought of something else. Wasn't everyone saying that Mr. Shen and Liu Man had something going on? Plus, they were alone last night. Mr. Shen stayed at the school every night, too. He was the most likely suspect.

That evening, he snuck into Mr. Shen's room while the teacher was at the cafeteria and planted the bottle of leftover poison on the dresser. No one would suspect Ma Li now.

The police searched the room and arrested Mr. Shen.

Thirteen days later, Mr. Shen died in the Demon Girl Zone.

Ma Li didn't know who killed Mr. Shen.

After living with the secret for years, Ma Li still thought of himself as the one who'd stabbed Mr. Shen first.

The Porsche stopped at Zhang Mingsong's building. He charged to the seventh floor and saw the door with its Fraternal Order sign. It was slightly ajar; heat and light came out of the room.

Ma Li pushed open the door and walked gingerly into the bedroom, finding Zhang Mingsong on the floor, tied up and naked.

Zhang Mingsong stared blankly at the man. He'd forgotten Ma Li's face after all these years, but Ma Li had never forgotten his.

"Mr. Zhang, do you remember me? You helped me get into Tsinghua in 1995."

"Ma—"

"Yes, I'm Ma Li. My homeroom teacher was Mr. Shen."

Zhang Mingsong squinted his eyes and nodded. "Why are you here?"

"Someone called me."

"Si Wang!" Zhang Mingsong shouted the name with disgust. "Did he ask you to save me?"

Ma Li paused and shook his head. "No, he asked me to kill you."

"What?"

"Didn't you kill Liu Man? And Mr. Shen, too?"

"You were the one who killed her! You also set up Shen Ming—that bottle of poison?" Zhang Mingsong twisted his pale body on the floor. "I never asked you to kill anyone!"

"All these years, the person I most regret hurting, other than Liu Man, is Mr. Shen." Ma Li tried not to cry, not wanting to show fear in front of Zhang Mingsong. "When his ghost showed up in front of me, when he possessed that boy, I knew this day would come. It's been a long wait."

"What are you talking about? Shen Ming's ghost? What boy?"

Ma Li smiled like a maniac. "Yes, he finally did it, and it's amazing! He sent all of you to Hell. All of you who abandoned him, who backstabbed him, who left him to die."

"You're talking about Si Wang?"

Ma Li smiled noncommittally and squatted in front of the disgraced teacher. "Mr. Zhang, I've had the same dream for years now—killing you."

Ma Li went to the kitchen, found a sharp knife, and returned to confront Zhang Mingsong. "I really hate myself. If I'd killed you earlier or told people what you did, you couldn't have ruined other boys' lives. It's too late for regret. I thought nothing else mattered as long as I could get into a top school, but I've already lost everything."

The knife's blade rested on Zhang Mingsong's throat, but Ma Li's fingers shook. He couldn't cut, no matter how he tried. In his dreams, he'd imagined this scene countless times right down to blood spattering everywhere.

After all, poisoning someone to death was different than stabbing someone to death.

"Damn it!" Ma Li dropped the knife and then slapped himself. It had been twenty years. Why had he become weaker?

"Kid, don't wimp out—kill me!" To his surprise, Zhang Mingsong started begging. "My student Si Wang has all the evidence already, and the whole school will find out tomorrow. Even if the principal and the teachers don't believe it, someone will talk to my former students. It will only take one of them talking for everything to come out."

"If I hadn't already killed one person because of you I would have exposed everything years ago!"

"It's no big deal being arrested. I'm afraid of the school firing me, just like they fired Mr. Shen. I'd be abandoned by everyone—teachers, students, and parents. I've trained the most successful scientists of the last decade. I'm the city's education star. Everyone respects me, even the stuck-up bureau chief and district chief beg me to tutor their kids."

Ma Li picked up the knife again. "I get it now, Si Wang got it a long time ago. Your only weakness is your vanity."

"I'd rather die than lose my reputation and be ridiculed by everyone. Born with nothing, die with nothing. Just kill me. Are you afraid? All pretty boys are as weak as girls."

Ma Li cut open Zhang Mingsong's throat.

CHAPTER 76

Spring.

There were many advantages to hiding in this small southern town. The fresh air made him feel better, even if he never recovered his manly ability; he was able to work as an appliance repairman, and he was an expert at fixing those things; and there were no posters with his face on them. In fact, there were no signs of cops anywhere.

He still woke up from nightmares many times a week. He would see that twenty-five-year-old face—a face full of life and passion, a face ready to be someone.

Lu Zhongyue dreamed about being killed by that face.

That face belonged to Shen Ming.

Blood flowed from his eyes, staining his clothes. He lay on the street, being gawked at by everyone, like a dog killed by a car.

Each time he woke from this dream, he rushed to the mirror and stared at his wrinkles, his thinning hair, and his bloodshot eyes.

The first time Lu Zhongyue met Shen Ming, both men were just fifteen. Back in 1985, Nanming High was in the middle of nowhere, forgotten by the world aside from those who worked at the steel factory. Only the teachers' building and the dorms were new. Nonetheless, getting into the school was highly competitive. Lu Zhongyue, an average student at best, had to use his dad's connections and a bribe.

Shen Ming arrived at the school wearing a faded white shirt and blue pants. His sneakers were washed so much they were gray. His book bag looked old, like a hand-me-down. But his eyes were special. He always avoided others—but if you made eye contact with him, he always made you a little afraid.

Compared to other kids the same age, his face looked more mature.

They were assigned to the same dorm room. Shen Ming was the poorest out of the six students. He didn't even have enough spending money to buy a popsicle for himself. But he was a great student with a great instinct for learning and easily understanding lectures. His Chinese and English scores were especially high. Other than the math teacher, Mr. Zhang, all the teachers liked him.

Lu Zhongyue seemed like an underachiever by comparison. He'd have been held back if his science scores hadn't been passable.

Yet he was Shen Ming's best friend.

Shen Ming was usually quiet. He only talked a lot when he was alone with Lu Zhongyue. Shen Ming liked to say, "In a hurry to reincarnate?" which Lu Zhongyue still vividly remembered. Whenever Lu Zhongyue needed help, Shen Ming always reached out. When Shen Ming needed money, Lu Zhongyue would help, too.

In eleventh grade, Lu Zhongyue dragged Shen Ming to play billiards somewhere shady and they ran into a bunch of thugs who wanted to rob them. Shen Ming fought off the guys, but his head was split open pretty badly. It took seven stitches to stop the wound from bleeding. He told the school that the injury was from a fall.

That night, Shen Ming rested his head on Lu Zhongyue's thighs and looked up at the starry sky. He said he'd never had an easy day in his life. All he remembered was being bullied and how no kids wanted to play with him. To come to school he needed to borrow a pencil from his grandmother's employer. He didn't even eat meat until he got to Nanming High.

He said coolly, "I don't want to live my life this way."

Shen Ming seemed depressed before the college entrance exams. He really wanted to go to Peking University, but he had no confidence in facing off with the tens of thousands of competitors.

Lu Zhongyue was more worried about just getting into any college.

One night in June, the squatters huts built across from the school went up in flames. Lu Zhongyue watched the commotion alongside other students. He didn't realize Shen Ming would go into the fire like a madman, or that he would burst out in a ball of flames having saved a young girl.

Lu Zhongyue didn't know he'd almost killed the same girl not long ago.

Due to his heroic feat, Shen Ming was guaranteed admission to Peking University—he became one of the lucky few.

After the exams, the two said their good-byes on Nanming Road. Shen Ming would go to Beijing while Lu Zhongyue would attend a local college. The two hugged and cried, then Shen Ming sang Li Shutong's "Good-Bye" song:

By the temple, next to the road, grass connected with sky
Night wind, sounds of the flute, setting sun on the mountains
Corner of the world, end of time, so many friends leaving
One cauldron of wine marks our good-byes, dreams get colder
The song ends, and we part.

That had been twenty-six years ago.

Now Lu Zhongyue was a fugitive. As he saw it, every obstacle in his life was thanks to his former best friend.

Lu Zhongyue had come to this remote village for Lu Jizong, his nineteen-year-old son. For a year he stalked Chen Xiangtian and Lu Jizong. The girl he'd once liked wasn't worth looking at anymore. But the son he'd wanted to abort had grown tall and strong. Most important, he'd inherited his father's looks.

Lu Jizong did nothing with his time. He either watched porn or played games all night at Internet cafés. He won a lot of virtual knives in the games, until his mom pulled him out of the place. He hardly talked to anyone, and had no friends except for the virtual ones he met playing games.

No girls liked him.

Lu Jizong always kept his head lowered because of the birthmark on his forehead. He watched others with a cool expression, putting fear in them. One night when he was playing *Defense of the Ancients*, someone sitting next to him at the Internet café called him a bastard and his mom a slut. As he beat up the guy, Lu Jizong looked like a man possessed.

Worried that if he revealed himself to his son he would be found out, Lu Zhongyue resisted introducing himself to Lu Jizong.

Sometimes a woman visited the apartment where his son and his mother lived. She always brought fruits and other gifts with her. She looked younger than thirty and dressed simply, but in clothes of exceptional quality. She was gorgeous. Lu Zhongyue didn't think Chen Xiangtian could make a friend like that. But Lu Jizong seemed to trust the visitor. From time to time they took walks together, looking like a young couple.

Lu Zhongyue was sure she wasn't local but from a big city. He followed her and found out that she taught in the Miao village, and that her name was Ouyang Xiaozhi.

But for the past month, Lu Zhongyue had not seen Lu Jizong, and the Ouyang woman had disappeared, too.

Where had his son gone?

Finally, Lu Zhongyue couldn't stand the question any longer. One late night that spring he knocked on Chen Xiangtian's door.

"Who are you?" After twenty years, the mother of his child didn't recognize him.

Lu Zhongyue hid his face in the shadow outside the door. "Where did your son go?"

"What?" Chen Xiangtian panicked. "What happened to him?"

"He's not in trouble." He stepped inside, letting the light expose his face—especially his birthmark.

Chen Xiangtian backed up and squinted, shaking her head in disbelief. "You are—it's not possible!"

"It is me." He locked the door behind him. The room was a mess and smelled greasy.

"Lu Zhongyue?" The woman clutched his shoulder, examined his face, and let go in fright. She cowered in a corner. "My curse!"

"Not happy to see me?"

Chen Xiangtian shook. "I—I—thought—"

"You thought I'd died?" Lu Zhongyue stroked her sagging face. "Sometimes, I thought of you fondly. When I first met you in that bar in 1995? That was a great time."

"Let go of me!"

"Didn't you miss me all these years?"

The woman slapped him. "I hate you!"

"Sorry." He found a place to sit. "I have to thank you for giving me a son."

"You don't deserve to be his father!"

"Where is Jizong?" He pinched Chen Xiangtian's neck.

She huffed, "He went out to work a month ago."

"Where?"

"The city where we met. He said he could find you there."

"He went looking for me?" he said, releasing her from his grip.

The woman coughed painfully. "Yes, he always wanted to know what his dad looked like. I told him you both had a forehead birthmark."

"Give me his phone number."

"His phone was disconnected a few days after he left. He hasn't called me. We've been out of touch for weeks, and I'm really worried!"

Lu Zhongyue paced back and forth. "What about that woman? The woman who's always here. Who is she?"

"You mean Xiaozhi? Isn't she your cousin?"

"Cousin? Do you have her phone number?"

"Yes." Chen Xiangtian took out her phone and gave Lu Zhongyue Xiaozhi's number. "I called her about Jizong but she said she wasn't sure."

"She's lying." Lu Zhongyue turned to leave.

Chen Xiangtian pleaded from behind him, "Zhongyue, please don't look for my son."

He noticed her eyes filling with fear. Though there were no warrants out for him in this city, she seemed to know he was a wanted man.

Maybe Ouyang Xiaozhi had told her about what he'd done? If he left, would she call the cops?

Lu Zhongyue flashed a rare smile and moved close to Chen Xiangtian to stroke her neck. "Xiangtian, maybe you've not missed me, but I've often missed you."

"Stop it."

"I did abandon you. I'm sorry about that." He clutched her neck as he said the last word.

His hands had killed before and now they tightened around her neck. Chen Xiangtian resisted and tried to kick him. But soon the sound of a slithering snake came out of her throat, until she shook all over and lost control of her bowels.

She'd died in the hands of the man she once loved.

Lu Zhongyue smoked as he stared at the dead body on the dirty floor. He thought she made an ugly corpse.

Sorry, mother of my son, he thought, brushing off some ashes that had fallen on her body.

He picked up the home phone and dialed the number Chen Xiangtian had given him. The soft voice that answered could have belonged to a college student.

"Hello, is it Ouyang Xiaozhi?"

"Yes, who is this?"

Lu Zhongyue hung up. He walked out of the murder scene, careful to lock the door behind him.

He went back to his rental room to pack and texted his employer to let him know he was quitting. He rushed to the long-distance bus stop and started on his way home.

In two months it would be the nineteenth anniversary of Shen Ming's death.

CHAPTER 77

"How many more storms can the flower weather? The spring passes so quickly. Pity the flower blooming too early. Wilted petals everywhere."

Ouyang Xiaozhi said this to the female student next to her as the two walked across the sports field. It was two months until the college entrance exams. The student reminded Ouyang Xiaozhi of herself when she was eighteen.

"Ms. Ouyang, why do you like this Xin Qiji poem?"

"Late spring and early summer are the best seasons for death."

A purple silk scarf draped her neck and her long hair flew in the wind, showing her distracted expression. Ouyang Xiaozhi had finished teaching the Miao village kids and returned to the city, where she was assigned to a downtown high school as a Chinese teacher who taught the liberal arts majors.

"Shen Min, why are you always following me?"

"Ms. Ouyang, you're very different."

The student was very interested in her. She was in that moody stage of idolizing her teachers.

Ouyang Xiaozhi laughed. "That's what everyone says, men and women."

"Why didn't you ever get married?"

"I've always liked someone, but he couldn't marry me."

"Is he married?"

Girls today mature too fast, Xiaozhi thought, smiling bitterly. "He's been dead a long time."

The high school senior's expression turned serious. "I like someone, too, but he can't be with me. He says he's a ghost."

Ouyang Xiaozhi whispered, "Don't believe what boys tell you. Now, go back to the self-study room."

Watching the teenager walk away, Ouyang Xiaozhi picked up the fallen petals by the garden and blew on them. She became sad watching them fly away in the wind.

Since returning to the city, she hadn't seen Si Wang. He didn't know she was back. But she was worried about running into him on the street, and she'd made it a point to avoid Nanming Road.

Dressed in her work outfit, Ouyang Xiaozhi left the school at four o'clock. She took the subway to the old part of town where small restaurants and shops lined the streets. It became really lively at night. She went into a restaurant serving Fujian-style food. The place seemed reasonably clean. It was too early for dinner and the waiters were chatting and playing cards. She ordered a bowl of wontons.

A tall, thin young man brought her food, hardly looking at his customer. Ouyang Xiaozhi put her money on the table and said, "If you're not busy, stay and talk a while."

The young man was startled and then blushed when he saw who it was. "Aunt, you're here."

"How have you been?"

"Not bad."

Lu Jizong wore a plain jacket, and his hair was stained with kitchen grease. He seemed in good shape, but his expression seemed mixed, as though he had many things he couldn't say.

"Hey, your pretty aunt is here," joked a chef who slapped him on the shoulder. "He likes it here and works hard every day. No idea where he gets the energy."

"Jizong, I'm very happy for you."

He shyly scratched his head. "It doesn't pay much—just two grand a month—but I'm happy. They're nice to me here. I want to work for another few years and then open my own place."

"That's great. I can lend you some money if you need help then, though I don't make much as a teacher."

Lu Jizong flashed a silly smile. He looked like a sunny young man, so different from the shy, introverted gamer from a few months ago.

In the year she spent in the small Southern town, Ouyang Xiaozhi had hoped to find traces of Lu Zhongyue by getting close to his son. If the fugitive was still alive, this young man was the only person he still cared about. When in the small town, she'd felt that Lu Zhongyue was nearby, hiding in some dark corner. She always carried pepper spray.

But the man was like a ghost, and he never showed up.

It had only been a month since Ouyang Xiaozhi had brought Lu Jizong to the city. The kid had begged her to do so. He'd had enough of the suffocating town. He knew playing games every day was like killing himself slowly. He wanted to go to a big city, even if there was a price to pay. His mom knew he couldn't be stopped and asked Ouyang Xiaozhi to keep an eye on him.

Lu Jizong had been excited and nervous about the move. Xiaozhi found him a job at the restaurant. The owner was an honest Fujianese man who also gave him a place to stay, even if it only had a narrow window looking out at the high-rise next door.

Lu Jizong changed his cell phone number right away and never contacted his mom. He asked Xiaozhi not to say anything if his mom called. Xiaozhi had never been a mom, but she could imagine how this would make Chen Xiangtian feel. Still, she promised him. She worried that lying to the young man would result in losing track of him, and her efforts of the past year would have been in vain.

"Jizong, I need to ask you something," Xiaozhi said, finishing her wontons. "Have you noticed anyone strange around you lately?"

He frowned and shook his head. "No."

"If anyone weird comes looking for you—or if anything odd happens—please call me right away."

He was Xiaozhi's bait.

CHAPTER 78

June 6, 2014.

Liu Man had been found dead on the roof of the Nanming High library nineteen years ago.

Now, it was Friday night just before nine o'clock. The streets were cooler than usual. Ye Xiao was wearing casual clothes and sitting at a street vendor's stall, eating fried noodles and seafood.

He saw Si Wang crossing the street toward him. The young man seemed more muscular lately, a very different person from the skinny kid he first met. Si Wang may have left the slums, but he still got into fights—though other people rarely started them. He was the only one brave enough to walk around at night, buying snacks from those Xinjiang cake vendors. Whenever he ran into thugs bothering people or pickpockets on buses, he always beat them up. He might have been brave, but he was no hero; people still treated him like a delinquent. He Qingying worried about her son. She was the only person who could still get away with slapping him.

If not for Ye Xiao's intervention, Si Wang would have been arrested and expelled from the school long ago. Ye Xiao had often told him to shape up.

Si Wang ordered a skewer of beef tripe from the vendor and sat down in front of Ye Xiao. "I snuck out."

"If your mom knew she'd break your leg. Shouldn't you be studying?"

Tomorrow was the first day of the college entrance exams; most students were at home cramming. Only Si Wang had the time to invite out Ye Xiao for a late-night snack.

"There is nothing to worry about. I'm afraid I'll do too well and end up with the highest score in the city."

"Well, good luck!"

"I didn't come here to talk about school." His eyes darkened. "Someone is always watching me lately."

"Who?" Ye Xiao looked around out of habit. People finished with their night shifts and nightclub call girls crowded around them to eat.

"I'm not sure. I have a feeling it's Lu Zhongyue."

Ye Xiao raised his eyebrows at hearing the name. "Does he have the guts?"

"Don't you want him to show up?"

"That's right!" The cop crushed the disposable cup in his hand. "If I'm not mistaken, the nineteenth anniversary of Shen Ming's death is in thirteen days."

"It was June 19, 1995—ten o'clock in the Demon Girl Zone."

"Lu Zhongyue is the most devious and luckiest fugitive I've ever known. He won't be stupid enough to come on that day."

"I've been waiting for it."

Ye Xiao noticed the young man's vicious gaze and clutched his arm. "Kid, listen to me. Don't go anywhere on June 19. Just stay home and protect your mom, OK?"

"What about you?"

"I know he won't show up, but I'll still go to Nanming High and the Demon Girl Zone."

"Let's talk about something else. What's the verdict on Ma Li?"

"The City Middle-Level People's Court announced their first sentence this morning."

As the officer responsible for the case Ye Xiao had been at the trial that morning. Liu Man's father was there, too, and the old man was very emotional. He asked for an immediate death sentence.

About six months ago, the city's elite math teacher, Zhang Mingsong, was killed in his home; the killer was his student and star pupil from years ago, Ma Li.

On the morning of the crime, Ma Li had turned himself in by dialing 1-1-0. He confessed his motive: Zhang Mingsong had molested him from 1994 to 1995. When his classmate Liu Man found out, Ma Li poisoned her and framed Shen Ming. Because this case involved the two other 1995 murders on Nanming Road, Ye Xiao quickly joined the investigation and interrogated the suspect.

Ma Li was calm during the questioning. He felt guilty about Shen Ming's death. He'd hated Zhang Mingsong for a long time. When he went to Zhang's home that night, he stripped and tied up his victim before cutting his throat with a kitchen knife. As to why the scene was so messy, he said he'd been looking for Zhang's photo collection. But Zhang claimed to have destroyed the photos long ago.

A few days later, everyone in the city knew about the Zhang Mingsong scandal. Graduates from many different classes spanning years came out in support of the truth. Five men said they were also molested by him. There was no telling how many victims would forever hide the secret.

The most crucial evidence, the photos Zhang Mingsong took, never materialized.

Ye Xiao and his colleagues combed the scene. The evidence they found mostly matched up with Ma Li's account: The knife matched the victim's wound; the knife handle was covered by Ma's fingerprints; and the blood on Ma's clothes matched the victim's.

Yet, Ye Xiao felt uneasy about one detail—Zhang Mingsong's apartment door had been left open. Why would someone do this? Even though Ma Li swore he was the only one involved, he couldn't explain where the rope had come from. At first he said he bought it online; later, he claimed to have found it on the street.

"Don't you find it odd?" Ye Xiao said to Si Wang.

"It is weird."

Ye Xiao was testing him, but he really didn't have much to go on other than a hunch. There were no third-person fingerprints and Zhang Mingsong's hallway didn't have surveillance cameras. The security guard only remembered seeing Ma Li, and it was easy for someone to avoid the lobby camera via the garage or stairs.

"I looked up Ma Li's cell phone records," Ye Xiao said. "The last call he got was an hour before the crime. It came from a nearby pay phone. Ma Li said it was a wrong number. I pulled the surveillance video for the phone booth, but unfortunately the person was out of range."

Si Wang remained eerily quiet, keeping busy with his noodles.

"Listen," Ye Xiao continued, "we also pulled Ma Li's phone records for the last couple years. Your number showed up, from about two years ago."

"I met him when I lived with the Gu family."

"Ma Li said he'd worked for the Erya Education Group. Before the Gu family went under, he worked as the GM assistant for Gu Qiusha. I asked him about you, and he said you were just an elementary school student he'd had no dealings with." Ye Xiao paused and watched Si Wang carefully. "Was he lying?"

"I want to know something first. What was the sentence?"

"Death." As someone who had caught countless killers, Ye Xiao made the declaration solemnly. "He confessed and didn't appeal. He wanted his sentence to be carried out as soon as possible. The Middle-Level Court will ask the Higher Court to review, and they'll file for final approval from the Highest People's Court."

Si Wang coughed through a frown and said, "This beef tripe is too spicy!"

"You still haven't answered my question."

"If he's been sentenced to death, what else is there for me to say? When will Ma Li be executed?"

"Seven days after the Highest People's Court confirms the sentence."

"Shot?" The young man bit off a chunk of the tripe.

"No, they use lethal injections now."

Ye Xiao's words startled Si Wang. He bit into his tongue and held his mouth in pain, mumbling, "*Les Misérables.*"

"What?"

"*Everyone who reads this book would be doomed. They would die, either by knife or needle!*"

CHAPTER 79

June 19, 2014.

It was early morning when Si Wang got up to wash. His nineteen-year-old face was already weathered with the character of a grown-up, especially his deep black eyes.

Ten days earlier, he'd completed his college entrance exams. He was the first to turn in his paper during almost every test. As the stunned teachers and students watched, he walked out with no expression.

After the exams, all he did was go online to watch horror movies. His behavior worried He Qingying a bit, though she thought it was better than him getting into trouble outside. Ye Xiao came by to warn her not to let Si Wang go anywhere on June 19. If Si Wang did leave the house, Ye Xiao told her to call the police.

He Qingying stayed up the night before and finally passed out at 4:00 a.m. She was sleeping soundly on the couch, having thought she'd hear her son if he did try to go out. But he walked noiselessly out of the building and rode his bike out of the neighborhood. The rainy season air was humid, making breathing difficult. The ground was soaked, and more rain was on the way.

Si Wang bought two egg pancakes and watched the crowds of morning commuters. He finished eating and headed for Serenity

Road. Ten minutes later, he pedaled onto the quiet block. The ginkgo trees were growing robustly. Several nice houses peeked out of the leaves, and birds chirped.

He stopped in front of the old house and could hear the sounds of face washing and toothbrushing. The basement window was covered in a thick layer of dust. He thought of Yi Yu and the old man from the last lifetime.

He turned to look at the house across the street, still empty after a murder committed thirty years ago.

Serenity Road Number 19.

He crossed the street. The rusty door sign was about to fall off. Chains and a big lock hung on it. He hopped over the low wall; no one was around to notice. He went into the yard and felt nauseated. He looked up to the second floor before crawling into the house through a broken window on the ground floor. The early-morning light trickled into the dim living room, which was still dusty and not very different from his last visit.

On a fall night in 1983, his mom He Qingying had killed her adoptive father here.

The symbols and lines on the wall were still there. Only the blood had faded.

He covered his nose as he walked upstairs. The second floor window was open, letting a breeze pass through the hall and pick up dust and cobwebs.

The first door off the hallway was the dirty bathroom, and the second room had that corpse-like big bed. Behind the last door was He Qingying's childhood bedroom.

He gingerly opened the door, and a familiar sensation washed over him—the same as the one he experienced on the night of June 19, 1995.

Was the Demon Girl Zone here, too?

Just as he was about to run, a cold gust blew past him and someone's shadow was cast on the opposite wall.

He had nowhere to go. He prepared to throw a punch, but before he could, a metal club hit him in the head.

It felt like the metal had entered his body.

Dizziness. He fell to the dirty floor as blood spurted out of his forehead and flowed into his mouth. It tasted salty and bitter, like death.

Heavy footsteps sounded, pounding in his eardrums. He opened his eyes, but his vision was clouded by blood. All he could see was a tilted, murky world.

Someone grabbed his ankles and dragged him into the small room; his chest and cheeks rubbed against the floor and burned like crazy.

A shabby dresser, a few naked wooden dolls. His mom's childhood playthings. They stared at him. Had the dolls attacked him?

A small bed frame was next to the dresser, on top of which was a thin bamboo mat, a pillow, and a blanket. A suitcase sat by the wall. There were a lot of instant noodle wrappers, a travel cooking range, and a big jug of water.

Si Wang tried very hard to move his neck enough to see that mirror by the wall. Someone had wiped it clean.

That someone was reflected in the oval mirror. It was a blurry shape in the dim room, but as the person moved closer, Si Wang could tell that it was a man.

"Lu Zhongyue?" Si Wang's teeth chattered as he spoke, and blood continued to fill his mouth.

The man found Si Wang's cell phone and went to the window. He pulled open the thick curtain to look outside. He went downstairs but came back up almost immediately.

Si Wang's body was stronger than most. The bleeding on his forehead had stopped, though he was still dazed and had no strength to fight back as the man used thick rope to tie him to a chair.

Si Wang was able to see the birthmark on Lu Zhongyue's forehead.

He huffed as he bent down, frowning and almost looking regretful. "So we meet again."

"You—you're still alive!" Si Wang's head throbbed with every word he spoke.

"I can't believe you came here. After eight years as a fugitive, I've learned to be careful, though. If not for my sharp ears, maybe I'd be the one tied up and bleeding."

"Were you waiting here for me?"

He held Si Wang's chin. "I'm not that crazy. I was freaked out when you brought that cop to track me down four years ago."

Si Wang closed his eyes and mumbled, "For Huang Hai."

"I've been back in town for two months. I have three IDs from my days on the run, but I don't stay at motels. This house was my uncle's. He was killed about thirty years ago, right down-stairs. It became a murder house and no one has lived here since. I didn't think you or the cops would ever think of it. How did you find this place?"

"June 19. You didn't forget this day, right?"

"You really think you're Shen Ming? Remember, Wang Er, I was your adoptive father. You're crazy paranoid. Plus, you're a liar who's controlled by others, like your mom He Qingying, and that bastard Ma Li. He wanted the Gu money, and then he wanted to take me out."

"Lu Zhongyue, you should thank me. I was the one who found out what Gu Qiusha was doing to you."

He slapped Si Wang, but then rubbed his cheek. "Sorry. You're pretty grown up now. I bet a lot of girls like you."

"I had no idea that you were hiding here! I wanted to visit the basement where Shen Ming lived, across the street. My mom lived in this house. This was her room. These dolls were hers. I wanted to go to Nanming High this afternoon and then the Demon Girl Zone at ten, just like how Shen Ming did back in 1995."

Lu Zhongyue's smile was odd. "Kid, you're more paranoid than ever. No one in the world knew Shen Ming better than I did. I knew him better than he knew himself."

"What else do you know?"

"Dying in the Demon Girl Zone was probably the best fate he could have met."

"What do you mean?"

"Even if Shen Ming had married Gu Qiusha and become Gu Changlong's son-in-law, do you think he actually could have made it? You think he'd get away from his pathetic pedigree? No one in the Gu family or the Education Bureau really respected him. Gu Changlong was just using him. He wanted to keep Shen Ming loyal and then toss him aside. In 1995, as soon as Shen Ming got arrested, didn't Gu Changlong ditch him? It was bound to happen sooner or later, even if Shen Ming never made a mistake. He'd have died a thousand times from other people's jealousies."

"Interesting."

"Only I treated Shen Ming like a real friend!"

"You still see him as a friend?"

"My best friend. I still miss him to this day." Lu Zhongyue fell to his knees and prayed to the wall. "Shen Ming, I'm sorry. I was truly happy for you. When you got sponsored admission to Peking University, when you got engaged, when you became a respected teacher. I knew you could be successful and no one would look down on you anymore. But this world doesn't like people like you. Hard work, being careful, and doing everything right doesn't matter. People's fates are set the minute they're born. If you wanted to change it, you'd be destroyed. Didn't you know? Everyone talked behind your back. They said, 'Shen Ming, that illegitimate kid, growing up in a maid's basement, how dare he have anything?'"

"You told everyone about Shen Ming being illegitimate?"

"I was always curious about Shen Ming. You never mentioned your parents or invited us to your house. I followed you once and saw that you lived in someone else's home and that your grandma was just a maid. A middle-aged man came to visit and gave you some money. He said something about being your dad. I found out later he was a prosecutor."

"This is how you found my secret?"

"Yes, I never told you about it because we were best friends. If I told people about it, you'd lose the last bit of self-respect you had and not be my friend anymore. I didn't want to lose you, so I kept the secret from you, too."

"But you still told people."

Lu Zhongyue lit a cigarette near the window. "At your engagement ceremony in 1995, I felt jealous for the first time. I watched everyone congratulate you. I knew how much they hated you, but they acted so friendly. They would have licked your shoes! You were going to have it all: status, power, money, and a pretty woman. My dad was a bureaucrat, but I didn't do well. I was just an engineer at an almost-bankrupt factory. Back in high school, I paid for you a lot. When I wore new clothes to school, you'd be envious, too. But at the engagement ceremony, it was the other way around."

"I'm sorry, I should have thought of how you felt."

"There was something else, too. After seeing Gu Qiusha at the engagement ceremony, I remembered that our families were old friends. We probably played together as little kids. After the party I dreamed about her. I tried to force myself not to think about her, but then I missed her even more. I started drinking at bars every night and met a girl. Guess it was meant to be. She gave me my only son."

"You have a son?"

"Yes, his name is Lu Jizong. He's nineteen, like you. Tall and good-looking, too. He'll be popular with the girls." He smiled but stopped when he saw Si Wang's expression. "Let's go back to 1995. I started to hate Shen Ming then, especially when he asked about my job and love life. I just wanted him to disappear from this world."

"You spread the rumor about him being born out of wedlock?"

"I only told the math teacher Zhang Mingsong, but I knew telling him meant telling the whole world. I knew how jealous he was of Shen Ming."

"What about that fake letter?"

Lu Zhongyue stubbed out his cigarette. "I wrote that! Only I knew how to fake his handwriting, because we were best friends. Funny, right? I got He Nian in on it. He made some mistake and was sent back to the city Education Bureau from Beijing. We worked on the letter together. I wrote it, then He Nian gave it to Gu Changlong."

"You killed He Nian?"

"Yes, we set up Shen Ming, and I became Gu Changlong's son-in-law. He Nian only got a management job at Erya Education Group. He thought that was unfair and wanted to make everything public. He blackmailed me. So I killed him. I hid his body in his jeep and drove it to a random place by the Suzhou River. Somehow you found it two years later. That's when I knew you were a scary kid."

"You killed Gu Changlong, too?"

"I didn't want to kill him. He broke into my place early one morning and pointed a knife at me. I don't remember fighting him but when I realized what had happened, he was a bloody corpse. It was self-defense, but I had killed before. If I'd ended up in Huang Hai's hands, they would have known everything soon enough. So I ran, but there were cops everywhere. Going to train stations was suicide. I also needed to do something before I went away."

"You wanted to kill Gu Qiusha?" Si Wang's strength was coming back.

"There was no one I hated more! My wife actually castrated me, slowly. What man would forgive that? Yes, I killed her. She was infertile so decided her husband had to be, too. Good thing I knocked up another woman before marrying her. If I didn't have Jizong, I'd have no reason to go on like this."

"Your kid is the most precious thing in your life."

He lit up another cigarette. His lips looked a bit purple now. "My life sucks. I've been living with rats like some rabid dog. Being executed would be better than my life now. But if I died, who'd protect my son? He'd be a fatherless kid and be discriminated against, just like Shen Ming was. I don't want my son to become like Shen Ming!"

"You'll ruin his life."

"No, I'll live with Jizong." Lu Zhongyue smiled indulgently. "You wouldn't understand."

"I have another question. How did you recognize me? I don't think I'd recognize myself from my elementary school days."

"When I got back to town, I visited your old address and saw that it's now a construction site. I asked around and found out your new address. I've been following you. In fact, I saw you eating with someone at a street vendor's cart two weeks ago."

"I knew it."

"Kid, I have to thank you for chatting with me. This is more talking than I've done in the last eight years combined."

"I'm not a kid."

"Sorry." Lu Zhongyue gave him another quizzical look. "Well, I need to go and find someone now. You'll stay here. Bye."

Shen Ming blurted out, "In a hurry to reincarnate?"

Lu Zhongyue didn't react, but his heart beat wildly. He took out a roll of tape from his luggage. Once he'd covered up Si Wang's mouth, Lu Zhongyue patted his face. Then he checked the room and windows—and he left.

Serenity Road Number 19. The murder house was as quiet as a tomb—except for the sounds of Si Wang panting like a wild dog.

CHAPTER 80

June 19, 2014—7:00 p.m.

It was getting dark and the thick clouds still hadn't shed any rain. The damp air felt suffocating.

Ouyang Xiaozhi hadn't gone out all day. She was debating whether to go to Nanming Road—just as she had two years ago—to burn some paper money for Shen Ming. But she didn't want to run into Si Wang.

She missed him.

She stroked her lips and neck and thought about how that young man's lean fingers glided across her skin. She looked at herself in the mirror, thinking about how her face would age. In a few years, maybe Si Wang wouldn't even recognize her.

She turned on the tap and carefully washed her face. She used toner and moisturizer, then added some foundation, and a bit of cream eye shadow followed by powder eye shadow, and then lined her eyes and added mascara. She gingerly put on blush and lipstick. The makeup was almost indiscernible, but men would notice. She picked up her comb and found a white strand in it. She plucked it away and combed her hair into a silky black waterfall.

She left home with the offerings she'd bought a few days ago.

Since moving back to the city, she'd been living in a rental apartment in a neighborhood where very few people were around at night. Even her coworkers didn't know where she lived. She walked down the dark hallway and felt panicked. She stopped and listened. She heard what sounded like crying. She knew it was a hallucination.

A hand covered her mouth when she reached the ground floor. Before she could struggle, a distinctive smell rose into her nostrils. Just as she lost consciousness, she thought, *Ether!*

She woke up at Serenity Road Number 19.

Her head felt like she'd slept for ages, like she'd already died once. She saw a tired-looking man with a smooth chin and a pale birthmark on his forehead.

It had been twenty-six years since she'd last seen him.

That had been in the late spring of 1988, when he was the senior at Nanming High and she was the disheveled young girl who stole a drumstick from his lunch.

If Shen Ming hadn't rescued her three days later, she'd have been a tiny, dried-up corpse.

For the last eight years, she'd looked for the man, hoping to kill him.

For Shen Ming.

Xiaozhi wanted to attack him, but she couldn't move. Her hands and feet were bound to a wooden chair.

She turned to see the bed nearby and the naked dolls on the dresser. When she was ten, toys like those were often found at the trash pile near the homeless huts.

Then she saw Si Wang.

He was even more solid and muscular than before. She wondered how he did on the college entrance exams. Where would he go to college? He was tied up, too, and she could tell he'd been hurt by the blood-stained tape covering his mouth. He was shaking his head violently, his eyes full of surprise and worry.

"Si Wang!"

Lu Zhongyue pinched her neck, and she tensed in pain. Si Wang looked as if he was going mad as blood flowed out from under the tape, like he'd bitten off his tongue.

"Ouyang Xiaozhi, I've spent the past few weeks here figuring out where you lived. I waited a whole day at your building. I was worried you wouldn't come out until tomorrow. But you came out ready to go to the Demon Girl Zone after all."

"You were the one who called me two months ago?"

"Yes, I got your number from Chen Xiangtian."

"You finally talked to her?"

Lu Zhongyue lit a cigarette. "I killed her."

Xiaozhi looked directly at Si Wang as she said, "You can kill me, too. Please let the young man go. He's innocent."

"I'm looking for another young man. You know where he is."

"I don't."

He found a phone in Xiaozhi's bag and scrolled through the contact list to find Lu Jizong's details.

Lu Zhongyue slapped her. "You hid my son."

He taped shut Xiaozhi's mouth. Watching her anxious expression, Lu Zhongyue took out his own cell phone and dialed Lu Jizong's number.

"Hello, is this Lu Jizong?"

"Who is this?" said the voice on the other end.

Lu Zhongyue calmly answered, "I'm Ouyang Xiaozhi's lawyer. She has some business she wants me to handle with you. Where can I meet you?"

"Now?" Lu Jizong sounded hesitant against the noisy background. "Fujian Snack Shop at Seven Spirits Bridge."

"OK. Will you still be there at nine thirty?"

Lu Zhongyue looked at the clock. It was 8:45 p.m. now.

"I'll still be working, yes."

"Please wait for me."

Ouyang Xiaozhi struggled as hard as she could, but the rope only got tighter. She cried from the pain. She saw that Si Wang's eyes were moist, too.

Lu Zhongyue had left the room, but a few minutes later he came back with jugs of gasoline and a weird black machine. He added two batteries to it, and when its red light flickered, he said, "It's enough for at least twenty-four hours."

Lu Zhongyue packed up, taking out all the trash, including the cigarette butts. There was nothing but the two of them, the gasoline, and the machine.

Si Wang and Ouyang Xiaozhi were alone in the Serenity Road murder house.

Ginkgo trees could be seen outside the curtains.

The smell of gas filled the room.

Si Wang breathed heavily through his nose and thought of his mom.

He tried to move the chair. His muscles could have burst, but he still couldn't get close to Xiaozhi. They were less than half a meter apart, and both their mouths were taped shut.

She said with her crying eyes—

You're Mr. Shen!

I am! his own eyes replied.

More tears blurred Xiaozhi's gaze. She remembered December 21, 2012—that cold night when she saw Si Wang's bright, naked body with a red birthmark on the left side of his back.

A wound from a past life?

On that supposed last night of the world, Xiaozhi had said nothing as she kissed his back with pity. Then the tides of desire submerged the both of them.

Staring at this other captive now, trapped in the murder house, she could no longer tell him and Mr. Shen apart. She knew there was something she owed him before death.

"Mr. Shen, I know your last question. Why did I want to see

you that night? I could tell that you wanted to kill someone,
so before you could I wanted to see you—in the Demon Girl
Zone—because that was where we first met."
"To do what?"

Xiaozhi wanted to slap him, but all she could do was keep
talking with her eyes:

"I wanted to give myself to you. That would have been my
first time. But you were killed that night. That my first time wasn't
with you is my biggest regret. The world knew your fiancée had
abandoned you, that everyone had abandoned you. If I could have
given myself to you that night, you wouldn't have wanted to kill
anyone. You would have always had me—right, Mr. Shen?

Tears poured from Si Wang's eyes. He understood that she'd
wanted to give Shen Ming a reason to live.

Xiaozhi nodded to affirm that she knew what he was thinking.

Xiaozhi had wanted to sneak out from the school to meet
Shen Ming. The students usually used a window on the ground
floor. But after Liu Man's death, the school had taken extra pre-
cautions and the window had been boarded up. The teachers kept
watch at the dorm entrances all night long. Xiaozhi cried in her
dorm room, kept awake by the thunder and her worries about
Shen Ming.

Yan Li's body was found the next day. There was no question:
Shen Ming had killed him.

The police were looking for him, but there was no news for
three days. Xiaozhi snuck into the Demon Girl Zone and found
Shen Ming's body underground. She didn't want to disturb the
scene. After crying there by his body, kneeling in the water, she
returned to the school and let it slip that Mr. Shen might have
gone there.

CHAPTER 81

June 19, 2014—9:30 p.m.

Thunder rolled outside.

Carrying his backpack, Lu Zhongyue walked through the busy Seven Spirits night market. The bigger the crowd, the safer he felt—just like the sea was the best place to hide a drop of water.

He touched the cell phone in his pants pocket. A push of a button decided two people's fates.

He'd prepared the jugs of gasoline and a remote explosive device at the Serenity Road house. The device was of his own design, requiring little more than two cell phones and some old circuit boards. One phone dialed, and the other one would start the explosion. It was worthy of a patent. At least Lu Zhongyue's electronic engineering degree was good for something.

There was only one Fujian Snack Shop in the area. Red-and-yellow lights adorned the door; cooking sounds could be heard. A few hair salon workers were having steamed dumplings and noodles. He ordered some wonton noodles and subtly looked around. A tired-looking teenager came out of the kitchen; he had a birthmark on his forehead.

"Lu Jizong."

The young man looked at Lu Zhongyue, who raised his head to show off his birthmark.

"You called me?"

"Yes. Are you done with work?"

"I just got off." Lu Jizong sat in front of him. He was taller than his father but still had a babyish face. Many people thought he was still in high school. "What did Aunt Xiaozhi need?"

"I'm not a lawyer."

Lu Jizong remained silent as he considered the old man who was looking at him as if he wanted to drill a hole in his face.

It was impossible to miss the man's birthmark.

His mom had always told him, "Jizong, your dad has that same birthmark."

Lu Jizong's lips were quivering. He had never met his dad, but he'd imagined this moment, this face. It had always seemed like something out of a movie.

Lu Zhongyue nodded, smiling. "Kid, I'm your father."

"Is this the first time we've met?"

The young man's hands balled up into fists as he remembered his maternal grandfather's raspy warning right before he died: *Your dad was a selfish bastard. He never even wanted you to be born.*

Lu Zhongyue stroked his son's hair. "Jizong, I've watched you grow up."

"I've never even seen you."

Lu Zhongyue was lying.

So was Jizong.

His mom had always kept a photo of his father; she'd look at it sometimes late at night. It disappeared after her Jizong started junior high. She searched for it everywhere, but Jizong had burned it. He'd never felt so good as he did watching the photo of his "dad" turn to ashes.

"I'm sorry. I had a wife, then I had to travel everywhere."

"Because you're a fugitive—a killer," Jizong said with quiet urgency.

Lu Zhongyue's face stiffened. "Who told you that?"

"Aunt Xiaozhi."

Lu Zhongyue's hand found the cell phone. He was was itching to press the button. "My cousin, she's a little paranoid, likes to say crazy stuff."

Lu Zhongyue ordered two sodas. The young man finished his in a few swallows.

"What did you want to say to me?"

"I just wanted to see you, to talk a bit. Then I'll disappear again."

"Have you been to see my mom?"

"I have. She misses you a lot."

"When I was growing up, everyone called me a bastard because you weren't around. All the kids bullied me. They'd hold me down on the ground and beat me. I'd be covered in blood but didn't dare try to get revenge. I'd tell my mom, and we'd cry together. I'd think, what was my dad like?" The young man's face looked like a dog about to be butchered.

"I'm sorry, but you must understand that there are many things in this world we can't change."

Lu Jizong recalled what his aunt had told him about any strange visitors. He asked, "Where is Aunt Xiaozhi? Why didn't she come with you?"

"She's tied up with something."

Lu Jizong pretended to straighten his shirt as he discreetly dialed that familiar number. Two seconds later, he heard the Hikaru Utada song "First Love."

Ouyang Xiaozhi's ringtone.

The sound came from Lu Zhongyue's backpack. He calmly opened the bag, realizing that the incoming call was from Lu Jizong. He pretended that he didn't notice anything unusual and just turned off the phone, and then took out the battery. He also had Si Wang's phone with him; he calmly took out its battery, too. No one could track them now.

Lu Jizong stood up slowly. "I need to show you something."

"Wait, Jizong." Lu Zhongyue said as he also rose from his seat. "Can you call me Dad?"

"OK. Come with me."

Lu Jizong led him into the kitchen. The teenager grabbed for something amid the steam and smoke. "*Dad*," he said, turning toward his father. Lu Jizong had never used that word before, though as a young boy he'd wanted to so much.

"Son!"

Happiness came so quickly in the kitchen of this unassuming restaurant. The hug was so tight, and Lu Zhongyue's face was right next to his son's. For the first time since becoming a fugitive, the man shed a tear.

Lu Zhongyue felt a burning stab of pain in his chest.

He wanted to speak, but his throat felt stuffed with a liquid warmth. His neck and face turned red.

The son let go of the father and stood panting by the kitchen counter. His shirt was now covered in blood, and he still held a kitchen knife.

Lu Jizong walked out of the kitchen. His father clutched his chest and backed out of the kitchen, too. Restaurant customers ran out screaming. Waiters scattered. Lu Jizong's only thought was that he hoped the place wouldn't go out of business because of what he'd done.

Three years ago, during the summer after junior high, he gave a neighbor girl a rose bouquet after much debating. It cost him six months of spending money. The girl gladly accepted the flowers but chose to date a Police Academy guy instead. She said to him, "My boyfriend said there's a dangerous fugitive who looks like you. Is that your dad?"

Lu Jizong swore to himself that if he ever met his father, he'd kill him.

Outside on the crowded street, thunder sounded overhead, but no rain came. Bats flew around. He glanced at the dripping knife—it looked like it came straight out of *Defense of the Ancients*. He was back in the small Southern town, and every stab he made with the computer game knife was at the man with the birthmark.

Monster, you finally came.

The man he'd imagined killing countless times before was lying on the street in a pool of his own blood. People stood around to stare, but no one came to help.

Lu Zhongyue blinked, watching the stormy night sky. Right now he missed the clear, starry sky above Nanming Road and the kid called Shen Ming. It had been twenty years, but he never stopped imagining what death felt like. What happened as the knife pierced the heart? Was there pain? Desperation?

He couldn't see his son's face, just the many faces of passersby: scared, cold, smiling, rushed.

He wanted to shout, "I killed myself. That kid didn't do it. He's not a killer!"

But the blood had filled his throat, and he couldn't say anything.

Someone in the crowd shouted that the police had arrived. Lu Zhongyue reached a bloody hand into his pants pocket to grab that cell phone.

In a hurry to reincarnate?

The last drop of his blood seemed to drain from him. A cop leaned over him, checking to see if he was still breathing.

He pressed the button.

CHAPTER 82

June 19, 2014—9:55 p.m. Serenity Road Number 19, second floor. He Qingying's childhood bedroom.

"If there was tomorrow, how do you want to make up your face? If there was no tomorrow, how do we say good-bye?"

A familiar ringtone sounded.

Si Wang didn't know what it meant, and though his mouth was sealed shut, in his heart he started singing along with the Han Yue song.

Ouyang Xiaozhi heard it, too, and her eyes widened with fear as she used all her strength to try to break free.

The ringtone played for about ten seconds before they heard a loud noise, like a firecracker. Sparks flew all around, some of them landing in the gasoline jugs.

Almost instantly, flames spread across the room.

They reached Si Wang's pants. He screamed, but his mouth was still blocked; the pain felt worse than death. He closed his eyes and thought, *Let me die like this with Xiaozhi. It's OK as long as our charred bodies are together.*

Burning tears and black lines streamed down Xiaozhi's face as the whole house began to burn. She and Si Wang were about to die in the fire. The smoke was making her cough, but she couldn't open her mouth. She nudged the chair leg and managed to topple herself over.

The flames reached her tied hands, singeing her skin and burning off the rope. She ignored the pain and fought to free herself from the chair. She didn't even rip the tape off her mouth before lunging to Si Wang.

Even if her hands turned to ashes, she was going to untie him first. But the knot was a complicated one and she couldn't undo it. She rolled Si Wang toward the flames in an attempt to burn away the rope, but it was fire resistant.

All she could do was rip off the tape covering his bloody mouth and kiss him as though that would lessen the pain.

Si Wang butted her away with his head, saying, "Xiaozhi, go!"

"No."

A terrifying sound came from overhead. The house was going to fall down.

If she ran out now, she might survive.

9:55 p.m.

Xiaozhi heard breaking glass. She dragged him and the chair toward the window.

Somehow she summoned the strength to throw the muscle-bound young man tied to a chair out the window.

His pants and hair on fire, Si Wang flew into the night sky over Serenity Road.

Then he fell.

The chair broke into pieces, and the rope unraveled.

The roof and columns of the house collapsed into a pile of burning ruins.

Xiaozhi was still inside.

Si Wang wanted to save her, but he couldn't get up. Two brave neighbors grabbed him and dragged him across the street.

He watched the reflection of the burning house in the grimy basement window.

There was an illusion of a teenage girl crying on the house's steps.

June 19, 2014—10:00 p.m.

The rain poured from above.

Si Wang watched the flames die down. He wanted to shout her name, but his throat was burned by smoke and couldn't make a single sound.

When the fire trucks got to Serenity Road, the fire was almost completely extinguished.

Ouyang Xiaozhi was buried in the ruins. She could neither see nor hear anything. Everything was gone but the endless silence.

Another ball of fire erupted, and suddenly she was surrounded by garbage and wooden boards. She was small and skinny, and wearing dirty clothes. Touching her hair and chest, she knew she was back to when she was eleven.

Nanming Road. 1988.

Dazed by the fire, a man appeared like a hero from the sky riding on colorful clouds, and he picked up his young bride and whisked her away.

CHAPTER 83

Midnight.

Ye Xiao was so busy that he was almost going mad. He'd been covering two murder scenes; the crimes had happened almost simultaneously.

The first scene was at Seven Spirits night market where a waiter at the Fujian Snack Shop had stabbed a middle-aged man to death. The victim was the fugitive Lu Zhongyue. The suspect was arrested. Lu Jizong was only nineteen and claimed to be Lu Zhongyue's illegitimate son. Ye Xiao contacted the police in the young man's hometown police and learned that his mother had been murdered in her home two months ago. The local police had been looking for Lu Jizong.

The second scene was at Serenity Road Number 19. A house abandoned after a murder thirty years ago had suddenly caught fire at 9:55 p.m. The house burned down in a few minutes. Inside, the firefighters found a charred body, which they were trying to identify. The initial impression was that it was arson; a lot of gasoline was at the scene, as was as a remote explosive device. There was one survivor. He'd suffered a broken leg and was sent to the hospital. His name was Si Wang.

He Qingying had looked for her son all day. She'd called Ye Xiao and even gone to the Demon Girl Zone. By the time the rain started at ten o'clock, she thought of another place—Serenity Road. While she was panicking, Ye Xiao got the call about the Seven Spirits murder. He went to that scene, and He Qingying took a taxi to Serenity Road, finding her childhood home in ruins. The firefighters and the police were cleaning up; someone mentioned a young man who'd survived.

He Qingying rushed to the hospital. Half of Si Wang's hair was burned away, and his forehead and mouth were wrapped in gauze. Severe burns covered his body. The doctor was putting a cast on his leg. The nurses said he was lucky not to be in the ICU. He was hooked up to an IV; after being unconscious in the ER for a while, he woke up and saw his mother, which made him cry.

She asked nothing, she only held him lightly as to not disturb his wounds. She whispered, "Wang Er, everything is over now."

Ye Xiao came to the hospital, too. He saw them hugging and wanted to give them privacy. Si Wang stopped him. "Is she still alive?"

Ye Xiao shook his head and Si Wang broke into sobs. The cop let the mother and son have their privacy. He walked out of the hospital. It was still pouring outside.

One hour later, He Qingying came out to talk to him. "Ye Xiao, Wang Er wouldn't go to sleep—he wanted to ask you something. Please make it brief."

The cop and the teenager talked for most of the night. By dawn, the rain had stopped.

Si Wang insisted on leaving the hospital. Ye Xiao drove them home. He wanted to carry Si Wang upstairs, but the proud teenager refused. He insisted that if his mom helped him, he could hop up the stairs.

6:00 a.m.

With great effort, He Qingying helped her son to their apartment. Someone dashed in front of them. Alarmed, she turned on the hallway light, revealing a familiar face. She rubbed her eyes.

The man looked at her and the young man. He was in his fifties, with white hair and a wrinkle-etched forehead. A giant suitcase sat next to him.

Si Wang sidled closer. He hadn't sleep all night, but he felt energized now. "Dad?"

"Wang Er!"

The man shook as he held Si Wang in his arms and asked how he'd gotten hurt.

He Qingying took out the key and opened the door.

It had been twelve years. On Pre-Lunar New Year's Eve in 2002, her husband had hastily come home and they had a big fight as he packed up. Some thugs were coming to collect on his debts, and he needed to get far away.

He never came back.

For a few months Si Mingyuan stayed out of town, at first just wanting to pay off the gambling debt and save his family from more trouble. Then he arranged to be smuggled into Brazil in exchange for becoming a contract laborer. After cutting sugar cane for eight years, he finally saved enough to pay off the smugglers. But he hadn't the money to come back and face his son. He opened a small store in Sao Paolo, working day and night to make more money. He'd sold the store last month and now had $500,000.

Three days ago, he'd returned to China. His old home was now a skyscraper. Si Mingyuan had to ask a lot of people before finally finding his family. He wanted to surprise his wife. The useless husband and pathetic father was at last a man, able to support his family.

Si Wang rested on the bed, listening to his dad recount his South American adventures. The man had been through a lot. His face had many scars.

Si Wang remembered once suspecting that his mom had killed his dad.

He'd never dared speak of that hunch, though he'd often been tempted to ask Huang Hai and Ye Xiao.

Si Wang fell asleep in his father's arms.

CHAPTER 84

July 7.

Si Wang received his college acceptance letter. Of all the liberal arts students at the high school, he scored the highest on the exams. He would start college in just a few weeks. The cast on his right leg had been removed, but he still had to be careful. It was a boring summer for him since he wasn't allowed to box. But now that Lu Zhongyue was dead, he had no reason to keep doing it.

His father opened a franchise supermarket next to Wilderness Books. During the days, he kept busy doing renovations in preparation for the grand opening. The two of them played Xiangqi; his dad played worse than ever.

Even with her missing husband back home, He Qingying rarely smiled. They slept in separate beds.

One evening Ye Xiao came by the apartment to speak with Si Mingyuan. Afterward, the cop wanted to take He Qingying and Si Wang for a ride.

"As long as you're not arresting them," Si Mingyuan joked. He was a simpler man after spending years abroad.

Ye Xiao drove to Nanming Road.

"If you have anything to say, tell us now." Si Wang seemed anxious in the front passenger seat. "Why are we here?"

"Wang Er, listen to Policeman Ye." He Qingying was in a serious mood. She rolled down the window to look at the unusually clear sky as the car passed Nanming High.

The police car stopped close to the Demon Girl Zone. Ye Xiao told them to follow him into the abandoned factory. He led the way with a flashlight, stepping around the trash and feces. Mother and son were hesitant.

"C'mon, are you scared?" Ye Xiao's voice echoed. "Let's go."

He Qingying patted her son's shoulders. They walked in silence until they arrived at the rusty hatch door.

Si Wang pulled open the door; the hinges creaked loudly. With Ye Xiao shining the flashlight into the Demon Girl Zone, Si Wang slid in, and was followed by the other two. The dank air made them feel like they were drowning in filthy water.

The foul smells grew even worse once they reached the Demon Girl Zone.

"I'm sorry to bring you here. But I wanted to tell you that after Lu Zhongyue died, I spent a month looking at a lot of people and more files. I found something. I thought telling you here would make it easier to accept."

"Just say it, Policeman Ye!" Si Wang backed up toward the exit, as if he would flee at any moment.

"In 1983, the victim of the Serenity Road murder case was a bureaucrat named Lu Jingnan. Lu Zhongyue's father, Lu Jingdong, also worked for the government. The residency registration papers showed that Lu Jingnan and Lu Jingdong were brothers—meaning Lu Zhongyue's uncle was the murder victim."

"Right, Lu Zhongyue told me about it. That's why he was hiding here."

"The only survivor and witness of the murder was the victim's daughter, Lu Mingyue. Oddly enough, her files disappeared. I spent three nights at the Archive Bureau looking for the missing files. Someone had moved her files to another index. Lu Mingyue was the victim's adoptive daughter. Her files being moved meant someone was trying to cover up her identity. Her new adoptive dad worked at the postal office. Her new adoptive mom worked at the Archive Bureau, so moving the files was easily done."

He Qingying's low voice rang out. "Yes, my adoptive father arranged the postal service job for me, and my adoptive mother hid my files so I could say good-bye to my past."

"In 1984, a coworker introduced you to Si Mingyuan. He worked at Nanming Steel Factory, and the two of you married the following year. That spring, the factory had an employee party. People remember you coming. Someone else came, too—the factory's youngest engineer, Lu Zhongyue."

"What are you trying to say?" Si Wang walked in front of Ye Xiao.

The cop pushed him away and stared at He Qingying. "I talked to many of the Lu family relatives. For two months during the summer of 1983, when Lu Zhongyue was thirteen, he stayed at the Serenity Road house—his uncle's place. You were cousins, close in age, and lived under the same roof. You couldn't have forgotten him."

"Yes." He Qingying paused a long time. "I remember him."

"Your husband also remembers Lu Zhongyue. He said you became depressed after that party, but he didn't ask why. He didn't want to pry. On more than one occasion I've asked you about Lu Zhongyue. You've always claimed not to know him. You said that even if Lu worked at the same factory with your husband, you rarely went there. Obviously, you've been lying to me."

"Mom, you don't have to answer."

He Qingying shook her head. "I'm sorry, I did lie. I do know Lu Zhongyue. But after the murder, I didn't see him again until 1995."

"Why did you lie?"

"It's my secret."

"Here is my theory. I don't think Lu Zhongyue killed Shen Ming. Destroying Shen Ming was all he really wanted to do, and he'd achieved that. Shen Ming became a killer on June 19—that's a fact. He was either going to be a fugitive or be caught and executed. Lu Zhongyue didn't need to kill Shen Ming."

"My mom had no motive to kill, either! She had nothing to do with Shen Ming!"

"Wrong. When Shen Ming lived in that basement across from the murder house, he could have had some interactions with Lu Mingyue or Lu Zhongyue. Furthermore, according to your uncle and aunt, when you were five, Si Mingyuan suspected you weren't his son. He was cold toward you and alienated your mom. He suspected that Lu Zhongyue was your father."

His face contorting like he'd been punched in the chest, Si Wang grabbed He Qingying and shouted, "Mom, who is my real dad? Please don't say Lu Zhongyue!"

"Please don't doubt me. You're Si Mingyuan's son. I swear it!"

Ye Xiao cut in. "Si Wang, I do not doubt your paternity. But why did Si Mingyuan suspect your mom and Lu Zhongyue? Was it because they lived together as kids? This is just my speculation. But there were many loose ends around the 1983 murder. A lot of people thought the killer wasn't an intruder. No one suspected the victim's daughter. However, I think the 1983 murder was done by one of these three people: He Qingying, Lu Zhongyue, or Shen Ming. Or maybe all three. The secret stayed hidden for twelve years, until someone wanted to expose it. Lu Zhongyue wanted to open it back up when he recognized He Qingying. There were threats and extortions. Someone wanted to use the secret to get what he wanted, and someone wanted to keep the secret hidden."

"You have no evidence."

"The person who killed Shen Ming is standing in front of me." Ye Xiao's flashlight shone on He Qingying's face.

Si Wang grabbed the flashlight and shielded his mom. "Ye Xiao, you're not speculating, you're imagining. This is not what the police do."

Ye Xiao effortlessly pushed Si Wang to the ground, making sure he didn't fall too hard on his bad leg, and retrieved the flashlight. "You're right, Si Wang. Most of the evidence is gone, including the murder weapon that killed Shen Ming. It's never been found. The most important witness, Lu Zhongyue, has taken all of his secrets to the grave. You two can deny everything. I have no evidence to arrest anyone. I just needed to say this tonight. I've known you two forever, and I needed to prove something so you can't call me a moron later."

"Can we go home now?" Si Wang said.

"Of course. Sorry to take up so much of your time. Go home."

Every pore on Si Wang's body throbbed. He tried to pull his mom out of the Demon Girl Zone, but she resisted, shedding heavy tears.

Raising her head calmly and exuding a haunting beauty, she said, "I killed Shen Ming."

CHAPTER 85

1983.

Teresa Teng songs were popular. The sounds of "Green grass, white fog, a beauty is waiting far away" could be heard from the second floor of Serenity Road Number 19.

The music came from a stereo Lu Mingyue's uncle got her as a birthday present. Since her uncle worked for the district government, he could always get nice things like this. The Teresa Teng tape came from a street vendor, and she wanted to fall asleep listening to it every night.

Lu Mingyue had just turned thirteen—she wasn't a little girl anymore. She liked watching the teenager who lived across the street, though she never talked to him. None of the neighborhood kids played with him. Everyone knew that his father had poisoned his mother and been executed for it. Many nights she could see the illuminated basement window and the boy reading in the faint light, his face painted golden.

She asked one of the older neighbors about him and learned that his name was Shen Ming.

The old man was over eighty and had a lot of stories. Important bureaucrats from Beijing visited him; some foreign reporters came to see him, too. At the other end of the block lived a woman in her sixties called Miss Cao. She and the old man often took walks under the ginkgo trees, talking in some foreign language no one understood. They'd part with a smile.

A year earlier, Lu Mingyue's adoptive mom had drowned herself in the Suzhou River, all because of her adulterous husband.

After that, happiness drained out of Lu Mingyue's life, especially on nights when her adoptive father got drunk.

She wanted to kill him.

That summer, a young man moved into her home. He was her adoptive uncle's son, Lu Zhongyue. His parents sent him there while they were on a two-month trip abroad.

Lu Zhongyue didn't like to study. He collected a lot of cigarette cards and played them with other kids. He liked to gossip and soon learned that Lu Mingyue was adopted and had no blood relation to the Lu family.

One night, the thirteen-year-old Lu Zhongyue told her that he liked her.

Lu Mingyue slapped him.

After that interminable summer ended, Lu Zhongyue's parents returned from their trip and took him back home. He still liked to visit his cousin from time to time. But he never used the front door, preferring to climb over the wall to scare her.

She was terrified whenever she saw Lu Zhongyue coming.

Late fall 1983.

It was raining lightly that night, Lu Mingyue was cornered by her drunk adoptive father. She fought him, grabbed a broken piece of glass, and slashed his neck.

As she was panicking, she noticed a face outside the window.

Lu Zhongyue had seen everything.

Her face covered in blood, she charged to the window, still clutching the broken glass. Lu Zhongyue was scared. "I didn't see anything! I swear I'll never tell a soul!"

He scrambled back over the wall and ran away.

Lu Mingyue cleaned up the crime scene, smashing the broken glass into pieces. She then walked out of the house and cried on the steps. She didn't know that Shen Ming was watching her from across the street.

The police interrogated her many times. She said she never saw the intruder and had only come downstairs after hearing strange noises. That's when she'd found the body.

No one doubted her.

The following winter a childless couple adopted Lu Mingyue and renamed her He Qingying. She moved into the house where Si Wang would be born.

Her adoptive mother worked at the Archive Bureau. After she begged repeatedly, her files were changed so there was no connection between Lu Mingyue and He Qingying.

She wanted to say good-bye to her past.

Her new family wasn't rich, but her new adoptive parents were very good to her. They supported her through high school, and then she was assigned a job at the post office. She didn't suffer anymore and never spoke of her past; no one she knew looked her up. It was a good thing her adoptive parents had few relatives.

When she was twenty-four, her adoptive parents died in a car accident. She met Si Mingyuan that same year.

He Qingying didn't know if she really loved him, but he loved her.

She married him in April of 1995.

Two weeks after their wedding, she went to a party at Nanming Steel Factory for employees and family members. Someone recognized her.

"Mingyue?"

The man with the birthmark on his forehead stared and kept asking her questions until Si Mingyuan stopped him.

She didn't admit to who she was, but that night she saw the Serenity Road murder house in her dreams.

Lu Zhongyue invaded her life. He'd wait in front of the post office or follow her home. One day, he visited her with an envelope. The addressee was in Beijing. He wanted He Qingying to make the postal stamp read six months earlier. She refused, saying it was illegal and could get her fired.

He said, "I know what you did on Serenity Road. I saw everything."

He Qingying had no choice but to give in to his threats. She altered the stamp on the alleged letter from Shen Ming to He Nian.

Lu Zhongyue made her meet him under the factory in the mythical Demon Girl Zone, where he'd often played during high school.

"Mingyue, you're my demon girl," he said, stroking her hair softly and staring into her eyes. "You've killed. I admire that. I'll keep your secret, in exchange for—"

He Qingying kicked him in the balls and fled.

She knew her secret couldn't stay buried forever. Lu Zhongyue wanted her and would just keep blackmailing her. She couldn't tell her husband about it.

She had to solve the problem on her own.

She wrote a letter to Lu Zhongyue, asking him to meet her at 10:00 p.m. on June 19, at the Demon Girl Zone. She said she didn't really like her husband and was making plans for the future.

She packed a sharp knife.

On June 19, 1995, she left home early in the morning and hid all day in the dark of the Demon Girl Zone, just waiting for Lu Zhongyue to appear.

10:00 p.m. Thunder rolled outside and was followed by the dull sound of steady rain.

The moment the hatch door opened, she saw the shape of a young man. As he was about to turn around, she stabbed him in the back.

The knife pierced the man's heart.

She turned on her flashlight to examine the body. It wasn't Lu Zhongyue.

He Qingying cried over her victim and begged his ghost to forgive her. She had to keep this a secret, just as she'd kept the secret from Serenity Road all of these years. She removed the knife from Shen Ming's body and made sure to clear the crime scene of anything that might incriminate her.

She quickly got out of there, leaving her victim in the dark cycles of reincarnation.

It was already midnight when she got home. Si Mingyuan was still playing mah-jongg somewhere, as she had expected. She washed all her clothes but burned her bloody jacket.

She thought sleep would elude her, but she actually had a vivid dream. In it she saw a young man. He was dressed plainly, and looked sad. Holding a candle, he cried next to her bed.

He Qingying remembered the face: It belonged to that boy who'd lived across the street on Serenity Road—Shen Ming.

Si Mingyuan came home at dawn and didn't act any differently than usual.

She found out she was pregnant on that day. Her husband went with her to the checkup; she was two months along.

The letter she wrote Lu Zhongyue was returned to the post office. The factory mailroom had made an error and Lu Zhongyue never received it.

Yet Lu Zhongyue never bothered her again.

As her belly grew and she could feel the new life move, she was filled with an unnamed fear.

She heard her husband talking about the man who'd been killed under the factory—Shen Ming, the disgraced Chinese teacher from Nanming High.

He Qingying thought about having an abortion but backed out at the hospital. It was as if she could hear the baby crying out to be kept.

The due date had been January of 1996, but the baby arrived early. She went to the hospital late at night and on December 19 gave birth to the son she had with Si Mingyuan.

When the nurse brought her the infant, she cried at the sight of his wrinkled little face.

She named her son Si Wang.

A few days later, she found a small birthmark on the left side of his back, right behind the heart. She thought it looked like a wound—as if he'd been stabbed in the womb. She couldn't help but think of that rainy night six months earlier.

She had endless nightmares while recovering from childbirth.

He Qingying never told her son or husband about the birthmark.

Si Wang learned to walk and talk very early. He Qingying felt uneasy. The kid was quiet, and when he played with toy cars and guns at home he didn't really make a mess like other kids.

Once, when he was still a baby, and she was sleeping, he climbed the bookshelf to read a copy of *Song Dynasty Poems*. Sometimes she'd find him staring into space by the window, mumbling to himself. His gaze was different from other kids' and he seemed to understand everything adults said.

Whenever Si Wang talked in his sleep, He Qingying tried to decipher. She heard him utter only grown-up words, like "Nanming Road," "Demon Girl Zone," "Serenity Road," and the name "Xiaozhi."

When Si Wang was five, the steel factory closed and Si Mingyuan became angry. One night over drinks another employee told Si Mingyuan about seeing the engineer Lu Zhongyue walking into the underground warehouse with his wife. It was true, but He Qingying denied it. For two years they lived under unspeakable strain until Si Mingyuan disappeared to get away from his gambling debt.

While watching television one day, she heard the Chris Yu song, "Meng Po Soup."

Suddenly, she heard a soft whining. Si Wang's face was streaked with tears.

"Wang Er, what's the matter?"

He went into the bedroom and locked the door. He Qingying unlocked it to find her son sobbing.

Meng Po Soup?

When visiting Gu Qiusha's house three years later, she ran into Lu Zhongyue. The two looked at each other awkwardly but didn't speak.

She didn't want her son to live with the Gu family, but with pressure from the debt collectors, and to save him from harm, she felt forced to send him to live with that awful man.

Lu Zhongyue secretly approached her. He was despondent and not at all like what he used to be. He said the Serenity Road thing had been a long time ago and he would never threaten her with it again. He had no desire for women anymore; he just wanted to be at peace with them.

He had no idea that she'd killed Shen Ming.

Si Wang returned to her not long after, while Lu Zhongyue became a fugitive wanted for murder.

The only man He Qingying ever loved was Si Wang, this kid who thought he knew everything and that his mom knew nothing.

Wang Er, your mom knows all of your secrets.

You don't know any of your mom's secrets.
You are no genius.
You're just a silly child.

There are no parents who don't understand their kids, only kids who don't understand their parents.

CHAPTER 86

July 7.

Ye Xiao took He Qingying and Si Wang out of the Demon Girl Zone. They got to the tallest chimney. It was now night.

He Qingying pointed to a dilapidated wall with a "No Trespassing" sign on it. "I buried the weapon here."

Ye Xiao looked for something to dig with but Si Wang had already started using his hands. The rain from the last few days had softened the soil. It didn't take long for him to dig down a few inches, but it was just roots and old animal bones.

"Let me." He Qingying pushed aside her son and dug until her hands bled. She found a blackish object that she wiped clean on the hem of her dress. It had rusted, but it was definitely a knife.

"This is the knife I killed Shen Ming with."

Ye Xiao dropped the knife into an evidence bag and made He Qingying leave in a police car bound for the precinct.

The police commander met He Qingying in person that night; Ye Xiao took extensive notes. She admitted to both the 1983 Serenity Road and 1995 Nanming Road killings.

When asked why she'd finally decided to confess after all these years—even though there was still no concrete evidence— she gave no answer.

Ye Xiao believed that He Qingying was worried about going to jail and leaving Si Wang to grow up alone. Now that he was grown and her husband had come back, those worries were gone. He Qingying could admit to everything and free herself from the burden of her dark secrets.

Si Wang got home at dawn. His father was up waiting for him; he'd already heard from Ye Xiao. He Qingying had called him, too. Si Wang was his responsibility now.

Si Wang leaned on his shoulder and softly said, "Dad, I really am your son."

"I made up my mind back when I was cutting sugar cane that, even if you weren't my son, I'd treat you like my own. Wang Er, you have no idea how happy I was when you were born."

Si Mingyuan took out a beat-up old wallet—a gift from He Qingying before they got married. During all his years of traveling, he'd always kept it with him. The faded photos included one of Si Wang as a precious infant with a moody grown-up gaze.

Looking at the photo, Si Mingyuan held his son tightly.

The next day, Si Wang visited Shen Yuanchao. But Ye Xiao had been faster, calling the old prosecutor to give him closure.

Shen Min got into her top-choice university, which was in another city. She was busy packing. She'd been very saddened by the death of Ouyang Xiaozhi. She still kept a photo of her with her teacher on her dresser.

Together with Shen Min, Si Wang lit three sticks of incense for Shen Ming's memorial.

As Si Wang hugged Shen Yuanchao to say good-bye, he leaned in and said, "Please do me a favor."

After some whispering, the old prosecutor's face paled, and he lowered his head. "I've always wanted to kill that man myself."

"I know."

"Kid, go home. Don't let me see you again."

Si Wang walked out the door but then turned around to say, "Please, I beg you. I'll wait for your call."

Shen Yuanchao said nothing in reply.

Shen Min caught up to Si Wang. As they walked downstairs together, she touched his arm. "What did you say to my dad?"

"It's a secret."

"When can we see each other again?"

"When you graduate college."

"Can I kiss you?"

Si Wang closed his eyes, and Shen Min gave him a light peck on the cheek.

He rode away on his bicycle without a backward glance. Shen Min cried.

College would start a month later.

On a crisp fall morning, Si Mingyuan hired a taxi to take his son to the university by the sea.

Si Wang carried a heavy suitcase. When they arrived, he waved to his dad and said, "Go home—I'll be fine!"

At the campus entrance a banner hung overhead welcoming new students. A slideshow of past university presidents showed various images, one of which was Gu Changlong.

Many girls paid attention to Si Wang, and some wanted to know his major. One senior was very warm; she offered to help him with registration and give him a tour of the classrooms and dorms.

Si Wang looked at her in confusion. "Yi Yu?"

"Do you know me?"

She was wearing light makeup and had on a knee-length floral dress. She showed no signs of being a tomboy. She was a bona fide beauty.

Her face looked the same as when they'd last seen one another three years ago—right before she'd been hit by the truck.

"Did you graduate from Nanming High?"

"Yeah, how did you know?"

"I went there, too. We also both went to May First Junior High. We were best friends."

"Really?" She seemed excited to see her classmate again. She flipped her hair and said with shyness, "Sorry, guess I forgot everything. I was in an accident right after exams."

"It was an out-of-control truck, right? I was there, I took you to the hospital."

"That was you? I was in a coma for four months. I lost all my memory. I was going to Hong Kong University but didn't like how crowded it was, so I came back. Since I did really well on the exams, this university accepted me. I heard that people used to call me a tomboy, but I don't feel like one. Is that true?"

"Yi Yu, you really forgot everything?"

"Well, sometimes I get these weird images and sounds in my head."

Looking at Yi Yu's blushing cheeks, Si Wang looked up at the sky and uttered, "Please give me another bowl of Meng Po Soup!"

How great it would be to forget.

EPILOGUE ONE

Three months later. Monday, December 22.

It was still dark at 7:00 a.m. The high-rise outside his window was long gone. Ye Xiao wore a uniform with a wool collar. Someone had ironed it yesterday. He found a cluster of white hair on his temple.

He arrived at the Middle-Level People's Court. There were two major cases today, both homicides on their first trials.

At 9:00 a.m. was the case of Lu Zhongyue being killed by his son. Ye Xiao sat in the front row as the investigating police officer. The suspect, Lu Jizong, was already eighteen; his attorney believed it was manslaughter, not murder. His argument was that the young man had been obsessed with the virtual world ever since childhood, and seeing his dad for the first time triggered in him an emotional breakdown that caused the tragedy.

He Qingying's case was tried that afternoon. The indictment said she'd killed Lu Jingnan on Serenity Road in 1983 and had also killed Shen Ming on Nanming Road in 1995. She'd turned herself in. Ye Xiao's investigation report showed the facts.

Ye Xiao sat in the last row and carefully watched the people in attendance. Si Mingyuan was there, as was Shen Yuanchao.

The suspect looked calm. Her hair was trimmed short, and she faced the judge and the public prosecutor with serenity.

Where was Si Wang?

During the interminable trial, the defense attorney presented a letter of forgiveness signed by Shen Yuanchao, Shen Ming's only biological relative. It asked the court to show leniency and concluded as follows:

> *I'm a selfish prosecutor, a man who didn't deserve to be a father.*
> *The real killer wasn't He Qingying—it was me.*
> *If you have to sentence anyone to death, sentence me.*
> *Please, for my child, and for her child, too.*

EPILOGUE TWO

Winter.

It was one of the shortest days of the year. The sunlight warmed him, chasing away the northerly wind's chill.

He'd just returned from Ouyang Xiaozhi's grave.

Si Wang visited Serenity Road for the first time in six months. He wore a black puffer coat and held something in his hand that stung.

Serenity Road Number 19 looked much the same as it had the night it burned to the ground.

Si Wang sat on the pile of rubble. The debris chilled him to the bone.

He closed his eyes and smiled into the air, saying, "Come with me."

Crossing Serenity Road was like crossing the River of Life and Death.

The old house across the street still had that window in the basement.

Half an hour later, he stood up. The ruins would be a green space come spring.

Si Wang squeezed onto a crowded subway train and made his way to Nanming Road. It was almost dark. He clutched the object in his hand so hard that his arm felt numb. He hurried to walk past Nanming High; the oleander branches peeked over the wall.

He knelt, with difficulty, on the cold ground and said with regret, "I'm sorry, Mr. Yan."

He then walked between two construction sites—to the tall chimney.

The dilapidated factory seemed even more desolate in winter, as if it was some forgotten ancient ruins. He limped to the Demon Girl Zone's entrance.

The hatch door seemed to be talking to him. After staring at it for about a minute, Si Wang pushed it open.

Demon Girl Zone.

Dust flew. He knelt in the dark and puffed into his closed fist. Unclenching his hand, he said, "I'm here."

There was no light at all, but Si Wang could count every single one of the beads on the necklace.

The necklace had hung in Shen Ming's room for years; it broke the day before he was killed and was never strung again.

June 19, 1995—10:00 p.m.

After Shen Ming killed Yan Li, he didn't think of running but came here holding the necklace.

Then he was killed.

Shen Ming clutched the necklace and lay in the muddy water for three days. When the police found the body, they couldn't open his hand. Huang Hai had to break two of his fingers to release the necklace.

Shen Ming's personal effects were given to Shen Yuanchao, but the necklace stayed with Huang Hai and was locked in the cabinet in his apartment. After Huang Hai died, Si Wang stole the necklace.

Si Wang held the necklace next to his ear. In these strange beads, he could hear a little girl's laughter.

"What's your name?"

"I'm Shen Ming." The senior sat in the wild grass and looked at the open sky in a daze.

"Thank you for saving me." The disheveled little girl looked no older than ten; she resembled a malnourished kitten. She leaned on the teenager's back and tickled him.

"Stop tickling me. What's your name?"

"I don't have a name!"

"OK, I'll give you a name." The teenager thought for a bit while holding her matchstick of an arm. Then he said, "Xiaozhi!"

"I like it!"

"You remind me of that Gu Cheng poem."

"I have a gift for you!" She stuck out her tongue and opened her hand to reveal an unusual necklace. "Look, this one is pearl, this one is glass, this is fake jade, and this wooden one is a Buddha bead. There are nineteen of them. I found them all in the trash. It took me three days to string them together."

The teenager held the necklace under the sunlight and watched it glimmer.

The little girl wrapped herself round his neck. Her skinny arms felt as suffocating as a snake. "Can you swear?" she said.

"Swear what?"

"That you'll always keep this necklace with you, until you die."

He smiled and held the necklace in his hand. Taking the little girl in his arms, he swore, "I, Shen Ming, will always keep the necklace Xiaozhi gave me—until I die!"

Until I die.

Suddenly, the sun ducked behind the clouds. The whole world turned gray, and it started to rain.

THE END

Author: Cai Jun

Monday, March 25, 2013—first draft, Suzhou River in Shanghai

Monday, April 22, 2013—second draft, Suzhou River in Shanghai

Tuesday, April 30, 2013—final draft, Suzhou River in Shanghai

AFTERWORD

In March of 2013, one late night in Beijing, at West Wudaoying Hutong near Yonghe Palace Temple, a friend gave me a copy of Zhang Chengzhi's *Journal of the Soul*. I felt joy as I touched the book. Flipping to the first page and reading the first line made me happy. My eyes seemed to grow moist.

I'd reached a watershed moment in my life.

I had been at this point ever since I finished writing *Murder in My Youth*. Anyone crossing a similar watershed would suffer as if crossing the River of Life and Death.

So the afterword for this book should start at the point when I was looking at the watershed.

Si Wang was a name that rhymed not only with "death" but also "lookout."

In 1985, I was in first grade at Suzhou Road Elementary School in Shanghai. The school was in an alley near Suzhou River in the Zhabei District, close to the Laozha Bridge (now Fujian Road Bridge). I remembered a school building that looked like an old-style mansion. My mom signed me up for an art class at the same school called Feifei Art Academy. A few years ago, the elementary school and my grandma's house (where I was living at the time) were both torn down.

When I was in the third grade, we moved, so I transferred schools. I started going to Longevity Road Number One School in the Putuo District. The Suzhou River ran behind the school; there is still a pedestrian bridge there. Everything seemed bigger when I was a kid. Now it all looks tiny. At the elementary school library, I read my first novel, Verne's *Twenty Thousand Leagues Under the Sea*. It was a condensed illustrated edition. The school had narrow paths reaching deep into a yard, where there was a three-story teaching building. I spent grades four and five there. People's houses were right next to the building; many bamboo and fig trees grew outside the houses; there was also a kindergarten.

In 1990, I entered May First Junior High School's prep class in the Putuo District.

Suzhou River flew past behind the school. A sports field was right by the school entrance. The teaching buildings sat to the right and in front. On the left was a coal slag–paved jogging track. There was a row of squat two-story buildings; they looked like a string of deserted islands, far from the teaching buildings and everything else. The school's medical office was in there. I was always afraid of the vision chart since I used my eyes hard every summer vacation reading all kinds of novels.

The PE teacher also had his office in those buildings. The male students liked PE class, and some of them were friendly with the PE teacher. They practiced long-distance jumping by the sand pits. The music classroom was there, too; its walls were sound-proof. The windows looked out at the sports field, where you could see the pale-green teaching buildings. An ancient piano made music like an organ. In seventh grade, a new music teacher arrived. She was young and pretty; she had just graduated from the teaching college. Her last name was Zhu; I still remember her melodious name. Every music teacher could play the piano, and so did Ms. Zhu. Schools didn't take music and art classes seriously back then. After ninth grade, I rarely had music class. My impression of music class was me hiding in the back row, listening to her play the piano. I was learning to play the flute at home and performed twice at school. Ms. Zhu didn't know I had the ability, and I was too shy to show off my flute. They were already teaching the staff in junior high music textbooks, so for a long time I used them to practice flute. The last music exam I had was singing a song with Ms. Zhu's accompaniment. Technically, we were supposed to pick a song from the textbook. A couple of the male students chose a popular song like the "New Mandarin Duck Love Song" or something from one of the four Chinese pop stars. I chose the song "My Motherland" from the textbook; it was old-fashioned, but I loved the melody. Too bad I stopped out of embarrassment halfway through. Ms. Zhu thought I did a good job in the beginning and gave me a medium score.

I never saw Ms. Zhu again after graduation.

The school library was above the music room. There was a young school staffer who worked there. I am not sure if she was a teacher or a library employee. I remember her for how she always wore a short skirt, even in winter. Her pale and shapely legs would make the high school boys scream. Back in those days, girls in short skirts were rarely seen, even on hot summer days. Once in seventh grade, I crept to the second floor and into the tiny library. There were just a few rows of books, but they were enough for me. I was excited to see those yellowed spines. I chose *The Adventures of Sherlock Holmes* by Sir Arthur Conan Doyle. I held it like a treasure and wrote my name on the book-lending card. As I walked gingerly down the steps, I was stopped by two older students. They saw what I had and said, "I read that—it's great!" I was even more overjoyed as I went back to class with the book.

Soon after I graduated, May First Junior High School closed. A nightclub opened outside the school entrance. It's now a well-known entertainment venue in Shanghai.

My music teacher was assigned to work at another school after the closing. One of Ms. Zhu's students eventually became the famous singer Shang Wenjie.

After that, I went to school in a faraway place. It was a rural factory area then, with a blast blower factory nearby. We often played soccer at school; whenever the ball went over the wall, we had to go find it. I heard the factory was once a famous cemetery where the legendary Chinese actress Ruan Lingyu was buried.

After that, I started working.

From 2002 to early 2007, I worked near Suzhou River in the Postal Plaza, which was to the north of the Sichuan Road Bridge. The plaza was built in 1924 in a style that combined Corinthian columns and Baroque domes.

After that, I became the person you see now.

It is a coincidence that ever since I was born I've always lived near the Suzhou River.

It's my River of Life and Death.

In 2012, one June evening, I went shopping at Carrefour with my family. While eating at Yonghe King, I suddenly had a thought. What do kids really think about? Do they remember things grown-ups can't even imagine? Things beyond their experience, or from another dimension? When kids are silent, are they remembering events from their past lives?

We all go through the same thing, even after we drink the Meng Po Soup by the Bridge Over Troubled Water. We all keep some past-life memories. We only start to forget as we grow up and are invaded and polluted by so-called education. We forget all the partings and the sorrows.

Then I started this novel.

In six months, I had finished 80 percent of the book; over 60,000 words of the book were already serialized in *Suspense World* magazine. But I suddenly thought of another plot, with a character none of you read, someone called Yu Lei, who was like

Julien in *The Red and the Black*. I thought the book's protagonist should have been him; why couldn't he cross the River of Life and Death?

I faced a difficult and cruel choice: either finish the book as planned and write the ending, or rewrite it with another protagonist, change the point of view for most of the book, and go from first person to third person. The book would have to be almost entirely rewritten, and I would have to stay up for dozens of nights.

This was a predicament I had never faced before. An easy road lay ahead, but it only reached Egypt, where one departed. If you wanted to reach the promised land of Canaan, you had to scale harsh mountains.

I believe a writer is fortunate to face such a crossroads.

I chose the more difficult path.

That was in the Lunar New Year of 2013. I gave up my holiday to write the second draft, as in completely rewrite the book.

It became the story you just read.

At the end of March, when I finished, I was so excited that I actually wrote my finish date as 2014 at first. It was as if my own life had time-traveled to Si Wang's timeline in the book.

I wrote a Weibo update that night:

I finished writing The Child's Past Life. *I really feel like crying. It's like having my heart crushed, glued together, crushed again, and then sewn back up. I remember the struggles I had. Right now I'm listening to Chris Yu's "Meng Po Soup." Please allow me to quote Gu Cheng's poem for the last line of the novel. Tonight, I think, life will never end, novels will never end, the pen lives on.*

I want to thank my publisher Motie Books, my publisher Shen Haobo, my planning editors Liu Yi and Bu Di—and you, the reader.

I want to thank every character in this book. You were all so vivid in front of me; you lived through the emotions with me. When Huang Hai died, I pounded the keyboard as I cried with Si Wang.

Last night, the friend who gave me *Journal of the Soul* visited me. I took him on a tour of my school, the same elementary school in the book. We were right by Suzhou River, where Si Wang found the body in the jeep.

There was a pedestrian bridge; we walked up the steps and looked down at the river. It was midnight and there was a spring breeze. It was hard to see the river in the dark, but I could imagine the quiet and deep waters.

Time passes just like the river—endless, every day and night.

Cai Jun
Wednesday, May 1, 2013
Suzhou River, Shanghai

ABOUT THE AUTHOR

 CAI JUN has published a dozen books and is China's best-selling horror writer. He started his writing career at twenty-two and was quickly awarded the Bertelsmann People's Literature Award for New Writers. His novel *19th Floor of Hell* won the Sina Literary Award and is one of three of Jun's novels to have been made into a feature film. Two of his books have been developed into television series, and his work has been translated into six languages.

ABOUT THE TRANSLATOR

 YUZHI YANG was born in Beijing, China, and arrived as an immigrant in New York when she was thirteen years old. Going through puberty and learning to live in a new country at the same time was a character-building experience. After attending a big state school in the South, she moved back to New York to work in online publishing. She did that for ten years before deciding to do translation full-time. She loves buffets, discount shopping, and playing with her daughter. She loves translation because, if the book is bad, she can always blame it on the author.